MACBETH'S NIECE

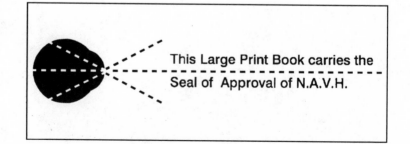

This Large Print Book carries the
Seal of Approval of N.A.V.H.

MACBETH'S NIECE

PEG HERRING

THORNDIKE PRESS
A part of Gale, Cengage Learning

GALE
CENGAGE Learning

Detroit • New York • San Francisco • New Haven, Conn • Waterville, Maine • London

GALE
CENGAGE Learning™

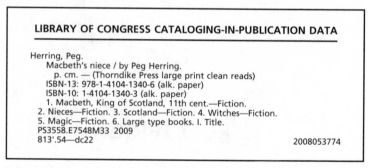

LIBRARY OF CONGRESS CATALOGING-IN-PUBLICATION DATA

Herring, Peg.
  Macbeth's niece / by Peg Herring.
    p. cm. — (Thorndike Press large print clean reads)
  ISBN-13: 978-1-4104-1340-6 (alk. paper)
  ISBN-10: 1-4104-1340-3 (alk. paper)
  1. Macbeth, King of Scotland, 11th cent.—Fiction.
2. Nieces—Fiction. 3. Scotland—Fiction. 4. Witches—Fiction.
5. Magic—Fiction. 6. Large type books. I. Title.
PS3558.E7548M33 2009
813'.54—dc22   2008053774

Published in 2009 by arrangement with Tekno Books.

To Kay: the first to know,
the first to believe.

PROLOGUE

Rain fell, but that was not unusual in the Highlands, and the three creatures making their way over the hills paid no heed to the weather. What they did take note of was unclear, for they seemed to sense things that were not there, answering voices unheard and peering at sights unseen. They were an odd trio: women, to be sure, but less and more than that term implied. Their hair, once different colors and textures, had faded now to the same matted gray. Clothing hung in tatters, long unwashed and uncared-for. The three cunning, leering faces seemed at once knowing and unaware.

The tallest, who led the way, suddenly stopped and faced the other two, bony face alight with enthusiasm.

"Shall we tell?" she asked. "What say you both?"

"Tell!" said the second, and the third echoed, "Tell!"

7

"If it be ill?" The crone's crooked finger pointed at them and her eyes narrowed.

"Tell!" the two repeated.

The smallest of the three, whose skin was gray with dirt and scaly from some vile disease, spoke. "They must make of it what they will. We are not to blame."

"No, not to blame," said the third, who lacked an eye, having only smooth skin over the spot where the right one should be. "They think themselves better, all of 'em. We shall tell and then see how it goes for them."

With nods all around, the three again made their way across the hillside, sometimes taking a dancing step or two, sometimes speaking to the air, and, as they melted into the nearby woods, muttering words that pleased them but would make no sense to anyone else: "Double, double, toil and trouble . . ."

CHAPTER ONE

"The problem with men," said Lady Macbeth, biting off a thread with small, white teeth, "is that they are too full of the milk of human kindness." She smoothed the stitch just completed with a finger and looked at it critically before continuing, her otherwise perfect face puckered between the eyebrows as she judged her work. "Oh, a man is brave when his blood is up, and he can kill in battle well enough, but ask him to do a task that requires more than brute anger and he will disappoint every time."

She spoke to the group as a whole, but Tessa noticed that when her aunt looked up, the direct gaze of her gray eyes fell sharply on her. The others were related to the lady herself, but Tessa was blood kin to the most likely subject of the comment, Lord Macbeth. Frustration that the lady could not express to her husband was diverted to the niece who sat before her,

9

not likely to argue the point.

Five women sat in the warmest place in Inverness Castle, the fireside, which in fact was not all that comfortable. The floor was cold, and Tessa's feet felt as if they were slowly turning to stone. The smoke curled out of the fireplace and into the room. Scotland had no chimneys, so a small hole in the roof allowed the smoke to escape. Periodically, a puff of noxious gray belched into the room and curled round itself as it drifted slowly upward. If the inhabitants wanted heat, they had to put up with the odorous byproduct. Sitting near the fire was both pain and pleasure. Tessa's fingers were stiff with chill, but her backside felt scorched by the blaze. She returned her gaze to her work, hiding rebellious eyes.

If she could move, do something she wanted to do, Tessa would not have felt the cold. However, she was being trained to behave as a lady should and therefore sat working on a tapestry under her aunt's watchful eye. Like others of its kind, the tapestry chronicled an event of interest to family members: a hunt in which Macbeth and his friend Banquo had distinguished themselves in the quantity and variety of game provided for the castle's use. Tessa was assigned a small piece of sky near the top while the others worked on the scene itself. The plain blue corner was simple enough that an amateur could hardly botch it, but the girl found the work tiresome and very slow, and her fingers hurt from a dozen pricks she had suffered so far.

Lady Macbeth shifted her stool away from the fire and re- threaded her needle. Her comely but haughty face twisted with the effort of seeing the needle's loop in the gloom, and it took several tries to succeed. The other three women sewed diligently, showing no reaction to the harsh comment on men in general. It was always thus. The dour trio of attendants worked at whatever was at hand, hardly looking up and seldom speaking. In the two months she had been at Inverness, Tessa had heard no friendly word from any of them. In fact, it was a singularly silent household when only the women were there. This was because Gruoch, her aunt, inspired respect but not love, obedience but not warmth. Although she said all the right words and was never overtly cruel or even unkind, Lady Macbeth was a woman who bent others to her will with a lifted eyebrow or the tiniest shift of one shoulder. Whatever was offered or done was never enough, failure somehow implied.

Tessa considered her aunt's statement,

understanding implicitly that it was aimed at the lord of the manor. Macbeth macFindlaech did not seem a timid man to Tessa. Before his twentieth birthday, he had taken up the sword in defense of his inheritance. A cousin had murdered Findlaech, the former laird, and briefly taken control of the small thanedom of Moray. Macbeth had gathered allies and regained his father's territory, burning to death the cousin and fifty of his men in reprisal. Then he had married the widow of the rebel, the striking woman who now sat opposite Tessa in the hall of Inverness Castle. She seemed to have captured his heart with her gray eyes and her lush figure, although Tessa — and the others, from their demeanors — found her intimidating. No one dared contradict Gruoch around the fire as they sewed. Neither did anyone sing, gossip, or make merry comments. They simply worked on and on, like mindless drones.

Lady Macbeth watched Tessa now, gauging the effect of her statement, and the girl felt compelled to defend her uncle. It would not do to take issue with her aunt's statement, so she took a different tack. "Perhaps a man may be both brave and kind as the need arises, Aunt. It seems that your husband is well-loved by the people of Moray, and even the king holds him in great esteem."

The look she received warned that she had spoken unwisely. "The king has no judgment of men!" Gruoch spoke bitterly. "He uses Macbeth and spreads fair words over his head, but when matters come to marching, he rewards his own." The lady stabbed her embroidery needle into the fabric as if it were Duncan himself who stood before her and not a stretched tapestry on a frame.

Tessa wished that she had merely nodded and stitched, as the others had. Gruoch obviously disapproved of King Duncan. How did a body learn to tread carefully in the maze that was Scotland's governing class? For the hundredth time since leaving home, Tessa wondered what her mother would say of her tendency to blurt out what was on her mind without taking into account those above her. She wondered as well what an encounter with three witch women meant for a person, because she was sure that she had met witches on the way to Macbeth's castle.

Kenna macFindlaech had sent her second daughter to Inverness two months ago out of what she termed desperation. Macbeth was the older brother of Tessa's father, Kenneth, who had died a year ago, leaving behind six daughters and a nearly penniless wife. Tessa was not deemed a good marriage choice among the practical, rather dour local Scots. Although lovely to look at, she tended to tomboyish ways. While other girls studied womanly arts of house-holding and discreet flirting, Tessa had roamed the Highlands, learning their contours and their secrets.

Worse, she would not hold her tongue in company and considered most boys in the area to be idiots. The sight of her auburn hair, fair skin, lithe body, and green eyes could turn men to idiocy, to be sure. Young Alan of the clan Maura, visiting with his father, had taken a shine to the girl and tried to force a kiss when he found himself alone with her in her father's byre. A bit over-sure of himself due to his status as the thane's only son, he had taken umbrage when Tessa refused him.

They had closed the gate after the last cow was herded in, and Alan found himself close enough to Tessa that her tumble of curls actually brushed his cheek as she stood up from fastening the loop of rope over the gatepost. He could not resist touching those curls, and then his hand of its own volition continued to her cheek, smooth as could be. The young man bent his head toward hers, encircling her tiny waist and pulling her toward him suddenly. Before his lips reached hers, twin pains shot through his forearms as Tessa's elbows came sharply down on them.

The boy involuntarily pulled back, and Tessa added a push to assure distance between them. "If I want your attentions, Alan macMaura, I'll let you know. Otherwise, keep your hands to yourself!"

Less in pain now than in anger, the boy growled, "Lassie, think well on your future! I may be the best chance a poor Highland girl like you will get."

"You're no gift to the world or to me!" Tessa informed him. "I'll kiss a man when I wish to, not when he chooses!" With that she turned away toward home, leaving behind one Scot less sure of his allure for women.

Others had tried to win Tessa's favor as well, but when she jeered at their longing gazes and overblown praise of her eyes, lips, hair, and form, bachelors took hasty flight. She was beautiful, but who would spend a lifetime listening to a litany of his faults from those lovely lips when she had not a penny to her name?

There was also the matter of her size. Tessa was as dainty as a songbird, and Scottish mothers took one glance and concluded that no strong sons would come from such as she despite her robust health. Current wisdom recommended tall women with large hips for healthy babies. Between the mothers' doubts and the sons' failure to impress her, the girl was an unlikely candidate for such marital bliss as the Highlands offered to those of her station.

Tessa's mother often berated the girl for her behavior, for her lack of interest in caring for the younger children, and for anything else that she could think of. "You are a disappointment," Kenna would tell her daughter. "Look at your sister Meg! She can weave a fine tartan, prepare an appetizing meal of venison or trout, she is as tall as ever your father was, and best of all, she can keep silent when silence is called for!" Tessa's older sister was "the good girl," according to their mother, cleaning and cooking and wiping small noses and bottoms without a word of complaint. Kenna discouraged Meg's chances of marriage, hoping to keep her most dependable helper, but Tessa she despaired of marrying off. It was no good pointing out that she caught the fish that her sister fried so nicely, or that Meg couldn't take credit for her height any more than Tessa could change hers. It was the silence that she needed to practice, and Tessa had done so, at least in that instance.

When Evan macCady pulled her into the pines for a kiss at Samhain that fall, she remembered her mother's advice and tolerated his embrace briefly, despite the fact that his leering grin gave her the shivers. However, when his hands began wandering places they should not, she reacted. "Mind who you put those big paws on, you great beast! I've bested better than you in a fight!" With that she thwacked him soundly on the nose and stomped back to the fireside.

The look on her mother's face at that moment presaged the tirade to come on how Tessa had ruined her last chance to get a husband. Never mind that Evan macCady was the lowest sort of oaf who would have made the girl's life a misery, as he had his first wife's.

"Mother, the man tried to have his way with me right then and there! Besides, he drinks more than even Laddie Ross, and he smells terrible! I could not marry such a one as that!"

"It's obvious that you'll never marry anyone at all, Miss Highboots! At least Evan has a fine herd of cattle and sheep and could have helped your poor mother put food in her children's mouths. You think only of

17

yourself!"

Kenna had changed over time in ways her children could not know. As a girl, she had been a beauty, trained to smile and say little. She had seemed meek and sweet until she married the handsome Kenneth. Once she had him well and truly snared, Kenna's true self emerged: a spiteful, whining woman who saw the actions of those around her only in light of how they affected her. People who once commented on her beauty now saw eyes squinted peevishly as she corrected imagined faults, a nose that had grown sharp as she poked about for reasons to be angry, and a mouth that curled in scorn far more often than in humor at the actions of those around her.

When the first scent of spring came to the air, Kenna informed her daughter that there were two possibilities for her future: her mother's brother, now thane of Cawdor; or her father's family, the macFindlaechs. Kenna sent the girl to Macbeth, making it clear that Tessa's task was to be agreeable so that her aunt would be willing to take on one or two of the younger girls as time passed.

"I do not know these people," Kenna told Tessa, "but it is their duty to educate you. Macbeth may even provide a dowry, if you

18

behave yourself —" Her tone dripped with threat. "There will be opportunities there to meet men who do not know your faults, unless you display them as carelessly as you have here." Tessa felt a pang of guilt at her mother's criticism. Had she been so difficult, then? Why was she not satisfied with the Alan macMauras or the Evan macCadys in life? Why did she imagine she was made for something — or someone — better?

The parting with her family had not been particularly sad. Only Meg showed any grief at Tessa's departure, since they had always been close. The other children were too young to grasp that they might never see their sister again, and Kenna had long ago lost any feeling for anyone on earth but herself, although she felt deeply there.

Having known no other kind of mother, Tessa accepted the contention that she was a flawed female, not realizing the jealousy Kenna macFindlaech felt for her own beautiful daughter. Kenna saw all of her children as burdens, but Tessa could not be tamed, and that she took as a personal insult. Almost gleefully, she said as they parted, "I believe you are a hopeless case, but here is one last chance. Do exactly as your aunt and uncle bid you and guard your reckless tongue, or you'll come to naught!" With those words, her mother sent Tessa off to foster with people neither of them had ever met.

Because propriety demanded a young woman of good birth not travel alone, old Banaugh went along as escort when Tessa came down from the mountains for the first time. The man seemed ancient, lacking most of his hair, many of his teeth, and any visible spot of unfreckled skin, but he nevertheless kept a steady pace all day, every day, at whatever he was doing.

When it was announced that Tessa would be leaving the Cairngorms, Banaugh cheerfully offered himself as escort to her uncle's castle. "I'll see th' lassie safely there, y' may be sure o' it," he promised. Even Kenna found little to criticize in Banaugh. He was loyal, respectful, and enterprising in all he did, so she merely warned him to return as soon as possible so as not to leave her shorthanded for too long.

Early on the designated morning, the old man showed up with a pack on his back containing necessities for the trip: food wrapped in cloths portioned for each day's travel, a few basic tools such as a knife and a small axe, his strong-smelling cumin liniment for his aches and pains, and flint and tinder sealed well to keep them dry in all conditions. Banaugh was swathed in his tartan, a four-yard length of rough cloth that served as cape, tablecloth, blanket, and various other things. He wore trews, or trousers, of wool and a tunic over a loose linen undershirt. Tessa had dressed for travel in the best dress she owned, a loose, sleeveless garment that fell over a long-sleeved linen shift and tied behind at the waist. Over it she wore a gray cape that served as her blanket at night. After a last quick hug for Meg and a pat for each of the four younger girls, the two travelers were off.

Banaugh led the way down the mountainside toward Inverness, to the north of their home in the Cairngorms. These mountains rise higher than any others in Britain, and on their slopes Tessa had learned something of the great variety of the Scottish Highlands. Her father's lands lay halfway up, in the pinewoods: slopes where huge Caledonian pine trees eventually gave way to acres of purple heather. Above were the shady corries, where odd little alpine plants grew, and still farther up, the plateau, where cushions of moss campion covered the rocky land with pink flowers in summer.

It was not until they had traveled downward for some time that Tessa realized how high was her home in the mountains, and not for some time after that could she look back and get some perspective on her former abode. The mountains were beautiful, but she wondered why her father had moved so far from his brother's lands. Were the brothers so different? She would know very soon.

CHAPTER TWO

The trip itself was pleasant. Tessa was fond of Banaugh, who often comforted her when her mother's mood was particularly spiteful. "Ye're a merry lass," he would tell her, "and tha's somethin' yer puir mother canna understand." Banaugh and Meg were the only things she would truly miss about home.

As the day warmed and the path led steeply downward, Banaugh entertained Tessa with stories of her clan, of glorious Scottish deeds and insidious English lords, some recited and some sung. She already knew them all, but it was good to hear his voice, drowning out her questions about life with her uncle.

Would she fit in? Would they be kind? Did they know she was "outspoken and hoydenish"? What would happen if she didn't suit them? Tessa was not expected to return home, ever. She was an extra mouth to feed, and her mother had solved the problem as best she could. If her uncle could not marry her off, she would make herself useful to the family in some way, tending children or sewing. That was not a pleasant prospect, since Tessa had neither the talent nor the patience for either.

Although unwilling to betray her nervousness, the girl could not help but ask Banaugh, "What sort of man is my uncle? Do you think he will like me?"

Banaugh chuckled as he walked ahead down the rock-strewn, winding path. "There's few men I culd think of tha' wuld not fall in love w' the sight of ye, lass." He walked on a bit and then continued, "Macbeth was ever serious, likely to brood on things, especially slights from others. He is one tha' wants to do well, and he seeks fame as yer father did not. When the twa were boys, Kenneth was angered by th' injustices o' the world and wanted t' right them, but Macbeth saw it differently. T' him life's injustices are unavoidable. Tha' is an honest man, t' be sure, an' brave as they coome, but when th' time came, I chose t' go wi' yer father int' the hills."

"And why did he do that?" Tessa asked, although she knew the story already.

"As youngsters, the boys saw the auld king

killed by Duncan in a fierce rebellion. Later, when yer grandfather was slain, his sons culd do bu' two things: fight back or leave Glames an' his thanedom o' Moray to Gilla-comgain, their cousin. Yer father Kenneth ha' seen eno' bloodshed betwixt Scot an' Scot. He went int' the mountains where life is hard bu' he culd choose whether he'd come doon to figh' or no. Macbeth stayed an' regained his father's land, bu' he's been constantly at war since: wi' the Scots, wi' the Danes, wi' th' English. I doot it has made him a happy man, but 'tis the way he chose. They say he is a hard man t' know, an' that only his lady is truly in his bosom. Still, as swee' a thing as ye will capture his heart, I ha' no doot."

Banaugh seemed sure enough, and he had once known Macbeth well. Watching her step on the treacherous hillside, Tessa hoped his judgment was correct.

Near the end of their journey the two travelers stopped by a tiny stream that tumbled down the last of the steep slopes and then ran away across a flat into a nearby wood. Tessa opened the pack and removed the last of their food: cheese and two fried scones. Banaugh dipped cool, clear water into a tin cup he carried on his belt, and they sipped from it companionably as they ate. When the food was gone, Banaugh went off without a word to attend to his personal business. Tessa sat wrapped in her cloak, waiting patiently. He was an old man and would be a while.

The day was somewhat cool, but she sat on a rock that had warmed in the sun, the rays also warming her face. Closing her eyes, the girl hummed a little tune, trying to picture her uncle in her mind. Her own father had been dark and strongly built, so she guessed his brother would be the same. She remembered Kenneth's warm expression, his craggy face with the many small lines etched onto it by Scotland's unforgiving weather. Her father had been sickened by the violence of Scottish politics, where brother slew brother and son slew father with no regret if it meant power. She supposed that no matter how much they looked alike, that was the fundamental difference between the brothers macFindlaech: Kenneth had rejected such practices, and Macbeth had accepted them.

A noise made the girl open her eyes. Before her, indeed too near for comfort, were three wild-looking women. They stared at her intently and she drew back, startled. They were an eerie trio, with disheveled hair, tattered clothes, and odd eyes like hooded lanterns letting out small but intense rays of light. They paraded around the rock on which Tessa sat, making muttered sounds and little mewling cries. Recovering from her surprise somewhat, the girl spoke with a hint of challenge in her voice to cover her nervousness. "Who are you, and what do you want?"

The muttering continued with no notice taken of her question. One of the three reached out and took a strand of the girl's hair in gnarled fingers. Annoyed, Tessa pushed the hand away. The skin felt like old paper, dry and likely to crumble. She repeated, "Who are you?"

"On your way to England, are you?" one woman rasped.

"Of course not," Tessa replied. "I travel north, away from England." Like most Scots, Tessa had no use for the English, who claimed that they ruled Scotland. They were usually wise enough not to try to prove it.

The crone smiled dreamily and repeated, "On your way, on your way!"

The second spoke, her voice high and keening. "Always seeking!" A long, grubby finger waggled under Tessa's nose. "You'll find happiness only among the dead!"

"What do you mean?" Tessa didn't like the sound of that at all.

The woman repeated, ". . . only among the dead."

The one who'd touched her hair now spoke, her face close to Tessa's. She was missing several teeth in front, and her tongue slid through the gap, making her words slushy and sibilant. "Two men who marry you, Pretty, will never be your lover, but your true lover will forget your name!"

Tessa tried to make sense of the words, but in the end her temper got the better of her. For one thing, each woman repeated a part of her statement, and the cacophony became irritating. For another, the foul odor that emanated from the women, a mixture of unwashed bodies, bad breath, and ancient, musty wool, was nauseating. Tessa tried for a polite tone, practicing ladylike meekness.

"I will remember what you've said, but please leave me alone. I prefer to rest in peace and quiet."

The trio laughed gleefully at this, gasping out, "Peace and quiet! Peace and quiet!" until Tessa shut her eyes in frustration. Suddenly there was silence, and she opened her eyes to find them gone. There was no sign of their departure, no rustling in the bushes or movement in the grass. They had simply disappeared.

Shortly after, Banaugh returned to find Tessa sitting dazedly and she told him what had occurred. "I can find no sign of them. They vanished," she finished.

Banaugh shook his grizzled head. "I ha' heard o' such. They speak t' folk o' the future. But," he warned, "they love t' play tricks on humans, as all fairy folk do, so they tell the truth a-slant."

"What do you mean?"

"There's truth t' it, no mistake," Banaugh averred, "but it's no' plain. Truth hides in the words they speak."

Tessa thought about that for a moment. "Fairy folk, indeed! They were only crazy old women. Why, Banaugh, think of it. The very first thing they said was wrong. I'm *not* on my way to England. Now let's get on, no more time for prophecies!"

Macbeth's castle wasn't far from Tessa's home as the crow flies, but it took several days on foot to make the steep descent. Built at the extremity of Crown Hill, on a plain near the junction of the River Ness and the Moray Firth, the stronghold commanded a view of both land and sea for a long way, an easily defensible site. As they came into the valley, the travelers saw its outline and heard the bell signaling the evening meal from a long way off.

Although not really a castle by European standards, Inverness was impressive. As young men, Macbeth and Kenneth had traveled across England and to the Continent. Macbeth's home was modern compared to the old Scottish brochs that were simply thick-walled towers, with design evident in its construction. Every advantage had been taken of the terrain, and the motte was stone rather than the usual wood. There were no windows on the ground floor for defensive reasons, and the outer wall was manned by well-trained troopers in leather tunics and trews. The round tower sat centered in a large bailey, or castle yard, both substantial and imposing. Despite its fortress-like qualities, the place fit harmoniously into the roughly hewn Highland countryside. Tessa's heart lightened at the sight of it, and she promised herself she would please her aunt and be biddable and feminine.

And now she had been a model of propriety for two months, Tessa thought, returning to the present and the fireside. Gruoch had patiently taught Tessa the rudiments of running a castle, which any good noble wife must know. Chatelaines were responsible for managing the household, supplying the needs of the various members, and even defending the place when their husbands were away. Gruoch ran her husband's property efficiently and with a firm hand, leaving him free to deal with other matters.

Macbeth was a strong man, handsome in a rugged way, with a strong resemblance to his brother that drew Tessa to him. He had welcomed her pleasantly enough, although he made no inquiry into either his brother's life since they'd parted or his death. He seemed distracted and distant, often walking alone by the Firth in the evening. There were rumors of war, but in Scotland that was not unusual. Something else bothered him, but the thane's worries were not the business of one insignificant household female.

One night Tessa met her uncle as she walked along the Firth, looking longingly across at the mountains that had been her home. Macbeth approached without seeing her in the dusk, starting when he saw he was not alone. Tessa hurried to identify herself. "I am sorry, Uncle. I did not mean to disturb you."

"You are no disturbance, Niece. I too like to walk. It helps me to sort things out."

At his gesture, Tessa fell in beside him and they walked in silence for a few moments, the only sound the crunching of rough stones beneath their feet. "Is it difficult to be a man, Uncle?" Tessa asked suddenly.

Macbeth smiled. "I suppose so. I have never been else, so I cannot compare."

"My father told me of the days when he was young, how the kingship was the source of much trouble in the land."

"True," Macbeth agreed. "We swore fealty to Duncan after he killed his grandfather and took the throne."

"His own grandfather?" Tessa shivered at the idea.

"Aye. In Scotland even close relatives can be traitorous. Your father would not admit it, but that sort of thing is common. Kenneth chose to avoid conflict." Macbeth's voice showed both a lack of understanding and a slight distaste for his brother's choice. "Strength holds the kingship. A weak king is worse than no king at all."

Tessa said nothing. It was actions like Duncan's murder of his grandsire, she suspected, that had sent Kenneth into the mountains, removing himself from the matter.

Macbeth continued as if he'd forgotten she was there. "Duncan was strong then, and Scotland loves a strong king." His face clouded in the moonlight. "Lately the old man has shown weakness sure to bring trouble among the thanes. The last uprising he left entirely to Macduff and me. We did our part, of course, but it has led to talk of the king's changed personality."

"The king is very old, then?"

Her uncle smiled. "Older to you than he seems to me, but yes. Old for a fighting man, and that has led to another problem." Macbeth's voice took on a teaching tone, as if explaining to Tessa was important, but she sensed he was clarifying things in his own mind as well. "You see, Scottish kings are warriors, expected to take the field during battle. Furthermore, kingship is not necessarily handed down to the son of a king, but to the strongest fighting man. Yet Duncan recently named his older son Malcolm to succeed him. The boy is not of age, which should have prevented his being chosen. Several noblemen are upset, having as good a claim as the boy by blood." Tessa knew that his own noble blood made Macbeth a possible candidate. It was obvious that her uncle wrestled with his own conscience in light of the king's weakness and Scotland's demands.

They reached the castle gate, and the guards snapped to attention. Remembering to whom he spoke, Macbeth concluded, "It is a coil, but nothing you must worry about, pretty Tessa. Scotland has gone on for a long time, and it will not end with you or me." With that, her uncle bowed slightly and continued up the stairs to his chamber.

That talk was the only real contact Tessa had had with her uncle, but it gave her insight as she sat now by the fireside with his wife. It was the possibility of kingship that Lady Macbeth considered when she criticized the weakness of men. Plainly she thought her husband should make a bid for the throne, and he had not. Tessa imagined her aunt's chilling touch on Macbeth's face as she spurred him toward ambition, and she shuddered.

The chemistry between Macbeth and Gruoch was familiar to Tessa, for her parents' marriage had been similar. The male was the head of the Scottish household, to be sure, but both Gruoch and Kenna macFindlaech made their husbands aware of their wishes in no uncertain terms. The difference between them was that Tessa's mother had been likely to rant and carry on, while Gruoch managed her husband with probing looks and cool little silences.

Watching her aunt now as she stitched on, Tessa said no more, since she didn't know enough about King Duncan to make a judgment. Was he cowardly? Senile? The business of kings was nothing to do with her, she reminded herself. Tessa sighed and returned to work on the tapestry that was supposed to be a lady's form of relaxation.

CHAPTER THREE

That night there were guests for dinner, and Tessa was introduced to her Uncle Biote, the thane of Cawdor. This man she regarded with some curiosity, since he was her mother's brother and she might have been sent to live with him. Three daughters of marriageable age gave him enough to handle, so she'd been sent to the childless Macbeth.

"I heard you were a beauty, and it was not a lie," Biote said as he kissed his niece's cheek in greeting. Gruoch had let Tessa make over one of her old dresses, since she'd had only two and neither very grand. The dress was of the softest fabric she'd ever owned, made of deep green wool that suited her coloring. The fact that she'd botched the sewing a bit in her haste to finish didn't show unless one looked closely. Uncle Biote was red-haired, like his sister Kenna, but thin-lipped and becoming paunchy. "I have all lasses meself, more's the pity. Ooch! The expense of those three! But they are dear to my heart," he boomed, offering his arm to Tessa as they went to the table.

The boards had been set up on trestles in the center of the great room, and here family, household, and guests met for the evening meal. Although they usually ate simply here in the north, there were enough people in the thane's household to make the evening meal a large endeavor, and extra care had been taken tonight because of Cawdor's visit. There was always meat, of course, but tonight there would be several kinds: venison, fish, beef, and fowl, roasted on large spits in the cookhouse. Bread and scones made fresh daily would be served with preserved berries and fruits put up by Gruoch herself, a source of pride for her. There would be a large pudding for dessert, and of course, haggis. The room hummed with good humor and smelled of a dozen tasty dishes. Tessa had a large appetite despite her tiny figure and looked forward to the meal with enthusiasm.

The evening soon became more interesting. Tessa sat next to her Uncle Cawdor as directed by the steward just as an amazing man appeared in the doorway, his clothes the finest Tessa had ever seen. A long tunic of gleaming white wool fell loosely over closely fitted white hose. On one shoulder hung a short cape, also of white and trimmed in some sort of fur. The toes of his shoes were pointed, and around his waist was fastened a belt of thin gold discs with a scabbard at the side for his knife. Tessa's own knife hung at her belt, but the belt was simply a leather strap, and the knife slipped through a loop of twine.

Apart from his wonderful clothes, the new arrival was nothing short of perfect in form and face. Over medium height, he towered above the servant who announced him, yet moved with the grace of an athlete. Blue eyes and black hair made an odd but striking combination. A wayward lock hung over his forehead, returning there immediately each time he swept it back with a hand. At one side of his mouth, a small line appeared and disappeared from time to time. Tessa would soon learn that its appearance signified repressed humor. His skin, browned from the out-of-doors, was smooth, his face cleanly shaven. *Handsome* was hardly a word to describe him, but in Scotland, no male would appreciate being called beautiful.

"I'm sorry to be late," the man said, and his accent gave Tessa a shock. He was

English! A great deal of her interest drained away. Handsome to be sure, but a waste of good looks and fine clothes if he came from such a place! She knew from stories, songs, and discussions around the fire in her father's home that the English were a cowardly, conniving lot who respected none but themselves. It was surprising that such a one was guest to her uncle.

"We were sitting down this minute," Gruoch answered, always the cordial hostess. "Come, sit next to me, sir. I am interested to hear of your travels." She made an imperious motion and the three people on her side of the table moved down the bench to make room for the Englishman.

As the young man obeyed, he was introduced to the assembled diners by Macbeth. "This is Jeffrey Brixton, who has brought us a new bull from his brother's herd near York, for which I am grateful." Tessa understood the need for new breeding stock for healthy cattle, even from England, so she supposed the man must be fed.

Brixton addressed the whole table. "Being the fourth of four sons, I am expendable and sent on all sorts of errands. Some might complain, but I appreciate the chances I get to see the world." He spoke in a silly, overdone manner that, Tessa reminded herself, one should expect from English-men. His head bobbed slightly from side to side as he spoke, and his voice was too high and drawling to convey masculinity. In spite of this, Brixton made himself the center of attention as he praised Macbeth's hall, his lands, and especially his wife. "I had heard of the lady's beauty," he gushed, "but it is beyond the rumors. Macbeth is the luckiest of men to have found such a treasure."

Macbeth thanked Brixton solemnly as Gruoch smiled patiently. She was used to such praise, being a beautiful woman despite her cold personality. She called a page to fill a cup for Brixton, Macbeth spoke to the steward, and the serving commenced with efficient clanks and chops. Only Tessa, still taking in the stranger's spectacular appear-ance, saw him glance around the room with an expression that belied his earlier friendli-ness. The unguarded look was calculating and unfriendly.

Something was wrong about this man. Contrary to appearances, the Englishman was not happy to be there but was watchful and alert beneath his pose of clownishness. Sensing Tessa's interest, he turned toward her. The striking eyes met hers for a mo-ment and by the merest movement man-aged to convey something she did not understand. Acknowledgement of her beauty? A jibe at himself? She had only the briefest sense of it and could not fathom its meaning. Brixton's attention returned to his hostess, who handed him a wine cup with her own hand in thanks for his compliment.

Jeffrey Brixton quickly became Tessa's greatest challenge since arriving at Inverness. While others at the table found him amusing, even hilarious, she grew less and less able to control her dislike of the man. Throughout the meal he entertained with stories of his travels, all told in a simpering manner with much waving of his hands and rolling of his eyes. His tales centered on himself, making fun of his position in life and the various circumstances he had gotten into while carrying out his brother's somewhat trivial and often complicated orders.

It seemed that the Brixton manor provided well-respected breeding stock all over northern England and Scotland. Jeffrey was often dispatched to escort the animals to their destination, sometimes with humorous results. According to one story, he had delivered thirty hens to a neighboring manor for an exchange that would serve to freshen each estate's stock. "The only problem was that the rooster, overcome with joy at the sight of all the hens, flew in my face with great enthusiasm, leaving two distinct claw prints on my best linen tunic," he finished with a moue that brought guffaws of laughter.

The company enjoyed the unexpected entertainment, and it seemed that only Tessa was irritated by the man's manner, his attitude, indeed, his very presence. She could not say why she disliked Brixton so. He was English, true. He was silly, also true. But something in the look she had observed earlier said he was dangerous as well.

The hall, of course, was noisy with the coming and going of servants, as platter after platter was brought in from the kitchen, a small building at the back of the castle, and placed at the head table. Before each place lay a slice of bread that served as a plate. Each person helped himself to whatever he liked, using the knife at his belt to cut chunks of meat, bread, or cheese from the platters, and laid it onto the bread, where bite-sized morsels were cut and carried to the mouth with the same knife. Bowls of gravy set along the tables were for dipping bits of meat or bread in, and small bowls of salt graced the main table, allowing the more privileged at the meal to sprinkle the precious stuff on their food.

When the meat was gone, the bread, soaked with the juices, could be eaten, too. Young pages stood by with pitchers of wine and cider to refill the tin cups at each place.

Laughing diners threw bones and scraps over their shoulders to the dogs. It was wise to be sure that these landed far enough away to avoid canine arguments under the table. The noise of dogfights sometimes became clamorous, but at a word from Macbeth the animals slunk away to a corner to wait more patiently. It being spring and the weather having broken, the ducks and geese that often wandered the hall, cleaning up the smaller scraps from the floor, had been shooed outside. Over all was the babble of many voices raised in the genial conversation that attends a good meal. Jeffrey Brixton's very different accent rose and fell among the others, and Tessa found herself more and more irritated by it.

When the meal was concluded and the boards and trestles stacked against the wall to clear the room, some of the household members brought out musical instruments for evening entertainment. Brixton volunteered to teach them dance steps from England. "I insist on returning value for my welcome by brightening the evening," he gushed, flopping his hands like a puppet.

"Of course, I am a poor dancer compared to others I have seen, but you must needs make do with me for lack of another." Despite the fact that this was something any polite guest might offer, Tessa found his manner insufferable, as if he were offering pearls before swine. He assumed that no one there knew the latest English dances and also assumed that they wanted to learn them. How like an Englishman to think himself above those who'd fed him!

"I'll need a partner." He paced the room dramatically for a few seconds. "You'll do." Coming out of her thoughts, Tessa found Brixton standing before her, indicating with open arms that she should dance with him.

The girl felt pulled in two directions. Her mother's voice commanded her to be lady-like and submissive, but her own inner voice rose up for the first time in months. She could not pretend that this man was as charming as he obviously found himself. Scottish men had been rejected for taking Tessa's assent for granted. Why should an English fop fare better? She raised her eyes to Brixton's, her chin high and her mouth a thin line. "I don't dance," was out of her mouth before she could stop it.

Immediately, Tessa sensed a chill like an actual draft from the general direction of her aunt. Girls did as they were told, even when they didn't want to, and a good hostess saw to it that the wishes of her guests were indulged. Something in Tessa rebelled still further as weeks of watching every word and facial expression caused a sudden break in her self-control. In Jeffrey Brixton's blue eyes glinted something that might have been a challenge, and heedlessly, she finished the thought. "And if I did, it would never be with an Englishman!"

"Tessa!" escaped from Gruoch at the same moment that a growl escaped the thane of Glames.

"Apologize to our guest, child, and leave us. If you cannot be civil, you'll bide by yourself."

Her uncle's face was stern. Thoughts of complying with the command formed, but Brixton's expression stopped her. He faced her, away from Macbeth and his lady, and the look in his eyes was not at all that of the character he had displayed thus far. There was danger, turbulence, and passion in it, and she felt something in herself responding to this man. Her response frightened her, angered her, and decided her. She would never apologize to this man, even if they beat her!

With head held high, Tessa stepped around

Jeffrey Brixton as if touching him would be odious, which it would. Fleeing the room, she heard her aunt making apologies, heard the words "young and untaught." She felt the heat of Brixton's eyes burning into her back and could picture the expression on his face, though she'd known him for only an hour. There would be that line of amusement beside his mouth, and the blue eyes would spark dangerously. *There, Mother,* the girl thought bitterly. *All your predictions for me have come true! My traitorous tongue has ruined two months of careful behavior!*

CHAPTER FOUR

The next morning Tessa slipped out of the castle early, unwilling to hear what Gruoch would have to say about her awful behavior the night before or to spend another day inside stitching harts and hinds onto cloth. There had been no response yet. That, she was sure, would be left for when the guests had gone. While she was still free to move about, Tessa looked upward, toward home.

In the mountains, she had learned to love the outdoors. With the lads who were her playmates, Tessa had learned to ride the shaggy Highland ponies, swim in the icy tarns and burns, and climb into the thick, prickly hawthorn trees to hide, escaping Kenna's wrath for a while. Now as dawn brought the first gray light, she found it calming to be outside, away from things that recalled her failings.

On this late April morning, fog hung thick overhead and wisped along the River Ness, making an odd, patchy landscape of brightly visible green spots and dimly perceived gray hills. Tessa walked down to the riverbank and stood looking across at her mountains as they peeped through the fog, remembering happier days from her childhood, now gone forever, among those peaks. She seated herself under a tree that overhung the riverbank, out of the cold wind coming off the water. The two men did not see her sitting there wrapped in her gray cloak for warmth as they walked along the river together, and since the fog muted all sound, Tessa heard nothing of their approach. She sat wondering if Banaugh had gotten home safely and if Meg was awake too, perhaps missing the secrets they'd shared. When one of the men spoke on the other side of the tree, Tessa came out of her reverie with a start.

"You'll sail to England with the tide, then?"

"Yes. I'll meet with Sweno as soon as possible. We'll return within the month with the necessary troops from Norway," came the answer in a very different accent.

"I will ready my men and join the fray when you attack Duncan's forces."

The second voice was recognizable even though this morning it was lower-pitched and stronger than the dandified tones of the night before. "You'll want to wait and see which way the wind blows, Cawdor, but fight beside us or you'll lose the reward you've been promised."

Cawdor! Tessa's eyes flew wide as she comprehended what she was hearing. Her mother's brother and the Englishman planned to attack the Scottish king! The night before Gruoch had mentioned that Tessa's funny little uncle spoke strongly against Duncan, but Macbeth had given him no encouragement. Now it was clear that Cawdor had made a bargain to side with a Norwegian invasion. And the Englishman Brixton was not what he seemed . . . of course. The English were ever deceitful, willing to undermine Scotland in any way possible, loathsome creatures that they were.

"Dinna worry, Brixton. Keep your part of the bargain, and I will keep mine. Duncan has gone daft, and the people won't stand for the boy Malcolm as king. If Sweno moves quickly, he can have his way. The thanes will fight half-heart or maybe no' at all for the auld man. For certes, Macdonwald and I will be with you, maybe more by the time you arrive." As he spoke, Cawdor stepped down the riverbank to pick up a stick, which he tossed idly into the current and watched float away. Turning back, he faced Tessa, who stared into his eyes in horror. The niece he had met only last evening at dinner had, from the look on her face, overheard his plan to turn traitor to his king! "Tessa!" His tone held both surprise and threat.

Cawdor made a lunge as, throwing herself sideways out of his reach, Tessa scrambled to her feet to make a getaway. Hearing Biote curse as he fell over a tree root, she dared not look back. She focused on getting to the castle, getting help, but before she knew it, strong arms caught her, lifting her off the ground. A hand covered her mouth as she opened it to scream, and a voice in her ear hissed, "Make one noise and I'll break that pretty neck of yours!" Unable to free herself, Tessa hung, struggling uselessly, at the Englishman's side.

"Well, now, Cawdor, what do we do with this?" Amazingly, Brixton's voice sounded amused again.

Cawdor had risen to his feet and was brushing off his clothing. "Damned if I know," was his first response.

There was a smudge of damp earth on his knee, Tessa noticed inconsequentially. She stopped fighting to better hear their discussion of her fate.

"Is she someone who would be missed?" Brixton asked, and Tessa thought, *I'm going to die. He's going to kill me and throw my body into the river.*

Cawdor looked distraught. "God's blood, Brixton! She's my sister's child."

Brixton understood the plea. "Well, then," was all he said. Although they planned treachery against the king, neither seemed willing to murder an innocent girl. Maybe they would try to bribe her. Tessa would lie, promise secrecy, and then run to Macbeth and have them both hanged for treason. Could an Englishman commit treason in Scotland? It did not matter as long as this wicked man died. Surely Macbeth could find a reason to execute him.

"We can't let her go," the Englishman said.

"Perhaps I can reason with her," Cawdor tried. "She is my niece, after all —"

"Have you ever known a female who could be trusted to do what you want her to?"

Cawdor had to admit that he hadn't. "But she's —"

"I heard you, man. What do you want me to do?"

"Could you take her with you?"

There was no amusement in the Englishman's voice at this suggestion. "Take her with me? You want me to sail to England with a half-grown girl and arrange a war for you? What's she to do while I collect Norwegian soldiers?"

"You could . . ." Cawdor had no idea and grasped at straws. ". . . drop her off somewhere."

"Do you know what you're saying? It would be kinder to snap her neck here and now than to abandon her in York or London. She's hardly civilized, doesn't even fit into Scottish society, primitive as it is." Tessa burned with indignation. Who was he to judge her? A spy!

"Please, Brixton! Think of someplace for her, just for a month or two, and then when the war's over, I'll take her off your hands, I promise. I'll marry her off to some young man who won't care that she's . . . damaged." Tessa's heart froze at the insinuation. This man could have her if he prevented her telling about Cawdor and the uprising. So much for family feeling. Her death might bother him, but not the ruin of her body, her reputation, and her life.

"I don't know what else we can do," said Brixton finally. "I don't like it, though, not at all."

"I know, lad, I know." Cawdor was sympathetic now that he'd got his way. "If there were any other way . . . but you're the one who's to leave this morning. I must stay and play my part with the Scots."

"Give me your kerchief, then," Brixton muttered. "At least I will see that she doesn't get away." Setting Tessa on the ground, Brixton kept one arm around her neck while her uncle tied her hands behind her back. Testing Biote's work with a sharp tug on the cloth, he spoke directly to Tessa for the first time.

"Now, girl, here it is. I do not want to take you with me, but I would rather not have to kill you. If you go quietly, I will not harm you, and I will try to treat you fairly when we arrive in England. If you give me trouble, I will drown you in the river. Do you understand?"

Unable to do anything else at the moment, Tessa nodded. Trying to convey with a look how vile she found them both, she saw her uncle cringe, which gave her some satisfaction despite her plight. Brixton arranged the cloak over her shoulders so her bound hands were hidden and pulled the hood low to cover her hair and face.

"How will you get her on board ship?" Cawdor asked. "They won't be planning for any women."

"I'll say I'm taking the girl to England as

a favor to the thane," Brixton answered. "The captain will be surprised, no doubt, but he's well paid to keep his thoughts to himself."

"Ah." Cawdor suddenly looked unhappy, chewing his lip and frowning. "I wouldna have the girl suffer," he began. "She is blood, you know."

Brixton sniffed. "You Scots have been spilling each other's blood for centuries, family or no. How did Duncan become King Duncan? How did our host last night gain his castle and his wife? Killing relatives, that's how."

Cawdor became angry, too, but on him it was less than impressive. His paunch quivered as he tried to draw himself up to full height, and his jowly cheeks shook. "And are the English any better? I think not."

Suddenly Brixton smiled sheepishly. "You're right. We English also kill each other, relatives and all, for personal gain. It is the way of men, I fear." His face took on a pensive look, but he shook it off and changed the subject. "Do not worry, sir. I will not abandon your niece, and I have no desire to hurt her. I will take her to my brother's wife, who may take on a half-grown brat, having no children of her own."

Tessa considered objecting that she

wanted no part of his wicked family, but in the end remained silent. She had to think of a way to reach Macbeth, who would save the king, or even Gruoch, who would never side with the English despite despising Duncan. She watched and waited for any chance as Brixton bade Cawdor goodbye and herded her to the pier, where a small ship was being readied for departure.

The morning was still gray, but the fog was thinning, its damp hold on the riverbank reluctantly letting go. She saw several sailors, all English judging by their harsh-sounding speech and unfamiliar clothing. Would any of them help her if she were to scream out that she was being captured? Looking into the eyes of one who stopped his labor to leer at her, she doubted it. They despised the Scots, she knew, and would side with Brixton against one who was both female and Scot. He had their allegiance, he had money, and she had nothing. Tessa's heart was heavy as she accepted that her situation was hopeless. She cursed Jeffrey Brixton silently as they proceeded in apparent amity toward the ship that would become her prison.

Brixton kept a hand lightly on Tessa's neck as they walked up the gangplank. He explained casually to the captain that there would be an extra passenger. Gold was exchanged, and the captain gave her the merest look of interest before returning to his preparations. Brixton led her into a tiny cabin formed by canvas sheets draped from the mast, the only private place on the ship. Once he'd pulled the curtain to shield them from curious eyes, he untied her hands and moved his belongings to a corner of the space, spreading a blanket on the floor.

"You may take the pallet, as much comfort as it will give," Brixton told her. "No one can help you. The men on this ship are in my employ and have no interest in what happens to a Scottish brat. If I have to beat you to keep you quiet . . . well, I will do that, too."

It was said in such an offhand manner that she knew that he meant it. Soon Tessa heard the men cry out orders as the ship left its docking and started out to the sea. There had been no chance to escape, no chance to warn of Cawdor's treachery. And now she was on her way to England.

Suddenly, the three crones' faces appeared in her mind, and she heard the first one repeating, "on your way, on your way, on your way . . ." Falling onto the tiny bunk, Tessa turned away, shivering despite the heavy cloak.

CHAPTER FIVE

A day later, Tessa's despair abated somewhat with the acceptance of change that youth affords and with the fact that her worst fears had not materialized. She was alive, though a prisoner; safe, though torn from all she knew well. To her surprise, Jeffrey Brixton had left her untouched; in fact, he had largely ignored her once the ship cleared Macbeth's territory. Good, she told herself. She had nothing to say to the man anyway.

Having never been on a boat before, Tessa took some interest in the vessel on which she rode, which smelled, not surprisingly, strongly of fish. It was clinker-built, which meant that planks had been overlapped to form its sides. A single square sail hung on the mast, and oars bristled from the sides as alternate power. It was maneuvered by means of a "steerboard" roped to the right side. The center was about fifteen feet across, and the mid-section was tented to provide their private space, about six feet square. The sailors weren't pleased to have a woman aboard, but gold counted for more than superstition.

Brixton stayed on deck except to sleep at night, avoiding contact with Tessa. From a small boy who came in to bring food and remove the slops, she learned that they were headed south to Grimsby, a fishing town at the mouth of the Humber River, where she and Brixton would travel west toward York, Brixton's home. Rob, who disliked the "Robin" most of the men on board called him, was from that area himself and enjoyed talking — and boasting — about home.

"There's a fine minster, as fine as you would see in London, I'm thinking," he told Tessa, bracing himself without effort as the little ship shifted. "And the town is full of shops where you can buy anything in the world."

Tessa, though a few years older than the boy, felt intimidated by his description. She herself had never been in a town of any size at all, although her father and uncle had traveled as young men, and she had heard tales of London and even Paris. What if one became lost in all those tiny streets and huddled shops?

The boy was a good source of information, although he feared a box on the ears if he stayed too long. "Now young Brixton," he told Tessa, using a term he'd heard the older men use, "he's got no prospects, you see. The estate went to his eldest brother, as is right, and there are two more brothers above him. So even though Lord Brixton has no children, this one will never see the title, more's the pity, 'cause we like him best of all of 'em, we do."

Tessa had her own opinion of Brixton, but unwilling to alienate her source, she merely nodded. Perhaps the older Brixtons were less despicable than this one, but she couldn't see how they could be. Did they all kidnap innocent young women and plot against neighboring governments? Of course, being English, they might.

Rob went on, picking up the porridge bowl she had emptied. "Master Jeffrey always treats us well, and he's generous when he gets a payday."

"And for what does Master Brixton get paid?" Tessa could not help but ask, wondering how much the boy knew of this man's perfidious vocation.

"Young Brixton's a soldier, miss," came the reply, "and a brave one too, I trow. He fights for armies that need men. A mercenary, he is, well paid sometimes but not often enough, he says. See, there're lots of young men of good family with no money, so they hire themselves out to fight, like Master Jeffrey does. Cap'n says he's making quite a name for himself, 'cause he's brave and smart."

A mercenary! That explained some things that had bothered Tessa. Brixton had seemed a simpering sort at her uncle's home, but that mien had been replaced with a stronger, harsher face the next morning. Now she understood that he'd played a part, acting the pampered English fool that the Scots expected, all the while beneath it gathering information and planning destruction. More detestable than she'd first thought.

She drank the last of her cider and handed Robin the tin cup. "So he's in the employ of the Norwegians at the English king's connivance?" she asked calmly.

Rob had the grace to look a bit abashed. "There's many in the North country as doesn't take to the Scots raiding our lands and stealing our cattle. If we can keep the thanes busy elsewhere, it leaves us in peace, y'see."

"Mm," was all Tessa could manage lest she let her anger spill out at the boy. Scottish raids were in reprisal for English attacks. She could have recounted generations of maltreatment the Scots had suffered from English troops, but she knew it was of no use. The boy, like most of the English, thought the Scots half-wild, half-wicked savages, fit only to be kept in their place with military might. If Rob could have seen the fine banquet her aunt had laid and her uncle had presided over that night when Jeffrey Brixton had falsely accepted their hospitality while plotting against the Scottish throne!

Rob finished his tasks and left, giving her a cheery nod. Alone in the tiny cabin, Tessa cast about for something to do, anything to pass the time. The sounds and feel of the ship had quickly become monotonous, almost hypnotic. She wandered aimlessly in a circle, all the space available for exercise unless she went on deck, where the sailors leered until her face burned red. Attractive she was — "bonny Tess," her father had called her — but the looks these men focused on her made her ashamed of her body, as if they were imagining what lay under the dress she wore. As a result she stayed below, all the while chafing with nothing to occupy her, not even the tapestry she had once detested.

In the corner where Brixton's things lay

she noticed a book's corner protruding from under the blanket. Despite it not being usual for females, Tessa could read. Her father had taught her, having no sons and no other child who was in the least interested. Although her mother considered it useless at best and evil at worst, Kenneth had worked with Tessa several evenings a week, teaching her to read the few precious books he possessed, proud of her progress. "It's because she wears herself out with being a tomboy and so can do nothing useful a' nights," was her mother's acrid response. Tessa loved the feel of books in her hands, loved deciphering the written word. She even had an understanding of the differences between her native Scots and English, languages similar but not the same.

Reaching to pick up the book, she hesitated. Would Brixton be angry? The thought itself was enough to urge her onward. So much the better if he was. He'd stolen her from her home and family. Let his anger have scope; she didn't care!

The book was homemade: a sheaf of papers folded together and fastened with string to a leather sheet that formed a cover. The pages were written in a masculine hand, forming clear, large letters. Almost at once Tessa realized it was Brixton's own writing, a journal of his activities, thoughts, and opinions, begun some two years back and continuing to just over a week before. Tessa paged through the book, reading bits here and there. A picture of the man emerged as she read:

May, 1037: I embark on my career, it being plain that my brother William wants none of me. Ethelbert has chosen the church as his vocation, and Aidan stays home despite William's broad hints and small discourtesies. I will have none of it. If the lord of Brixton Hall wants me gone, then gone I shall be. I aim to win for myself a name and perhaps even a title. Both are possible as strong men seek support for their various causes. One day I will no longer need my brother's grudging providence of my equipment for campaign. Then I will pay him back and bid him farewell. Aidan will probably drink himself to death by thirty years anyway, and then William will be alone. My heart aches for Eleanor, though, left by herself in that crumbling house while her husband plays the courtier in London. Perhaps that's why he dislikes me so. Eleanor is fond of me and it makes him uncomfortable. It is ironic that he is jealous of what he holds so lightly. He treats her with cold politeness when she wants so much to be loved.

Tessa stopped reading for a moment. So Brixton was in love with his sister-in-law. No wonder his brother wanted him somewhere else. And he had the nerve to deplore the turmoil in Scotland! She scanned more recent entries.

November, 1038: I have offered my sword to nothing, it seems. There is no real king of England. Hardecanute is more Dane than anything, and the court is full of foreigners. One must speak Norman French, Norwegian Danish, and Anglish simply to eat a meal in the hall. There is much dissention among them, and while there is plenty of opportunity to fight, I wonder what it all means. They tell us we must subdue the Welsh, so we go east and make a show of force. Then we must sail to Denmark to help the king with unrest there, then to Norway and west again to Scotland. It is certainly enough to keep a man busy and earn him his keep, but to what avail is it?

Our little island seems destined to be ruled by one foreigner after another. My own people were Saxons who, with

Angles, Jutes and other tribes of wanderers, took the land from the Celts who lived there after the Romans left, then the Vikings came with their terrible raids and settled the coast, pushing us inland. Even the Normans in France make noises about claims to the throne of England. For whom do I fight, or for what? Is there a nation called England, or will it disintegrate into small warring kingdoms as it has done before? I have little faith that the current rulers can keep control.

Tessa stopped reading and considered. The boy who left home anxious for glory had changed in less than two years into a man who saw the world differently. She thought of her own family: two uncles, both unhappy with their king. One would betray him, and the other had probably considered it. Was there anywhere in the world where people lived peacefully?

The curtain parted at that moment and Brixton came in, taking in with one glance what she was doing. Tearing the book from Tessa's hands, he threw it to the rough plank floor and grabbed her, his strong fingers digging into her arms. He pulled her to him, her face close to his, and hissed furiously, "You snooping little Scottish bitch! Is nothing safe from you? I only left it because I assumed you could not read, but you *were* reading, weren't you?"

Tessa felt momentary guilt, knowing she had violated the man's privacy, and fear, thinking he might strike her. Despite both, her temperament asserted itself, and she spat back at him, "I was not asked if I wanted this voyage, Englishman! You brought me against my will! Nothing is safe from *you* — not my family, my country, nor my life! It matters not to me what you do now, for I can never go back home after your hands have been on me!"

Jeffrey's blue eyes blazed. "My hands on you? Why, I wouldn't touch you at all if I didn't have to! Hell kite!" He still held her close, and Tessa felt an odd sensation she had never known before. It was a kind of heat in the center of her, like melting from inside out. Fighting it back, she concentrated on her anger.

"Then let me go, Englishman," she said as calmly — and as haughtily — as she could.

Brixton looked in confusion at first his left hand, and then his right, as if they disobeyed him. Finally they opened and released Tessa, who stepped back, face flushed and heart pounding. Neither said a word. Brixton bent to retrieve his journal, his face red but expressionless. Tessa stood rigid where he'd left her, feeling a mix of emotions that she did not understand. Anger was there — she clung to that — but underneath was the heat of his touch. Her mind whirled with an unusual urge to apologize, to say that she understood his disillusionment with life. She, too, had been rejected — by her own mother. She hadn't seen the treachery of political struggle that he had, but she'd begun to understand at Inverness Castle the false smiles and hidden hatreds between those who had power and those who wanted it. Should she tell him she was sorry she'd read his private thoughts?

Tessa found it difficult to form such words. She'd never apologized to anyone except her father, and she'd always been sure of his forgiveness. "Master Brixton, I . . ." She turned to face him and found that he'd recovered himself, replacing the look of anger with the one she had disliked from their first meeting, amused scorn. His blue eyes gazed directly into hers, and one eyebrow rose in a sort of question as his lips quivered with humor and the tiny line appeared beside his mouth. It was his way of saying she hadn't hurt him, and nothing ever could.

Any desire Tessa might have had to apologize fled. "Master Brixton, when next you enter this cabin, the civilized thing would be to give warning. A lady shouldn't have to abide unannounced visits, even from an Englishman, who, of course, knows no better." With that she lay down on the bunk and turned her back to Jeffrey Brixton, who stared in disbelief for a few seconds, then exited the cabin in disgust.

CHAPTER SIX

By the time the little ship sailed up the Humber, the weather had warmed considerably. They were far south of Inverness, of course, and spring was farther advanced. Flowers had begun to peep out of the hedges and roadsides, many Tessa had never seen before, and their fragrance wafted over them as they journeyed along to the west.

They left the ship at Kingston upon Hull and traveled on in a small fishing boat Brixton hired to take them up the Ouse to York. Brixton Hall was actually south of the town somewhat, so Tessa did not glimpse the sights young Rob had described so glowingly. The home of the Brixtons was made of stone, as befitted their station. Rising two stories in height, it was stately but not ornate, large but not grand. Set back from the riverbank far enough to avoid floodwaters, it was near enough for convenient travel and provisioning. Trees as yet only lightly green formed a backdrop, making a charming frame for the house. At the east side were gardens and on the west various outbuildings.

Although not truly a castle, the house was defensible enough, with strong outer doors that led into an entryway with a second set of doors. There being no immediate threat, both sets stood open, facing the river so that Tessa could see directly into the great hall.

Jeffrey Brixton straightened and dusted his tunic with both hands, then helped Tessa out of the boat and led her up the path to the house. She felt very nervous, as she had when approaching Macbeth's castle, only worse, since these people were not family, but enemies.

"Say nothing at all until I've had the chance to explain," Brixton ordered. She resented his tone, but the anger that welled up helped her face her fears. "It's not that she won't take you, but she shouldn't think I assumed she would. Even if I did," he admitted.

Tessa recalled that Jeffrey's journal had revealed he loved this Eleanor who was married to his brother. She ignored him as if he had not spoken.

The great hall, the home's center of activity, was a large, sparsely furnished room where everyone passed on their way to everywhere else. The ceiling was two stories high, useful for dispersing the smoke in winter. Around the edges of the hall were small rooms, or closets, where various people slept. A spiral staircase circled up one side of the room, and there were more closets upstairs, these slightly larger, for family members. No room was terribly large, for that would make it hard to heat in winter. At the back of the hall were the fireplace and a door to the cookhouse outside, where meals were prepared.

Later a servant would explain to Tessa that Brixton Hall, like other modern homes, had a specially designed "water closet" on the second story, where the back wall of the house was extended a few feet and a board with a hole in it laid across the span. Tessa would come to appreciate this improvement to the outhouses she had experienced all her life.

At that moment Eleanor Brixton appeared on the stair, and Tessa saw why she held Jeffrey's heart. Here was a lady from a fairy tale, one Banaugh might have described in his stories of Tristan. Tall, willowy, and fair, she seemed to float downstairs as she hurried to embrace Jeffrey.

"Dear little brother!" She laughed as she

greeted him, and well she could laugh, for she didn't look a day older than he. Her blue eyes sparkled and her skin was perfectly white with only a faint flush of happiness at his appearance. "I wish you had warned us of your arrival. I have made no preparations, and William is away."

"All the better," Jeffrey answered deliberately. "I would have neither of you go out of your way for me." But he embraced her warmly, and Tessa could see affection in his eyes. A very different man than she had seen thus far.

"And have you brought home a wife, then?" Eleanor stepped back and examined Tessa. Her gaze was good-humored, and no jealousy showed in her face. Tessa knew her appearance could not be flattering after days aboard ship, and she blushed under Eleanor's gaze. The lady herself was elegantly turned out in a dun-colored dress with long, tight sleeves and softly draped skirt. A simple garment, but on Eleanor it was transformed into loveliness. While Tessa had hurriedly braided her thick hair into two long plaits as the best she could do, Eleanor's blond hair was gathered smoothly at the back of her neck and tied up in a snood of the same color as her dress. To her credit, the lady seemed not to notice Tessa's disheveled state.

"No, this is no wife of mine," Jeffrey responded to Eleanor's question. "She is the niece of a friend, who asked me to watch over her while he is on business."

Eleanor's eyebrows rose. "This friend left a young female in the care of a man only a few years older? Is he mad? He can't know you as I do, and trust that you would not harm her." Tessa, searching for clues to their relationship, reacted to the lady's assumption. Was she so sure of his love that she had no doubts as to his fidelity?

Tessa almost spoke, but Brixton's grip on her arm tightened. "The Scots' ways are different from ours."

"I would say so," was the woman's reply. "But Jeffrey, she cannot travel around England with you willy-nilly. She must stay here with us until it is time for her to return to her family."

The grip on Tessa's arm relaxed a bit. He'd got what he wanted. Tessa guessed he was used to it, with his looks and the charm he exuded when it suited. "You are kind, Eleanor, as always." He smiled wryly. "Truthfully, I hoped you would ask. The girl is a detriment to my work."

"Then it is settled. Will you introduce us, or must we acquaint ourselves?"

Jeffrey's handsome face showed consternation and his feet shuffled nervously as he struggled for an answer and finally gave up. "Acquaint yourself with her, Eleanor, for I'm blessed if I know the girl's name."

Eleanor looked confused, then incredulous, then amused. "Jeffrey, Jeffrey," she admonished. "What other man could travel from Scotland with a lovely young woman and never think to ask her name?" She turned to Tessa. "I apologize for my brother-in-law. He thinks only of war and combat and has no time for the fair sex. I am Eleanor Brixton, and I welcome you to Brixton Hall."

Tessa responded unconsciously to the first kindness she'd experienced in days. "I thank you, madam. I am Tessa of the clan macFindlaech, and I appreciate being in the company of civilized folk once more." She glanced at Brixton as she said this, and he rolled his eyes in aggravation. Eleanor saw but went on without comment, taking Tessa's arm and leading her into the house.

In a very few minutes, Tessa was established in a small closet off the main hall, which held a pallet, a stand with a pitcher and basin, a peg for her cloak, and a stool. Eleanor, noticing she had no personal belongings, gave Jeffrey a probing look and promised a hairbrush and other items she would need. She then left Tessa to rest, telling her that a bell would ring when the evening meal was ready. "You must sit beside me, Mistress macFindlaech, so I can learn more about you," Eleanor said in farewell.

Tessa found that she actually needed rest, for although she'd had little activity on the two boats, she'd slept fitfully due to the movement of the waves and her own disquiet. Nodding, she wondered briefly what Jeffrey Brixton would tell his sister-in-law when they were alone. How would he explain her to his lover?

When Tessa awoke, there was a small pile of items on the stool beside her pallet. She was delighted to find a clean dress and undershift, both long for her, which she took to mean they were Eleanor's own. The dress was a deep blue, and a girdle of bleached hemp was folded inside it. There was a rough cloth to wash with, and the water in the pitcher was warm. She washed, put on the clean clothes, and brushed her hair, putting into its heavy waves two combs made of some type of shell. The last gift, a pair of soft slippers, were also too big, but she could keep them on if she shuffled a bit.

As she finished her toilette, the bell rang

for dinner, and Tessa pulled back the curtain to find the hall transformed. The trestles had been brought out, and the boards laid across them were laden with food. Some people milled about, some hurried back and forth with more trays of food, and still others were already at table, their knives ready.

Eleanor spotted Tessa and gave her brother-in-law a push in her direction. Reluctantly, Jeffrey approached Tessa and offered his arm. He spoke sidewise to her as they moved to their places. "Eleanor knows your story, for I could not lie to her. She will tell no one else the truth and will treat you as a guest. If you insist on airing your troubles, I will take you off in the morning and leave you in an alley in York where you may fend for yourself. It is your choice."

What choice was that? Tessa asked herself as she looked at the tables crowded with alien, curious faces. No one here was going to help her get back to Scotland to warn her uncle that the English and Norwegians were plotting with rebels to overthrow the king. She was alone in a country of enemies, or at the very least, not friends. "I understand," she told Brixton. "But *you* must understand that someday I will repay you for the ruin of my life. I have nothing now, no family, no home, and no reputation, and that is your doing." This last was whispered in a hiss, as they kept the appearance of amity between them.

Jeffrey, his face a mask and his arm stiff beneath Tessa's, seated her next to Eleanor and went to his own place across the table. When she looked at him next, the expression of amused scorn was back, as if to let her know that Jeffrey Brixton was not one to succumb to threats or worry about earning the hatred of one small Scottish girl. She turned to the meal, but the food was oddly tasteless and the wine bitter on her tongue.

The next morning Tessa awoke early, before most of the household was astir. She had always been an early riser and liked the quiet time in the morning when no one else was about. After briefly exploring the castle, she decided to walk outside and orient herself so that if the chance to escape ever came, she would be familiar with the grounds and the habits of the workers. Pulling her cape from its peg by the door, she stepped out into the mist.

Being a mountain girl, Tessa was used to morning fog, thick and damp, which chilled as one passed through it. The difference in York was the elevation. The fog was thinner, more ethereal, like dust settled on the countryside. She expected it would pass off more quickly than at home, since the land was much flatter hereabouts. Once that happened, she saw, the day would be pleasant. Passing buildings they'd come by the day before, she saw all the crafts essential to country living: a blacksmith, a leather worker, a brewer, and various others. Most had begun to stir, opening doors and checking the weather, some sniffing the air testily, others peering at the sky with speculative eye, a few apparently with eyes not yet focused. Farther off, on the riverbank, was a mill operated by the power of the flowing water, and behind the house were the stables, far enough removed to lessen the odor of manure but close enough for convenience.

Between the river and the house was a vegetable garden, as yet unplanted but showing evidence of preparation: turned soil and tools scattered about. Closer in was a low wall separating the house from its surroundings, and here lay the flower garden. Again, not much variety yet, just early daffodils and jonquils, but it was quite large, with stones laid out for walkways and trees and bushes of various heights to provide interest and privacy. It would be lovely when the sun shone and one could see the whole without the tendrils of mist that obscured parts of it. Someone cared deeply about encouraging the beauty of nature, and Tessa knew instinctively that it must be Eleanor herself.

Following the pathway with head down, the girl almost missed the sound of murmured voices, which she later thought would have been most embarrassing — to be caught eavesdropping on Jeffrey Brixton a second time! As it was, she stopped short and stepped between two lilac bushes already green with early leaves. The two people who passed her unknowingly, just a few feet away, were Jeffrey and his sister-in-law Eleanor, walking arm in arm and talking softly. Tessa heard the words, ". . . doesn't understand me at all," from Eleanor.

"No, and it's a pity for a woman such as you to be unappreciated," was Jeffrey's answer. "My brother is a fool." It was said with decision, but no vehemence, as if he had said it many times before.

Eleanor sighed. "Oh, it could be worse. He doesn't beat me or force me to live in London and watch his affairs. I am content to be here where I am free to do as I please each day. Still, it is a pity that he is not on better terms with his brothers. To keep you all penniless is his shame, not yours. He should at least provide for your needs so that you have the means to take your rightful place in society."

"But he'd have to give me a few acres of land then, and that he will not do," Jeffrey growled. "It doesn't matter. I'd rather earn my way with my sword than attend him as Aidan does." His voice changed to a different tone. "I don't mind the soldier's life, really, except that it leaves so much work for you to run this place alone."

"And I miss you when you are away and worry for your safety. But that is life, and one may as well accept what one has and find the good in it. You were here for a day, and you have left me a companion, little Tessa."

Jeffrey snorted and the sound of their steps paused. Tessa jumped as a small rock came clattering toward her. She froze, but Jeffrey had thrown it idly, unaware that she stood on the other side of the lilac. "Companion? Problem. I hope the minx does not annoy you too much."

"She seems intelligent despite her rural speech and ways," was Eleanor's reply. "We'll get on well enough, I think." Eleanor had spoken to Tessa kindly at dinner the night before, adroitly explaining her appearance at Brixton Manor to the household. The story was that Tessa had come to visit, being the daughter of an old friend of Eleanor's. She had traveled with an elderly waiting-woman as chaperone, but the woman fell ill near York and therefore stayed behind. Tessa had come on in Jeffrey's protection, being anxious to arrive, and the other lady would return to Scotland when she recovered.

Tessa had been surprised at Eleanor's calm spinning of this string of untruths, and it sounded totally believable when accompanied by the lady's serene composure. Tessa was grateful for the lie, for Eleanor had made it possible for her to keep her reputation, at least as far as anyone in England knew. It seemed the lady of the manor would do anything for Jeffrey.

"I can't tell you how grateful I am that you will take her off my hands," Jeffrey said now as he turned to Eleanor and took both her hands in his, "but I must go. Old Matt should have my horse brought round by now."

They moved off, and Tessa digested what she'd heard. First and foremost, she was stung by how glad Jeffrey was to be rid of her. Second, she'd confirmed to her satisfaction that he and Eleanor were lovers behind the back of her husband, his brother. What sort of man cuckolded his own brother? The sort who abducted helpless girls, that's who. She imagined the tearful farewell taking place at the manor gate, Jeffrey leaving his love to go off to war. Eleanor would surely be a wreck at breakfast.

On the contrary, Lady Eleanor was composed when they met for the morning meal, which consisted of oatmeal, a rasher of bacon, milk, and aromatic, freshly baked bread. Eleanor merely announced that Jeffrey had left for Norway very early. Tessa was oddly disappointed that he was gone, and oddly content that Lady Brixton was her usual, gracious self. She ate heartily, watching Eleanor and copying her manners, remembering the comment about her rural ways.

CHAPTER SEVEN

Despite herself, Tessa could hate neither life at Brixton nor the Lady Eleanor. She was allowed to explore the house and grounds as she liked, and within a few days she had fallen in love with the place. The countryside was not as ruggedly beautiful as Scotland. The hills rose more softly and the grass was a lighter green. Sheep and cattle abounded, of course, the cattle calling intermittently from their pasture, while sheep dotted the hillsides like clouds in the grass, choosing their spots and moving only when the dogs insisted.

The manor house was warmer and more colorful than any she had seen before. Even the stone it was made from was a golden, inviting mineral, less forbidding than the stone at Inverness. She and the other ladies of the house sat in the afternoons with Eleanor, reading and gossiping as they sewed or performed household necessities.

Due to the tutelage of her aunt, Tessa could contribute modestly to these activities. However, the sessions were much more lively than those at Inverness had been, with frequent laughter and substantial learning exchanged. Eleanor encouraged all those around her to take interest in the world, and with genuine curiosity drew information from each person she spoke to. Her family was accustomed to Eleanor's questions, and each person strove to find interesting bits to amuse or amaze her. It was lovely to hear her laugh, satisfying to see her frown in concentration as a new idea became clear to her.

Tessa was of course a fountain of fresh information for discussion. At first shy, she soon became willing to share stories and facts about her homeland. "The Scotti, the tribe for whom you name Scotland, actually came from Ireland," she informed Eleanor and the other women as they sewed.

Brixton Manor's household was largely female: three cousins and a maiden aunt. William and his younger brother Aidan spent their time at a townhouse in London. Now the five ladies listened as Tessa explained that Scotland was not so alien as they might think.

"We share many legends with the Irish

and the Welsh, since the Romans drove many Celts north and west into those areas."

"Are there not monsters in the lakes of Scotland?" asked Mary, one of the cousins.

"I've never seen any," Tessa said, smiling, "but I know better than to deny something simply because I haven't seen it. Some of our lakes are very deep, and who knows what might lurk below the frigid waters?"

"I don't believe in such things as monsters," said Cecilia, another cousin. "I only believe in what I can see, not fairies or witches neither."

Tessa's brow furrowed, and Eleanor noticed. "Have you seen a fairy or a witch, Tessa?" she asked teasingly.

"I cannot say. I . . . I would have agreed with Cecilia until recently, but now I am not sure. You see, I met three weird women several months ago, when I was traveling to my uncle's home, and they told me strange things. I did not believe them because what they said seemed unlikely."

"Oh, tell us, please!" Mary, the most excitable of the three cousins, fairly bounced with anticipation.

"Well, the first one said that I was bound for England, but I had no intention of coming to England — ever." Tessa stopped lest she say too much and betray her lack of choice in being where she was presently.

"Circumstances often change," Eleanor put in smoothly. "It's not necessarily magic, but it was a lucky guess."

"What were the other two predictions?" Mary's delight was unfazed by Eleanor's logic.

"Oh, something about marrying two men," Tessa was now faintly embarrassed by the conversation. She was not about to tell these nice but rather prim ladies that the actual words of the prediction had been that two men she married were never to be her lovers. "And that a man I love would forget my name, whatever that might mean."

Tessa saw a look pass over Eleanor's face, and she remembered with a jolt that Jeffrey had been unable to introduce her to his sister-in-law. No, she told herself, he had not forgotten her name. He had probably never known it. They had never been formally introduced, and if he had heard her name it was in passing only. Besides, there was little likelihood that she was in love with a man who had ruined her life — or ever would be. Jeffrey Brixton was to her the worst sort of man, and she hoped never to see him again. She shrugged off further discussion of the three odd women and took up her sewing again.

In the course of their conversations, Tessa had discovered that all the females in the household, not just Eleanor, doted on Jeffrey. Auntie Madeline, older sister of William, was tall and spare, with iron gray hair and a rather horsy face, but her eyes lit up when Jeffrey's name was mentioned. "I wish the boy were not away so much," she mourned. "He brings life to the house, and we are a sorry lot without him, a bunch of hens with no rooster to preen ourselves for." Tessa could see no likeness between Jeffrey and a rooster, but Auntie Madeline did resemble a hen, albeit a very thin one.

In addition to the old lady's fondness, in at least two of the cousins there was longing for a glance from Jeffrey, which he seemed never to have noticed. The girl of about Tessa's age, Mary, was quite open about her feelings for him and sighed over his absence until the rest of them became impatient with her.

Cecilia declared, "Mary, you drive him away with your mooning looks and your simpering ways. Jeffrey is not a man to be snared by such things. In fact, he once told me he doubts he will ever marry at all." Mary had looked sad for a moment, but the third cousin, Alice, assured them all that men often changed their minds about such things as they grew older.

"Why, Father didn't marry until he was thirty-five," Alice said earnestly, "and then he chose a cousin who lived on a farm nearby. Perhaps it will be well for us that Jeffrey has known us all his life when he looks to wed."

Tessa watched Eleanor, wondering what she thought of Jeffrey's marrying. Eleanor gave Tessa a little smile with upraised brow, as if to say, "Who can tell the future?" She certainly didn't seem to be worried about it.

Days, then weeks, passed, and Tessa began to feel more at home than imprisoned. The men of the family never appeared, which the women seemed to take for granted. Sir William preferred London, and Aidan, the third brother, served as his agent, acting in reality the part Jeffrey had played as his disguise in Scotland. The last brother, a monk, was seldom seen by his family.

Eleanor went out of her way to help Tessa learn English ways, never criticizing hers, but simply explaining how things were done differently in her country. Tessa's speech improved as they talked. Her accent was still Scots, but she became more careful of her grammar and spoke more slowly, with fewer gutturals and fewer swallowed vowels.

One day the two women had a conversation that changed Tessa's way of thinking about her future completely. She had been drifting, not thinking about where her life at Brixton might lead or when it would end. It became evident that Eleanor had thought about it seriously, however. She waited until they were alone in the garden to announce, "I had a letter from Jeffrey today that is rather disturbing. He says I may share it with you, since you are interested in events in Scotland." She took a rolled paper from her skirt pocket and glanced at it to refresh her memory.

"Jeffrey's side has been defeated. Duncan's generals, including one Macbeth he told me to mention to you, met the rebels and the Norwegian troops on two fronts and defeated both. He says the thane of Cawdor was executed as a traitor and his lands given to this Macbeth."

So odd little Uncle Biote had lost his gamble for power. Tessa did not know how she felt about his execution. Jeffrey claimed that he had died bravely, but Macbeth emerged the hero of the matter. Because they had become friends, Tessa explained to Eleanor what Jeffrey's information meant to her. After listening to the full explanation, the older woman put her arms around Tessa's shoulders. "How sorry I am that this happened to you. You did nothing at all, and your life was completely changed. I wonder that you don't hate us all."

"I could never hate you," Tessa assured her.

The faint emphasis on the word *you* was not lost on Eleanor, and she turned down a side path among rows of pinks just coming into bloom. Stooping to pull a weed from between them, she slapped the dirt from her hands.

"I don't approve of Jeffrey's actions," she told Tessa, "but then, men often do things we women would not do, because they think only in the direction of a goal. I believe that women, who are not given credit for much intelligence, are actually better at examining all the results of an action, while men simply choose the action that suits them and accept its consequences. Our deliberations may make us seem indecisive, but men often seem cruel when they ignore what may happen to others as they act decisively."

Tessa didn't respond. Knowing that Eleanor, although she might criticize Jeffrey's actions, also loved him, it was safer to keep quiet. Turning, Eleanor faced Tessa with serious purpose. "Because of Jeffrey, I suppose you are now a woman of no reputation in Scotland?"

"Yes. It will be assumed that he . . . dishonored me, and no man will want me as wife after that. Not that anyone did before," she said in a burst of honesty.

"Why would no man ask for a beautiful, clever girl like you?"

"I've a brassy manner and tomboyish ways," Tessa confessed, using the terms her mother had often employed to describe her. Humiliated to admit her faults before this woman she admired, she waited for the shocked reaction.

Instead, Eleanor laughed, a warm, lovely sound, and once more put an arm around Tessa. "I believe I know *exactly* what you have suffered!" She put her face close to Tessa's, her eyes dancing. "They said the same of me once. It's the reason I am married to William Brixton!"

"I don't understand." Tessa frowned, shaking her head. How could this paragon be considered unladylike?

The paragon's face was full of mischief. "As a girl, I preferred riding to sewing, being outside to learning wifely chores. I had prospects, but I said too much of what I thought, and men were offended by it."

"Why that is what my mother said of me!" Tessa exclaimed in wonder. "My face should have been my fortune, she told me, but my tongue ruined all."

Eleanor's face grew solemn. "Could it be our parents who were wrong, and you and I merely more independent than some might wish their children to be?"

Tessa laughed. "That is what Father used to say, that I had too much spirit for the local boys. But after he died, my mother hoped to marry me well to ease her way in life. I was a disappointment to her with my wild ways."

Eleanor nodded. "Because she couldn't control you as she wanted to. My father, a very stern man, found me too outspoken. My mother died when I was four, and without her influence, I did grow up rather wild. Once he bothered to notice me, Father became determined that I would be taught how to behave properly. At ten I was sent to a convent where I was trained" — here her eyes turned hard and she folded her arms as if a chill passed over her — "sometimes with force, to become a 'suitable' female."

Tessa gasped, but Eleanor went on calmly. "In addition, my father searched long and hard for a strong husband who would quell what he saw as my rebellious nature. He found William Brixton, heir to Brixton Hall" — here her voice became bitter —

"who sought only a wife of great beauty. We never spoke until the day of our wedding. Jeffrey was sent to interview me and appraise my suitability, since William was newly Lord Brixton and too busy with his affairs to take the time. Jeffrey and I liked each other at once, and I was silly enough to believe that his brother might be somewhat like him."

"So you had no idea what sort of man your husband was?" Tessa was intrigued. She'd had few choices of a mate in her home in the mountains, but she knew each of them, both their strengths and their weaknesses.

"None. It pleased my father to exercise his right to control me in that way. William is much like him, a man who believes women should have no thoughts of their own. He took a wife because it is expected of the lord of Brixton Manor. He chose me to give him fine sons and make other men jealous." Eleanor looked sad at this. "I failed to produce sons for him, but I doubt if it would have made him any happier in the end."

"It isn't fair that you were given like a prize," Tessa blurted out, outraged for Eleanor.

"It is the way of things," Eleanor soothed,

patting Tessa's arm comfortingly. "The irony is that I love Brixton. Here I can ride, walk, or boat when I like, toil in the orchards and gardens with the workers, and" — she grinned impishly — "avoid the boredom of endless parties, my husband's glowering looks, and his frequent affairs. So you see, I have won, despite the plots of men. I have the life I want, at least most of it, and can do as I please."

Tessa stared at Eleanor. Was she boasting that she had outwitted her father to become relatively free of male influence, or was it her husband that she enjoyed fooling? Did pompous old Sir William not realize that his own brother was in love with his wife? Suddenly uneasy with the conversation, Tessa began to speak of flowers.

Later that same week Eleanor again brought up the subject of Tessa's supposed failures. Although the day was fine, Eleanor had claimed fatigue and chosen to stay in when the others went to pick the delicate wild strawberries that made such delicious jam. She and Tessa sat together in a small room warmed by the afternoon sun, which Eleanor used as a sort of retreat. Under the stone stairway and therefore not much use for any other purpose, here she kept books and games like *tafl,* which she was teaching

Tessa to play. The board that sat between them contained pegs carved from wood. One player had a king and only a few men to protect him, while the other had no king but more pieces with which to capture the opposing one. It was a game of strategy, but neither woman cared much who won or lost.

In the intervening days, Tessa had observed Eleanor with a new perspective, and she had to admit that life on the manor allowed activities that did not require genteel manners or prim ways. Life here was actually the best of possibilities for Eleanor. She was removed from the husband she did not love, and in a place where her lover could visit without scandal. She indulged in her enjoyment of the outdoors and was respected as lady of the manor.

Eleanor lent a hand in whatever work was being done on the manor. She oversaw the planting of crops, herded cattle, and made rushlights right along with the servants, dipping rush tips into pitch to make cheap, if smoky, torches. She spoke honestly with her workers and her neighbors, bargaining, mediating, and giving orders as needed. Eleanor was as true to her nature as could be, yet neither Tessa nor anyone else ever thought of her as anything but a lady. New awareness of Eleanor, her mother, and herself meant changes that left Tessa unsure of what the best course for a female was in life, and she found herself thinking on it often.

Now Eleanor sat still for once, her eyes a bit cloudy and her posture less erect than usual. She really was tired, Tessa thought, but she seemed anxious to explain what it had taken her years to learn on her own.

"I tell you this: the secret of the tomboy must be timing. You can be feminine and sweet, even simpering if need be, when the situation requires it, mostly during courtship. When you are married and secure in your future, become what you want to be. Married women are more free than you might think, *if* they marry carefully.

"When my father gave me to William, he thought he had done what was best for me, and perhaps he had, but not in the way he intended. William is so full of himself that he all but ignores me, which has allowed me to lead a life I enjoy. A happy woman needs either a dull husband who ignores her after a year or a clever one who understands her and respects what she is. The first is much easier to find, so I propose to help you accomplish it."

Tessa was aghast. Here Eleanor sat, calmly defying custom and belief, claiming that women had a right to find happiness through subterfuge and deceit. Tessa had never considered choosing a husband with cold calculation, never thought of appearing to be something she was not in order to capture a man. Still, she knew that her Aunt Gruoch and even her mother had manipulated their husbands. In a society where women had no choices, clever ones employed the means at their disposal.

"Are you saying I could have a husband who would let me live life as I choose?"

"He will have to be a little stupid, as mine is," Eleanor replied coolly, shifting a bit with a grimace. Menstrual cramps, Tessa guessed, and wondered if there was mistletoe available to soothe them. "William, you see, thinks he is clever, living in London and having affairs. He doesn't realize that as long as I have my home and my freedom, I don't much care what he does. Now Jeffrey is not stupid. He would expect more from a woman than appearances, but he will never marry anyway. The lands in England have been divided and divided until there is no more to be gained. You don't want a landless younger son like Jeffrey, so we must find you a husband who is rich."

As if Jeffrey Brixton would be on her list of potential husbands!

"I can teach you how to dress, walk, and speak properly, how to converse with a man without intimidating him, and" — here her eyes sparkled — "how to charm his mother, a very important thing that many young women forget. Without a dowry, you must offer something attractive to the man, which is fairly easy with your looks, but also to his mother, which is a little more difficult. It doesn't do to please only one or the other."

"Was your mother-in-law pleased with you?"

Eleanor smiled at the memory and the pinched look on her face relaxed somewhat. "I liked Lady Brixton very much, but I'm afraid William was born selfish. She tried to provide for all her children, but when she died, William ignored her wishes." Eleanor looked out the window, her face bleak. "When I first met my husband I thought him dignified, but I learned later that dignity is what he holds around himself so that no one sees his empty heart."

Forgetting the game board before them, Eleanor rose, her arms wrapped around her middle as she paced the room. "The law of primogeniture brought William all the property, and he keeps his brothers paupers, begrudging every penny he spends on them. Ethelbert, the second son, entered the priesthood, but William refuses him the funds to get a decent posting, saying clergymen should observe poverty, as Christ did." Her tone held a sneer at her husband's choplogic. "Aidan you will meet soon. He's treated more as a servant than as William's brother. When Jeffrey saw how the other two fared, he offered a deal. If William would outfit him for soldiery, he'd take himself off and never ask for another cent. It was all William could do to keep from chuckling as he gave Jeffrey an aging horse and the worst arms from the storehouse. Still, Jeffrey has done well, becoming a respected soldier and a trusted aide to those who pay his hire."

Tessa felt a pang of unexpected sorrow for Jeffrey, cheated of his inheritance, and for Eleanor, married to a man she obviously despised. No wonder they found solace in each other's arms.

Eleanor looked at Tessa directly, as if trying to make a decision, then reached down to put a hand on the girl's arm. "Do you wonder why I tell you all this?"

Tessa had indeed been wondering. When others were present, Eleanor never criticized her husband, in fact, seldom mentioned him. Why had she told Tessa her true feelings? Sitting again, she leaned against the stone wall and answered her own question.

"I never had a child. I am thirty-five years old and never even conceived one. I was ashamed at first, but although William has many other women, none has had a child, so it is probably not my failing. William wants sons badly, but I wanted a daughter to talk to, nurture, and perhaps help to a life better than my own. Now you arrive, not my daughter, true, but in need of help. And you are just in time."

Tessa looked questioningly Eleanor, who hesitated again. "If I could help you to find a wealthy husband in London, would it be a life you could accept? Would you make a home for yourself in England and perhaps never see Scotland again?"

Tessa considered it. All her life she had been termed a misfit by her mother, but she *had* known love: her father, her sister Meg, even old Banaugh had held her dear. That life was gone now, for they probably thought her dead. If she made a successful marriage in London, what more could she ask? It was her fate to be stranded in England. The weird old women had spoken the truth, although she'd dismissed their words then. The English were no better and no worse than the Scots; some she liked and others she avoided. In the situation Eleanor proposed there would be security, protection, and possibly a measure of happiness.

Once again the image of the crones arose before her, and the words of the second repeated in her mind: "You'll find happiness only among the dead." That settled it, then. If in truth she would never be happy while alive, then she'd best take the prospect of security.

"Yes," she told Eleanor. "There is no reason to return to Scotland now. I may as well settle as best I can and hope for children to love. I will try to be a good wife to whoever will have me."

Eleanor nodded. "That is wise. I have too long neglected the other girls' prospects, hoping William would take pity on them, but they must have their chance in London as well. Your arrival has decided me — that and something else."

Now the blue eyes met Tessa's directly, and Eleanor leaned toward her. "Now I'll tell you the rest of the bargain. Although no one knows it, I am not well. A few months ago, I noticed a bulge here." She indicated her abdomen. "At first I thought after all these years I was with child, but soon I knew it was not so. There is no life there, and there is pain."

Tessa was shocked at the revelation. "We must get a physician! You must be given some medicine —"

Eleanor shushed her and said calmly, "My own mother died at thirty of a similar disease. There is nothing to be done." She touched Tessa's shoulder lightly. "What I want most is to help those I love before I die. If I make some difference in your lives, I will go contentedly enough. All I ask in return is that when I say it is time, you must fetch for me a bottle that I shall have ready."

"A bottle?" Tessa asked, uncomprehending.

"Something that will help me end the pain."

Realization dawned on the girl's face. "Poison?"

"To some." Eleanor smiled. "But if one is in great pain, it is a blessing to stop it."

Tessa gulped to quell the lump that rose in her throat. If this was what Eleanor wanted, when the time came she would be strong for her.

CHAPTER EIGHT

Eleanor wasted no time beginning Tessa's transformation. The first thing she did, though daring, effectively ended any question of Tessa's stature in the house. At dinner one evening, Eleanor declared that Jeffrey had brought Tessa from Scotland after discovering that the two were half sisters. It was true enough, Eleanor informed Tessa privately, that eighteen years before her father had gone to Scotland as the king's agent and later died there of a sudden illness. The story she invented was that he'd married a Scottish woman and fathered a daughter before his death. Eleanor had kept it to herself until she was sure, but Tessa was in fact her younger sister, and they were all going to London for her introduction to William.

Auntie Madeline had some of her eldest brother's disapproving outer manner, but was not unkind at heart. After a moment of shocked silence, she gave Tessa a rather formal hug, enfolding her in bony arms, and welcomed her to the family. The three cousins were a little surprised that Tessa was now on equal footing with them, but did not seem upset. Being poor relatives sent to Brixton, much as Tessa herself had been sent off to Macbeth's household, none of them had much expectation for the future. They would have deluded themselves to suppose that Sir William would settle more than a tiny dowry on them, so there was not much to be jealous about. And in truth all three were kind-hearted girls with no rancor in them.

The weeks that followed were a whirl of constant activity. Tessa must be taught English dances. Luckily Alice, the cousin who was sister to Cecilia, was a very patient teacher. Next she must walk like a lady, not on her heels, and she must watch her table manners. For example, it was important for a lady to dip her meat gracefully just halfway into the gravy bowl so as not to soil her fingers, and then bring the portion to her lips quickly so the liquid didn't run down her arm and onto her sleeve. In London, she was told, people ate from metal plates, not the wooden trenchers used at Brixton Manor. Ladies carried on their belts jeweled knives of intricate design with which to cut their portions and carry the pieces to their mouths. She was given one of these, modest but well made, as a gift from Eleanor.

Bolts of fabric were found in the storeroom with which to make new dresses. Cecilia was good with a needle and helped Tessa cut two basic shapes and sew them together. In the front of one dress they cut a squared neckline and edged it with braid salvaged from an old curtain. The other they rounded and edged with embroidery. Over these plain shapes the girls wore tunics of various colors and styles. Tessa made herself a pair of soft velvet shoes, and a leather worker on the manor made her boots for foul weather. The old gray cloak she'd worn from Scotland was cleaned and mended neatly, and clever Cecilia embroidered it with red designs that changed it from plain to majestic.

Tessa had a basic knowledge of music and a good singing voice. Eleanor taught her some English ballads, tactfully leaving out those that dealt with Scotland, and encouraged her to accompany herself on the lute. "Nothing melts a man's heart as does a woman who sings and plays the songs he loves," she told the girls, "unless it is a woman who cooks and serves his favorite foods." And so there were cooking lessons. Although Tessa could clean fish and fowl, she'd never taken much interest in cooking them. There was the English way, too, which although not the best of the world's cuisine, was still better than most Scottish food, which was plainly prepared, to say the least.

"And haggis, my dear," Eleanor said. "I've heard of it, but I can't imagine anyone actually eating it."

"Then you probably wouldn't like black pudding, either," Tessa told them. "You start with twelve cups of pig's blood . . ." The other women squealed, but they all laughed together. Tessa thought of her own sisters, and wished their lives could have been more like this, with laughter and joy rather than the peevish carping that was all the littler ones had ever known of their mother. She at least remembered her father's kindness as he had attempted to ease Kenna's sharpness. "Now, lass," he often said to his wife, "don't let the world make you sad or mad, for it's only yourself that you're listenin' to."

Tessa reminded herself that it was she, and she alone, who could make herself sad or mad. Despite recent misfortune, she had found kindness in England and had begun to understand that her own behavior had contributed to her downfall. If she hadn't insulted Jeffrey Brixton the night she met him and been sent from the hall in disgrace, she'd have been sleeping peacefully in her bed when he left Scotland the next morning. Had the crones seen that angry streak in her and in their odd way tried to warn her of it?

Barely two months after her arrival Tessa said goodbye to Brixton Hall and set off for London. Even so, she went as a quite different person than the one who'd arrived, well dressed and so full of advice on proper behavior that she feared her eyes would cross with the strain of remembering it. They journeyed to London in a two-wheeled cart so loaded with female accoutrements that there was hardly room for the six of them: Eleanor, Tessa, Cecilia, Alice, Mary, and Blanche, whom they shared as lady's maid. Aunt Madeline had stayed behind to see to the house, having no desire to go to London. "Been there once," was her disdainful comment. Two sturdy peasants walked behind the cart and two armed bondmen rode before on horseback to protect the party from outlaws and wild animals. They slept on the ground, making nests in the tall grass beside the road and washing in brooks and rivulets still icy cold despite summer's arrival. Inns were scarce and usually unclean, and Eleanor preferred to avoid them altogether.

The journey passed quickly with stories and songs, and they arrived at the outskirts of London on the fourth afternoon. As they walked behind the wagon for a while to stretch their legs, Eleanor confessed privately to Tessa the trick she'd used to assure that they would be able to make the visit. "William will not be pleased to see us, since he says London is much too expensive for a gaggle of women. If he'd had a day's notice, he'd undoubtedly have sent someone to order us to stay home." Eleanor paused, enjoying her own boldness. "Therefore, I sent a messenger ahead just a few hours, telling him of our arrival on an important matter. There won't be time for him to frame a negative response before we're there, and then what can he do but let us in?"

"But won't he be angry with you? What important business do you have that requires all this?" Tessa indicated the wagon brimming with women and their finery.

"Once I'm there, I'll convince him to let us stay. I will relate the story about your background and explain to him that you

108

must find a husband or he'll be saddled with another mouth to feed next winter." Eleanor said with a chuckle. "I may have to make you sound quite ravenous. He'll want to let you all be seen in order to get offers of marriage, so he'll cooperate, *if* you have learned well the game that must be played."

"To smile and say sweet things even when men bore me to tears?" Tessa said sardonically. "I believe I can."

"Good. I have in mind several men with large fortunes who will fall so in love at the sight of you that offers will pour in despite your lack of a dowry." With that, Eleanor hopped back up onto the wagon. A quick flash of pain crossed her face, but she conquered it and held out a hand to help Tessa in beside her.

The house that William kept in London was smaller than Brixton Hall but much grander. Here William entertained important people, so his concern was the impression it made. The house was made of wood, as were most in London, despite the town fathers' pleas for brick or stone to lessen fire danger.

Tessa and Mary shared a bedroom in the upper story, small but comfortable, with a slanted ceiling and a rug on the floor instead of the rushes used at Brixton. Mary was ecstatic over the windows, which had real glass in them. Looking out was difficult because the thick, bubble-pocked glass made things wavy and distorted, but it was better than the greased hides that covered the narrow slits of Brixton Hall in winter. There was even a small charcoal brazier that could be lit on cold nights.

Tessa had grown fond of Mary, an orphan whose father had been William's cousin. He had taken her in, albeit reluctantly, when both her parents died within a year of each other. Although no great beauty, Mary was sweet-faced and pleasant to be around. Her best feature was her round, luminous eyes. The rest of her face lacked proportion, her chin being too small, but the eyes dominated when she was happy, transforming her into an attractive young woman. Although the other cousins, Cecilia and Alice, were friendly enough, as sisters they were close to each other. It was natural that Mary and Tessa sought each other's company.

Tessa never heard how William Brixton took their arrival. He was out when the party of excited females arrived, and Eleanor sent them up to unpack, urging them to be at their best for dinner. When the two girls came down the stairs, William stood at the landing, framed in the heavy oaken doorway to the great room. Behind him on the wall a painting hung depicting a martyr's gruesome death, and William and the martyr wore the same glum expression. Tessa saw a resemblance to Jeffrey, but where the youngest brother had a strong bone structure and a clear, direct gaze, William had the same features with less substance. His face sagged into itself, leaving pouchy eyes and a heavily jowled chin. The eyes seemed to judge everything they saw and find it wanting. He was dressed well, with a robe of deep blue and a close-fitting cap that showed only a few graying hairs below its edge.

Lord Brixton greeted the two girls tersely, looking hard at Tessa before remarking in a casual tone, "You don't much look like a sister to Eleanor, Mistress macFindlaech."

"I'm told I favor my mother, sir, God rest her," Tessa replied, keeping her eyes downcast and trying to appear both demure and marriageable.

"Ah, then," was the reply. "Go along to dinner."

He indicated a direction, and Tessa took Mary's arm and went off with relief. At least she wasn't to be set out on the street tonight. Mary whispered encouragement as they went: "He's always like that — quite stern is William."

Stern indeed, Tessa thought. She could feel those cold blue eyes at her back, the color of Jeffrey's, but much less human.

The party at the dinner table consisted of the five women, Lord Brixton, a local priest, a businessman who spoke of nothing but linen prices, and Aidan, the brother closest in age to Jeffrey. Aidan was something of a surprise. With Eleanor's remark that he was treated badly and the notation in Jeffrey's diary that he would drink himself to an early death, Tessa had expected a pathetic little man with a red-veined nose and slurred speech.

Instead, Aidan was quite handsome. He wore a red and black tunic with black hose that showed off well-muscled legs. His long face was rounded somewhat by a neatly trimmed beard. Aidan resembled his brothers very little, having brown hair and eyes, but they were nice eyes. With an engaging manner, he teased the other girls about their foibles, having known them from childhood. To Tessa he was charming and attentive, listening to her half-true, half-concocted story of how Jeffrey had found her, realized who she was, and brought her to Eleanor.

"How clever of Jeffrey to find a beautiful addition to the family in Scotland of all places," Aidan remarked. Tessa bristled, but remembered her role in time to bite back a response to the slur on her native land. Aidan had seen it, though; she could tell by his look and the raised eyebrow that brought Jeffrey to mind. They shared, she thought, a quick understanding of the feelings of others, betrayed by that eyebrow's arch.

"I'm sorry, Mistress macFindlaech — may I call you Tessa? Your name is quite a trial for my poor tongue." Tessa had already heard Englishmen refer to Scotland's tongue as half cough and half speech. Eleanor had explained that Tessa was known by her stepfather's name, macFindlaech, which required the Scottish glottals used less and less in English these days.

Tessa was gracious. "Of course, Master Brixton."

"I am most grateful, Tessa. And grateful to Jeffrey, for bringing you among us." He smiled at her directly, and she decided that brown eyes were very nice indeed.

As the meal progressed, Tessa could not help but notice William Brixton's sour personality and demanding manner. At one point a very young serving boy spilled a few drops of wine in his anxiousness to keep the glasses full, and William barked to the housekeeper, "Get that lout out of here and find someone who knows how to properly serve at table!" The boy fled in disgrace, and William turned to Master Conklin, the linen merchant. "I apologize. It is impossible to find people of the standard that I require in servants."

"I understand," the merchant hurried to agree, flattered to be invited to dinner at the house of a nobleman. "We find also in my trade that good help is hard to find. It's what drives the prices up . . ." and he was back on his favorite subject.

Later in the meal, Master Conklin mentioned his approval of the roast fowl they were served. William, in a generous mood because the man was about to make him even wealthier with the deal they had concluded that afternoon, smiled. "I raise them on the manor," he told Conklin. "I will see that you have a brace for dinner some evening." Without looking at his brother, William said curtly, "Aidan, see to the matter. And mind, don't be slow about it." The tone was peremptory, not a request but an order to one clearly regarded as subordinate.

While the other ladies at the table pondered their plates, Tessa glanced at Aidan, whose face showed no emotion. He simply replied, "Of course," and made a slight nod of his head to the merchant. So this was how William treated his brothers. No wonder he was regarded with disdain by his wife.

Up in their room after dinner, Mary told Tessa a family secret. "Master Aidan is only half-brother to the rest, which is why he's so different looking," she said with the air of one who knows her news will bring surprise. "You see, the old Lord Brixton had himself a leman, an Irish woman he met on campaign. He kept her in a little house just the other side of the wood at the manor house. She had Aidan, then sickened and died. The old man brought him home and told Lady Brixton that she would raise him as one of her own, and bless her, she did it. No one's allowed to speak of it, though, by her own wish. Eleanor says that Lady Brixton was truly a great woman, and when she took the boy in, she made him her own.

"And the present Lord Brixton? What does he think?"

"I daresay he finds it convenient having someone to do his errands. To his credit, he never calls Master Aidan anything but brother."

Tessa was glad, for Aidan's sake, that William accepted him. It was not much, since he treated all three brothers badly, but at least they were equals. Remembering a comment from Jeffrey's journal, she asked Mary, "Does Aidan drink overmuch? I heard somewhere that he did."

Mary nodded, her eyes round. "Well, he did in the past. I believe William spoke to him about it, and he's thought to be mending his ways. He were an awful one when he were in his cups, I can tell you."

"Is that why Jeffrey is your favorite then? A miser, a monk and a drunkard. I suppose even young Master Brixton must appear well next to those three."

Mary was instantly defensive. "Jeffrey is superior to all men, not just his brothers."

"And how many men do you know?" Tessa teased.

"As many as you, I'll wager," was Mary's laughing response, but then her face sobered. " 'Tis true, though. I think poor Eleanor would have gone mad except for Jeffrey. He's always stood between her and Sir William, making the old stick ashamed when he deprived his wife of small things while he lived in London in this fine house. Not that Eleanor cares for finery. She'd as lief plant a garden as attend a feast. Still, William was cruel to her in small ways once he found he'd get no son from her. Jeffrey has always protected her and been good to us, too, the poor cousins."

Tessa had an idea of what it must be like for the three Brixton girls with little hope for a bright future. William's penny-pinching might leave them old maids, or at best wives to younger sons of poor noblemen, working themselves to death on five acres.

"Mary, this is our chance to see what London offers in the way of husbands."

"I'm not such a beauty as you —" Mary began, touching her thin, mousy brown hair, but Tessa interrupted.

"Don't be silly! You're as pretty as one of your English daisies, and men differ in their tastes in women. After Eleanor's instruction, I'm sure we will each succeed." She turned impish, taking on a lecturing tone. "You must get the attention of two or three young men, and then set them each thinking you might be interested in another. Nothing makes a man more ardent than the thought you mightn't want him."

"Are you sure?" Mary said, wide-eyed.

Tessa wasn't sure how she knew it to be true, but she did. She'd seen men in the hills of Scotland who chased only after the girls who ran away, or appeared to, and figured men were the same in England despite fine clothes and manners. The girls practiced flirting with their eyes until it became too dark in the room to see. They pinched out the tallow candle and went to sleep, each dreaming of the days to come and the men they would conquer.

CHAPTER NINE

The next week was a busy one. Once he saw the chance to marry off his harem of female relatives, William arranged with alacrity invitations to several parties. "It's not that he cares for anyone but himself," Eleanor admitted to Tessa, "but it works for our purposes. I'm guessing that my thrifty husband is plotting a mass wedding for all four of you." Eleanor put on a droll expression and spoke in imitation of William's usual sonorous tone. "One banquet, one priest, a great savings."

"Perhaps we could share the dress too, if we arrange the ceremony cleverly enough," Tessa said with a chuckle.

Eleanor laughed too, but then her face tensed and she gripped her stomach. Tessa ran to a small bag they had taken to having nearby and fetched a small bottle of painkiller obtained discreetly from an apothecary. Beside it was an earthen orb with a cork stopper, the one Tessa tried not to think about very often. Eleanor drank the medicine and waited for the pain to subside. Her color alarmed Tessa, and she was frustrated at her helplessness.

"Are you sure —" Tessa began, but Eleanor put up a hand, signaled she wanted no discussion.

"This is what I want, Tess. Don't fret about it."

"Eleanor . . ." Tessa longed to say how much this lovely woman meant to her. This whole trip was Eleanor's attempt to settle Tessa's life, and though she had doubts about marrying a man she didn't love, she was realistic enough to see the necessity of it. She'd heard it said that a woman's first marriage should be for security. If fate decreed, she could look for love in the second one.

"I know, my dear. Your face is like a book. Now let us dress for tonight's banquet. Perhaps you will capture the heart of Hardecanute's eldest son." Eleanor was joking, of course. Rumor had it the man was a boor, interested only in falconry and racing horses.

Tessa joined in, keeping her voice light to match Eleanor's lead. "I'd as soon marry an ape as a Dane, and I have my heart set on an Englishman, as you well know."

The first party was a great success. For it Tessa chose her gown of green and set it off with a small cap of matching cloth sewn all over with small beads that caught the light, showing her hair to advantage. Whispers began as she entered the hall, eyes downcast and framed by Eleanor and William. Behind them came the three cousins, also beautifully dressed and coifed. The message was obvious: here are likely candidates for wives. Within minutes, young men found ways to be presented, and although Tessa was the obvious favorite, the other girls had their attendants, too. This invasion of attractive country girls was not popular with the local females, who clustered like threatened chickens and mumbled among themselves. Tessa murmured polite responses to queries and danced with men until she could no longer keep track of names and titles but merely smiled and nodded as they vied to impress her.

After an hour Tessa's head spun from unaccustomed stimulation. The room was warm with the press of bodies and the heat of the torches necessary for light. The people in attendance dazzled in the variety and sumptuousness of their apparel, so that everywhere she looked there was color. The room had been freshly decorated with cut flowers, branches of sweet-scented woo- druff, blossoms, and ribbons of every sort. The room itself was grander than anything she had ever seen. Its dimensions were huge, its walls covered with the finest of tapestries. The high ceiling had been deco- rated with delicate carvings, and in a corner of the room three musicians supplied a sweet-sounding background for the buzz of conversation. There was so much to take in, so much to remember, that she found herself at a loss to notice details, could only register a sense of movement and grandeur.

Remembering Eleanor's teaching, Tessa managed to ingratiate herself to several mothers in the room, chatting about sewing and gardening, making sure to appear mod- est but responsible, charming but chaste. She noticed two formidable-looking ladies watching her critically, and eventually a friend of Eleanor's introduced her to them.

"Lady Acton, Dame Ballard, may I present Tessa macFindlaech, late of Scotland but now here to visit her sister, Eleanor Brix- ton." The man, having obviously done as he was told, now backed away, leaving Tessa with two very opposite personalities.

Lady Acton was square and substantial. Her expensive gown could not make up for the distinctly masculine shape of her body and looked more like a disguise than a dress. Her hair was completely hidden in an elaborate and unbecoming cap that accentuated the size of her head with horns and veils and swinging beads. Her face was flat and pugnacious, inviting no familiarity, and the eyes swept over Tessa continuously, taking in her hair, her clothes — everything about her — giving the impression she was judged as never before.

"How nice for you to come to London before everyone leaves for the summer." Lady Acton's voice was surprisingly low and feminine. "Much better than Scotland, I'm sure. I'm told it's always damp there."

Biting back the reply that begged to be spoken, Tessa merely answered, "I find London most interesting. I notice flowers that I have never seen before, and they are quite beautiful." Having been tutored by Eleanor, Tessa knew that Lady Acton was inordinately proud of her gardens and would talk about them forever if allowed to. For some minutes after that, all Tessa had to do was listen, nod, and smile from time to time.

When Lady Acton finally finished her glowing description of Mirabeau, the country estate to which she would soon be retiring to avoid London's summer heat and the dangers of disease that accompanied it, Tessa murmured, "It sounds breathtaking. I'm sure it is a great deal of work for you, but what rewards you must reap when you survey your labors." She doubted if the woman ever got her hands dirty. Her "work" would consist of telling servants and gardeners what to do each day. Even that was probably unnecessary, since her servants were undoubtedly closer to the earth than their mistress could ever hope to be, more able to coax from it the finest blooms.

Lady Acton was sure that her own toil was exhaustive, and she warmed to Tessa due to the girl's interest in her garden. "Oh, yes, my dear, but it is such a joy to see one's labors come to fruition. I hope to leave the world a more beautiful place than I found it, and therefore I am willing to sacrifice as needs be." Leaving the world might indeed make it more beautiful, Tessa reflected, for Lady Acton was no beauty. Her strong chin was mirrored in her son Cedric, with whom she had danced earlier. On him it was manly and somewhat attractive, but on his mother it predicted strong opinions, rather like a bulldog.

Dame Ballard, the woman with Lady Acton, had been patient as long as she could, and now began what could only be termed an interrogation, delving into every area of Tessa's past.

As Lady Acton's opposite, one could hardly have found a more perfect choice. Everything about Dame Ballard was tentative and frail, or at least appeared so. She was very slight and hunched herself together in such a way that she seemed even less than she was. Her tiny face was all bones, with deep-set eyes and pale skin that added to the wraithlike impression. It was somewhat surprising, therefore, that this lady had no qualms about voicing her curiosity and no restraints on what she considered was within her right to know. Asking questions that Tessa found both invasive and rude, the old lady proceeded to what must have been a mental list of questions designed to satisfy herself as to Tessa's suitability as a candidate for marriage. The old desire to speak out threatened to emerge, but she remembered Eleanor's caution that it was the mothers who were her most critical challenge in securing a favorable match.

The dame's youngest child, Bolton, was eligible, as was Cedric Acton. Their mothers obviously had an interest in her, so Tessa swallowed her objections and answered Dame Ballard's queries. Soon Lady Acton joined in, and the two women poked into Tessa's life until she struggled to keep up with her manufactured past. Lying was against her nature, so she and Eleanor had kept to the truth when possible, simply leaving out facts that would mar her prospects. One such fact was her relationship to Macbeth, to whom the English were naturally antagonistic.

"Your mother was of good blood?" Dame Ballard asked.

Tessa felt a slight flush of anger but answered calmly, "My mother's father was a thane — what you would call a lord — in the Highlands. He was well respected as a leader, and our people are known for their metalwork. If your son owns a long-sword, it may have been made by my grandfather's craftsmen. They also make excellent targes — what you call shields — of wood studded with iron."

"I know little of such things," Dame Ballard admitted. "Does your line run to sons or daughters?"

Tessa knew this was an important question, and she chose to omit mention of her father's six daughters. "My father had but one sibling, a brother, and my mother is one of three children, she the only female."

Both ladies nodded their heads in satisfaction, the effect comedic as the absurd fripperies on their headpieces bobbed and swung in response. Both looked at Tessa speculatively, and she felt like a ham in a butcher shop. As soon as was polite, she excused herself and returned to the much easier task of charming the young men who flocked to her.

Cecilia was faring well, having the most self-confidence of the three cousins. Mary listened wide-eyed to a young man who had a terrible stammer. She never blinked an eye as he struggled to speak, and his gratitude showed in his face. Alice, the quietest cousin, stood against a wall, looking near to tears. Tessa managed to maneuver two of the nearest gentlemen over to where Alice stood, chatting animatedly for a few minutes. Finally, she turned to one (either Alex or Alan, she didn't remember which) and said, "I would be pleased, sir, if you would teach me the form they're dancing now." Inclining her head toward the dance floor, she begged, "Alice, please you and Walter" — she hoped that was his name — "join us or I shall feel quite foolish." The men, well trained in courtesy, did as asked, and soon Alice, an excellent dancer, was laughing up at her partner, face pink with success, quite changed from the terror-stricken creature of a few minutes before.

Eleanor caught Tessa alone for a brief moment and whispered in her ear. "I overheard Lady Acton telling Dame Ballard that you are quite the most charming girl she's met this year. Her son is the one in the scarlet cap, there on the right." Tessa nodded. "Dame Ballard says she's never seen such a beauty since her own daughter Beatrice was young. The Dame holds her daughter to be the standard of womanly perfection against which all others are measured. Being mentioned in the same sentence with the lovely Beatrice is a great compliment."

It was true that Tessa was exceptionally striking that night. With Eleanor's guidance, her natural beauty had been enhanced with subtle additions of color and shading. Her green eyes sparkled in response to the admiration she'd inspired, and her thick auburn hair shone in the candlelight. With some satisfaction, she judged she had performed well, remembering the steps to the dances and managing to smile at each man who circled around her in time to the music.

It was a bit of a jolt when a strong hand gripped Tessa's elbow as she stood alone for a moment, her current partner having gone to get her a cup of wine. Turning, she found

Aidan Brixton's face close to hers, his brown eyes for once harsh.

"How goes your foray onto the marriage market, Tess?"

Brixton was not himself. His words slurred and his body swayed slightly despite attempts to hold himself erect. Gone was the charm, and in its place was an anger that she had never imagined.

Tessa suddenly saw two things clearly: Aidan despised being his brother's lackey, and he was attracted to her. Just as certainly, she understood the hopelessness of Aidan's cause. William would hardly relish the prospect of Aidan's marriage, which would divide his time and require the support of a wife and children. To make matters worse, Aidan could not compete with the glittering men who sought Tessa's attention this night. Strangely, his anger focused on her rather than on the unfairness of his brother.

"Does it not sicken you to smile at these calves and picture yourself in the marital bed with whichever one makes the best offer?" Aidan's smile twisted and his grip on her arm tightened as he struggled to keep his swaying body still. She caught the scent of wine on his breath, and remembered Mary's statement that he was not the same when he'd been drinking.

"Master Aidan. Good evening." Tessa kept her face expressionless lest others around them see her disgust.

"As you say. I find it not particularly pleasant."

"And so you have medicated yourself to improve your own disposition?" She spoke between clenched teeth, angry with Aidan for destroying her fondness for him.

He smiled wickedly. "So, the polished young lady is not the role you play with me. Is it because I have no prospects that you can afford to be so blunt?" The handsome face curled in self-mockery.

"It is because I consider you part of a family that I care about that I warn you, sir, to take yourself off before Sir William sees the state you are in. I will always be honest with you if it saves you trouble."

He stared at Tessa for a few moments then straightened himself, as drunken men will who want to seem in control. "I will remove myself from your presence, since I obviously displease you. Your servant, mistress." And with a satiric bow, he was gone.

Tessa thought about following but decided he was used to looking after himself, even when intoxicated. The third Brixton was a cipher. Although full of charm, there was a dark side to him that she had glimpsed tonight. She wondered which side she would see when next they met.

The answer came swiftly in the morning, for as she came down the stairs to breakfast, Aidan waited in the hallway, his face knitted with worry. When he saw that she was alone, he spoke pleadingly.

"Tessa, I was unforgivably boorish last night. I was awake for hours wondering how I could have let myself get into such a state, and how I could have spoken so to you."

Immediately her heart went out to Aidan, who was obviously very embarrassed at his behavior. "Think no more of it."

His face flushed. "It is shameful to me to admit it, but I cannot take strong drink. It transforms me into a different person, and my brother has often taken me to task for it. The only remedy is to take no drink at all. I had been successful until last night . . ." He paused, about to say one thing, and then finished differently. "Last night I slipped back into old ways. I would give anything to be able to have it back to do differently, and I hereby vow to you that I will never again allow myself to sink to the state of drunkenness that you observed last evening."

"I have said, Aidan, you must think no more of it," Tessa chided him gently. "All of us make mistakes, and only a churl would hold it against you when you have made your apology and promised never to repeat it."

Gratefully, he grasped Tessa's hand and kissed it. "You are as good as you are beautiful," he told her. "I thank the heavens that they have sent us such as you to be a part of our family." With that he led her in to breakfast with the others. As they took their places, Tessa reflected that she now understood the family's references to Aidan's drinking, and she applauded his efforts to change. Aidan was a man who set a standard for himself, and though he had fallen short of it last night, he seemed determined to make himself a better man. For that, she believed, he should be admired.

Chapter Ten

By the end of the week, Tessa was tired of parties. Although she was the center of attention, it had become a strain to keep quiet when men around her said and did the same stupid things that had annoyed her in Scotland. Just months ago they would have received the sharp edge of her tongue, but now she forced herself to pretend they were fascinating.

"Perhaps this is not the life I want after all," she moaned to Mary one afternoon. "It's one thing to say you will marry some dull fellow for his money and his name, but it's another to go to parties and be told I am as beautiful as the goddess of the moon, Hera. I'm an ignorant Scot, and a female, and even I know Hera isn't goddess of the moon. Still, I must bat my eyelashes and murmur how sweet he is to say it, all the time trying to remember if this one is Charles or Cedric."

"But it is how one meets men so that families may arrange marriages. Once that's done, you can retire to an estate somewhere and milk cows or whatever it is Scots lassies do for fun," Mary teased.

They had left the house and were strolling idly through the streets, looking at things they had no money to buy but enjoying themselves anyway. The streets of London were an adventure. Shop windows were crowded with things neither girl had seen before, and in the street itself were offered all sorts of things from barrows present from dawn to dusk. They were encouraged to buy everything from "good Scots metalwork" to "le-e-e-e-mons fresh from Spa-a-a-in." They laughed together, pointing at this and that, until Tessa came to a dead stop, staring ahead of her. Coming out of a gateway was Jeffrey Brixton, dressed in traveling clothes muted with dust and boots caked with mud. He looked weary and defeated, eyes glazed and dull.

Mary saw him a second later and screamed with delight, "Jeffrey! Jeffrey, over here!"

As he raised his eyes, there was a flash of recognition. For a moment his eyes lingered on Tessa, taking in her becoming new coif, her attractive rose-and-cream outfit, and —

she found herself hoping — more ladylike bearing. There was a flash of appreciation in his eyes, and his mien lightened. Mary fairly twitched with delight as he crossed to them. "Jeffrey, we have come to London to visit, and William is to find us husbands, all of us!"

"Husbands?" Jeffrey seemed slow to comprehend, his brow furrowed in thought. Turning to Tessa, he asked, "Are you to have a husband?"

"Of course, she is," Mary babbled on. "Sir William will see to it that his sister-in-law is well married."

"Sister —" Jeffrey began, and Tessa gave him a look that interrupted the thought and he stopped.

"Your brother has been very kind to all of us," she said, looking directly at him. "My half-sister has prepared me to be a good English wife as best she can in so short a time."

Jeffrey still struggled to understand; it was plain from his expression, but he kept quiet.

Mary noticed nothing, so happy was she to see her cousin. "You must come with us to the house. Eleanor will want to see you." His face showed indecision, and Mary added, "I believe William has gone out for the day." Jeffrey smiled for the first time.

"Good, then. If you care to wait, I will be a few moments, and then we will walk while you apprise me of recent events." With a look at Tessa, he added, "I am interested to hear what brings you all to London."

After Jeffrey had arranged for his horse to be fed and stalled, the three of them made their way to the town house. Eleanor was joyful to see Jeffrey safe once more, but he disappointed her immediately. "I must be off tonight," he said. "My ship sails with the tide."

"Where now?" Mary asked, but Jeffrey would not say.

"Well then, I will at least see to it that you have a decent meal before you go," Eleanor insisted. She went off to find the cook, Mary trailing behind as they began a list of things to get for Jeffrey's journey.

Tessa watched them go, uneasy now that she and Jeffrey were alone together. He stepped closer so that they could speak in low tones, and his eyes held an odd expression, maybe anger, maybe something else.

"You are now Eleanor's sister?" he asked coolly.

"A story she made up to explain my presence."

"I should have guessed that Eleanor's ingenuity would solve all problems. But you will stay here now?"

"I cannot return to Scotland with any reputation after . . . what happened. It seems best to attempt to make a life here. Eleanor has given me a chance to remake my future."

"And have you done well here in London?" he asked, his voice tired. He slumped into a nearby chair, his eyes watching as she moved nervously about the room. "Eleanor has made you into a social success?"

His words stung, but Tessa chose to ignore what she interpreted as sarcasm. "I have come to love Eleanor, and she has done much for me," she answered.

"Do you forgive me, then, for what I did?"

Tessa looked sharply at Jeffrey. He seemed to speak in earnest, and she turned away, unable to decide what the question meant. Was he mocking her? Did he think ill of her for turning her situation to the best advantage possible? Whatever she had done, he had begun it, taking her by force from her homeland.

Anger flared, and she felt her face growing warm, but Jeffrey went on. "I've thought about it, many nights. You did no wrong, and I — your uncle and I — we caused you great suffering for our own ends."

"Was it awful, the fighting?"

"Yes." No more.

"I am glad you did not succeed." She was defiant.

"I was sure you would be." He paused. "Will you marry an Englishman, then, and become an obedient wife?"

"What else have you left me?" It was more strident than she'd intended.

Suddenly, he sprang from the chair, his weariness gone, and came to her side. "I *have* thought of you," he said softly. "The way you struggled to get free of me on the riverbank. The way you shouted at me in the cabin of the ship, unafraid even though your life was in my hands. And I remember your vow that you would repay me for ruining your life. Sometimes it seems that I think of nothing but you, who never once cried, never once begged for mercy. If Scotland has more like you, she will never be defeated."

Tessa's throat closed with emotion. As Jeffrey put his arms around her and drew her to him, her mind refused to function. Half-formed thoughts were interrupted by the sensation of his touch and the feel of his coarse beard as his lips found hers. The kiss brought again that sensation of heat, of melting, that she had first experienced aboard ship as his captive. The world receded for a long moment, but finally a voice drifted into her consciousness.

"Well, Jeffrey, it seems you are not as fatigued as the Lady Eleanor had imagined."

The two sprang apart guiltily. "Aidan," Jeffrey managed, but it was all he could say.

Tessa stood mute, wondering what had just happened. How did she feel about Jeffrey Brixton? She'd thought until a minute ago that she hated him. Now all she could feel was the blood that rushed through her body, the lingering traces of his touch on her skin.

Finally she gathered her dignity around her. "If you will excuse me, gentlemen, I will leave you alone. I'm sure you have much catching up to do." She met neither man's eyes as she left them, running straight up the stairs to her room and closing herself in.

Tessa sent Mary down alone to supper, saying that she had a headache. Eleanor dispatched a servant with a tray and a cold compress soaked in witch hazel, and the girl sat miserably with the food before her, untouched. What had she been thinking, to let Jeffrey Brixton kiss her? And what was Aidan going to do about it? Would he tell Eleanor? William? Sick with dread, she considered her reaction. She had responded to the kiss of a man who'd torn her from home as if she did not matter. But he'd thought of her. Her heart held on to that confession despite her mind's objection: *Sometimes it seems that I think of nothing but you.*

A few minutes later, as she sat by the window staring at nothing, Tessa came to her senses, reminding herself that to a man like Jeffrey Brixton, words were used to get what he wanted. They meant nothing. Within half an hour she had convinced herself that she was a fool to react to a man who made love to his own sister-in-law and then had the gall to say that he thought of her. If he did, it was with lust, wishing he'd taken advantage of her when he had the chance. He would never have such an opportunity again, for she would see to it that they spent not one moment alone together in the future. She even convinced herself that she was grateful for Aidan's interruption of what was an unfortunate and unwanted encounter.

The next morning things were as usual, and Eleanor showed no knowledge of a change between Tessa and Jeffrey. Aidan treated her politely, as did William. She guessed that no one had even told the head of the household of Jeffrey's visit. Once they were alone, the women talked of Jeffrey, how tired he had looked, how soon he'd had to leave, and how dangerous his life must be. Tessa noted with amusement that now that Mary and Alice had other prospects, their erstwhile mooning over Jeffrey was replaced with mere affectionate concern. Mary's stammering young man was the only son of a prosperous merchant, and Alice had caught the eye of a widower with two sons and a thriving business. A penniless cousin, fourth in line to inherit, was not such a glittering prize by comparison, no matter how much they liked him. Eventually the talk turned to the evening's entertainment.

Tessa had indeed captured the attention of Lady Acton. Her son, Cedric, was everything Eleanor had described: good-looking, wealthy, well taught . . . and deadly dull. Cedric was dull not so much from a lack of intelligence, but more from an inability to think of anything but himself. His mother's dotage, his good looks, and his vast fortune had convinced him that he was peerless among men. His hair, seldom covered, was his pride and joy: thick, wavy, and honey-colored. His posture was so erect as to appear uncomfortable. And Cedric certainly had enough chin for a lord — perhaps for a lord and a half.

Although she could not deny his good looks, Tessa secretly longed for a personality to accompany them. Cedric considered himself a catch, and it didn't help that most of London agreed. He was the type of man whom Tessa in her former days would have sent off in less than three minutes with scathing comments resounding in his ears. As it was, she smiled through clenched teeth when he told her for the third time about the last hunt he'd gone on. He thought it masculine to laugh loudly and often, which made Tessa's head ache; he used an exaggerated courtesy that she found irritating; and he endeared himself to her, or so he thought, by calling her Tessie, loudly and often.

Cedric assumed that any girl would be flattered to be the object of his attention, and perhaps she should have been. Although she tried, Tessa could not feel flattered; the best she could achieve was resignation.

Eleanor often caught Tessa's eye as Cedric droned on and winked to let her know she understood. He was far from her perfect mate, but what could she do? If Sir William ever discovered that she was not family, she'd be homeless in a trice. She had to hope for a match quickly, before her secret was out, or before something happened to

Eleanor, who weakened daily. The others had begun to comment that she was losing weight, looking tired. So far, Eleanor had laughed it off or used some excuse, but Tessa could see that she was very ill.

Lady Acton was herself a formidable pill to swallow, manipulative and opinionated, especially where her son was concerned. In Eleanor's view, she was well disposed toward Tessa precisely because she had no dowry or strong family ties. "She wants control, and her son wants a beautiful wife to show off," Eleanor told Tessa as they washed their hair in rainwater, softer and less drying than regular water. "They have all they need of money, houses, land, and servants. You will always be under her thumb, and she will hold it over you, too. Oh, my dear, can you abide it?"

"I believe so," Tessa answered, toweling her thick curls thoroughly. "I am dishonest in entering into marriage with Cedric — if he asks me — since I want the security of his name and wealth, not Cedric himself."

"That is how marriages are made."

"Cedric's mother is a gargoyle, to be sure. I will manage as best I can to be where she is not, and I will give her grandchildren, which will soften her, I hope. As long as we all get what we want, is it so bad?"

"Not so bad," Eleanor said sadly, "but I wish you could wait for the man who makes you feel alive."

Tessa looked up in surprise. "You knew such a man?"

Eleanor's blue eyes clouded. "Once, yes. But my father would have none of it. The man I loved was merely one of his knights, far removed from inheriting anything."

Like Jeffrey, Tessa thought, but she pushed it aside.

"Did you love him?"

Eleanor smiled sadly. "Oh, yes. And he loved me. He hoped money would change my father's mind, so he went off to win his fortune, to Normandy."

"Where is that?"

"Across the Channel. Miles hoped to get a grant of land as a reward for helping the duke."

"And what happened?"

"I never heard from him again, but it wouldn't have mattered. My father had made his bargain with Lord Brixton. I pleaded with him to delay the marriage for a year, but he would not."

Tessa felt sad that Eleanor had been treated so, but the latter smiled brightly.

"As I told you before, I have come to understand that we must make our own happiness. William allows me to do as I wish up in York while he stays here in London. Mine is a better lot than some." She grinned at Tessa. "I'm afraid with your temper, you'll have to convince Cedric to be where you are not, or you will end up braining him with a firedog."

"Oh, no," Tessa said, joining in the jest, "it would take at least a pike to pierce through all that hair!"

CHAPTER ELEVEN

After a month in London, Tessa was sure that Cedric Acton would soon ask William for her hand. Lady Acton had deigned several times to speak to her, and others of the older ladies treated her in such a way as to indicate their understanding that she might soon be someone of importance. One evening at a dinner, she was seated across the table from the two gargoyles, as she privately called them, Dame Ballard and Lady Acton.

Lady Acton set her rather nearsighted gaze on Tessa, her eyes narrowing as she tried to focus. "William says that you will soon return to Brixton."

Tessa knew nothing of this but gave no sign. Leave it to William to hint that they were to leave soon so Cedric would ask for Tessa's hand. The old lady continued, her voice giving the distinct impression that she bestowed a great favor. "You must visit —

with your sister, of course — and see my gardens for yourself."

"Thank you very much, my lady," Tessa answered as sincerely as she could. "I consider it a great privilege."

"Yes," the lady drawled in agreement. "You must plan to come in August, when the dahlias are at their best."

"Of course. I will speak to Eleanor of it as soon as possible. Thank you for your kind invitation."

"I'm sure she'll be glad to come," Lady Acton pronounced, the over-sized jaw setting firmly as she finished speaking. Irritated by the lady's assumption that Eleanor would come at her call like a puppy, Tessa forced a weak smile and turned the conversation to the weather, which had grown very warm. This woman might become her mother-in-law. She must learn to accept her, pomposity and all.

Eleanor's plans for the girls proceeded well. Mary's young man, Francis Hope, had stammered a proposal in the second week, and Alice and Cecilia moved sedately forward in their friendships with several young men. Plans were made for a celebration at York in the fall, to which many of their London friends would be invited, but Tessa feared it would be too much for Eleanor, who had admitted now to the others that she felt unwell. Her husband took this as an excuse to send them all home and end the unexpected expense of their stay.

Tessa happened to be in the solar with Eleanor when William made his decision known to her. He entered the room abruptly and began without preamble. "Wife, it is time these females returned to Brixton. I have made every effort to please you. The women have had their moment of celebrity, for which they should be thankful. You are obviously unwell and will fare better at home where Madeline can see to your recovery."

"I am resting as much as possible, William," Eleanor replied. "Cecilia has not yet met anyone she cares for —"

"Enough of this silly idea that girls should have a say in the choice of their husbands! I allowed it for your . . . sister" — here William's tone said something of his suspicions concerning Tessa — "and I believe she will be settled with Cedric ere long. That is good, since both families will benefit from such a union. The others may marry as I arrange for them and be grateful for it. You will return to Brixton at the end of the week."

For a moment Eleanor seemed about to

argue, but she did not. Her face was pale, and her usually bright eyes had lost their sparkle. Over the past few weeks she had become terribly thin, and when only Tessa was present, she sometimes let down her guard and admitted to the pain she now lived with constantly. William took her silence for agreement and turned on his heel, leaving the two alone.

"I hope we have done enough for Cecilia and Alice," Eleanor said softly. "You have captured Cedric. The invitation to Mirabeau is proof of that. And Mary is set on Francis and he on her. Just a few more days . . ."

"We have been given the best of opportunities, and it has all been your doing," Tessa told her, pressing her hand softly. "You have been more than caring to all of us, but especially to me, and I'm very, very grateful." With that Tessa went to tell the others, leaving Eleanor weak but with a small smile of contentment on her face.

The ride home was quieter and more somber than had been their coming. Eleanor felt pain with each jarring of the cart-wheels on the road, and Tessa silently cursed William for sending them away, although she had to admit he did not know the extent of his wife's illness.

By the time they reached Brixton Manor, the whole party was quite exhausted. Auntie Madeline took one look at Eleanor and paled. She ordered two strong servants to carry her inside and told the girls to see to the unpacking. Later she stopped Tessa on the stairs. "She says you know."

"Yes," was all Tessa answered.

"I don't know why she's kept it a secret. Perhaps there could have been help —" The old lady's eyes misted. "What shall we do without her? She's been the light of this house for twenty years. I have loved her like a daughter, and now . . ." Tessa's eyes filled, too. Dear Eleanor, keeping up appearances until they'd all had their chance at happiness.

Auntie remembered something and tottered down the stairs. Returning in a few minutes, she put a letter into Tessa's hands. "I believe it's from Jeffrey," she said. "Read it to her. She loves to hear from him." Tessa opened the letter with trembling hands. It was a large sheet, folded and waxed, and inside was a smaller sheet that bore the words: "For Tessa, who can read and sometimes should not." Unwilling to open it with anyone else present, she thanked Auntie Madeline and went to her room. Breaking the seal, she read:

My dear little Scot,

I feel I must apologize for my behavior on both the occasions when we have met. I don't seem to be able to do anything correctly where you are concerned.

Yr Servant, Jeffrey Brixton

Tessa stared at the letter for some time. What did it mean? Was he sorry he'd abducted her or that he'd kissed her or both? The man was quite maddening, never saying anything that made sense. And what of Eleanor? He couldn't know how ill she was. Tessa decided Jeffrey was merely clearing his conscience. He had treated her badly — twice — and probably didn't want Eleanor to know about the second time. Would Eleanor be jealous of Tessa? That was impossible to tell, but Tessa had to admit she resented the love between Jeffrey and Eleanor, although she would not ask herself why that should be.

Her thoughts went to the other letter, the one addressed to Eleanor. Slipping her letter under her pallet, she hurried to Eleanor's room. Pale and weak, Tessa's supposed sister lay on a large, curtained bed in the center of the room. The curtains were open, since it was a warm day, but at night they

151

would be closed to keep the sleeper's body heat inside. The bed sat on a raised platform to escape the chill floors. Lady Brixton looked much smaller than when Tessa had first met her. She had lost weight but seemed also to have shrunken, so that even her frame seemed smaller and more fragile than when she had been in health. Eleanor opened her eyes and smiled at Tessa, but it was a tiny smile.

"I've brought you a letter from Jeffrey that came while we were away. Auntie just gave it to me. Shall I read it, or are you too tired just now?"

"Please, read it."

"Dearest Eleanor," Tessa began. *"I hope this letter finds everyone well."* Tessa's eyes filled with tears and she choked on the words, but she gathered herself together and continued. *"I am about to board a ship for the north again, and I wanted to give you what peace of mind I can about my task. I will not be fighting this trip. I go to visit the new king of Scotland, Macbeth."*

Here Tessa stopped in amazement.

"Is that not your uncle?" Eleanor asked.

"It is."

"Why, that is good. Perhaps you can go home if your uncle is the king."

Tessa had read ahead, and she frowned.

"The old king, Duncan, was murdered in his sleep while visiting Inverness. There is no proof of who did this thing. Some suspect the king's sons, but others say Macbeth himself did it. The oldest of the sons, Malcolm, fled to England to beg help in taking the throne from Macbeth. I am sent to see what I can find out. I know you will speak of this to no one except Tessa, but I want her to know that it is not safe for her in Scotland at this time. It is whispered that Macbeth is not himself, that he suspects all those around him of perfidy. Nor is it safe for relatives of Macbeth in England. For this reason, I am glad that you have provided her with your protection and that none know her true identity. Keep her safe, I ask you, although I know you love her and will do so for her own sake. Yr Loving Jeffrey."

The two women sat quietly for some time, taking all this in. What did it mean? Perhaps nothing, since Tessa had given up hope of returning to Scotland. Her most prominent feeling was joy that Jeffrey cared at least a little about her welfare. These thoughts were interrupted by Eleanor's voice, frail but determined.

"We must burn this letter, my dear, so no one can discover your secret." Tessa obediently made a spark from the flint at Eleanor's bedside and lit a candle, putting the edge of the letter into it until it caught fire. She took it to the window slit, laid it there until it was ash, then blew the ash outside.

"I have a favor to ask, Tessa." Eleanor's voice was even weaker, her breathing more ragged. Tessa thought of the bottle she had promised to bring when Eleanor could stand the pain no more. Was it time? Could she be part of this woman's death? But Eleanor had something else in mind. "Jeffrey. What do you think of him?"

Tessa was at a loss. She couldn't bring herself to speak well of Jeffrey Brixton, who had taken all she had from her and played with her emotions in the process, but she couldn't speak ill of the man Eleanor loved. "I . . . I do not think of him at all."

Eleanor's eyes focused for a moment on Tessa through her own pain. "I want you to promise that when next you see him, you will give him something."

"What?"

"A wooden box where I keep a few things. I would like you to get it for me now from my trunk in the storage closet off the hall."

"Can we not get it later?" Tessa worried about Eleanor tiring herself fretting over minutia as her body weakened.

"Best do it now. For one thing, my father's will is in the box. William mustn't see it when I'm gone. It makes it quite clear that I am the only child my father had at his death. He wrote it out himself just before he died, leaving me all his worldly goods. There was nothing much to leave, and I only kept the document because it was in my father's hand. At the time William was only interested to know there was no money, but if he finds it now and reads it, he will deduce that you are not my sister. The will you must burn as you did Jeffrey's letter. Give the rest of it to Jeffrey when you and he can find a time to be alone. Go now, please, and get it."

Tessa did as she was told, slipping into William's closet and pulling closed after her the curtain that served as a door. Luckily, servants and family alike were busy unpacking the cart. People passed by but no one looked in on her. Searching quietly through the trunk, Tessa finally located a small wooden box with an "E" carved in the top. It was beautifully wrought with great care and detail. Attached to top and bottom was a red ribbon that secured it with a neat bow. Turning it over, she found the initials "M.T." in tiny letters on the bottom. Miles? she wondered.

The box held just a few pieces of paper, most of them sealed with wax imprinted with an "E." The bottom one had simply been refolded, the wax around the broken seal old and crumbling: the will. Tessa put the other papers back as she had found them and closed the box, tying it shut with the ribbon as before. Listening at the curtain until the hall was quiet, she went back upstairs.

"I have it, Eleanor," she said softly, and then stopped. Eleanor lay, white and still, on the bed. Beside her was the tiny earthen bottle Tessa had so often looked upon with dread. Later, when Auntie Madeline found them both, Tessa was holding Eleanor's head in her lap and crying softly, "You didn't want to ask me, I know. You didn't want to ask."

Chapter Twelve

Poor Madeline was heartbroken at the loss of her sister-in-law. Tessa and the other girls did what they could to comfort her, but the old lady had indeed looked upon Eleanor as a daughter. She insisted on preparing the body for burial, staying up all night in a prayer vigil.

Tessa felt empathy for the aunt's loss, for without Eleanor's intercession, she could have become like Madeline: childless and alone, living on the edges of a household with no one of her own to love. With Eleanor's help, there was hope she would find peace with Cedric and joy with the children they would someday have.

The most helpful person of all was Aidan, who returned with some speed to York and oversaw the arrangements for a grave but elegant funeral. For once Lord Brixton didn't stint on cost, and the house was put into good order as much as possible in the brief time available. Tessa thought angrily that it would have been kinder to let Eleanor herself buy new curtains when she still could have enjoyed them, but she tried to see William's actions as a tribute to his wife.

Aidan worked efficiently, without fuss or pretension, to make the preparations. The result was a tasteful ceremony that proclaimed to the world, whatever the truth might be, that William's wife had been his dearest treasure. Eleanor received in death the tributes she deserved, but it was Aidan who was most responsible. The family found themselves depending on his judgment, which was faultless, and his kindness, which was unfailing.

Tessa was surprised at the number of people who came from London for Eleanor's memorial. Midmorning on the day of the service, a large carriage arrived at the gates of Brixton Manor. It was like a box on wooden wheels, and although efforts had been made to decorate it, the ride could not have been comfortable. From a distance Tessa recognized the Acton colors. Touched that Cedric had made the journey from his lands near Beverly, she was surprised when he assisted not only his mother but also Dame Ballard from the carriage.

Lady Acton descended upon her like a large goose, arms extended in what might have seemed a threatening gesture if she hadn't known the lady. Tessa was soundly enfolded in mixed scents of pomander and the normal human reaction to a warm summer day. "Oh, my dear child, if only we had known how ill poor Eleanor was! A shock, although I told Cedric she looked terrible. Didn't I say that, Cedric?"

"You did, Mother." Cedric stepped up to Tessa and kissed her cheek. "I am so sorry that you have lost your sister after finding her only recently." He was for once focused on her emotions, and his words were genuine. These people were making their best efforts to comfort her.

Not willing to be forgotten, Dame Ballard stepped up behind Cedric. "I am so sorry, my dear. Eleanor was loved by us all," she pronounced formally in her little-girl voice. Then as her curiosity could be stayed no longer, she added, "Did she die on the road? I suppose it was most unnerving if she did, for then you had to travel with a corpse in the cart, did you not?"

Ignoring the dame's misplaced inquisitiveness, Lady Acton took Tessa's arm and proceeded to the house. "I felt I had to come. I am sure you have need of an older

159

woman's support at such a time."

Tessa thought she heard Auntie Madeline, who had been largely ignored thus far, sniff in disapproval. As if she could not comfort her own family! Lady Acton noticed nothing. "I, of course, am never ill, but I realize that some become quite overcome with grief, and their health suffers accordingly. I will assure myself that you are able to manage before I leave this place."

Tessa tried to appear at once grateful for the offer of help and capable of managing on her own. Considering William's increasing coldness, she did not need the strain of Cedric's overpowering mother staying under the same roof as well. She should have been heartened by the presence of these people, for it indicated their commitment to her and meant that Eleanor's plans for her were likely to be successful. All she could think of, though, was that Eleanor herself would never see them come to fruition. Eleanor was gone.

The funeral itself was a blur. She remembered little except William's stiff presence beside her as they took their place as chief mourners. Servants and estate workers were grief stricken. No one had been more beloved to them than the Lady Eleanor. They crowded outside the chapel and lined the pathway, heads bowed and silent in respect.

When it was over, Aidan again smoothed the way for Tessa, tactfully suggesting that she needed time to herself and escorting the guests to their various conveyances. Although Tessa sensed that Cedric would have made his offer after the funeral with any encouragement from her, she simply could not face the prospect of deciding whether to marry him at that point. She sent him off with a look meant to portray fondness and the suggestion that he return in a week. Aidan sent him and the ladies off with just the right mixture of friendliness and respect.

"I must say," she told him as the carriage bumped away down the dry cart road, "you've been wonderful. I hope Sir William appreciates you enough."

"It's a fact he doesn't," Aidan said, but his brown eyes sparkled. "Nobody knows what I can accomplish when I put my mind to it." His face sobered. "I had to do it, you know. She made life bearable for me when Lady Brixton died. William, I think, might have sent me on my way. I'm sure you know the story?" Never having been able to lie when asked a direct question, Tessa nodded. "I don't mind making myself useful, but I was afraid I'd be sent to become a soldier, like Jeffrey. It may be his way, killing masses of people, but it isn't mine."

He stopped, as if remembering. "Sorry, I didn't mean to make Jeffrey sound . . ."

"It's all right," Tessa told him. "I've never explained that day to you, because I don't know how to explain it. I know that Jeffrey and Eleanor were . . . fond of each other —" She stopped, not knowing how much Aidan knew and unwilling to tarnish his memories of Eleanor.

Aidan's eyes were on her, and again she got the feeling that he was sensing her thoughts. He looked blank for a moment, but a look of understanding finally appeared. "Oh, you know about Jeffrey and Eleanor." He stopped, evidently unwilling to put words to the thought. "Yes, I'm sorry you had to see that. It was . . . distressing to me. I tried to talk to Jeffrey about it once, but he felt he was getting a bit of his own back from William for the poor treatment he'd received. It was sad to see him so bitter."

"I am sure it was. But my awareness of — of that —" She tried again. "What you saw between Jeffrey and me was an accident. I have no hold on him, nor he on me."

Aidan's smile got wider. "That's good,

162

then, isn't it? Room for the rest of us, perhaps." And with that, he left the hall, whistling.

The second blow to the peaceful life Tessa had found in England came just a week later; in fact, on the day that Cedric was to visit. Tessa had not slept well. Grief for Eleanor and her knowledge of the decision that awaited her combined to prevent slumber. Could she marry Cedric? Eleanor had accepted an arranged marriage and made the best of it, but she had not been happy *with* William, only *without* him. Did Tessa want a life such as that?

A sudden memory came into Tessa's mind of a servant in her uncle's castle at Inverness who had done something terribly stupid. "Cream-faced loon," Macbeth had called him, and the name fit Cedric as well, at least to her. She was faintly repelled by the man, which did not bode well for a happy marriage. Still, what else was she to do? Other men made it clear they found her attractive, but most found her lack of property an insurmountable problem. Could she afford to delay Cedric in hopes that a man more to her liking might appear? Probably not now that Eleanor was dead. William would be anxious to have her gone.

The box now hidden in her room also occupied her mind. What had Eleanor wanted Jeffrey to have, and why did she choose Tessa to present it to him? She decided the answer was that Eleanor had trusted Tessa not to reveal their affair, which of course she would never do. It was their secret, and she had to preserve it. Aidan had confirmed it, surprised, it seemed, that the secret was known to someone else. Did Auntie Madeline know, she wondered? Unable to decide who might be able to explain the box, Tessa kept its existence to herself.

Because she was awake, Tessa heard the knock at the door first and went down to answer it. A boy of about ten stood there, shivering in the morning chill. He was wet from travel through damp fields and muddy from last night's rain. His thin linen smock and coarse breeches could not be much protection from the elements, and his nose ran. "Message for the master of the house, mistress."

Tessa took the proffered paper. "Come in and we'll give you breakfast and let you dry. Have you come far?"

"Flamborough Head, mistress. They said there that the master here should get that paper right away."

"I'll see that he does if you rest and eat before starting for home. Will you do that?"

"I will," came the sturdy answer, and she pointed him toward the kitchen where the fire was already kindled and the breakfast started.

As she turned back, William came down the stairs, a heavy robe wrapped around him against the morning chill. He stopped on the last step, waiting wordlessly for an explanation of the noise that had woken him. "A boy has brought this for you," Tessa said, handing him the paper. "From Flamborough Head. Isn't that on the coast?"

Without answering, he broke the seal. Tessa watched his face and saw shock as he set his jaw.

"My brother Jeffrey is dead, it seems. Lost from a boat during a storm on the North Sea. They don't suppose — What's this?" for Tessa had fainted dead away on the cold stone floor below him.

When she awoke Tessa was surrounded by the four Brixton women, all in tears themselves but also concerned for her. "Are you all right, dear?" Madeline asked.

She meant to say that she was, meant to get up and behave as if nothing had happened that should concern her except as a mild sorrow that the family had lost another member so soon after Eleanor. Instead, she wept bitterly.

It was three days before Tessa could get off by herself to think. The cousins, especially Mary, were concerned that the two deaths so close together had unhinged her mind. Tessa had to fight to maintain control, fight to assure them that it was only the shock of the news that had caused her fainting spell, fight to avoid Aidan's eye when he looked at her with sorrowful concern. Jeffrey was dead. Life would go on, she told herself. He had never been anything to her, should in fact have been her enemy, so now she must go on without him and pretend his death didn't matter.

But it did matter somehow. "You will find happiness only among the dead," the old woman had said. And now it did feel like her happiness was dead, as if the life that stretched before her could offer nothing.

In a daze, Tessa went through the motions of another funeral. In a fog she heard Cedric promise to make her forget her unhappiness if she would say yes to him. In a dream she said yes and heard those around her say it was for the best. A wedding would dim the memory of Eleanor's death and her brother-in-law's drowning. But Aidan's brown eyes watched her, and she knew it was not a dream.

Preparations for her wedding began immediately. William had his way, at least partially, and there were to be two ceremonies combined, hers and Mary's. Cedric argued for a Christmas wedding, but good sense — or in this case his mother's opinion — prevailed, and it was decided that spring was soon enough. Mary theorized privately that William hoped Alice would be settled by then and he could toss in a third bride and groom for the money.

The winter was mild, and Tessa occupied herself with her trousseau, sewing and embroidering with the help of Cecilia, making over dresses that had been Eleanor's. This made her feel sad and yet satisfied somehow to keep bits of Eleanor near her. The family, in deep mourning, did little outside the home, and the holidays were observed in somber mood. Eleanor's room was closed off. After a month, William returned to London to resume his presence at court. A new king ruled England, Edward, and Lord Brixton wanted to be in the midst of things. Aidan made trips back and forth as necessary, so they saw him often. He never mentioned Tessa's wedding and was always polite, but his eyes said he thought she was wrong to marry Cedric Acton.

The weather broke in April, and they had

three days running that were warm and dry. William came home for a week to meet with his staff about the year's crops and the tenants' duties. On the third day, although the ground was still damp, the four girls went walking, just to be outside in the sunshine for an hour. As they returned to the house, a man came out, closing the heavy wooden door behind him with a disgusted thud. He was dressed in Scottish fashion, a huge, ferocious specimen with wildly tangled hair and a full growth of beard. On his left hand the last two fingers were chopped away, as if he had raised it to ward off a sword blow. He ignored the women and went on with some speed, as if glad to be away.

"Who was that?" Tessa asked William as they entered the hall.

"Only a rascal that I have sent on his way," was his answer, and he said no further word.

At the end of the week of William's stay, the rain began again. Aidan rode in just before supper, looking tired and out of temper. He said nothing to Tessa and very little to the other women of the household, but he spent an hour closeted with William, their voices low and incomprehensible. Dinner was a silent affair, although the girls had planned special dishes for William's last evening with them. He appeared not to notice and when the meal was over spoke brusquely to Tessa. "I would see you, Mistress macFindlaech, in my office."

Eyebrows were raised and shoulders shrugged. None of the cousins could decide what the audience was about. Tessa had an idea, but she said nothing. Aidan avoided her eyes for once and said he was going for a walk, even though rain dripped noisily from the roof.

The "office" she was called to was really just a closet that had been converted for the brief times William spent at the manor. At other times it was a storeroom, so during his residence the stored items were piled out of his way and a table was set up for his use. The result was rather chaotic, with bags of flour and pots of ink vying for space. For all his strictness with those around him, William was not prone to neatness himself, and the place was littered with apple cores and the shavings of pen nubs. A candle burned beside him, since the room had no windows, and Tessa noticed that the wax had made a stain on the table that would probably never come out.

Sir William sat on a stool behind a table littered with papers and the paraphernalia of writing. Most landowners were illiterate, depending upon clerks to do their paperwork, but since William did not trust easily, he had taught himself to read and write in order not to be cheated. Aidan had whispered to Tessa one day that his brother's eyesight was not what it had been, however, so he depended more and more on Aidan for his information. Now he held before him a paper, looking down at it rather than at Tessa. Knowing that he could not read it with his poor eyesight and the dimness of the room, she concluded that he was unwilling to face her directly. She was not invited to sit and so stood before him like a disobedient child.

"Mistress, I have had a letter." He swept his hand across the rough surface. "I don't suppose you read?"

"As a matter of fact, sir, I do." Tessa held out her hand, and, with some surprise, William handed the letter to her. She scanned it briefly, having guessed its contents. It was from a lawyer in Scotland who had investigated "as requested" the background of one Tessa macFindlaech and discovered no relationship between the girl and Eleanor, *nee* Ardonne, the late Lady Brixton. The lawyer reported that the macFindlaech clan was now the ruling clan of Scotland, under Macbeth macFindlaech, the king.

Tessa returned the letter to Brixton with

no comment. He did not look up but set it aside and began to write on another sheet. "I have no idea why my wife made up this lie, but I blame you as much as Eleanor, for you have continued it even after her death, allowing me to support you, a stranger: sleeping in my house, eating my food, even taking the clothes on your back from my kindness, all the while knowing you had no right to them."

There was nothing to say. He was correct, and no argument she could make would change his view that she had taken advantage of him. He would not care that she had had no choice but to seek the protection of marriage or starve in the streets. The only two people who could corroborate her situation were now dead, and William was not interested anyway. "I am grieved that I must make Lord Acton aware of your treachery, for I will not have a valued friend take a snake into his bosom unknowing."

More likely he feared the loss of Cedric's support with England's king more than anything else. "If you will allow me, I will tell Cedric myself when he comes here tomorrow to accompany you to London."

There was a snort of derision from William. "No doubt you will want to couch your confession in terms that make it seem less vile. Rest assured, I will speak to him of it as well, and he will see you for what you are, a Scottish Jezebel sent by her evil uncle to undermine England."

Tessa almost laughed aloud at that. If he only knew how unwillingly she had come to England! As for her uncle, she would have liked to reply that Macbeth had no cause to bother the English if they would leave him alone to rule his own country. But again, there was no sense talking to William.

"I will speak to Cedric in the morning, sir, and I will be gone from your house anon." She spoke calmly although she had no idea where she would go or how.

"See to it, then. I'll not have you here with my nieces any longer." As if he cared about them, she thought bitterly, but she turned and left the room without further comment, keeping her head high until she was out the front door and into the garden, where it was quite dark. Here she broke down and wept: for Eleanor, for Jeffrey, and for herself. All had started life eager to find happiness, and all been thwarted in some way by William Brixton and others like him who sought only their own ends. Perhaps there was happiness only among the dead, as the crone had predicted.

Not the type to mourn reality for long, it was only a few minutes until Tessa pulled her tattered emotions back under control and repaired the visible damage to her person. She wiped her eyes, blew her nose, and composed her facial expression. She would never betray to Lord Brixton any sign that she suffered.

Her mind tossed about for options. What was she to do? There was no money to pay for passage back to Scotland, and it was plain Sir William did not intend to help her. She paced back and forth across the garden, cool as it was, examining possibilities.

"Tess?" a voice stopped her and she turned. Aidan stood uncertainly at the edge of the walled enclosure, barely visible in the fading light. "Are you all right?"

"You know better," she challenged, and saw his head droop in embarrassment.

"Yes. I knew William was investigating your relationship to Eleanor. I didn't know whether to tell you or to keep silent and hope that nothing could be found." Distress was evident in his voice.

"I must leave, Aidan. I cannot stay here now."

"You don't have to go." His voice was low, and she thought for a moment she had misheard.

"Of course I do, Aidan. William just said —"

"You could marry me." Tessa was speechless, but Aidan rushed on, coming closer in the fading light and grasping her hands in his. "Oh, I know it is not the same as marrying Lord Acton, but I will provide for you. I shall ask William to give us the little house where my mother and I once lived. It is not grand, but we could be comfortable there. And someday I shall be the Lord of Brixton Manor, and then you would have a title."

"Aidan, it isn't the title!" How could she explain? "I don't want that or the money —"

He grunted with disgust. "No, of course you don't. *Everyone* wants the title and the money, Tessa, even younger brothers. Do you think William gives me a penny for myself? Never! I am to do the work he sets me to and be glad I get meals, a bed, and a new suit each year so I don't shame him in public." His voice was bitter, more than she had imagined it could be. "But he has no children, and I am the only one left now. That is the reason I don't show him my back."

Tessa realized that this was what Aidan held on for, a future that had recently become more of a possibility. A brother in the church, a brother dead, and William with no heir. It would all go to Aidan, the bastard son, if he were patient — and servile — long enough.

"When I am Lord Brixton, Tess . . ." There was a pause as he searched for the words. "I — I know you loved Jeffrey."

Surprising herself, she admitted it. "Yes." Eleanor's words came back to her: ". . . a man who makes you feel alive." That had been Jeffrey. She had felt alive in his presence, even when she thought she hated him.

"Perhaps if you look hard enough, you will find something in me to love." Aidan's tone was earnest, and he stepped closer. "And if I do become Lord Brixton, you would be Lady Brixton. That would have made Eleanor very happy, I think. Perhaps Jeffrey too." He was using all his persuasive powers now, but Tessa turned away.

"I see things in you that might inspire love, Aidan, but I don't love you as a woman should love her husband."

His face flushed in the fading light. "And you do find things to love in Lord Acton?"

"No, I don't." She understood the difference but wasn't sure she could explain it to Aidan. "But Cedric doesn't love me either. He wants me. That isn't the same as love. We each would have gained something from marriage with no harm done, a business arrangement of sorts."

She stopped, realizing how cold it all sounded when put into words. "If Cedric does not want a wife who has misrepresented herself, it will not be hurt he feels, only regret that he must find another suitable candidate. But you, Aidan, would seek love in return for your own. I would do you a great wrong."

"Perhaps today's Lady Acton sounds better than someday's Lady Brixton," he said, his voice changing to bitterness again.

There was no talking to these Brixton men, Tessa thought. "I'm sorry you don't understand, Aidan."

"Tessa!" His tone was sharp, but the next words softened it considerably. "Think about my offer. You don't think you can love me now, but you may come to do so in time. I am willing to take that chance, but time is what you do not have. You must make a decision, and I am the best choice, for as you admit, Cedric does not love you, only the image of a beautiful wife."

"But don't you see, Aidan? That is all that I can be now, the image of a wife, for there is no love in my heart for any man."

You will find happiness only among the dead.

The crone's words came from the very air around her. There was no one living who made her feel alive. The man she could have loved was drowned in the sea, and the man who stood before her, humbly pleading for her love, could not replace him. Better to leave this place forever than to stay where their frequent meetings would only be a source of discomfort to them both. "I'm sorry, Aidan," she said softly, and left him standing in the garden alone.

Chapter Thirteen

As Tessa stepped quietly into the manor, she saw Auntie Madeline standing before the fire, still as a statue, arms wrapped around herself as she stared into space. "Is anything wrong, Auntie?"

"I sent the girls to their chambers so that we could talk. He's sending you away, isn't he? William." The old lady looked forlorn. Having lost Eleanor and Jeffrey, she had become very fond of Tessa, who now, she seemed to know already, would be taken from her as well.

Suddenly ashamed of the lies that she'd allowed these people to believe, Tessa shuddered. "Yes. But he is right to do so. There is something I must tell you."

Auntie Madeline's lined face took on a knowing look. "You are not the sister of my Eleanor, or even a relative," she said matter-of-factly.

"How did you know?" Tessa breathed.

"Eleanor and I had no secrets from each other."

"Lord Brixton has found it out. Now I must leave this house and make a new life for myself." Tessa turned, speaking mostly to herself. "I just don't know how."

"Will Aidan help?"

"He offered marriage, but I could not accept."

"No. Aidan is not Jeffrey." The old lady's eyes showed understanding. "Aidan has always been in the shadows, you see. William has power over men, Ethelbert has a goodness about him, and Jeffrey had a strength that attracted people to him. There was nothing left for Aidan but to be William's tool, but I have never felt it fit him well. Eleanor . . . we . . . oh, but it doesn't matter now." Her gaze sought Tessa's. "What about Cedric?"

"When I tell him tomorrow, I expect he will release himself from our engagement. After that, I will get to Scotland somehow and find my uncle. He is king now, and perhaps despite my adventures he will take me back once I tell him the facts of the matter."

"How does a woman alone make such a voyage?"

"I could travel as a male. I'm short

enough, and I spent my youth acting like a boy. The disguise would eliminate most dangerous situations."

"But the trip is long. It will take days," Madeline protested.

"What else can I do?"

There was another pause as they both considered the prospect. "If you must take this chance, I have some money," the old lady finally declared. "My father and William were much alike, and once it was clear I would not marry, my mother wanted me to be able to live on my own if necessary. She sold some of her jewelry and gave me the proceeds as a sort of emergency fund. I have kept it all these years but never had need of it here on the manor. It is unlikely now that I will ever need it. With Eleanor gone, William will appreciate my presence. It saves him hiring a chatelaine." Her plain face showed some measure of pride that she could at last earn her keep in this way. "If Cedric rejects you tomorrow, you must take what money you need for your trip home."

There was no use in polite refusal. They both knew it was Tessa's only chance. Hugging Madeline's bony shoulders, the girl felt relieved and warmed by the offer of help. "If ever I can, I will repay you."

"Oh, be off with you! I want nothing for it. Come, let's find some breeches and a shirt. We must tear some rags, too, for wrappings that will hide your more feminine qualities. You must be ready in case things do not go well with Cedric." They went up the stairs together, both more cheerful than they had been moments earlier. The old lady chuckled, "I almost hope things do not go well with Lord Acton. He isn't worthy of a hair on your head, I say."

William was noticeably absent when Cedric arrived the next morning, having stayed in his bedroom with a tray brought to him. Tessa asked for a few moments alone in the hall, and, although curious, the girls stayed away.

Cedric was dressed for travel in an array of decorative, but on the whole useless, accessories done in his family's colors, argent and verte. His tunic was green trimmed with silver, and a matching cape hung nearly to the ground although the day was fine. Silver spurs and elbow-length leather gloves completed an ensemble intended to impress, but Tessa had other things on her mind.

"Cedric," she began when they were alone. "I must tell you something I should have told you before. Because of circumstances that I shall not explain, I misrepresented myself to you and to the Brixtons. I am not related to Eleanor. I am from Scotland, that is true, and I am of the clan macFindlaech. In fact Macbeth, now king, is my uncle."

Cedric's large jaw dropped with surprise, and she hurried on. "Eleanor and I thought it would be better if Sir William felt . . . obliged to sponsor me. Now that he knows the truth, he will contribute nothing to my wedding nor have any more to do with me." It came out in a rush, and she wondered if she was coherent.

Cedric's expression, at first confused, finally cleared, and a bob of his head indicated understanding. He looked surprised, interested, and, if she was reading him correctly, calculating. "You are related to the king of Scotland?"

"He is my uncle," she repeated.

Cedric was thoughtful, and for the first time, Tessa saw the light of intelligence in his eyes. However, that was not as heartening as it should have been, for she sensed a shrewdness that belied Cedric's apparent shallowness. "I have heard of Macbeth as a general."

"He is considered a great warrior among the Scots, where warriors are plentiful."

182

"Some claim he murdered the old king."

"I have heard that, but the man's own sons may have killed him, to reach the throne all the earlier."

Cedric went on, speaking almost to himself. "One of the sons, Malcolm, has come to England and convinced King Edward of Macbeth's guilt. He is raising an army to take Scotland." What had this to do with her? Cedric's next question was telling. "He has no children, this Macbeth?"

"Why, no, he has not."

"Is it possible he will have?"

"I doubt it, but what — ?"

"Nephews?"

Quite puzzled, Tessa answered, "None. My father was his only brother, and we are a family of six daughters."

Again there was a pause as Cedric stroked his chin and paced the hall a bit. Finally, he came briskly back and stood in front of Tessa. "I feel, my dear Tessie, that although your confession upset Lord Brixton, it need not concern us. I have more than enough money to pay for our wedding, and I would see it through. I have admired, may I say, desired you, since our first meeting, and nothing you have revealed today changes my intention to marry you."

"But —"

"Please, do not worry your lovely head over it further. I only ask that we be married without delay, which should please you well if you no longer feel welcome at Brixton. I will inform Lord Brixton as we journey, and instead of going on to London, return to Beverly to inform Mother of my changed plans. I may be able to convince William to allow you to remain here for the short time it will take to make our final preparations."

Cedric briskly clapped Tessa on the shoulder, his posture becoming, if possible, even more erect. "Now, my love, I must be off, so that I may return to you at the soonest possible moment." With that Cedric kissed her hand and left, calling to a servant to hurry his master along.

In a few moments William came down the stairs, also dressed for travel. Throwing Tessa a black look, he went out after Cedric, his poor page half-running to keep up. There was hubbub in the courtyard for a few moments and then silence. Tessa stood trying to make sense of what had happened. Was it so easy, after all her plans and worrying? She would still become Lady Acton, then, still have security and wealth, despite her lies? She replayed the scene with Cedric in her mind again. What had it meant?

Auntie Madeline entered the hall rather timidly.

"What happened, my dear? What did Cedric say?"

"He says we shall be married as planned."

"That is an answer to prayer," the old lady breathed. "I would have been quite mad with worry if you'd had to go back to Scotland alone. Cedric must love you very much."

But the word he'd used was *desire*, and that was much closer to Cedric's true nature. He was much like William, concerned only with himself and what he wanted from life. Tessa felt disquiet at the thought, but what choice had she now? If Eleanor could bear this sort of life, then so must she.

Going back to her room, she considered the purse of money and the borrowed boys' clothing that lay rolled into a blanket. On an impulse, she stowed them at the bottom of a trunk filled with trousseau items. She would explain to Auntie Madeline about keeping the money. The dear old lady would understand that it was necessary to be prepared for anything in the next few days.

A moment that evening did much to relieve some of the burden on Tessa's heart. Aidan, who had not gone with William but stayed one more day to finish some business, took Tessa aside after the evening meal.

He looked very handsome that evening in a suit of deep burgundy that, although plain, complimented his lean build and warm skin tones. Seating her beside the window, he stood facing her and made a speech that Tessa realized he must have practiced carefully.

"Tessa, I would like to congratulate you on your wedding to Cedric, and I wish you all the happiness in the world. It seems to me, however, that it would be best if I do not attend. I would not for the world bring discomfort to you on such an occasion, and therefore I ask you to understand if I return to London tomorrow morning."

She smiled warmly at him. "Of course, Aidan. I will miss you there, for I have come to count you as a close friend, but if you feel it is for the best, I am content."

Secretly she was relieved. Aidan's confession of love had made subsequent meetings awkward. It really was better if she did not have to go through the strain of this hasty marriage with Aidan's dark eyes watching her every move.

He came over and kissed her cheek softly. "You know I wish it were otherwise," he said, "but I accept what you have chosen to do and will be ready to answer when you call on me for help — always." With that he was gone.

Cedric returned with the proper documents the next day. "I'm sorry you won't have the large wedding we'd planned, Tessie, but I must tell you that Lord Brixton is quite adamant that you leave his home at once. The only way we can accomplish that with honor is for the two of us to be married today, which I have arranged with a priest in York. It will be quite informal, I'm afraid, not the large wedding we had planned, but you shall of course have the company of the ladies here. Can you be ready in an hour?"

Tessa hardly had time to think as she was shepherded away from Brixton, perhaps forever, and on to the minster at York. As they approached the church, she remembered young Rob, the boy on the boat that had brought her from Scotland, and the pride with which he had described it. Dedicated to St. Olaf, a Norwegian king, the church's architecture showed evidence of the Vikings who had settled along England's east coast. The pale stone shone in the sunlight as the small party entered the arched gateway of heavy stonework. They turned left into the church itself, a huge structure with thick walls topped with decorative spires and pierced with tall, gracefully arched windows.

Tessa had invited the women of Brixton to her wedding, and they stood in a small knot in the huge sanctuary: Tessa, Mary, Cecilia, Alice, and Auntie Madeline on one side, Cedric and two of his retainers on the other. Cedric had sent the news of the wedding to his mother, who had journeyed to Dame Ballard's house in Grimsby after Eleanor's funeral and could not return in time. Tessa hoped she was not too angry to have been robbed of the huge wedding she had envisioned.

After a brief ceremony Tessa was pronounced one with Cedric, Lord Acton. Auntie Madeline sniffled a bit, and the girls looked awed and confused. Were they to be happy or not? Tessa herself didn't know the answer to that. They now knew her true identity. She had told them herself, being unwilling to lie any longer to these people she considered friends. The girls watched solemnly as the ceremony concluded. Cedric kissed her gravely, Auntie Madeline congratulated her, and no one seemed to know what came next. Finally Alice said they'd best be going, and Tessa walked with them outside, telling Cedric she wished to say goodbye to them alone.

Outside she received hugs from all four, but the mood was not at all the happy one she'd hoped for all those months ago when she and Eleanor had imagined her wedding. Although everyone tried hard to seem cheerful, there was no true joy in this hasty pairing. Tessa was determined that they should not pity her, though, so she tried to appear content and promised to see them whenever possible. As soon as they had gone she returned to the church, feeling dread rather than anticipation for her wedding night.

As she entered the coolness of the apse, her slippers made no sound, and it was thus that she overheard the end of Cedric's conversation with his man. "So when the king dies, there will be his beloved niece, who has married an English peer and given him sons. Who better to sit on the throne of Scotland than someone who represents the interests of both English and Scotsmen? Of course Macbeth may want to settle a dowry on his beloved niece once he learns she's alive. A grant of land would show his appreciation." The two chuckled together at the joke.

Tessa stopped short, calling herself all kinds of a fool. She should have realized that Cedric had motives other than the desire he'd admitted to. He loved nothing, and he had all that wealth could buy him, but he still desired many things. Power was evidently one of them, and he'd seen in Tessa a chance at power — and the creation of a dynasty, it seemed. Although he was dull company for a woman, Cedric had a grasp of politics. Macbeth's niece was to become a pawn in his ambition to control her homeland. Penniless and disgraced, she was still kinswoman to the king, and her sons would have as much right to the throne as anyone. She wondered just what Cedric and William had discussed on the road to York. Had this hasty wedding been forced upon her so she would not have time to think and perhaps change her mind?

Suddenly the way ahead was clear to her. The mist that she had wandered in since Eleanor's death disappeared in a flash of determination. Leaving the church quickly, Tessa hurried to the carriage where Cedric's driver had fastened her box. The man offered to help, but she dismissed him. "I need to find something . . ." She let her voice indicate that it would be indelicate of him to see what it was she sought. The man backed away in embarrassment, turning his back as Tessa rummaged through the trunk until she found the things she wanted. When the man asked politely if there was anything he could do to help, there was no answer. She had disappeared around the side of the church.

By the time Cedric and his men missed her, Tessa was far away, running with a small bundle of clothing and the bag of money Madeline had given her. Finally realizing that people stared, she slowed her pace and tried to control her gasping breath. A finely dressed woman tearing through the streets was sure to be remembered. She tried for a more leisurely pace, although she could not help looking behind her. Unsure of what to do, she found herself outside a small shop. Before it sat an old, old woman, so tiny that her clothes hung loosely and her head seemed too large for her body. The woman gazed blankly into space, paying no attention until Tessa spoke. "Can you tell me how far I am from the river, mistress?"

The face swung around toward her. The woman was blind, her eyes coated with a milky film. "Not far," the woman told her. "This is Whip-ma-whop-ma-gate, and just a bit that way" — a bony hand pointed the opposite direction Tessa had been heading — "are the docks."

Tessa couldn't resist, despite the hurry.

"What did you say the street was?"

"Whip-ma-whop-ma-gate," the old woman repeated. "It means 'neither one thing nor the other,' a long name for a short street." She chuckled at the joke, showing toothless gums. "You are young, are you not?"

"I am," Tessa answered, then had an idea. "My name is Tom Thomson, and my father sent me to find my uncle on the docks and bring him to our house." If the old woman were questioned, she would report that no female had passed her resting place in the sun.

"Well, then, Tom, be off like a good lad and do what you were told. Boys these days do not mind their elders as they should." Without further ado, Tessa thanked the woman and headed off in the direction indicated. That night she lay hidden in the rafters of a barn, constantly on guard, but no one came near. In fact, Cedric's men didn't find the fine wedding dress until two days later, lying under some straw where a cow had stepped on it and ruined it beyond repair.

CHAPTER FOURTEEN

The captain of the *Bonnie Blue* chuckled to himself at the greenness of the boy who booked passage on his little ship. Dressed in oversized clothes that must have belonged to an older brother, nervously touching the auburn hair that had been hacked off with no skill whatsoever, the lad was quite undecided about how to approach him. Finally he stammered out that he needed to get to Inverness, and would the ship be stopping there? Of course it would, but the captain made as if he thought hard about it, wondering how much money the boy had and how much he could get of it.

"How much have you got, lad?"

The boy opened a small purse at his belt and spilled out a few coins. The captain, seeing the thinness of the purse, named a reasonable figure, and the boy carefully counted it into his outstretched hand. The hands were dirty but very delicate, with long, slim fingers. There wasn't much left in the purse after the fare was paid, but the captain did not know that the "boy" had been clever enough to keep only a few coins in the purse. The rest were secured in the lining of the clothing.

On the voyage the boy kept to himself, although he seemed friendly enough when spoken to. He watched the sea for hours on end, apparently thinking deep thoughts. When one of the sailors commented that he ate and drank very little, another responded, "Never takes a piss, either. Wonder where the little runt keeps it all." Because they were not men accustomed to thinking about anything very deeply, that was as far as it went. In fact, Tessa suffered agonies in disguising her femininity and was happy for a multitude of reasons when the little ship landed at the very pier she and Jeffrey had sailed from the year before.

Gathering up the few things she had brought from Brixton Hall, she wrapped them in her cloak: a few extra clothes Auntie Madeline had scavenged, the knife and toiletries Eleanor had given her, and the wooden box, which she'd brought for no real reason. Her promise to Eleanor had been that she would give it to Jeffrey, but both Eleanor and Jeffrey were dead. She'd considered burying it at Brixton, but she had no intention of ever returning there. She might have given it to Auntie Madeline but feared it might betray the love between Eleanor and Jeffrey, which would have diminished the old lady's memories of both of them. Although Madeline claimed Eleanor had told her everything, Tessa doubted that Auntie would have approved of the affair. She considered reading through the papers in the box herself and then burning them, but somehow could not make herself do it. She'd carried it along, delaying any decision about what should come of her promise and Eleanor's last wish.

Not knowing how best to proceed and wondering how things stood with the household, Tessa went to the castle kitchen and asked if there was work. The cook declared she could use a boy if he knew how to work, not like most of the boys nowadays. Tessa, or Tom, as she named herself, vowed to work hard and was set to various kitchen tasks. Her childhood ways stood her in good stead, because her first job was killing and plucking chickens for the evening meal. After that she watched others and copied them, managing to satisfy the demands of the first day. When the evening meal was eaten and cleared, she was allowed a corner to sleep in. Exhausted from the work and the stress of watching every word and deed to keep up her disguise, little "Tom" found it no trouble at all to fall asleep on the rush-covered stones in the great hall.

Macbeth was not at Inverness. The kingship made demands on him that kept him at Scone or elsewhere. The atmosphere in his home was tense, and hardly anyone spoke except from necessity. Several of the women she'd known before were still in attendance upon Queen Gruoch, but the lady herself never showed at dinner that first night or the next. Tessa kept to her disguise, unsure how to proceed. Something told her not to approach her aunt, but to wait for her uncle's return.

The second night she was asleep, again exhausted from the day's work, when she was awakened by the sound of someone speaking. Being the newest member of the household, Tessa's sleeping spot was on the floor farthest from the fire and closest to the entryway, which required vigilance or she might be stepped upon as people got up in the night to go to the privy. Opening her eyes, Tessa saw the glow of a candle on the stairs. Squinting in the darkness, she discerned her aunt, dressed in nightgown and cap, descending the stairs and mumbling.

She couldn't make out the meaning of the words but thought she heard the word "blood," then some singsong phrases. The look on the lady's face in the candlelight was totally blank. She was asleep, unaware of her surroundings or her behavior.

As Tessa watched, an attendant came and gently turned her so that Gruoch went back up the stairs, still muttering. The woman stood aside to let her pass, then followed her out of sight. Around Tessa several heads had raised at the sounds, silhouetted in the firelight, but no one said a word, and one by one the heads sank back into the general shape of the room. It did not do to take notice of such things.

The next morning she sought out Jamie, a boy who'd been friendly about showing where things were and how the cook wanted tasks done. "Is the queen ill?" she asked.

He looked around to see if anyone was listening. "Best no' speak o' it, Tom," he said. "Her is sick, well enough, but 'tis sickness o' the mind, nae the body. They say 'tis guilt for things done sae her husband should come t' rule Scotland."

"You mean . . ." He shook his head to indicate it must not be said aloud. "And the king? How does he?"

"He ha' nae been himsel' neither, talkin'

to shadows and rantin' aboot things we canna see. We pretend along wi' him or he becooms mae violent." Jamie passed a dirty hand through his unruly hair, which returned immediately to its upright position.

"This is not a pleasant place to be," Tessa remarked.

"True enough. Many has left a'ready. Tha's why ye got a job sae quick, though, so ye shud be grateful." With that Jamie returned to his own tasks.

After two more days, Tessa feared approaching either Gruoch or Macbeth. The king had returned to Inverness in a foul mood, speaking as little as possible, though he looked every inch a king with his dark, brooding looks and his tall form clothed in robes much finer than those he had worn as soldier and thane. Something had changed him. He seemed unable to feel anything for his wife, ignoring her almost completely.

By day Gruoch walked the castle in a sort of daze. When she saw her husband, she made pitiful attempts to reach him, caressing his face and holding his arm, but Macbeth seemed unable to abide her touch. He had no patience for anyone but spent his time alone with his own thoughts, glaring at walls or mountains alike. Tessa felt sorry for him, for he had changed greatly in a year.

Although Cook would scold "Tom" for it, Tessa went for a walk along the hillside one afternoon, feeling the need to escape the atmosphere of dread prevalent at the castle. From the distance she looked back. It was hard to believe how the place had deteriorated in a year. Although still a handsome edifice from the outside, things were different inside. Without her aunt's strict hand and with as many servants leaving the place as could arrange it, the hall had become dirty and the remaining help slovenly. The rushes hadn't been changed since she left, so the place smelled of dogs, mice, and decaying food. Only the cookhouse remained fully functional, and that was due to Cook, who kept her own standards there but dared not intrude on the main house.

As she walked, Tessa was glad for fresh air. Spring was extending even to Scotland by this time, and buds and flowers greeted her on every side. In the year she'd been gone, Tessa too had become a different person. She had experienced so much: love, gaiety, grief, and despair. What was left to her? she wondered. Would she return to the Cairngorms, those beautiful peaks before her? Would she find a place with her uncle here? Only time would tell. Sitting down in the open meadow and resting in the sunshine, Tessa soon felt sleepy, having had little enough rest the night before in her cold, busy corner.

She didn't know how long she dozed, but a sense that someone was there awoke her. Opening her eyes, Tessa saw the three crones standing before her as they had so long ago, smiling and nodding as if she'd said something clever. They said nothing until she spoke to them.

"Well, it seems you were right," she said to the first. "I did go to England. How did you know?"

"Question not," croaked the woman, her breath causing Tessa to recoil in disgust.

"Her happiness is dead," grinned the second.

"Dead but not forgotten," added the third. "He has forgotten her name."

She spoke in the present tense. Someone had forgotten her, but who? These odd creatures would say what they had to say, whether she spoke or not, so she merely looked directly at them to indicate interest.

"He has forgotten much," said the first woman.

"And he will remember much." The third woman touched Tessa's arm.

"Look for him where the lands meet." This one's eyes didn't both look in the same direction, which was disconcerting, so Tessa didn't comprehend her meaning right away.

"Look for him?" As she realized the import of what she heard, her heart leapt. "For whom should I look?" The three only grinned stupidly and joined hands, backing away at the same time. As they retreated, the first one spoke again. "He took you away, and he brings you back."

"Please, tell me what you mean. Is Jeffrey alive?" Taking a step toward them, she tripped over a large stone and went down on one knee, catching herself with her hands before she fell all the way to the ground. When she looked up, the three women were gone, but her mind spun with the message they'd left behind. Jeffrey Brixton was alive!

Returning to the castle, Tessa decided she had to speak to her uncle. After the evening meal, she waited in the passageway until his step sounded on the stairs, heavy and slow, like that of an old man. She heard him dismiss the attendant who would have followed him into his chamber to assist with preparations for bed. Giving the man a moment to be gone, she peeped around the corner to find Macbeth alone in the hallway that led to his room. He started when he saw her, and she made haste to assure him that the boy she appeared to be was no threat.

"Sire, a moment of your time. Is there somewhere we can talk about your family and one you once knew?"

He was distrustful at first, making her walk ahead of him into a small closet where linens were kept. She had brought a candle, and she lit a torch that hung on the wall, then turned to face him in the light. "Look at me, closely, sire. It is I, Tessa macFindlaech."

Macbeth squinted at her, then his eyes widened. "Niece! We thought you dead, drowned in the river."

"I was captured by my Uncle Cawdor, who sent me to England so I would not tell you that I'd heard him treating with the Norwegians."

"England! You've been there?"

"Yes. Malcolm Canmore is there, trying to raise an army against you."

"I have heard the same. Has he had success?"

"I fear that he has. The English are always ready to come to Scotland to war, it seems."

"How did you escape those devils?"

"A kind lady took me in and treated me as her daughter. She is dead, but another lady gave me the money to come home. I traveled as a boy for my own protection, then found work here to wait for your return."

He nodded. It seemed as they talked that he became more like his old self, less tense and wild-eyed. His eyes focused not unkindly as she gave him the details of her capture on the night of Jeffrey's visit. Finally he spoke. "It seems you have managed well despite your troubles. Now what do you want of me?"

Tessa sighed. It was important that he understand her reasoning, but she couldn't judge his mood. Macbeth seemed under control at the moment, but she'd heard of wild rages and rash actions when he felt that someone was against him.

"Sire, I seek a certain Englishman, the one who came here that night with Cawdor. I know he is not your friend, but I made a vow that I would find him." The heavy eyebrows lifted, then lowered threateningly. "I'm sorry, Uncle. The man's family was kind to me, and I owe them word of him if I can find it."

There was a long silence. Macbeth seemed to lose interest, and his gaze went to the floor. Tessa felt she would burst with apprehension. She admitted that she had been befriended and in turn had befriended the hated English. The Macbeth who was now a king had reportedly killed people for less than what she had confessed. Desperately she tried to find the words to convince him. "His family thinks him drowned, but I met three weird women in the meadow today who say he is alive. I *must* try to find him."

Macbeth's head came up suddenly and his eyes locked on hers. "You saw the weird sisters?"

"Twice now. Before I arrived here, they told me I would go to England. I thought them mad."

His eyes glazed and he looked past her. "They called me thane of Cawdor and king. I thought them mad, too, but their words haunted me."

Tessa seized on their similar experience. "Today they told me Jeffrey is in the mountains. I must look for him. Uncle, can you give me a letter of protection? It is all I ask, just your name so that I may travel unmolested."

Macbeth's eyes focused again, and he nodded his understanding. "I can help you in no other way. I must ready for battle with Malcolm and the English, and I will need every loyal man. I will give you my order of safe conduct and a bit of gold, perhaps more valuable among the outlaw clans who call no man their king. If they have your Englishman, they are holding him for ransom and should already have sent word to his family."

Tessa's mind conjured up a sudden picture of a rough, bearded Scotsman leaving Brixton Hall in disgust, the man William had called a rascal. Had he brought news that Jeffrey was alive and would be returned for a price? It was common enough practice among some clans, holding prisoners of war or even unlucky passers-by for ransom. How would the Scots know that William didn't want his brother back, at least not enough to part with any money?

"Sire, where should I begin to look?"

"I don't know, lass, but you know the hills better than most. Why don't you start at home?" When he saw her look of dismay, he added gently, "Your mother is dead. She sent your sister Nettie to serve my wife —" Here he stopped and his eyes saddened for a moment. "But she went home when the news came, some three months back."

"Mother is dead?" Tessa waited for grief but felt only regret. Having known Eleanor, who longed for children to love and treated everyone kindly, Tessa could feel little sorrow for one so un-motherly, could only feel sad that life had been so unhappy for Kenna macFindlaech.

Macbeth went on, "Your oldest sister . . ."

"Meg," Tessa supplied.

"Yes, Meg — has married and inhabits the house my brother built, keeping your younger sisters with her." He tactfully didn't mention that Tessa might be welcome at home now, but he must have understood it.

"Thank you, sire. I will go there first, then. Tomorrow at first light."

"Take a pony if it will help. But I have a request in return. On the way, will you show me where you met the weird sisters? I would speak with them about my own future." His face held a curious vulnerability, and she saw again a tortured man. His eyes narrowed and he leaned forward eagerly, reaching out a hand in unconscious appeal.

"Of course, Uncle." Tessa led the way out of the small room. She wanted to warn him, to plead caution, although she sensed he was past caring. "You know, I am sure, that they speak in riddles, and only tell as much as they will and no more. But I can show you where I met them last." With that, Tessa bade him goodnight and started back to the hall and her place near the stairs. She glanced back once at her uncle, who sat staring into the dark corner of the corridor,

his lips working as if speaking to an unseen
visitor.

Chapter Fifteen

The next morning Tessa and the king were up and away early, passing through grass so wet that their clothes were soaked within minutes.

Macbeth didn't seem to notice, but watched her eagerly for identification of the place he sought. "I must know if I will defeat the English," he said, absently pulling his tartan closer around him, but it seemed he spoke not to Tessa, but to someone unseen. "If I am to be defeated, there is nothing left for me. The people despise me, my wife is beyond earthly help, and I have done things I am sorry for. All that is left to me is to be king of Scotland."

"I'm sure you intended to be a good king, Uncle," was all Tessa could think of to say. Stories of his misdeeds hinted at how far he had missed the mark.

His attention returned to Tessa when she spoke, and he seemed surprised at her remark. "I did," he mused, but his face hardened. "But the wanting to be king was stronger than the wanting to be good. I have made enemies."

"Perhaps you could regain the respect of your people. You could —"

"First I must defeat the English," he interrupted, and she saw that his attention was again fixed beyond her. "They say old Siward comes with Malcolm. He is a fine general, and I have lost many soldiers of late. They join Malcolm's army. Even Macduff, who once was my friend, has gone to England." His voice took on a strange quality. "I was most wounded by his treachery."

They had come to the spot Tessa sought. "Here it is, Uncle. I sat near that rock, and the three appeared before me. They seem to be clever at hiding and disappearing, like magic."

He looked at her strangely. "Yes, like magic." His manner turned brisk. "Go on. I will bide here a while and hope that the weird sisters take note."

He seemed unsure of how to take leave of her, probably thinking an embrace was proper between relatives. Tessa took a few steps backward and waved a hand, feeling sorry for him. He was frightening; was that what kingship did to people? She called a goodbye and hurried up the hillside, pulling behind her the pony Macbeth had ordered loaded with provisions for her trip. He was an odd mixture of kindness and ambition, and perhaps that was the problem. As his wife had commented with eerie premonition, he was too full of human kindness to live with the things he'd done to achieve that ambition.

It was two days later when Tessa began to feel that she was home. The woods looked familiar. There was where she had built a tree house to hide from her mother's anger, and there was a brook that she'd waded in, seeking such simple childhood delights as frogs and interesting stones.

Another hour brought her to the house that now belonged to her sister. Just as Tessa stepped from the wood line into the clearing surrounding it, Meg came out of the doorway, a basket under her arm. Although she must have suffered sorrows over the last year, losing her mother and her closest sister, Tessa's sister appeared at this time to be content.

Meg was not as striking as Tessa, her hair less bright, her eyes less expressive, but she had quiet beauty and a serenity about her that was more pronounced as a wife. Perhaps it was the gentle swell of a child in her belly that lent her the added look of contentment. Now she looked at the stranger in a friendly but curious way. It was not often they had unknown guests. Tessa pulled back her hood and let her cropped hair spill out, laughing with delight at seeing her beloved sister.

"It's me, Meg, back from the dead!"

Meg's reaction was first total surprise and then great joy. Running to Tessa, she hugged her for a long time, as tears streamed down both their faces.

"They told us you had drowned in the river by mishap."

"They were mistaken. I am well, though I have been a great way. Let us go in and I will tell you all of it."

That night Tessa met her brother-in-law Donwald. He was a typical Scot, brawny with reddish blond hair. Tessa imagined from his broad shoulders and large arms that on festival days he tossed the caber, a huge wooden pole held upright and thrown end over end. He was probably good at it. Donwald welcomed his sister-in-law to the house, although Tessa knew Meg had given him a slightly edited version of her adventures. They had found proper women's clothing for her to wear and Meg had pulled

Tessa's butchered hair back into a small knot, managing to make her look feminine once more. She certainly didn't mention to her husband Tessa's quest for an Englishman. It had shocked Meg enough when she heard of it.

"And what would you be doin' with this Englishman if you find him?" she had asked, making Tessa laugh.

"Oh, I have no plans to bring him home to meet the clan," she said with a twinkle in her eye, but her face sobered. "I owe a debt, Meg. This woman befriended me when I was left in England without anyone to care for me. She gave me fine clothes, a roof over my head, and friendship. Her dying wish was that I give this man a small box, which I have with me. I thought him dead and did not know what to do with it, but now I believe he may be a prisoner of one of the outlaw clans. His brother won't ransom him, being a jealous and miserly sort, and I feel a debt to Eleanor to find him if I can and take word to someone who will help, perhaps his commanders or his friends in the English army."

"You would do this for a man who captured you and took you away from home and family?" Meg asked skeptically.

"I do it for Eleanor," Tessa responded, but

then added, "although to be fair to the man, he could have snapped my neck and thrown me into the Firth. It would have been far easier than carrying me to his home. And he did ask Eleanor to treat me as a guest."

"Pooh!" was the response. "An Englishman who doesn't rape and kill young Scotswomen may be unusual, but kidnapping and plotting are no great credit to him, I say."

That seemed to end the conversation. Tessa was not going to convince Meg that such a man was worth time and effort.

The happiest moment of the evening was when Tessa was reunited with Banaugh, who looked not a day older than when he's escorted her to Inverness a year before. He was most joyful to see "his lass" again. Meg said privately that he'd grieved for months when he heard of her disappearance.

The next day Tessa spent getting re-acquainted with her younger sisters. Surprisingly, they were no longer the whiny brats she remembered. Her mother's disposition had made them all feel miserable. Under Meg's kind care, the girls had blossomed. They smiled more often and though they had little, they seemed content with their lives.

Nettie, the one who'd been at Inverness, confided to Tessa her relief to be away from the king's home. "Uncle was seldom there, and when he was it was all we could do to keep him calm. And his wife . . ." She paused, there being no loyal way to put into words what she had observed.

Tessa nodded. "I saw her walking about the castle at night like a ghost."

"Aye, but waking she does not remember it. We took turns watching to see she didn't harm herself, and what she said, Tess! Things about blood and stained hands."

"Best forgotten, I think," Tessa cautioned. "She is the queen, at least for now, and it's best not to know what such people face in their dreams."

The girls were learning to sew and cook and keep a house. "Donwald comes from a large family," Meg whispered to Tessa. "He has cousins enough for all the girls to get a husband."

Tessa sighed. England or Scotland, it seemed getting a husband was all a woman was supposed to think of. Would she ever be happy as a wife? Eleanor had said only two kinds of husbands allowed women the freedom they needed, those who truly loved their wives and those who tired of their company. Would she have been happy with Cedric? She doubted it. Perhaps the old crones were right and her happiness was with the dead, although precisely what that meant she didn't understand. Had Eleanor's plotting to get her a husband been her chance for happiness? Or had Jeffrey something to do with it? She shook herself at the thought. There certainly would be no happiness for a woman with a man such as he. Ruthless, arrogant, and unfaithful as well, since he'd kissed her while Eleanor's back was turned. Still, she'd made a promise to Eleanor, and something inside her wanted to know if Jeffrey Brixton still lived, although she didn't like to consider why his life was so important to her.

At dinner Tessa questioned Donwald about captives in the area, saying Macbeth wanted news of possible spies.

"Nae, I know of none in the Cairngorms," was his answer. "It sounds more like somethin' ye'd find Lowlanders at. We ha' no truck with the English at all, i' we can manage it. If the king wants tae locate sae as that, he should send someone south through Perth an' then follow th' coastline. If an Englishman was brought to Scotland, it's most likely he's in Fife or Lothian."

Although Meg pleaded with her to stay a few more days, Tessa was determined to be off the next morning, promising to return when she could. As she took her leave, Meg

215

kissed her sister with tears in her eyes. "To have you back and then lose you again is hard, but I can see you are decided. I shall say a prayer to Saint Julian for you every day." Julian was the patron of travelers, and it seemed Tessa might be traveling for some time in this undirected search. Hugging her sisters, she promised to return someday.

As Tessa readied the pony, Banaugh appeared with a bundle rolled up in his tartan. "I canna let you travel a' alone int' the Lowlands," he announced, his accent as thick as hers had once been. "T'was bad enough when yer mother bade me tak' ye north to yer uncle, but at least tha' was still the Highlands. Now ye go south, where they ha' no idea how civilized folk behave. Ye'll need someone to watch yer back, lass."

What could she do? No one had the nerve to tell Banaugh he was too old to go, and truthfully, tears of relief filled her eyes at his offer of help. Up to now Tessa had felt very much alone in her search. Still, she told Banaugh the whole story before leaving, not wanting the gentle old man traveling under any misconceptions.

"So ye'll track all over Scotland to find a man for some other woman, then?" he asked ironically.

"I promised her I'd give him the box,"

Tessa repeated.

"Seems t' me there's more to 't than a promise made to a dead woman," he said with surprising acumen.

"I don't know, Banaugh. I just need to find him. Perhaps I'll know then why I feel I must."

The grizzled face wreathed in a smile. "Och, you're a slow one, then. I know 't already, and I've never laid eyes on the lad."

Two months sped away as the Tessa and Banaugh wandered the Lowlands seeking information about captured Englishmen. They made a competent team, both experienced at finding food in the wild, and Tessa took up the trapping and fishing skills she had developed as a young girl. Her boy's disguise made traveling easier, and no one questioned a man and a boy looking to ransom an English soldier.

Some of the less honest border lords made money by holding unfortunate men until their families paid for their return. Although the process was usually discreet, being of course illegal, the locals knew and even approved, since ransom meant gold to benefit everyone involved. Scotland was a poor country, especially in the hard currency that brought in goods from elsewhere. Any wealth gained tended to trickle down to all levels eventually, so people who knew about such things kept quiet. The travelers heard of one prisoner who turned out to be English but not Jeffrey, and his family had ransomed him by the time they found the castle anyway. At every town they asked about English guests or travelers, sometimes hearing a promising item only to have it lead to nothing.

It was September before they had their first real news. In an inn south of Edinburgh about thirty miles, they took a room to escape a rattling thunderstorm. It was a tumbledown affair in the Pentland Hills, not overly clean but dry at least. Sitting by the fire as their clothes steamed, Banaugh suggested a game of Nine Man's Morris, to which the landlord agreed. As Banaugh set board and pegs up, arranging the fox and the thirteen geese it would pursue, he began a running conversation, as he usually did with those they met.

It was instructive to watch the old man casually bring the talk around to the subject he wanted as they moved the pegs around the board. After discussing the stubborn stupidity of sheep, the best medicines to treat common ailments, and of course the weather, he mentioned the English.

"They say they are on their way to Inverness and will try Macbeth's army before winter."

"Aye, no' that it matters much to us down here. If they are in the north, they'll nae be watching us so close," grunted the landlord, taking his turn.

"True, true," Banaugh agreed. "Of course, there's always a bit o' money to be made on a war. The king himself has provided gold for news of the English. He wanted to know of prisoners held for ransom, for fear they'll be released and tell th' English what they know."

"And what could they know, poor clods? They haven't a brain to think with!" The landlord laughed loud and long at his own joke, and Banaugh joined in rather lamely.

"Well, some, you know, might be smarter than they appear, and then where would we Scots be?"

The man snorted. "We Scots? Since when does a Highlander care what happens down here? The bordermen serve as a buffer, so ye haven't had to face th' English, at least until now. Malcolm's invited them in, for good or evil, but they'll strike north, at Macbeth's strongholds, and perhaps leave us alone for once."

Banaugh knew when to keep his peace, so he merely nodded. There was a pause in which only the crackling of the fire was heard. The man moved his game-piece, then spoke again. "Ye say the king pays gold for Englishmen? What aboot those that might only point the way?"

Banaugh appeared to consider. "I could offer this." From a worn purse he removed one gold coin.

The landlord considered for a moment. "And when ye find the Englishman?"

"We are to warn the laird who holds him that he is nae to be released until th' English are defeated. Of course," here he spoke in a conspiratorial tone, "after the fightin' he may still be ransomed, no matter who the winner may be."

This decided the man. Evidently he had not wanted to make trouble for his neighbor. "South of here a day or so, outside Jedburgh, lives Ian Hawick. He may have a guest who is English, although I'm sure he's not held against his will." The man smiled to signal the lie. He would not accuse Hawick of kidnapping. "Still, Macbeth may have interest in keeping Hawick's guest where he is till the troubles with the English dogs are over."

"Indeed," Banaugh answered. Tessa sat silent beside him, but her excitement fueled at this news, and Banaugh understood. "I will pay you now for our lodging, for we will leave early, I'm thinking." He handed over the gold piece, five times the inn's fee.

In the room they shared, Banaugh was enthusiastic. "This is yer Englishman, Tess. I feel it in ma bones."

"I don't think I shall sleep a wink!"

"Ye must, lass. It'll be a long trip for one day, and I know ye won't want to make it two," Banaugh teased. So saying, he rolled out his tartan on the floor and turned his back to allow Tessa a measure of privacy and the plank bed. In three minutes he was asleep, while Tessa lay for some time pondering the possibility that she would, in less than a day, see Jeffrey Brixton once more.

Chapter Sixteen

Jedburgh was a lovely little town on the bank of the River Teviot. An old Celtic church loomed over the whole town, ruined but still impressive. The road leading out of Jedburgh and on to Hawick, however, was little more than a cow path that followed the riverbank. Not many people of the town went there, it seemed.

When Tessa and Banaugh reached the place a few hours later, they approached a castle of the old motte-and-bailey type. A large stone structure, a motte, had been built on a small knoll for easy defense, then surrounded by an area fenced with upright wood pilings called the bailey. They passed one set of guards at the outer gate then walked onward, passing several small cottages where people plied their trades. Leatherworkers, smiths, bakers, millers, and weavers sat in the mid-September afternoon, finishing the day's work as their wives and children moved around them, tending to the attendant tasks of the trade. A couple of young churls polished armor by dropping each rusty piece into a barrel of sand and then rolling it vigorously between them until the sand scraped the rust away. It was a busy group, but Tessa sensed a difference in their demeanor from other demesnes they had visited. No one sang, few even talked, and there was about them a watchful quiet that spoke little of happiness and much of fear.

More armed men stood guard at the castle doorway, and Tessa had to show her safe conduct from the king for a second time in order to get inside. Even then the men seemed loath to let them pass.

At the main hall, they had to show the paper yet again, this time to a blank-eyed, reed-thin seneschal who was only a shade more courteous when he saw Macbeth's seal. Hawick was out hunting, the man told them, and would not be back until dinner. Somewhat grudgingly he assigned them a place at the evening meal and showed them a corner where they could leave their bundles. Tessa took the opportunity before dinner to wander through the hall, hoping for a glimpse of Jeffrey, but she had no luck.

The meal was impressive, though not in

its pomp and splendor. As soon as the bell rang, ten or twelve burly men appeared from several directions and took their places at the head of the table. One of them seemed familiar to Tessa. His bushy beard and broad shoulders reminded her of something, but she could not decide what it was. In contrast to the people Tessa had seen working, these men were noisy and full of hilarity at each other's antics. They tripped an old woman as she carried in bread for the table, then passed a young serving girl among themselves, each man kissing her in his turn. She stumbled off, looking close to tears, but no one seemed able — or willing — to control the actions of these rowdy jacks.

Behind them came various lesser types, men and women of the household, Tessa guessed, who seated themselves at the two sideboards. Banaugh and Tessa were led to their places near the head but just barely above the salt, in recognition of their status as king's messengers. For the first time in months, Tessa felt fearful. Something about the place made her uneasy. She noticed that Banaugh kept glancing about also, ever watchful and on guard.

At the last, three people entered the hall to signal the start of the meal. The first was a huge man with a barrel of a chest that seemed to precede him rather than form part of his frame. The chest continued into a large belly that hung over the rope belt that cinched his black velvet tunic. The rest of his body looked small by comparison, especially the legs, which were encased in black stockings and seemed far too slim for such a torso. His undertunic was bleached linen, and over the whole he wore a tartan cloak pinned at the shoulder with a large gold brooch. The man had light brown hair and eyebrows, a wide, flat face, heavily jowled although he was not yet thirty-five, and small eyes. The lower lip jutted out from the upper, its shiny inner surface showing red against his skin and giving him an arrogant expression. With mouth turned down and eyes glaring, he strode in, then seemed to make an effort to appear genial as an afterthought. Speaking with several people as he made his way to the head table, he clapped the men on the back and teased the women. This was their host, Ian Hawick.

Behind him came a woman of striking beauty with dark hair set off by a skin so white as to be worthy of the overused comparison to alabaster. Almond eyes tilted slightly at the corners, and her lips were so red that Tessa knew they weren't naturally possible. She was taller than Tessa, but not by much, and exquisitely formed. The clothes she wore were carefully chosen to enhance her looks. The gown was crimson with creamy accents, and she wore a matching cap with pearls sewn onto it so that they dangled bewitchingly around her face.

In the doorway the woman turned back and smiled encouragingly at someone, and Tessa's eyes followed her gaze. She had to stop herself from crying out.

It was Jeffrey!

He was certainly alive and seemed in good health as well, dressed in a brown tunic of wool, green stockings, and a linen undershirt. None of these garments fitted him well, but their condition was good. If Jeffrey was a prisoner, he had not been mistreated. He even took his meals with Ian Hawick and his companions. Jeffrey seated himself at the head table, next to the woman in red. The look in his eyes as he spoke softly to the beautiful woman confused Tessa, for the look said more than any words could that he was captivated by this glorious creature. At Tessa's side, Banaugh studied the girl's expression, confirming his opinion of her unconscious purpose at this place. His wizened face settled into disapproval of the man who caused the pain he saw in his Tessa's expression.

Later, on the rough plank floor, Tessa tried yet again to find a comfortable way to lie, but it wasn't really the hardness of the boards that kept her awake. Beside her Banaugh slept peacefully, and on the other side a young servant snored, his mouth open slackly. The events of the evening replayed in her mind. She and Banaugh had been introduced and formally invited by Hawick to stay the night, as was proper due to their letter from the king. They said nothing of their mission, making an appointment to speak with Hawick the next morning in private. Once that was settled, they had been ignored for the rest of the evening, for Hawick had as guest a traveling bard, and all were anxious to hear his performance.

He began, of course, with a listing of all the clans and their chiefs who were part of his story. It was important to be mentioned, and everyone waited eagerly to hear the names of his own forbears, nodding happily when they occurred. Then the rather rambling account began, much less of a narrative than rhythmic boasting, overall quite confusing. Still, the audience knew the events already and were mainly concerned with cheering their heroes. Tonight's rendition was a tale of battle, magic, and emotion mixed together and told in an extended, singsong style, and the bard pleased his listeners greatly.

Tessa heard very little, for she watched Jeffrey Brixton. He sat next to the beautiful creature, who, they were told, was Hawick's stepsister, Mairie. The man on Banaugh's left explained that this sister had been born and raised in France, coming to Scotland rather unwillingly when her mother had married Hawick's father. Mairie considered herself above the Scots, and the man admitted grudgingly that she was unusual in these parts. She spoke several languages, danced and sang prettily, and even wrote poetry. "Not my style of woman," the man grunted. "Still, I wouldn't mind bedding her onct or twict, hey?" and he'd elbowed Banaugh knowingly.

There was no doubt that Jeffrey was enthralled by her. His eyes never left Mairie, and he helped her with each course of food that was brought in, first cutting off choice portions of venison for her and then slicing an apple to hand to her piece by piece. Mairie accepted this as her due and smiled into Jeffrey's eyes a look of promise.

Tessa was sickened by the whole picture. His family thought him dead, she had thought him a poor captive among ruffians, and here he sat at a full table, dallying with a pampered, Frenchified doll! Anger flaring, she'd excused herself and walked along the Teviot until the evening was concluded.

Now as she lay sleepless in the early morning hours, Tessa tried to decide what to do. The landlord at the inn had been correct. Jeffrey was no prisoner, except perhaps to love. She had come all this way for nothing. Despairing of sleep, Tessa contented herself with letting her body rest while her mind conjured ways to murder Jeffrey Brixton without endangering herself or Banaugh.

Early the next morning Tessa spoke to her old friend about their meeting with Hawick. "It will do no good to offer to ransom Jeffrey," she told him. "It seems he's free to come and go as he pleases."

"Perhaps he has given his parole," Banaugh suggested. "In these situations, if a man gies his word tha' he willna escape, he is oft treated as a guest. No nobleman wuld break his vow t' another, even an Englishman."

"I'm guessing it's the woman Mairie who keeps Jeffrey here." Still, Banaugh's words made her consider other possibilities for Jeffrey's meek acceptance of his captivity, and she sighed. "You are right. We should be certain before we leave that he is not a prisoner."

"You mus' speak wi' him before I mee' wi' the laird o' th' manor. Then we shall know how best t' proceed."

It was only fair to give Jeffrey a chance to explain himself after coming all this way to find him. Determined to give him one last chance, Tessa waited near the stairs as he came down from his chamber. He certainly didn't look deprived, she thought grimly. Today he wore a simple tunic of plaid with blue and green dominant. The trousers were the same blue as the tartans and were tucked into boots of soft deerskin. Approaching Jeffrey with head down, Tessa spoke in the boy's voice she had adopted as part of her disguise. The appearance of one of Hawick's men on the stairs above Jeffrey caused her to be brief.

"Sir, may I speak to you alone? I have news that you will want to hear, from a certain lady in England."

Jeffrey's face showed puzzlement. As the man on the stairs above began his descent, the familiar look of amusement took its place on his features. "You have nothing to say that could interest me, boy." He clapped her on the shoulder and started past, then playfully tickled her ribs. Outraged, Tessa almost fought back, but as he ducked toward her, apparently tussling, he whispered, "Outside the stable's east wall in ten minutes." Before she could reply Jeffrey released her and sauntered on.

It was more like twenty minutes before she saw Jeffrey approaching the stables. Tessa had wandered slowly through the manor's outbuildings, trying to look like a curious boy, and had taken up a place that was outside the view of most people. She took out her knife and began whittling, a common enough pastime for a young lad, and one that a gentleman might stop to observe, giving them a few minutes' time to talk. The only problem with her scheme was that Tessa had no idea how to whittle or any talent for it. She hoped that no one asked to see the finished product.

Jeffrey appeared to be casually wandering also, and he went round the other side of the stable, admiring the morning, which was fine; the trees, which were no more than ordinary trees; and even a horse that was being groomed by a boy of perhaps eight. Finally he approached Tessa and stood some feet off, still gazing at the view.

"So, young man, what have you to tell me of England?" he said, not looking at her at all.

"I come from your family, sir. They thought you drowned when you were lost overboard."

"Luck was with me that day. I must have been in the water for some time, but some fishermen picked me up." Jeffrey paused, his tone changing as his face tightened. "My life was saved, but my luck was not all good. Something happened, no one knows what, but as a result, I forgot everything of my former life. I would not even know my own name except for some documents wrapped in oilskin that they found on my person."

"I am sorry to hear it, Jeff— sir," she answered, remembering her role as a boy.

"I was brought here a prisoner. These fishermen deal with Hawick when they find cargo or such as might be sold. Hawick pays them and then turns it to what profit he may."

"Even people?" She was revolted by the callousness of dealing in others' misfortunes.

"Even so."

"Did you not think of escape?"

"To go where? I cannot wander the Scottish countryside asking if anyone knows who I am. Hawick leads me to believe that I am not safe doing so, since it seems I am an enemy of the king."

"So you remember nothing of yourself?"

"Well, not exactly. Over time, images have returned. There are many things I don't remember, but I sometimes see pictures in my mind, a house, I think my home —"

"Brixton Manor."

"Yes, I suppose so. And some people . . . a blond woman."

"Eleanor."

"Is that her name? I see her, but not clearly. Is she my wife?"

"She is your brother's wife."

"Ah." He didn't even seem upset by this piece of information. "And she sent you?"

A hesitation. Tessa was confused by what she'd just heard. Jeffrey didn't know about his past. He had forgotten home, his family . . . had he forgotten her? "Your lover will forget your name" sounded in her head. The old women were wrong. This man wasn't her lover. Still, she had to ask. "Do you remember me?"

Jeffrey looked at her directly for the first time, a frown of curiosity on his handsome features. "No, lad —" he began, but then his face changed as his eyes met Tessa's, taking in the face and not the disguise. Caution seemed forgotten as he spoke to her earnestly and with force. "You are no lad! You are the face that appears in my dreams!

Who are you? What are you doing here?" In his excitement he grasped Tessa's arms and pulled her close, his eyes searching hers.

"Jeffrey," a voice called from behind them. "Is anything wrong?" The look on Jeffrey's face changed to alarm. Tessa saw him fight for control. A look of mute appeal crossed his face as he released Tessa, then the old look of amusement appeared like a mask, covering everything Tessa was trying to read, and he turned to Mairie, who stood several paces away in the sunlight, looking as fresh and youthful as the artful application of cosmetics could portray. She wore clothes much too fine for daily use, in Tessa's opinion: a rose-colored silk that draped attractively over her full hips. She did not approach, for to do so would have meant leaving the hardened path where she might dirty the slippers dyed to match the dress.

"Nothing, my dear." Jeffrey smiled at Mairie. "The boy spoke harshly to his mother, and I cannot abide an ungrateful child." To Tessa he hissed, "Meet me in an hour by the large oak tree along the river. Please!" Straightening, he raised his voice and commented with lifted brow. "Be careful whom you speak to and what you speak of, boy, and things will go better for you." Offering Mairie his arm, he escorted her back toward the house without a backward glance.

Jeffrey's last words seemed a warning, so she and Banaugh said nothing of English prisoners to Hawick. Their meeting with him that morning centered on Macbeth's preparations for war with Malcolm and the English forces. Having heard of their letter of safe conduct, Hawick assured them in his bluff manner that he would fight, "willing and strong," for his king when the time came. Although he was cordial in a condescending way, Tessa found that she could not like the man. His greed was obvious, and she wondered about the truth of his words.

"I hope that you will take to the king good reports of my loyalty and my hospitality," he told them. "We border lords have much trouble with the English, and we dinna feel, sometimes, that the king understands our predicament. We are poor men who must make our livings as we can."

Tessa knew that meant that Hawick expected the king to turn a blind eye to raids across the border, which infuriated the English and made things more difficult for the king and for Scotland as a whole. Looking around the manor, she didn't think that Hawick and his people suffered much poverty. Some border lords were not above raiding their own neighbors and blaming it on the English from time to time, and she would bet Hawick was one such.

Keeping their faces blank, she and Banaugh listened to the man's boasting. They learned that Hawick was, in his own opinion, a canny man of business who saw himself as a go-between at some time in the future, making peace with the English. "I have dealt with some Englishmen from time to time, being so close to the border, you see," he told them, "and I have learned their ways. The king might remember that when it comes time for him to deal with them." Here he turned sly. "That is, after Macbeth has beaten the English dogs back over the border, where they belong." It was clear he hoped to set himself up for a post in Macbeth's court. Banaugh was amiably noncommittal, listening politely for an hour, at which time the interview was ended and the seneschal came to escort them out.

They found a private spot outside the hall where they could make their plans. Tessa told Banaugh, "Jeffrey's memory of England is gone, and there's nothing there for him anyway with Eleanor dead. It is best we go on."

"Well, then, that's what we shall do," Banaugh replied. "But do ye not want to try again, lass? Perhaps he will remember ye a second time."

"Jeffrey is taken with this Mairie, and it matters not whether he remembers me, since I am nothing to him anyhow."

"Lass, I believe he is something to ye, is he no'?"

"Of course not. I made a promise, and I've done my best to fulfill it. That is all."

"But ye've come all this way, and to speak only a few words t' this Brixton hardly seems fair to the mon!"

Part of her was only too willing to be convinced. "All right. I'll meet him and give him the box. It won't mean anything now, but I will have done what I came to do."

Banaugh nodded. "I'll pack our things and be ready t' depart when ye've taken care o' that last thing."

"Wait for me by the crossing." Banaugh had given her an idea. If Jeffrey had truly lost his memory, perhaps seeing Tessa in her own clothing would jar his memory. It was so hard to know what to do, or even what she wanted to do. How could she rescue a man who didn't know who he was and had nowhere to return to anyway? "I'll join you at the first river bend after I've seen him. I will know by then . . ." Her words trailed off. What would she know? Banaugh asked no questions but moved off to get the pony ready. Tessa stood biting her lip, almost ready to follow the old man and forget the whole thing. What purpose would it serve if he did remember her, the girl he had foisted off on his old lover? And now he had a new one. As if on cue, a voice spoke at her elbow.

"Jeffrey's walking along the river, no doubt trying to remember who you are."

Turning, Tessa faced Mairie. Before she could answer, the woman went on, the pretty face she showed to the world hard now, revealing her true character. "Don't bother to lie to me. You deceived the others, but I knew from the start you were no boy. In the first place, your eyes never left Jeffrey's face last evening. Second, you're too graceful for any boy in this primitive country." Her tone dripped loathing for her adopted homeland. "I began wondering, why would a woman come disguised to my brother's castle? Then I saw you with Jeffrey this morning, and I had my answer. You're from England, and you've come to rescue him from the uncivilized Scots."

Tessa found her voice, picking up on the one part she could truthfully deny. "I am a Scot. And if I came for Jeffrey, it appears he doesn't want to be rescued."

Mairie frowned in consternation. "Perhaps. He was quite docile at first, so weak and confused. As time went on and healing began, he became very . . . sociable and has kept us quite entertained. But our Jeffrey has remembered little things lately that make him restless. Today, he's quite agitated, no matter that he tries to be attentive."

Mairie looked around to assure herself that no one was listening. "Jeffrey is the only reason I haven't gone insane in this godforsaken place. Everyone here is crude and disgusting except him, even my brother. Ian believes that my presence in his so-called court adds nobility and grace — as if anything could grace this sty!" She paused for a moment. "I suppose Jeffrey is a younger son?"

"His brother is the lord of Brixton," Tessa replied. "Jeffrey is the fourth son."

"I thought as much when no ransom was paid. It's too bad. I could fall in love with such a man if he had prospects. Still, Jeffrey amuses me, and I prefer that he stay here until I can convince my brother to let me return to France and live among civilized people again."

"What happens to Jeffrey then?"

"I couldn't say," was the airy reply. Tessa

had begun to see the ugliness beneath this beautiful exterior. Now Mairie grasped her arm tightly, nails digging in. "I warn you, I shall have him for as long as I want him, so you'd best be off and forget him as he has forgotten you." With that she released Tessa and strode off, gradually regaining composure as she went until her walk again became feminine and sedate. Tessa watched with disgust. It was like seeing a glimpse of a worm disappearing behind a perfect leaf.

CHAPTER SEVENTEEN

More determined than ever to complete her task, Tessa circled the bailey and approached the river from the northwest, keeping out of sight as much as possible. Slipping into the woods, she changed into the soft linen gown she'd kept rolled in her blanket. Combing her hair, which was growing out again, she finally put on slippers of leather that her sister had given her. Finished, she left the cover of the trees and stood on the bank beside the dead oak Jeffrey had mentioned.

The tree was huge, leaning out over the river as if ready to fall any second, but she knew that such trees often spent decades that way. It seemed likely that the diversion of water for Hawick's moat had killed it, drowning its roots and washing away the soil around them gradually. A low branch swept outward, and for a moment Tessa was tempted to climb out on it and sit suspended over the river, forgetting everything but the flow of the current beneath her. It was something she would have done when her mother's jibes had become too much for her, hide from trouble and wait for it to go away.

Now she had changed somehow, and escaping from a troubling situation was no longer what she chose to do. She wanted to face Jeffrey, not to blame or berate him, but to know what the truth was, so that she could accept it and go on with her life. Was this what maturity did to a person? It was good to face life's questions, but the fear that in this case the answer would not be the one she wanted made her long for the past, when hiding from trouble seemed possible.

Tessa looked along the bank for Jeffrey, but there was no sign of him. Maybe he had changed his mind, decided that his past life didn't matter anymore. Then he appeared, coming down the path from upriver. Slowing for a moment when he saw Tessa in women's attire, he made a gesture of adjustment and came on determinedly. Glancing past her to assure they could not be seen from Hawick's stronghold, he returned his gaze to Tessa, his blue eyes taking in her face with curiosity, and, she detected, approval. Now that he was close, she noticed a scar at his temple, a jagged white line that testified to the injury he had suffered. She longed to touch it, feel the roughness of it, but she did not.

"It is easy now to see that you are not a boy," he said with some amusement.

"No. I am Tessa macFindlaech, niece of Macbeth, king of Scotland."

"I see." He looked closely at her face, frowning in concentration. "I have seen you in my dreams, but have no memory of you. How do we know each other?"

Tessa avoided the question. "That is not important. I am glad to know that you live. I will tell your family that you are well."

"The woman Eleanor whom you spoke of?"

"Eleanor is dead."

"Ah." He seemed to be trying to decide what it should be that he felt. "I'm sorry. My brother?"

"You have three, all well when I . . . left Brixton."

"Three brothers! It is odd to hear these things, to hear of a family and a life that I have no memory of. As I said, I see images, but nothing is clear. That is why I had to speak with you again."

"It is why I have come," Tessa answered. "That, and this." She handed him the box, its carved "E" catching a stray beam of light that penetrated the leafy awning.

"What is it?"

"I don't know. Eleanor wanted you to have it."

Jeffrey's face showed nothing but curiosity. "The blond woman, Eleanor, sent you to give me this?"

"Well, yes and no. She died not knowing that you were lost at sea. She thought you would come back for it. I brought it home to Scotland with me, where I heard you might be alive. I've looked for you ever since."

"Why? To give me a box of letters?"

It seemed to Tessa an inadequate reason, too. Why, indeed? "I'm not sure."

"Tell me your name again, please. Now that I see you clearly, I know we have met before. Your face has appeared often in my mind, but I could not put a name to it."

"I am Tessa. Tessa macFindlaech."

"Tessa." Jeffrey said it with a half-smile. "And Tessa, were we two lovers?"

"Quite the opposite, not even friends. It is only my vow to Eleanor that brought me here." She lied when she said it, but pride would admit to no more.

He looked at her for a long time but said only, "I see. Perhaps the letters will help me

244

to remember more. Would you mind if I read them alone?"

"Of course not. I am ready to depart, actually. My friend and I will be gone when you return to the house."

"Well, then." Jeffrey looked thoughtful for a moment, seemed about to say something, then thought better of it and said only, "I thank you for your trouble. I must put together bits and pieces of my life until I have a past, and you have helped with that."

Tessa stood, uncertain what to do. Should she warn Jeffrey that Mairie was playing with him, using him only for amusement? Should she try to make him remember the night he'd taken her prisoner on a riverbank much like this one? Or should she go and leave him to this new life, where he seemed content? In the end, she chose the latter. It was not her affair, and who in England looked for the return of Jeffrey Brixton? With a smile she hoped was casual, Tessa walked off, never looking back. Had she done so, she would have seen Jeffrey standing where she'd left him, a curious expression of pain on that striking face.

Banaugh stood waiting beside the pony, and though his eyes sought hers briefly, he said nothing as Tessa approached. In mute agreement they started for Jedburgh. They had gone no more than half a mile, however, when the sound of horses made them turn to look behind.

Four mounted men came down the path at full speed, pulling up only when they reached them. One was Ian Hawick, looking out of breath and angry, his piggish eyes even less attractive than usual. Two were henchmen, who kept their faces impassive. The fourth was Jeffrey Brixton, who did not meet Tessa's astonished eyes, but said to Hawick, "It is as I said. The boy is no boy, but the niece of the king, Macbeth, sent to spy on you. She will prove a valuable bartering chip, so treat her well."

"You villain!" Tessa spat at him. "After —"

"Remember to keep your tongue silent, and you will live longer!" This time Jeffrey looked directly at her, his eyes intense. Then his face relaxed and the look she hated most settled. "My friend," he said to Hawick, "why is it that women need to speak when they are most useful, and certainly more attractive when they do not?"

Hawick's anger dissolved into hilarity. "True, Brixton. Perhaps we should gag the wench. 'Tis true, the best of a woman's uses do not require speech. Dougal!" he spoke to one of the men.

It was the one who had looked familiar to her the day before, and seeing him on horseback, Tessa remembered why. He had left Brixton's manor house in disgust after having spoken to William. Her glance went to his hand, missing the last two fingers. He must have been sent with Hawick's ransom demand, which had been rejected. "A rascal," William had said. So was it only Mairie's amusement that kept Jeffrey alive, or had he become valuable to Hawick in other ways as well? Certainly he had betrayed her easily enough. Why had she not seen it coming?

The man urged his horse forward. "Take this lass to the house and lock her in the storeroom," Hawick ordered.

"What about the old man?" asked the other rider.

Hawick looked briefly at Banaugh. "Kill him." The man grinned and fingered a sparthe, a long-handled, broad-bladed battle-axe that hung at his side.

"No!" Tessa screamed, but the burly Dougal bent easily down from his saddle and scooped her up in front of him. She fought until he cuffed her just hard enough to make her head spin and her mind go blank. She slumped against his chest, dimly aware that terrible things were happening, but unable to stop the whirling in her head. Dougal turned his horse and headed up the hill to Hawick's Castle, and she knew no more of what happened on the road.

When Tessa came to herself, she was in a dark room. Feeling cautiously around she found jugs, sacks, and crates: the storeroom Hawick had mentioned. No one came for many hours, and she spent the time half in crying and half in bitter anger. Banaugh's death had come from her chasing after Jeffrey Brixton, and he had betrayed her to Hawick to ingratiate himself further with the outlaw. She hoped terrible things happened to all of them, and soon.

Tessa stayed locked in the room for two days, maybe three. From time to time a servant girl came to attend to her needs. The girl was kind but terrified of doing anything to make Hawick angry. Tessa considered every possible avenue of escape, but there was no way out of the room except the locked door, and when the girl came, a manservant accompanied her and stood outside the door until it was locked again.

After time had become impossible to judge, Tessa was awakened from dozing as the door opened. No accompanying ray of light entered. In the black of night, someone had entered her prison. She scuttled to a corner and sat as still as possible, seeing only a dim male form in the darkened passageway. The door closed behind him and she heard the key in the lock.

"Tessa?" She recognized the voice as Jeffrey Brixton's, and immediately began to figure how she could kill him. He was totally lost in the blackness, and she had the advantage. He didn't know her location, but she knew his.

"Tessa?" he said again. Without further thought she launched herself from the corner, fists doubled and teeth set. He was farther into the room than she'd figured, however, so they connected before she expected it. Still, Jeffrey went down with a satisfying grunt of surprise, and then she was on him, beating his chest and face with her hands. She heard a low growl without realizing that it came from her own throat. With all her strength, she tried to punish the man who had hurt her so much. Sobbing, all of the tension of the past few days coming out at once, she focused on revenge, on hurting him as much as possible before his superior strength prevailed and he killed her.

Jeffrey's response was quick and strong once he recovered from the initial blow. In moments Tessa lay pinned beneath him while a whispered, "Stop that and listen to me," hissed in her ear. Since there was nothing else she could do, she stopped struggling, but anger pounded in her ears and her heart, and she gathered her strength for another attack if he gave her any opening whatsoever.

Jeffrey relaxed somewhat and gingerly released his hold on her. "I have come to explain something to you," he began, but Tessa reacted furiously, punching him in the face with her little fist, thumb tucked under her fingers the way her father had taught her. She couldn't see in the darkness, but her aim was good nevertheless, and she heard a strangled oath from Jeffrey. Once again he grabbed her wrists in one hand and pinned her to the floor with his body.

"Stop that, hellcat! I tell you I've come to help!"

"Like you helped me before, you fiend? I loathe you!" Despite her anger, Tessa kept her voice low, following Jeffrey's lead.

"If you will let me explain . . ." She could tell he was rubbing the eye that she'd hit, and for the first time in days she felt almost good. "You must believe that I did what I had to do to protect you."

"I want nothing from you, Jeffrey Brixton.

Neither your protection nor your lies — nothing! All I've ever had from you was pain and heartache, while you take what you want without considering the result. I've watched you make love to Eleanor, your own sister-in-law, and leave her to die alone, and now you have Mairie, who is every bit your equal in evil and cruelty. You deserve her, and you can go back to her bed this minute and leave me to my own company, for while I may be an uncivilized Scottish brat, I would never betray anyone the way you have betrayed me!" Her voice shook, and Tessa knew she was close to tears. "And now Banaugh is dead because of you!"

A noise in the passage interrupted the reply Jeffrey was about to make. They both froze as footsteps, soft scuffles like those of a woman's slippers, came to the door and stopped. Someone tried the handle, stood listening for a long time, and then moved off. Tessa felt Jeffrey's tension slowly relax, and he whispered, "Tessa, I know what you think of me. It is not safe for me to stay here now. If that was Hawick or Mairie, I must be found soon or they will be suspicious. I cannot tell you all, but please understand that I will release you at the first opportunity. It will be difficult, for the gate is closed at night and guarded all the time, but I will find a way." Suddenly the tone of his voice changed to almost a plea for understanding. "I would never . . . I could not . . ." He pulled her to him and kissed her hard, the kiss betraying more emotion than she could have imagined in a man like Jeffrey Brixton. Her mind began to whirl, and she responded despite herself. When it was over, he touched her cheek and helped her up gently, releasing her hand with reluctance. She heard the door open quietly, saw in shadow Jeffrey's silhouette as he checked the passageway, and then he was gone.

Tessa stood staring into the blackness, trying to sort out the truth of Jeffrey Brixton. Was he the man who had just left her, gentle and loving, or the sardonic betrayer who had smirked as Hawick took her captive? At that she remembered Banaugh and her heart sank. No one who cared about her could have been responsible for the death of that beloved old man. Tessa surrendered to tears once again and cursed Jeffrey Brixton for the destruction of her friend — and her heart.

Chapter Eighteen

There passed another day of anxious waiting, Tessa nearly out of her mind with nothing to do but go over and over the events of the last few days. The little maid who brought her food smiled shyly but dared not speak. It was clear she feared punishment for any sign of friendliness. The door opened again unexpectedly at evening, which Tessa discerned by the torchlight in the passageway.

The same burly man who'd carried her on his horse stood in the dimness. "Come with me," was all he said.

Tessa obeyed, hoping against hope that it was Jeffrey she would be meeting, but the man led her to the hall, where dinner was in progress. There were no important guests in the hall this night, just Hawick's own and the bard who had been invited to stay, having pleased the company. The outlaw himself sat at the table head, dressed informally in a rough brown robe. Mairie shimmered beside him, making Tessa feel all the more disheveled and grubby. Tonight the lady wore a dress of sky blue that managed to make her appear vulnerable and provocative at once. Jeffrey sat on Mairie's right, looking down at his food, which made Tessa wonder what discussion had preceded her presence. Mairie looked excited, which did not bode well for Tessa. She did notice with satisfaction that Jeffrey had an angry-looking purple bruise under his right eye.

Hawick's eyes traveled up and down Tessa's frame in a way that made her blush. "So this is the king's niece?"

"I have said so." Jeffrey's eyes came up and met Tessa's briefly, but she could read nothing in them. "She says that I met her at Inverness when I visited Macbeth, but of course, I remember none of it."

"My sister has had an idea that I find interesting. The last invasion of Scotland failed, did it not?"

"I have heard it said," Jeffrey answered.

"It is true enough, Brixton. You sold your sword to the wrong side in that instance." Hawick had no delicacy, no tact, when an opportunity came to belittle one who could not challenge him on it. "Macbeth was largely responsible for Scotland's victory, being a capable soldier and a strong leader of men. So the present question is, which side of this . . . disagreement over the kingship should I be supporting, Macbeth as king in fact, or Malcolm as the one named to succession?"

Jeffrey said nothing, but Tessa thought he looked pale. Had he some idea of where Hawick's thought was going? She herself had no idea.

Hawick tore a piece of bread from a nearby loaf and ate it while he continued. "My sister is by many considered a perfect example of feminine beauty, but those who know her well understand that she possesses a mind that rivals her appearance. She has suggested that if I were married to a close relative of the king, say his niece, I would be doubly blessed. First I would have a comely wench in my bed, and second" — here he looked at Tessa — "I would have access to the king of Scotland himself." His own perceived cleverness made Hawick's flat face shine with delight.

Tessa almost laughed aloud. He had vastly overestimated her importance to her uncle. She opened her mouth to tell the man his mistake, but Jeffrey caught her eye and flashed a look of such vehemence she almost heard the words, "For once, Tessa macFindlaech, keep quiet!" Perhaps it was her own mind that spoke them, because she realized in the next instant that her value as the king's niece was all that kept her alive at the moment.

"So I consider the institution of marriage," Hawick said smoothly, and the assembled company buzzed appreciatively. Finally the man who had fetched Tessa chuckled, and soon general laughter filled the room. Everyone seemed to know what was going to happen except Tessa, but Hawick soon let her in on the secret. "I keep a pet priest nearby for such 'holy' needs as I might encounter, so we will knit this matter up quickly. Prepare yourself, woman. You have one hour. We will wed this night, and I will be king of Scotland someday because of it."

There were cheers from his men, and Hawick ordered more ale be brought out. Conversations broke out among small groups as people discussed the news and what it might mean to them. Tessa stepped closer to the table so that only Hawick, Jeffrey, and Mairie could hear her.

"The Scots would never accept you as king," Tessa spat at him. "You are an outlaw as well as a swine."

There was a flicker in Hawick's eyes, and

Tessa knew that if he had his way she would pay dearly for that insult. But he recovered himself and smiled again. "Macbeth has no children. If he defeats the English and remains king, what better heir to the throne than his niece's husband? I may be an outlaw today, but I'm willing to work my way to the kingship, as your uncle himself did." He and Mairie both found this remark funny.

Jeffrey smiled rather weakly and late at the jibe, then spoke languidly from his seat, keeping his gaze hooded and away from Tessa. "What if the English win, my friend? You'll be saddled with a wife whose family is disgraced."

"Not likely," Hawick replied. "None but we know she's here, and none but we will know or care what happens to her if Macbeth is defeated."

Tessa's blood froze as he coolly admitted that he would kill her if she became useless to him. Her eyes sought Jeffrey's, but he did not look up. Mairie was at the moment tempting him with sweetmeats from a plate before her. As he took one, Tessa imagined that the smile he managed was less than sincere.

Hawick noticed Tessa's gaze. "Do you suppose this one is a virgin, Brixton?"

Jeffrey's smile froze and he spoke only after a moment's pause. Tessa saw the look on Mairie's face and knew she had taken note of his discomfort. "I don't know m'lord." With Mairie's eyes on him Jeffrey threw off the look of unease and displayed his mask of amusement. "I have no memory of her morals . . . or my own, for that matter. But seeing her makes me hope that if the opportunity arose, I was able to relieve her of that state."

Hawick tensed for a moment at the thought that Jeffrey might have done just that, but he relaxed with a chuckle. "I say it matters not, for if she is a virgin, then I alone will have the pleasure of her, and if not, then I hope you taught her well."

Tessa's face burned to be discussed in this way, and once more she wondered at the man who could bring her such shame after promising to help her. Jeffrey continued to accept sweets from Mairie, who glanced once at Tessa with a haughty smile then returned her attention to her lover.

Hawick spoke to the little maid who'd waited on Tessa. "Take her away and make her presentable." To a man at his left he ordered, "Have the priest here in an hour. I will become a complete man tonight."

The girl put her hand timidly on Tessa's

arm, and seeing no other option, Tessa left the room with her. A few voices called out bits of marital advice that they thought humorous. Tessa feared she would be sick but controlled her nausea for the sake of pride.

Once they were alone, the girl, whose name was Brenda, was as kind as she dared be. There were clothes already laid out, fine ones. "Mistress Mairie was told to provide ye with a wedding gown, but she didna like it much. Fine clothes are hard to come by here, but she dares not stand against Hawick's wishes. 'Tis a pity your hair's chopped off, but it ha' plenty o' curl, so t'will look well enow."

Tessa had no one to talk to but this frightened, ignorant girl. She spoke to herself as much as to Brenda. "I am already married."

Brenda's eyes widened in fear. "Oh, miss, is it so?"

"I was married in York last summer. If I tell —"

Brenda's hand was on her arm. "No! He'll kill you!" The girl knew well how ruthless her employer was.

"You are right, but what can I do? I can't speak the words again."

"True, t' would be a deadly sin, I'm

thinkin'." Brenda considered for a moment, her freckled face earnest in the rushlight. "Say nothing. That's the best. If ye say nothing, perhaps ye'll not really be married this second time." It wasn't much. Would Hawick force her to say the words, or would it be enough for him to go through the sham of a wedding ceremony? Tessa had no better idea.

For such an occasion a bath was called for, which felt good despite the circumstances. Brenda then helped Tessa dress and adjust the gown of creamy white satin with full sleeves and a fitted bodice. It was meant to have a colored tunic over it, Brenda said, but it was fine enough to be worn alone for such an occasion. The skirt was a bit long for Tessa, but her breasts were fuller than Mairie's so the top was tight. Brenda managed to make it fit by slitting the bodice a bit lower, an effect that embarrassed Tessa when she looked down. "I'm sorry, mistress. It's the best I can do with sae little time."

"What does it matter? I am to be married by force, and in the company of men who are hateful and lawless. There is little sense in worrying about how much of my bosom shows."

When they'd finished Tessa's toilette to Brenda's satisfaction, the two girls sat quietly in the chamber, nothing to say. Finally a knock came on the door and a man almost as large as the other came to fetch Tessa. He grinned when he saw her and with exaggerated courtesy bowed her through the door. At the last moment Brenda remembered and brought a length of sheer fabric that she draped over Tessa's head to serve as the traditional bridal veil. She looked back at the girl, whose face showed sympathy for her plight. "Thank you for your kindness," she told Brenda, who answered with a smile and a blush.

As she descended into the great hall again, Tessa noticed one change. Neither Jeffrey nor Mairie was at the table. Where had they gone? She had little time to wonder, for her attention was taken up with her own predicament. Before her stood Hawick, who had not bothered to change or even wipe the grease from the meal out of his beard, and a priest who looked half-frightened yet half-eager, probably for the payment he would receive for this unusual wedding.

As Tessa was led reluctantly through the crowd of waiting people, Mairie slipped back into her seat at the head of the table. When she gestured with disgust at the mess left from the meal, two servants cleared it away.

"Well met, Mairie. I thought you might miss my wedding altogether with your dallying," Hawick teased.

"I would not miss it for the world," Mairie responded, "but I fear Master Brixton has become lost in the castle yard. He will not be joining us."

Hawick chuckled. "We must only hope he does not black the other eye stumbling around in the dark. Now, let us begin. I grow weary and would take to my bed." General laughter accompanied his remark, and Tessa's stomach tightened. For a moment she imagined Hawick's hands on her body, but with determination she shut out the image. It was too much to consider. She would face the disaster when it happened, not before.

The method suggested by Brenda to avoid the marriage vows worked. Tessa never said a word. It seemed the priest had not even bothered to learn her name, referring to her only as "this woman." When the old man asked if she took Hawick to husband, she stood mute until someone bawled, "Of course she does, ye ninny!" and the priest went on with a flinch. Hawick, for his part, tried at least to be half-serious about the matter, but it was hard with the snickers and jibes from the men of his company.

There was not much to it, and the ceremony was over in minutes. Tessa found herself dizzy and a little confused. Was she married to this outlaw baron or to Cedric? Oh, Eleanor, this was not what either of us planned.

After the ceremony, such as it was, the health of the couple was drunk many times. Tessa sat stonily beside Hawick, who at one point planted a greasy kiss on her lips, to her horror and to the enjoyment of his men, and then paid her no more attention whatsoever. Mairie and her brother discussed their plans for the future.

"The honeymoon must be short, I fear. I will leave with my troops in the morning and march to Inverness."

"Perhaps the plan should change a bit," Mairie purred. "Methinks your wedding will explain well why your troops do not arrive to help the king until it is too late." She smiled as she waited for Hawick to catch on.

"I see," he mused. "I am so in love that I delay my departure, and if our English informant is correct, things will be decided before I arrive."

"That would be much easier for you," Mairie said.

"True. Once we see which way the battle

has gone, I will join the winning side. If Macbeth wins, I come to him as his newest kinsman, willing to help but a little too slow. If the English win, I join Malcolm, claiming my intention was always to fight on their side."

"Once things are settled, you can decide what to do with her. Malcolm may be won over if you deliver to him one of the tyrant's family as a token of your loyalty." Mairie hardly spared a glance at Tessa, listening to her own death discussed for the second time that evening.

"What about Brixton? You say he remembers nothing, but is it wise to have him about?"

"He's easily led if one has the right weapons." The smile Mairie sent Tessa's way was arch.

"My English friend tells me he's a dangerous man in a fight. I've only kept him because you enjoy his company," Hawick growled. "Once I saw there was no ransom, I'd have slit his throat. What say you, Mairie? Do you trust your Englishman while I am gone north?"

Mairie's sly eyes rested on Tessa for a moment before she spoke. "You are right to be concerned. I wager we can no longer trust him at all. He has begun to remember his past, although he pretends otherwise. Besides, he has begun to bore me. Do with him as you like." Her eyes went to Tessa again, waiting.

Hawick glanced about the room, seeking his henchman Dougal. Seeing it, Tessa knew what he would be told to do unless she thought fast. Calling herself all kinds of fool, she spoke, hoping to save Jeffrey Brixton's life, for no matter what he had done to her, she could not see him murdered in his sleep.

"My lord," Tessa said, hardly trusting her voice to stay even. "Brixton's family may not pay ransom for him, but some would pay in gold."

"And who might that be?"

Tessa put forth the strongest argument she could think of. "If you want to gain favor with Macbeth, you would benefit from delivering an English spy to him. Why do you think my uncle sent me here? It was to find this Brixton, who plotted with rebels and invaders while he was a guest in Macbeth's own home. The king would pay well to get his hands on Brixton."

"Fie! Why would he send a girl and an old man to capture an Englishman?"

Tessa remained calm, at least outwardly. "Not to capture, only to find where he is. My uncle knew I could identify Brixton, having traveled with him for several days when he held me captive."

"Brixton abducted you?"

She looked directly at Hawick for the first time. "I'm afraid you've made a bad bargain, for I speak the truth. I journeyed to England as Brixton's prisoner, the two of us alone. I'm sure I need not tell you what I suffered. I for one am glad the man has lost all memory of the past, but my uncle has not forgotten. You know how he repays his enemies." Tessa guessed that rumors of Macbeth's revenge on those who betrayed him had reached Hawick's ears, and the look on his face confirmed it.

The man's face tightened. Mairie's jaw clenched and she nodded involuntarily, as if to say she'd known there was something between Jeffrey and Tessa. After a moment, Hawick regained control and let out an ironic laugh. "Well, my dear, it seems we both made a bad bargain. I am to have used goods, and you may well have a very short future." Tessa felt the blood drain from her face, but she forced her expression to remain unchanged as Hawick continued, wagging a finger under her nose, "Unless you behave very, very well."

He laughed at his heartless jest and pushed his bulk back from the table. "So, now we will forget the past and make our way to the bridal chamber." Mairie smiled slyly again, and Tessa felt a wave of fear. "But I thank you, lass, for the information. There is yet time to be rid of Brixton if he gets in my way, but for now I shall let him live. Perhaps I shall take him with me to Inverness, for he is an amusing fellow, and I like a man who might be worth a bit o' gold." He raised his voice and announced that he and his new wife would retire to their chamber.

With much merriment and many ribald comments, Tessa and Hawick were escorted to a room on the second floor. Hawick made a great joke of carrying Tessa across the threshold, to the delight of his men. Tessa did not resist, knowing that was futile, but held rigidly still as she was set back on her feet inside the room. Hawick dismissed the crowd of raucous attendants with a mock-gallant bow and a lewd wink. Because of his status, the chamber had a real door, which he shut and locked, pocketing the key. Sounds of laughter died away in the passage. A few last comments floated back as the party retreated. The outlaw turned to face Tessa, who stood where he had set her, frozen with dread.

"Now, lass, let's see what I've got in this

bargain," he growled. His eyes went to the front of the gown, and Tessa put a hand to her chest involuntarily. Then anger replaced fear and her old fire returned. For once Kenna might have approved of her daughter's indomitable spirit.

"I cannot stop you, outlaw, and you will do what you will do. But understand that you will never be able to turn your back on me, nor will you ever have a kind word from me, even on your deathbed," Tessa hissed.

"Words, my dear, were not what I had in mind from you. I care not for your heart or your mind, but I will have your body, and as you say, you can do nothing to stop me." Hawick chuckled deep in his throat, advancing upon Tessa and pulling her to him. Frantic now, she tried to push herself away with both hands against the man's huge chest, but he was strong and soon held both her arms tightly at her side, his face close to hers. She made an involuntary sound of distress that amused Hawick.

"Never be shy about making noise, lass. The household will enjoy hearing your screams, for they are a rowdy lot."

Tessa knew there was no hope. Hawick's hands tightened on her arms, and he pulled her even closer, his lips nearing her own. His eyes, staring into hers, gleamed with amusement . . . and then they crossed, uncrossed, rolled up into his head, and closed. After teetering for a moment, his grip on her arms loosened and his oversized body dropped to the floor in an undignified heap.

"She can't stop you, but I can," said Jeffrey Brixton, and Tessa almost fainted with relief.

CHAPTER NINETEEN

Amazed, Tessa stood looking down at Hawick's prone figure for a moment. Finally she raised her eyes to see Jeffrey, wrapped in a black cloak that had served to hide his presence in a shadowed corner of the room. He clutched what looked like the leg of a stool in one hand. Directing his now-familiar look of amusement at Tessa, he asked, "Have I done the right thing, or were you expecting a night of bliss with this fellow?"

His cool manner irritated Tessa after the tense events of the evening. "Of course not," she snapped. "They forced me to marry the man."

"Well, then, we must do what we can to get you away from here before they discover your objections to being an outlaw's wife."

Tessa said no more, although she understood nothing. Jeffrey seemed to change from one moment to the next, but if he was willing to help her escape, she was certainly no worse off to go with him than she had been moments ago. She moved to assist him as he gagged Hawick's mouth with his own belt. Together they tied the limp hands tightly with strips of cloth torn from the bed linen, then lifted him onto the bed, tying him to the slats so that he would not be able to move when he woke.

"Now, how are we to get out?" Jeffrey mused as he checked the tension of the knots. "The gates will be shut by now, and I may be missed at any moment."

"Where were you?" Tessa asked.

"While you were being prepared for a fate worse than death, the lovely Mairie suggested we go for a stroll in the autumn evening, actually more a command than a request. She was very cool about it, I must say, but I had my suspicions. Still, she got me out of the hall with no one to wonder where I might be, so I went along. She locked me in the stables, having some suspicion that I might interrupt your nuptials, which it turns out she was quite correct to conclude." Jeffrey grinned in the torchlight.

"It serves you right for chasing after that painted wench," Tessa began, but a thought cut short her tirade. "Oh, Jeffrey, I can't be married to this man!"

Brixton misunderstood her meaning. "Well, they did get a priest, but I believe your uncle will see to an annulment when he understands that you were coerced into marriage." It was a hopeful thought, although Jeffrey didn't know everything. Tessa could not bring herself to mention her first marriage at the moment. It was too complicated, but the thought that Macbeth could arrange an annulment might work as well for Cedric as for Hawick.

"I hope my uncle does not tire of my explanations. I have been nothing but a problem to him. First he must take me in, then I reappear from the dead, and now I'll be needing a marriage dissolved."

"He has problems to deal with much larger than you," Jeffrey grimaced. "Still, we must get you away from here and back to him, which won't be easy."

As he spoke, Jeffrey searched Hawick's pockets and recovered the key. Unlocking the door, he peered into the passageway then signaled Tessa to follow. He locked the door behind them and set the key high on a rafter, out of sight. They crept down the narrow stone passageway toward the stairs that led down to the great hall, where they could hear the revelers still drinking and talking, their drunkenness obvious from the volume and tone of the proceedings. A smaller, darker passage led off on the other side of the stairs, and with great care not to be seen, they crossed the open space and entered it.

"The servants' quarters," Jeffrey whispered. "If we're lucky, they're still at work downstairs."

They were not that lucky, for a moment later Brenda came out of a room, her brown eyes widening at the sight of the two of them. Jeffrey motioned for her to be quiet, and Tessa felt his body tense to grab the girl if she disobeyed. Quickly Brenda made up her mind. Pointing over her shoulder, she bade them follow.

A few steps down the corridor was a small room mostly taken up by a spiral staircase. Brenda whispered quickly, "This stair goes down the back o' the house. If ye are careful, ye can go through the scullery t' the bin where th' peat is stored. Above it is a chute that leads outside. Once there, ye must be watchful, for folk are about and the gate is already shut for the night. I dinna know how ye macht ge' oot o' the place."

"I have some ideas on that," Jeffrey told her. "But I thank you for your help."

"We are very grateful, Brenda," Tessa whispered.

"Master Brixton has a' been kind t' me," the girl said simply, "and it hurt me t' see ye forced to marry Hawick, even if ye be not really married to 'im. Tha's an evil man." Jeffrey gave Tessa an odd look but asked no questions, his mind focused on their escape.

With a quick hug for Brenda, Tessa followed Jeffrey down the back stair. They found the scullery easily enough, and the chute, though a tight fit for Jeffrey's shoulders, was big enough to allow passage. Once outside, Jeffrey wrapped Tessa in his black cape to hide the white of the gown, not so white now as it had been a few minutes before. They slipped through the shadows toward the stables, staying close to walls and objects in the courtyard to hide themselves from sentries on the parapet.

Since the guards' attention was focused on what went on outside the bailey, not inside, no one noticed them as they approached the stable end where a small shed housed grain for the animals. Jeffrey indicated where he had escaped by loosening a board on the side wall. They entered the same way and were soon out of sight.

"We are safe for a few hours," Jeffrey announced softly. "Mairie promised she'd let me out in the morning. I suppose she believed I would lose interest in interceding once the wedding had been consummated."

"And why did you intercede?" Tessa asked him. "You say you don't remember me yet release me from a man who will kill you if he finds out. At times it seems you care nothing about me, then you risk your life to help. Why?"

"I don't know," Jeffrey spoke honestly. "I know that I care what happens to you, no matter what we have been to each other in the past."

A rather nervous cough sounded just then from a haystack in one corner of the room. "Who's there?" Jeffrey called out. He still clutched the stool leg, his only weapon. Tessa smiled as the smell of cumin arose.

"Never fear, I am a friend," said a voice, and Banaugh's face appeared in the gloom.

"Banaugh! Oh, Banaugh, I thought you were dead!" Tessa ran to the old man and embraced him, delighted to find that he lived. "I thought they had . . . How . . . ?" She stopped in confusion.

Banaugh chuckled in the darkness. "Thank yer young man there, Master Brixton. After Hawick told his tame wolf t' kill me, he rode off. Jeffrey stayed behind, and ye should ha' seen the show he put on. I was convinced m'sel that he were a monster.

'Let me kill the auld man,' he says, cool as you please. 'I have a score to settle with him and with the girl.' " Banaugh caught Jeffrey's clipped accent with the skill of a practiced storyteller. "He even slipped th' man a gold coin as a bribe!"

"I steal them from Hawick's coffer. How else can I make friends among these mercenary types?"

Banaugh chuckled. "He was a' so convincin'. The man agreed t' it, can ye imagine? I though' I was done then! Jeffrey guides me off into the brush and then tells me t' let out m' death yell. I was willin' enough, and he throws a rock into the river, like it were m' corpse, y' ken." Although she could not see the old man's face in the darkness, Tessa could picture the grin that spread across it as he described Jeffrey's cleverness. "So he saved m' life, and I ha' been hidin' here until I could think of how t' rescue ye. Now that he's got ye away from Hawick, we shall a' get out o' this den o' thieves somehow."

Tessa turned back to Jeffrey, whose face was becoming slightly visible as her eyes got used to the darkness. "So you haven't fallen in with these people?"

Jeffrey let out a sound of mixed laughter and disgust. "If you knew how I've lied, flattered, and smiled to stay alive all these months! When the men who took me from the sea brought me here I was quite help-less with what was probably a broken skull. Hawick almost killed me then rather than go to any bother, but little Brenda nursed me back to health, at least in body. Once I recovered, Mairie decided she found me interesting, so I was allowed to live. They had my papers and sent a ransom letter to my family — to my brother?" He stopped, a question in his voice.

"Your brother William holds the Brixton title."

"And he hates me?"

Tessa tried to be tactful. "Not hates, I daresay. I believe William loves only money. You and he did not see eye to eye, and you left home to be a soldier. He probably feels that he owes you nothing."

"Not very brotherly, to leave one at the mercy of this lot." Jeffrey's tone was angry, and Tessa could not blame him. William, in his safe dwelling in London, could not imagine what it had been like for Jeffrey to live in constant danger of having his throat cut the moment Hawick ordered it. But then, according to what she knew of William, the affairs of anyone other than himself seemed to be of little concern to the man. Had he not ordered her out of his house knowing full well she had nowhere to go? Cedric had saved her then, but it was only Cedric's lust for power — and for her — that had made him take her part. Were all men concerned only for their own desires?

Still, Tessa had done the same thing: used what was available to her to survive. Could she blame Jeffrey for dallying with Mairie when it had kept him alive? If she did, then Aidan was correct to condemn her marriage to Cedric. Both were choices made for survival, not for love.

"He's not an overly kind man, your brother," was all she said. "I believe I saw the one they call Dougal at Brixton shortly before I left, looking angry. I suppose William had dismissed him, thinking him a liar."

"And why did you leave Brixton?"

"After Eleanor died, William discovered that I was not Eleanor's sister, as she and I had led him to believe. He requested that I leave."

Jeffrey's face told her that he understood immediately the predicament she had been in, the unwelcome guest of a man such as William. She wondered how much of his memory had returned, but he made no reference to his role in her abduction. "As you say, my brother is not overly kind," he said with great irony. "What did he expect you to do, on your own in a strange country?"

Again Tessa left out the marriage to Cedric, acknowledging her own cowardice in doing so. "Your Aunt Madeline helped me to return to Scotland. At my uncle's castle, I learned that you might be alive."

"And so came to rescue me?" His voice took on the tone of amusement that never failed to irritate Tessa. How dare he sneer at her efforts to help!

"Only to be betrayed by you to Hawick and his henchmen. How could you do such a thing?" As anger returned, her voice rose.

"I meant no sarcasm," Jeffrey assured her. "I've never before been rescued by a contentious Scotswoman, and I must adjust my masculine pride accordingly." This time the amusement was directed at himself, and Jeffrey put a hand on Tessa's shoulder to calm her. "I did not want to betray you, but I had to tell Hawick something. After you left, I returned to the castle to find them preparing to ride out. Hawick was pleased with himself, I could tell, and he let slip that he expected to find 'a bit of gold along the road to Jedburg.' It seems a local innkeeper reported to him that a man and a boy who came through had the king's gold in their

279

possession. He was smart enough to let you be seen leaving his property, so that when you came up missing later, he could swear you'd departed in safety. The intention, though, was that you'd not get far."

"So you betrayed my identity to keep me alive," Tessa said, realizing the danger she and Banaugh had escaped.

"I had to think quickly to save your friend," Jeffrey said with some pride in his acting ability. "But then, Hawick doesn't hire his men for their impressive brains."

Tessa felt she had misjudged Jeffrey badly, and she tried to atone. "I am sorry. If I had known, I would not have . . . struck you in the eye —"

Banaugh's cackling laugh sounded beside her. "She hit you, did she? Ah, the lass can fight, always has done."

Jeffrey cut him off, embarrassed by the topic. "Now you know why I acted as I did."

Tessa related Hawick's comment of the night before that he might rid himself of Jeffrey. She tried to spare his feelings, being tactful about Mairie's comment, but Jeffrey saw the truth of it and laughed.

"Do you think I don't know what a treacherous liar Mairie is? I have used her to stay alive, knowing her brother will deny her nothing, but I never deluded myself that she has even one genuine feeling for me or anyone outside herself in that beautifully coiffed head. They are quite a pair, the two of them: he grotesque and rotten, she lovely and even more so."

Although surprised, Tessa told herself she should have known. Jeffrey, who could himself act many parts, would be the first to recognize the actress in Mairie.

"Still, I can delay them long enough for you two to get away," Jeffrey mused.

"No!" Without analyzing why, Tessa was unwilling to be separated again from Jeffrey. "We came here to get you out, and you must come with us."

Jeffrey's face was visible now that her eyes had adjusted to the darkness, but after a pause, she could hear the old amusement return to his voice. "It was just a thought. If I must come with you to get you to leave this place, then I must. Now get some sleep. We must be ready at first light to make our escape."

She was surprised that he gave in so easily, but perhaps it was just as well. The tension of the evening had drained her of all but the tiniest bit of energy to make this last demand. Gratified that Jeffrey gave in, and finding that she really was quite tired, Tessa did as he suggested, although doubtful that she could actually relax. Some time later, she realized that sleep had indeed been possible, in fact, inevitable. Awaking as light began to creep into the stable, she saw Banaugh and Jeffrey talking quietly on the other side of the room. They stopped when she sat up and rubbed her eyes.

"Jeffrey —"

"Hush," was his answer. "We're listening for someone's coming to release me. It could be any time now."

Tessa spent a few minutes combing the straw from her hair with her fingers. Soon a carefree whistle was heard outside. Someone was coming to let Jeffrey out of his makeshift prison. Her attention was focused on the door, so she never sensed Banaugh coming up behind her. Before she knew it, his wiry arm was around her waist and the other hand clamped firmly over her mouth. Dragging her into the corner behind the door, he held her tightly while Jeffrey watched with approval.

At that moment there was a rattling from outside as the latchpin was removed from the catch. When the door opened, Jeffrey rushed out in a feigned rage, knocking the servant who had opened the door backward and slamming the door behind him.

"Where is the woman? I will tear out her

hair by the roots! How dare she leave me to shiver in there all night with only mice for company?" His voice grew fainter, but he continued his tirade all the way to the house. Tessa realized in despair that he was making sure no one looked into the tiny storage room where the two of them hid.

Once it was quiet again, Banaugh released Tessa. She said nothing, knowing they had done this for her, but her heart quailed for Jeffrey's safety. "He will mak' his escape and mee' us on the river," Banaugh soothed her. "We ha' arranged a rendezvous place."

Picking up the pack with her boy's clothes inside and handing it to her, the old man turned his back. Tessa quickly dressed in her disguise, reflecting that for a second time she was exchanging an exquisite wedding dress for rough boy's clothing. The crone's prediction suddenly rang in her ears; "Two men who marry you will never be your lover." So far that was true; maybe it meant that they would escape Hawick's clutches. "Your true lover will forget your name," the third one had said.

Jeffrey had forgotten her name, but he was not her lover, was he? He claimed to care about what happened to her, had seemed at times to be attracted to her. Tessa could not decide what kind of man Jeffrey Brixton was. It could simply be that he was grateful for her attempts to find him, or maybe he was a man who loved adventure and women too well to resist either, or, most likely, she didn't understand him at all. Pulling her hair back into a knot, she covered it with the hood that hid its color and shine, then said to Banaugh, "I'm ready."

"We must get t' the river if we can," Banaugh told her. "There's an old rowboat there tha' I ha' patched as best I could, and in the mornin' mist, we should be able to ge' far enow downriver t'escape th' scoundrels. We must ge' t' Jedburgh an' book passage on a ship. 'Tis the fastest way t' put distance twixt us and Hawick."

"But we have no money!" Tessa protested.

"Och, but we do," Banaugh replied. "Tha' day when I heard the horses comin' behind us, I dropped the purse into the bushes at the side o' the road. Ye never ken wha' t' expect i' these parts, bu' ye can usually expect trouble. Later I went back an' picked it up again." Tessa smiled at his canny forethought. What would she do without Banaugh?

Their first task was to escape Hawick's courtyard. "How are we to get out of the gate? It may be open, but it will be guarded.

They'll be looking for me soon if they aren't already."

"Yer Master Brixton thought o' that." Banaugh left the stable, first checking to see that no one was around, and returned shortly with a barrow. "It is sma', but then, so are ye. Ge' in an' I will cover you with straw."

Tessa did as she was told and soon was bumping along the path toward the gate. It was terrifying to lie there, unable to see what was happening. A coarse voice called for Banaugh to stop. The old man had pulled his cap low and bent over to hide his face, appearing to be an ancient worker from some nearby farm.

"Where do you go so early, old man?" said the voice.

"Home, to the west o' here," Banaugh squeaked. "I ha' straw for my dovecote, and I ha' paid for it, too, with pigeon eggs for the master's table. My ladybirds will ha' soft bedding this night." His voice sounded so querulous that Tessa herself almost didn't recognize it. Then he began to sing, "Coo, coo," in an idiotic manner.

"Go on with you, then!" the guard growled. As Banaugh plodded on slowly, so slowly that Tessa thought she might go mad, the gruff voice growled, apparently to another standing nearby, "Crazy as a bedbug."

Banaugh continued down the path until they were far enough away to not be heard. "The benefits o' lookin' ancient, lassie, which ye wi' not know for some time yet. An' seemin' a bit addled doesna hurt, either."

Finally they reached the trees that lined the Teviot River, and Banaugh wheeled the barrow into some trees, out of sight of Hawick's castle. Tessa jumped out, brushing off her clothes as they hurried to the riverbank. Banaugh untied the rowboat, which did not look at all serviceable to her with its gray wood and the green slime growing on the bottom. "Dinna worry, lass, we've not far to go in it," Banaugh encouraged as he helped her in. Taking up two crudely made oars that he had fashioned from driftwood, he guided the boat into the current.

Water began immediately to seep in around the rags and grass Banaugh had used to stop the holes. Without a word he handed Tessa his tin cup. She bailed as he rowed, and they were away.

CHAPTER TWENTY

As they floated toward Jedburgh, Banaugh did his best to convince Tessa that Jeffrey would be all right. "Tha' is a clever man. 'E has a plan for 'is own escape, and will mee' us if 'e thinks it safe. 'E hopes they will be sae int'rested in findin' ye tha' they won't watch 'im close."

They found the spot that Jeffrey and Banaugh had agreed upon, a bend where the river was shielded from the road by thick gorse and scraggly trees. The river had cut into the bank and then receded, leaving a hollow that allowed them to hear passersby on the road above while hidden from view. Just above the place they pulled the boat up onto the bank and into the underbrush, its bottom fully waterlogged now. Their journey had been spent with feet soaked as the porous old boards allowed in more and more of the river. Still, the boat had accomplished its purpose. Their means of escape would not be easily detected since no boat was missing from the castle's supply. Hopefully, pursuers were searching for them along the roads, where they would find no track or sign.

They sat quietly, surrounded by the smell of damp earth and leaves, and waited for the sound of Jeffrey's approach. Tessa felt her stomach growl and remembered that she'd had nothing to eat since noon yesterday. Banaugh wordlessly unwrapped a bundle he pulled from his pocket and offered her a carrot. She grinned at him, and he murmured, "I didna suppose the horsies in Hawick's stable wuld miss a few o' the sma ones." Grateful for anything, Tessa concentrated on munching quietly.

They waited several hours, dozing in the morning sun. Autumn was advancing fast, but their place of concealment was sheltered from any breeze, and the midday sun soon made it comfortably warm. It was not easy, though, to lie idly while thoughts of Jeffrey's situation kept disturbing the quiet around her. Was he coming? Had Hawick caught him while trying to escape? Had they killed him? Banaugh too was worried; she could tell by the way he looked in all directions every few minutes, chewing his bottom lip.

Finally they heard noises on the road

above. With a finger raised, Banaugh signaled she should stay where she was and crept quietly away. As she listened, Tessa's heart sank. There were two horses. She prayed they would pass by, but they stopped just down from her. A saddle creaked as someone climbed down, and shortly after came an unmistakable sound as he relieved himself not ten feet away.

"I still think she went north," said a voice. "She'll want to find her uncle the king and tell on us." She recognized the voice of Dougal, the man she had first seen at Brixton Hall.

"Hawick thinks she'll head to Jedburgh," came the reply. "A girl alone would have little chance traveling overland. She'll have to find passage on a ship." That was good. They had no idea Banaugh still lived, so they sought only one person.

"I still don't see how she managed to overpower Ian, tiny thing that she is."

The other man guffawed. "He dinna want to dwell on it, did he? I'd wager his second head distracted him! Right shamed he was, though, to be o'ertaken by a lass, and in his own bedroom!"

"Dinna let Hawick hear you laugh at him, or he'll have your guts for garters," Dougal reproached the other. Sounds of metal meeting metal accompanied the conversation. The men were eating something, judging by the way their words distorted from time to time. Dougal's next statement came between chews. "We are on a wild goose chase."

"Someone had to go to Jedburgh on the chance she heads that way," the second man said reasonably. "I'd rather be here than on the way to meet Macbeth with Hawick and the others. He takes a great chance with this business."

"Hawick knows the risk," Dougal assured his friend, "but the Englishman's newest idea is a good one. The best way, I ken, for Hawick to prove his loyalty to young Malcolm is to kill Macbeth."

Below them, Tessa gasped. Jeffrey had plotted with Hawick once again. It was a terrible blow to the faith in his character that had just begun to grow in her. The man's voice went on. "He has the girl's letter from the king, which will gain him entry, and he will go as her husband, offering his services against the English and Malcolm. Once inside, he can dispatch Macbeth, signal the English, and hide until the battle is over. Once the king is dead, the castle will fall easily, I'll wager."

"All we must do is catch the girl and see

she doesna live to tell a different tale," the other added grimly.

Sounds indicated that the two were about to remount and be on their way when a splash sounded from the river. Both stopped and listened, and a second splash followed soon after. Stepping into the brush, Dougal peered down at the water but could see nothing. He turned back to his companion, and immediately another splash sounded. Now the second man joined Dougal. They carefully descended the steep bank, slippery with vegetation. As they reached the water, a decrepit rowboat floated around the bend and toward them. Someone in white huddled on the floor of the thing, obviously trying to avoid detection. With a shout, Dougal waded in as the second man stood on the bank shouting encouragement. For the tall Dougal, the river was only chest deep at this point, and he easily intercepted the old boat in mid-stream.

"Come now, lass, get up. I've got you now," he called, but the figure did not rise. Grabbing the fabric of the fine dress he had last seen the macFindlaech woman wearing, he found it stuffed with an old horse blanket, empty of any human form. Staring openmouthed at the man on the bank for a second, Dougal realized their mistake. "The horses!" he cried. The other reacted quickly, scrambling up the slick bank as best he could. He was too late. Both horses were gone, and even the sound of their retreating hooves was drowned out by Dougal's roared curses at the slip of a girl who had bested Hawick's clan a second time.

It was an exhausted and bedraggled pair who several days later approached Scone, the ancient site of kings close to the center of Scotland. Macbeth now resided in an imposing castle overlooking the River Tay, north and east of the town of Perth. The travelers had learned in bits and pieces as they journeyed that the king maintained a large household at Scone comprised of paid troops as well as Scots still loyal to Macbeth. Anxious to reach the place, the two had ridden their horses almost to death, the beasts' only rest in days being when they ferried across the Firth of Forth. Tessa and Banaugh dozed in their saddles as the autumn rains drenched them.

Tessa's emotional state teetered between manic determination and sheer despair as she encouraged her exhausted horse onward, the smell of his sweat mingled with her own unwashed scent. That Jeffrey could plot the death of her uncle was a betrayal she could never have imagined, even if, as Banaugh tried to convince her, he had done it to save his own life. She was determined to get to Macbeth's castle before Hawick and warn her uncle. No matter what he had done, he was her blood kin, and he did not deserve assassination.

As a result, the old man and his "grandson" had taken every shortcut possible, no matter how treacherous, sleeping little and eating less. Banaugh, wiry and tough to begin with, had grown even more spare, and Tessa found it necessary to use rope to hold up the breeches she wore.

As they journeyed, the pair had heard worse and worse news of Macbeth's chances of success. The king was despised, and his soldiers had deserted in large numbers. His behavior had gone from merely odd to totally unpredictable, and those around him served only from fear or greed. People spoke in whispers the rumors that had gathered around him for a year now: he had murdered not only the old king but his best friend, Banquo; he had put to death many people who had done nothing more than question his actions; and he had ordered the murder of the entire family of one Macduff, a former comrade who had fled to England, refusing to acknowledge his former comrade-in-arms Macbeth as king.

When she heard this, Tessa remembered her uncle's words concerning Macduff. "I was most wounded by his treachery." But to take revenge on wife and small children? If the rumors were true, her uncle had lost himself completely to ambition, and the Macbeth who once existed was no more. She considered turning back at one point, but something of family loyalty prevailed. Perhaps she could convince her uncle to give up the throne and go into exile. At least she could warn him of Hawick's plan, for she would not let the outlaw succeed, no matter what. Let Macbeth die in battle if he must, but not on Hawick's knife. And certainly not by Jeffrey Brixton's plan.

It was about ten miles from their destination, as they broke camp early one morning, that Tessa and Banaugh saw English soldiers for the first time. They were chilling to see, disciplined and businesslike as they made their way to war. Walking stolidly over the rough ground, their conical helmets bobbing as they stepped, their leather tunics shedding the rain as they were intended to, the troopers' eyes seemed watchful and emotionless.

They steered clear of the soldiers, since it was dangerous to be seen riding two fine horses in their present condition. They had received a few questioning looks as it was, an old man and a boy, neither one prosperous-looking, mounted on well-trained, well-bred steeds. They skirted wide of the troops, therefore, and through a forest Banaugh said was called Birnam. Once they judged themselves far enough away, they dismounted and sat for a few minutes, letting their sore muscles rest from long hours in the saddle. Their one blessing all this way had been the gold that Macbeth had given Tessa months before. They had been sparing with it, and Banaugh had kept it safely hidden, bringing out only what was needed. As a result they had been able to buy food now that they had no time to hunt or gather it. As they shared a breakfast of cheese and a small loaf of bread, neither spoke much, being tired to the point of semi-consciousness.

It was because of this silence that they heard the first sounds of chopping far off to their right. Soon the noise grew, and the sound of many hatchets filled the wood with a rhythmic pattern. Tessa was too tired to care, but Banaugh crept silently off to see what it meant. He returned with a confused look on his face. "The soldiers are chopping the branches off the trees," he told Tessa. "I dinna know what it could be for."

"Nor do I, but we'd best be on, in case they come this far," Tessa replied. Wearily they climbed into the saddles once more and headed north with a leftward slant to avoid being seen by the men whose actions continued behind them, the chops growing more distant as they rode.

A drizzling rain fell all day, and noon brought them to the castle, which had the closed look about it that signified preparation for war. No one moved outside the walls, no sheep or cattle grazed in nearby pastures, and the cottages that stood on the outer perimeter were shut tightly, no smoke trailing from their roofs.

Scone Castle sat before the Grampian Mountains like a gray obstacle to the green beyond. Poised above the River Tay, the palace overlooked the routes north to the Highlands and east through Strathmore to the coast. Across the river stood the town of Perth.

Five hundred years before, the Romans had camped here, at the very limit of their empire. They had never defeated the war-like Picts, who later came to rule Scone, but Christian missionaries had more success a few centuries later. The Culdees, or servants of God, had established themselves at Scone in the seventh century and converted the Picts. Now Scone was the place where Scotland's Christian kings were crowned. By tradition the king sat during the ceremony on the Stone of Scone, a stool of rock that sat atop Moot Hill, a knoll at the front of the castle. Tessa imagined her uncle accepting the crown of Scotland. It had been his greatest desire, but had it made him happy? She doubted it.

They rode around Moot Hill and boldly up to the castle gate. Removing the hood she had used to hide her hair, she called out, "I am Tessa macFindlaech, come to see my uncle the king on urgent business."

Several heads peered down at them over the wall, and someone must have recognized Tessa, for a few moments later the door opened enough to allow them entrance. A brusque soldier took in their muddy boots and bleary eyes with a practiced eye and sent someone to tell another someone inside the castle of her presence. Banaugh went to see to the exhausted horses. Tessa was surprised to see young Jamie, the boy she'd served with at Inverness, come to meet her. His appearance was no cleaner than it had been before, and he had a harried look about him unusual in one so young.

"Jamie, is it not? I am Tessa, whom you

once knew as Tom. I must see the king."

"Tom? But you . . ." He stopped and digested what he was seeing. Probably the boy had seen stranger things in the past year, for he adjusted well. Tessa saw reluctance in his expression. "I cannot say that he will treat you well, miss. He is sometimes himself, but not often these days. He talks to the air and starts at shadows."

"I have heard it. How does my aunt?"

"Dead." The boy's eyes stared past her and gave away nothing. She did not ask more, unsure if she wanted to know. Had the king — ? No, that was impossible. More likely Gruoch had been unable to bear the terrible dreams any longer and had found a way to put an end to her unhappiness. Her death was nothing but justice if the tales were true, that she had badgered Macbeth into murder, perhaps even helped do the deed. Still, Tessa could find it in her heart to be a little sad for her. Macbeth's lady had simply not understood the consequences of so terrible an act. Murder for political reasons might seem the nearest way to one's ambitions, but such things could not be done without grave damage to one's own soul.

"Jamie, I must see him. I will take the chance."

The youth led Tessa into the hall, once grand but now in great disarray. Rushes lay rotting on the floor with scraps of food, dirt, and worse. The trestles had not been cleared away, and the boards were littered with dishes. Overturned cups had spilled their contents onto the floor. She had had a moment's fear that her uncle might berate her for her appearance, dirty, unkempt and in dress improper for a female, but she saw at once that none of that would matter. Before a weak fire sat a large chair where Macbeth slumped, wine cup in hand.

Jamie stopped well out of range of the king's arm and announced, "Tessa macFindlaech, sire, your niece. She brings important news." Then he was gone, without waiting for dismissal, and they were left alone.

Her uncle was greatly changed, much worse than before. His eyes, which had once been steely and direct, were watery, and the lids drooped as if it were too much effort to keep them open to the world he had created for himself. His hair had gone from richly dark to shot with gray, and strong streaks of it stood up from his forehead and sprang from his temples. Where once he had appeared taut and vibrant, a man of power, now his muscles were slack and his movements slow and feeble. The wreck of the man who once was sat before her, and she despaired for him.

"Uncle," she began. "I have come to warn you of a certain treachery. One of the border Scots, more an outlaw than a laird, plans to gain entry to the castle and kill you, using my name. This Hawick stole the safe conduct you gave to me when last we met, and he will claim that I am his wife. He is the worst sort of man, and I barely escaped him with my life."

Macbeth seemed not to have heard her. His eyes squinted, and he tried to focus on her face. "Tessa? My brother's little Tessa?"

"Yes, Uncle, it is me," she replied, frustrated by his torpor. "You must listen! He will kill you if he can, to gain favor with Malcolm."

Macbeth's droopy eyes took on a glint of slyness. "Ah, my dear, he may try, but kill me he will not."

"Uncle, please listen."

"No man can kill me, you see," he continued without acknowledging her. *"No man of woman born shall harm Macbeth."* He said it in a crowing, crooning tone that Tessa recognized. The three weird sisters. He had found them, it seemed, and now parroted their words.

"Uncle, the three women who told you this — remember, I have heard their words as well. Their truth is slanted, as your old friend Banaugh warned me when first I saw them. One cannot believe the words themselves but must look beyond them. There is truth, but not the truth that seems to be." She stopped, unable to put it as she wanted to, but Macbeth paid her no mind anyway. He seemed far away, and Tessa extended a consoling hand.

"Uncle, your wife . . . I am sorry she is dead. She was . . . helpful to me." Tessa would not lie, so she could not say *kind.* Gruoch had been neither kind nor unkind, merely efficient, cordial only to those above her, and neutral to everyone else.

"She took her own life," he said in response. "She could not stand the dreams, you see. I have them too, but I am a man. I have screwed my courage to the sticking place —" He spoke as if to convince himself, but he could not complete the thought.

Jamie appeared again. He seemed to be the only personal attendant Macbeth had left, or perhaps the only one brave enough to approach the king. "Sire, a man is at the gate. He says he comes from your niece," here he glanced at Tessa, "and he carries your safe conduct."

"Kill him," Macbeth said calmly. With a start, Tessa realized that something of what she said had penetrated.

"Uncle, I . . ." she didn't know what to say.

"Tell the guard to kill him," Macbeth repeated, and Jamie left the room with a nod of assent. "Now my dear, you must go to a place of safety. There will be a battle soon, perhaps today, and I would not have you nearby." Suddenly he spoke rationally, as if he had no care except for her protection. "I suggest you make your way upriver about three miles. There is a hamlet where you will be safe. When the battle is over, you may return. I will have more time for you then."

Tessa looked sadly at this madman who could calmly order the death of a man he had never seen, the deaths of Macduff's wife and children, and even the death of his best friend, and now calmly take precautions for her safety. She thought briefly of insisting that she stay with him, but what could she do? He must fight this battle, and she must hope it would be his last. There was nothing for Macbeth now but an honorable death. She had given him a chance at that.

Jamie returned, stopping in the doorway this time, obviously not happy about what he had to tell. "Sire, when I returned, the man was gone. The guard said he had forgotten something, and that he would return shortly."

Tessa had a thought. "The old man who came with me, is he presently in the courtyard?"

"Why, yes, miss," the boy replied. "He sits waiting for you just inside the bailey gate."

Hawick had taken one look, recognized Banaugh, and made a hasty retreat, Tessa deduced. She pictured the barrel-chested outlaw hurrying away from the castle, sweating lest an arrow take him in the back as he did.

"He has learned I am here," she told Macbeth. "At least that plan is foiled."

"As I have told you, my dear, I cannot be harmed." The king was confident. "I have done what I have done, and I have lost much. But I have been given assurances. I shall live until a man not born of woman faces me, and who could that be? Furthermore, I cannot be defeated, no matter how many Englishmen come, until one Birnam Wood, which is miles from here, rises up and moves up the hillside of Dunsinane."

Tessa felt a sinking in her heart as the import of the words and what she had recently seen drew her to a terrible conclusion. "But the soldiers! We saw them, Banaugh and I. They were cutting boughs from the trees of Birnam. We did not know why they did so."

At that moment a soldier came skidding into the room, his face white. "Sire! There is . . ."

"Speak, man," Macbeth growled, his face showing that he understood the message before it was given.

"There is a forest moving toward the castle! I swear it, sire! I saw trees moving!"

Macbeth rose, his listlessness suddenly gone. It was as if a shell fell away, and the warrior behind the madman emerged. He took Tessa's shoulder and repeated his earlier words, this time with the air of command.

"Go! Now! Get into one of the boats and make your way to the hamlet. Jamie will show you the way. Stay there until this thing is decided." Suddenly he softened for a moment. "I have no one left to me, Tessa. You are the last person who has shown care for me, and you are of my blood. I have become what I never intended to be, but I am still man enough to protect a woman of my clan. Jamie!" he called, and the boy appeared. "Take this woman to Dunangus and stay there with her."

"I shall fight, sire," the boy protested.

"You shall not," the king roared, but his voice softened again. "I have chosen you to protect my niece. It is a boon that I ask. Anyone can fight, but you must be clever and brave to save her life. Can you do that?"

Jamie's stubborn look faded as he understood that he was not being banished because of his age. "Yes, sire."

Macbeth went to a box set into a wall niche and took out several gold coins, some of which he gave to the boy. "Go and get the boat ready." Macbeth stepped toward Tessa and took her into his arms. She remembered the last parting, when he had been unsure about an embrace. Now his arms held her strongly but briefly. He placed a kiss atop her head and thrust the rest of the gold into her hand, saying, "Go with God, Tessa." She felt tears on her cheeks, but her uncle never saw them, for he was off, calling for his armor and giving orders to prepare for a battle he now knew he would not win.

Tessa found her way back to the courtyard, dodging soldiers headed for their posts and serving women trying to find a place of concealment. There was chaos as people shouted and screamed, animals scrambled out of the way, and orders were called from officers to men and down the line of defenders at the wall. "We will attack!" Tessa heard as she looked frantically around for Banaugh. He appeared at her side and she clung to him in relief.

"We must be away from here, lass," Banaugh told her. "Why would he attack when he has a stout castle wall to stand behind?"

"He is mad," was Tessa's answer. "He will wager all on this last attempt, but I believe he knows now that it is for nothing. He has provided us a way out, though. We are to take to the river."

Banaugh nodded briefly and fell in behind Tessa as she led the way. They fought their way through the bailey and out the river gate, jostled and passed by others who also made their escape. On the riverbank, she looked frantically through the knot of people pushing their way into whatever crafts were available. Jamie waited beside a rowboat similar in size to the one they had stolen at Hawick's, but this one was much sturdier. A stout cudgel in his hands, he brandished it at those who tried to join him in the boat, shouting, "No! On the king's order!" People backed away and chose other means of escape while Banaugh helped Tessa into the boat, giving it a shove into the water before jumping in himself. Jamie took to the oars, navigating upstream, away from the others, who chose the easier method of floating with the current.

Soon Tessa was looking her last at Macbeth's stronghold. The sounds of the battle's onset carried clearly across the distance, making her wish she could shut her ears to them: screams and shouts, the clang of metal on metal, and the thud of metal on wood — or something softer, she imagined. Banaugh put an arm around her, and she wept for the last macFindlaech, one who had not understood that the power to rule that he had wanted so badly would bring about his ruin.

CHAPTER
TWENTY-ONE

Jamie did not follow the river's main course for long but steered into a smaller stream. Here the current was stronger, and Banaugh joined him on the seat, taking an oar. Working together the two guided the boat upstream, where after an hour's hard rowing they entered a small tarn, or lake, formed by a low-lying swale that the river passed into and out again several hundred yards later.

Tessa stared in amazement, for on the east side of the tarn stood something she had never seen before. "What is it, Banaugh?" Floating like a mirage in the center of the lake was a castle, a rather small one to be sure, but impressive in both its simplicity and its placement.

" 'Tis a crannog," the old man answered. "Once there were many sech across Scotland, bu' they ha' gradually been replaced by more modern fortresses. Tha' one is a jewel of an example, I mus' say." He spoke truly, for the small fort apparently defied gravity, sitting on the surface of the water. "They were built tha' way for safety, o' course. Wood pilings are driven int' the water, then a platform spans th' pilings an' th' fort is built o'er th' platform. Difficult t' do, o' course, but difficult for an enemy t' reach as well. The walkway o' th' far side, between th' gate an' th' lake edge, can be taken up for defense."

Tessa saw that the feature Banaugh indicated was made of wooden sections roped together. These could easily be pulled back if danger approached, effectively protecting the inhabitants from any threat on horseback or afoot.

"What do you know of this place?" she asked Jamie.

"Tha' is Arleigh. The auld laird died some time back, so th' runnin' o' th' place is left to 'is wife, th' Lady Miriam. Tha' is a strange one, folk say. A body nae kens hae she will tak' visitors. " 'Tis best t' pass by quiet."

"Is this lady not in danger with English troops so close by? We should warn her."

"Ach, miss, tha' will know it all," Jamie averred. "Lady Miriam is hersel' nae one t' leave th' crannog, bu' she hears ever'thing an' kens ever'thing. She is said by some t' be a witch!" He made the sign to ward off evil as he spoke, and his young face pinched with earnestness.

Tessa cast a glance at Banaugh, who shook his head slightly. They had no need of more strange acquaintances. Nodding, she signaled her agreement that they pass by, and the two pulled at the oars again. By tacit consent the crossing was silent, and they skirted the far side of the tarn, hoping to enter the river without attracting the attention of those in the crannog.

It was not to be, however, for when they neared the mouth of the river, two small rowboats appeared at either side of it, pushed from places of hiding on the shore. The men in them must have circled the tarn's rim quickly and stealthily and boarded boats stored there for the express purpose of intercepting travelers. Each craft held two armed soldiers who knelt menacingly fore and aft, arrows nocked in bowstrings half-taut. Two sturdy rowers sat ready to move into place at the river's mouth, blocking passage. One of the men, a strongly built fellow with pale hair, hailed them. He alone wore the long sword some Scots preferred. Most fighting men chose the bow or the spear, cheaper weapons to make and maintain.

"Travelers, who are ye and where do ye travel?"

Banaugh nudged Jamie to answer, hoping they could pass for locals. "I am James, son o' James the Shepherd. I travel upriver t' Dunangus, m' home village."

The man, Tessa could now see, was young but square-jawed and stone-faced, giving no indication of amity. "And who are your companions?"

Banaugh spoke for them. "We are on our way t' Loch Lomond. The laddie here offered space i' his boat for help wi' th' rowing, the better for us a' to arrive quickly."

The man showed no sign of belief or disbelief, waiting until Banaugh finished and then demanding, "My lady begs your attendance upon her so she may speak with ye."

"We wuld nae at another time refuse a lady's request, bu' we needs must continue on our way before night catches us on th' river. We hae some urgent business at Loch Lomond tha' argues our traveling onward." Banaugh tried for firm politeness.

Just as firmly the soldier answered, "Your business must wait. As for a night on the river, there is no need to concern yourselves with that. My lady will provide you with food, drink, and a place to rest comfortably. She insists that you accept her invitation."

It was no request, however politely it was phrased. The men stood ready to stop them if they tried to pass, and their manner conveyed determination to conduct the three of them to the lady of the crannog.

"I think we must go with them, Banaugh," Tessa murmured.

"Aye, lass, ye hae th' right o' it," he muttered back. "I hope tha' th' Widow Miriam is nae so hard t' deal wi' as young Jamie here has heard."

The three were escorted to a water gate on the lake side of the crannog. An opening in the wall allowed Jamie to row right into the structure and up to a pier guarded by two more men at arms. Tying up the boat, the men assisted the three of them up wooden steps to the platform level. As they stood wondering what would happen next, the pale giant alighted from his own boat and joined them. "This way." He opened a door at the back of the boathouse and ushered them through it.

A short passageway led to an open hall where the man stopped and waited, no expression on his face. Tessa looked around her in some wonder. One would not guess that they stood on water, for the inside of the place was warmer, drier, and more comfortable than many castles she had been in. The walls were hung with tapestries the like of which she had never seen, not pictures as she was used to, but geometric shapes portrayed in beautifully deep colors. The furnishings, too, were different from the ordinary, with curves where most pieces had corners.

Movement in a doorway opposite caught her eye, and there stood a young woman of extraordinary and exotic beauty. She had large, almond-shaped brown eyes, dusky skin, and hair as black and shiny as obsidian. Her plain blue dress was traditionally cut, but she had added a trailing scarf and a necklace of intricate design, lending a foreign look to the ensemble that matched her appearance. Tessa and she were about the same age, but clearly not of the same race or background.

The young woman pushed before her a chair on wheels, another surprise. In it sat a pathetically shrunken form swathed in rich black. Even the head was covered so that only the face and two gnarled hands showed. The limbs were twisted cruelly and the back so curved that the afflicted woman had to hold her head at an acute angle to see before her. The face that met Tessa's, though, was intelligent and curious, with black eyes that shone with interest and features that revealed first the ravages of years of pain, but beneath that traces of former beauty, before illness had ruined it so completely.

The woman looked carefully at each of the newcomers, her gaze settling on Tessa in some private moment of decision. At a sign from the chair's occupant, the stone giant spoke, and Tessa detected a different note in his voice, some human warmth. "The Lady Miriam of Arleigh gives you greetings. You two" — he indicated Jamie and Banaugh — "will go with Ayla, who will attend to your needs so that you are pre . . . pared for the evening meal." He had almost said "presentable," and Tessa knew that they must be offensive to both the eye and the nose. "When the interview is over, Ayla will also see to your needs," he told Tessa. With a curt nod, he left the room.

The old one in the wheeled chair said nothing. The other, who stood with eyes downcast until the blond man was gone, now looked at them with frank curiosity. Finally she spoke to Jamie and Banaugh, her voice low and pleasing. "Please follow me. The Lady Miriam wishes to speak to your companion alone. You are quite safe and will be reunited at the evening meal."

The question foremost in Tessa's mind at this point was, should she reveal her sex to these people or attempt to remain disguised? Instinct told her that if they had meant her ill, she would already be dead. On a moment's decision, she spoke for the first time, choosing to trust her first impression.

"I am Tessa, late of the king's household. I will be glad to answer the lady's questions, and grateful if you can show my companions a place to rest."

Surprise flickered across the girl's face, but the older woman's face showed satisfaction that she had chosen correctly. She said nothing, but on Ayla's face a shy smile bloomed. "Tessa," she repeated. "I will provide hot water, clean clothing, and refreshment. If you will come with me, sir" — she bowed slightly to Banaugh — "and the other gentleman will go with this lad . . ." A serving boy who had stood back until this moment came forward, trying to maintain a dignified air but clearly excited to be given responsibility for the needs of guests. For his part, Jamie straightened visibly at being referred to as a gentleman. Banaugh started to object at being separated from Tessa, but she stepped in.

"Go ahead, Banaugh. It will be all right."

She smiled at Ayla, who for some reason inspired trust. The two left with their escorts, and Tessa found herself alone with the pitifully deformed woman, who had as yet not spoken a word.

Recalling Jamie's warning that Miriam was "odd" and believed by some to be a witch, Tessa tried to look past the obvious ugliness and find the personality beneath. The woman let her form her own impression, saying nothing. She supposed this place could be another like Hawick's, where travelers were held for ransom or perhaps murdered for their goods, but she did not think so. In this woman's eyes Tessa saw only interest, not the greed so easily read in Hawick's expression or the self-interest in Mairie's. Truth would do here, not all of it, perhaps, but most.

"You seek news of Macbeth?" she asked the woman.

"Yes," the voice was surprisingly strong, belying her physical weakness. "It is important to my people that we know what lies before us."

Did the woman hope to see the king deposed? Many did, judging from talk she and Banaugh had heard on the trip north. The woman interrupted her thoughts with an assurance, for the first time showing some humanity. "You should know, whoever you may be, that I wish the king well, and I care not who knows it. He has been for many years our friend, and lately our liege lord. He and my husband traveled together as young men, to Spain, where we became friends. He was present at my wedding to Arbeen Arleigh."

Tessa's surprise must have shown plainly, for the lady chuckled. Her explanation explained the odd differences in the castle's furnishings, the exotic look of the servant girl Ayla, and the stories and rumors that Jamie had heard of this place and this woman. Her foreignness alone would have been enough to convince the superstitious locals that she was a witch. Digesting the information about her friendship with Macbeth, Tessa revised her assessment of the situation. Here was an ally who might be trusted with all of the truth. Still, she was cautious.

"I cannot tell you the final outcome, but I was with the king when the battle began. The English troops, supporting Malcolm Canmore, came upon his castle in great strength. Many of the king's troops deserted him in the days before, and many fled with us as we escaped. The king chose to leave the castle and . . . meet his enemies." Here the image of her uncle's despairing mien as he made that decision overpowered her, and her eyes filled with tears.

"He sent you to safety?" The dark eyes showed understanding that this girl disguised as a peasant boy was somehow valuable to Macbeth. Tessa wondered how she had guessed that of the three visitors, this one was more than appearances indicated.

"Yes. He . . . had lost so much, he said. He wanted me to live. I —" The tensions of her last encounter and the escape caught up with her again, and Tessa fought back tears. "I doubt he has survived, although he had some hope of it, claiming he cannot be killed."

". . . by a man born of woman. Yes, he told me." The old woman's tone revealed disbelief in Macbeth's claim, and Tessa's eyes widened at the information. "Perhaps I should explain who I am, and that will give you some idea of how much you will want to trust me." This was said in a matter-of-fact tone, acknowledging the need Tessa might feel to lie, or at least withhold some facts. "Twenty years ago, more or less, I lived in Spain. I am a Moor. Are you acquainted with my people?"

Tessa blushed and admitted that she knew little aside from the fact that the Moors ruled Spain and were of a religion other than Christian. She had vague memories of her father's stories of his travels and of the Islamic Spaniards who had befriended him. She recalled tales of their odd customs, their interesting religion, and their impressive accomplishments.

Miriam smiled. "My people came from Africa three hundred years ago and conquered the Gothic tribes of Spain. Although we are Muslims, followers of the Prophet Mohammed, we gained the respect of many Christians because of our devotion to learning. Still, our empire has begun to fail of late, and it is only a matter of time until we are driven from Spain. The vizier, Almazor, struggles to keep his power, but there is dissention within the government and strong movements outside it to Christianize Spain once more. It is sad to see the end of an era when Christians and Muslims lived together in peace."

Miriam examined her clawlike hands for a moment. "Of course, I cared little about history and politics as a girl. I grew up in a beautiful city called Granada where my father's wealth provided me with lovely things, a good education, and a happy childhood. When I was fifteen, three young men came into my life. They were on a sort of

319

discovery tour, traveling through Europe as knights-errant, winning tournaments and sampling the delights of each city they visited. They would never have come into contact with us except for an unusual circumstance.

"As my father returned from a business trip, word got out that he carried a large sum of money. A band of brigands attacked his party, killing the two guards he'd hired. He managed to ride off, but the robbers pursued and would have overtaken him except for the three young men I mentioned earlier. Seeing his situation they came to his rescue, defeating all six bandits and killing two. My father was so grateful that he invited these young men to stay in his home, where he rewarded them and ordered a banquet in their honor."

"And there you met them?"

The woman smiled and her ravaged face was transformed. "Not at first. It is not the custom among Muslims to introduce females of the household to guests. Still, my father was very proud of me, and especially of my musical talent. He was not as strict as some, and after several visits, when the young men had shown themselves to be honorable sorts and good companions, he asked me to sing and play the lute for them.

I did so, completely veiled, of course, but I became enthralled with these three giants, Arbeen in particular.

"I arranged to play for them more and more often." She stopped momentarily and looked again at her hands, now twisted and useless with huge lumps at the joints. "I was a good musician — before this. Arbeen was always soothed by the sound of my lute, and he used to beg me to play in the evenings, until he saw how much it hurt me. My husband was always concerned for my comfort, even at the last, when he was in such pain himself."

Her voice took on a dreamy quality, as if she had forgotten Tessa was there. "His heart failed him, and he slowly faded from the man I fell in love with in Granada to a pitiful shell, unable to cross this room without tiring. Still, I loved him just as much . . ." With an effort, Miriam pulled herself back to the story.

"At any rate, much to my father's dismay, I found myself in love with this pale-skinned, red-haired Scotsman, and he with me. We began meeting in secret, with his two friends playing Cupid by distracting Father's attention. They would ask him to take them hawking or riding, and Arbeen would claim prior engagements. I would tell my chaperone that I simply must visit the marketplace, and there he would be. The poor woman didn't know whose anger to fear more, mine or my father's, but in the end I won."

Miriam shifted her body to a less painful position, and the chair squeaked in protest. "I was a headstrong girl, you see, determined to have my way. In the end I told my father that I would marry Arbeen and no other. At first he raged, threatened to lock me away, threatened to marry me to the first Muslim who would have such a witless woman, but I knew him well. Father could deny me nothing, and in the end I got my Scotsman."

Tessa imagined the shocked reaction of Miriam's friends and family. The Moors considered themselves more advanced than Europeans in general, but Scots were seen as mere tribesmen with no culture whatsoever. The wedding must have been the talk of Granada for months.

"My father gave in," the lady continued, "on the condition that Arbeen agreed to live in Granada. His two friends returned to Scotland without him. He tried to be happy there, but I knew he missed his homeland. When my father died, I suggested we come here to live, and I have never looked back."

The lady's lips closed as if she could tell more but would not. Living here had probably not been easy for her.

Clarification was needed on one point, though Tessa thought she knew the answer. "The two companions who accompanied your husband to Granada . . . ?"

"Macbeth and Kenneth macFindlaech," came the brusque answer, "as if you did not already know. Did your father not tell you of his friend and his Arab wife?"

Tessa blushed. "He did, but it was like the fairy tales he also told. I was never sure it was true. He did not know that you had come to Scotland."

Miriam nodded. "Kenneth had by then rejected Scottish politics and moved into the hills. He was always the gentler of the two, careful of everyone's feelings and concerned with the wrongs of the world." She smiled. "He fretted over our marriage, fearing we would be outcasts."

"And were you?"

Miriam considered her answer. "We were, but it meant little to us since we wanted only each other's company. The Moors snubbed Arbeen's lack of sophistication, and the Scots refused to accept my race and religion. Aside from your uncle and a few others, we were left to ourselves."

"How did you know he is my uncle? I never said so."

Miriam smiled slyly. "You wonder if the tales of witchcraft might be true? It is not magic, merely deduction and years of observing people's behavior. You have your father's eyes and his way of tilting your head to one side when you ask a question. Macbeth took pains to get you away from danger, which means he cares about you. I know he has but one brother —" She shrugged expressively.

"Had. My father died several years ago."

"I am sorry. Kenneth was a good man." She smiled in remembrance. "I think I could have fallen in love with any of them back then. They were so big and full of life, so different from what I had known."

"I'm sure they were impressed with you as well."

"In those days I was not as you see me, of course. I was thought a beauty. Even the Scottish bigots admitted that: 'Poor Arbeen — blinded by the charms of a heathen.' This . . . affliction came on slowly, over the years, first just stiffness in the joints, then more and more difficulty, until I could no longer walk, or weave, or even hold a book." It appeared that the last was the most difficult to accept.

324

"You saw my uncle recently?"

"Yes. He had not been here since Arbeen's funeral, but about ten days ago he appeared at the lakeshore, looking lost and half-dazed. Hamish brought him across in a boat, and he stayed a few hours, telling strange things."

Tessa nodded. "About three weird women?"

Miriam's eyes showed interest. "You know of them?"

"I have met them."

"They said he could not be killed by an ordinary man."

"He said something of the same to me. I don't remember the exact words."

" 'No man of woman born shall harm Macbeth,' " Miriam quoted.

"When they predicted my future, I thought them mad," Tessa said, biting her lip, "but the things they said came true. Not in the way I imagined, but true, nonetheless." Suddenly she felt weary beyond speech. So much had happened to her since she first met those three. They had foreseen, if not engineered, the ruination of her family. Tears stung her eyes.

"I would be interested in hearing more about that," said Miriam, her face softening at the girl's unhappiness, "but I have worn you out with an old woman's babbling."

Ayla appeared in the doorway, where she probably had awaited some signal from the lady of the manor. "It is almost time to eat, and you have had no chance to refresh yourself." Miriam gestured to Ayla, who moved to a small closet directly off the large room, gesturing for Tessa to follow. "We will continue our conversation later, if you are so inclined," Miriam said as a servant came forward to assist her, pushing the chair from the room.

Once inside the smaller room, Ayla pulled a curtain for privacy and invited Tessa to sit on a small cot while they waited for the things she had arranged for her guest's comfort. She sat on a nearby stool.

"You will feel better when you have bathed and changed. I've had your things brought up from the boat."

"You are very kind." Tessa breathed a sigh of some depth. "I've had so many surprises today I don't know how I feel. We were not sure if our presence here would be welcome or not." She didn't say what she had heard.

"The lady allows tales of her prickliness to circulate. It discourages visitors." Ayla smiled. "Mystery and dark hints are her way of protecting her territory. I am sorry if Hamish frightened you on the tarn. He is utterly devoted to our lady, but he is sometimes formidable." An understatement, but it was good to hear that he was loyal to Miriam. "Hamish is responsible for our defense, but you will see that we are very few in number. This has made him rather more serious than he was in the past, when he was only one of Arbeen's lieutenants."

"I'm sure it is a strain to be in charge of the lady's lands as well as her safety."

"Laird Arleigh trusted Hamish completely. Because he was away much of the time from his lands in his younger days, he refortified this old crannog to make it difficult for invaders to reach. Since it lies upriver and away from main travel ways, there aren't many passersby, and we have had no trouble. Still, since the laird's death, Hamish spends much time inspecting, repairing, and watching." She sounded almost angry at her protector's industriousness.

A servant appeared at that moment with a ewer of hot water, which she poured into a basin, mixing it with cold from a pitcher already there. "I will leave you to yourself," Ayla told Tessa. "You will hear a bell when dinner is prepared, and you will see your friends again at the meal." Then she was gone, the servant following with a quick bob of respect.

CHAPTER
TWENTY-TWO

Tessa had the forgotten luxury of washing herself all over with warm water, a soft cloth, and fragrant soap — much nicer than the hurried splashes in cold streams that had served for weeks. Afterward, she dressed herself in a clean linen shift over which she pulled a light blue dress, its edges decorated with embroidered flowers. Her hair she arranged as best she could. It was too long to look boyish now but too short to be truly feminine. Without a polished brass mirror she had no way to know what the effect of her preparations amounted to, but in truth she looked charming with her tumble of auburn hair stopping just over the white and blue of her costume.

When the bell rang for dinner, Tessa stepped through the curtain and into the great hall with curiosity. It was a small household that greeted her. Only about twelve people gathered for the meal, the soldiers she had seen earlier and several ladies who seemed likely to be their wives. A long table was set for sixteen with real plates, real glass goblets, and something Tessa had never seen before, forks beside each place.

A servant indicated her place by pulling out a chair for Tessa, not the usual bench, and she seated herself just as Banaugh and Jamie entered the hall. The eyes of both lit up to see her, and they looked quite changed, being clean and neat. Jamie had probably never been so well groomed in his life.

As they took chairs on Tessa's right, Banaugh rubbed his beard thoughtfully. "They sent a wee foreign man t' trim me up," he told her with a grin. "He was clever an' quick as a squirrel, an' th' blade he used was somethin'. D' ye no' think me twa sae handsome?"

She laughingly assured him that he had never looked better, then complimented Jamie's appearance as well. For once his hair did not stick up like bristles from his head, and his plain face shone with pleasure at Tessa's attention.

There was a small stir among those at the table, and the three looked up to see Ayla, pushing before her the wheeled chair in which Lady Miriam sat. She had changed for dinner into a robe of silk, beautifully patterned in blues and greens, with a blue headpiece again hiding her hair and forehead. It was a brave attempt, but her body was still pitiful in its unnatural shape.

Ayla maneuvered the chair up to its place at the head of the table, then seated herself beside the lady. At a gesture from Miriam, platters of astonishing variety were brought in and placed on the boards. No one moved to begin the meal, however, and Jamie's anxious eyes sought Tessa's, wondering what they waited for. The answer came when, at a signal from Ayla, the assembly stood as one, Tessa and the two males hurriedly following custom. A dark-skinned man in strange clothing began without preamble a sing-song chant that Tessa recognized as a prayer, although she had heard nothing like it before. After the chant, Miriam and Ayla washed their hands and feet in a silver bowl held by a servant while another servant handed each one a small towel on which to dry them.

When this was finished, Hamish, standing on the lady's left side, said a simple prayer of thanks for the meal, one that Tessa and her two companions understood. Afterward there was silence as every head bowed for several minutes. Finally, a movement from Ayla ended the silence. With a chanted "Amen," everyone was seated once more. That grace had been asked was apparent, but the style was unusual to say the least, a mixture of Christian and Islamic customs. Immediately the meal began, with accompanying chatter and good humor. Food was offered, drinks poured, and things began to feel more normal.

Tessa was delighted with the fork, which she used after watching Ayla's deft movement. It was vastly superior for keeping one's fingers clean, but she noticed that bits of cloth were placed beside each plate for wiping hands that did become greasy. Much better than grease-spots on the clothing, she thought, and resolved that if ever she had a home of her own, forks and these useful bits of cloth would be part of its furnishings.

During the meal, Miriam chatted with various people, but her eyes wandered often to Tessa. Clearly she hoped they could speak further. At one point she leaned toward the girl, who was on Ayla's right. "You have Macbeth's way of watching and learning," she said approvingly. "Those anxious to learn make the best companions. Your uncle helped me to learn your language, never laughing at my mistakes and always explaining clearly why a thing was so."

Tessa's mind flashed back to Eleanor Brixton, who had done the same for her, teaching her how to behave like an English lady with no disparagement of her Scottish ways. She understood the gratitude Miriam must have felt for one who helped make a strange society less confusing.

Miriam finished, "I will always remember that he treated me well when others avoided me, calling me 'foreign witch' and 'heathen.' Macbeth macFindlaech was a man who could see more than two feet from his nose."

Tessa could have argued that Macbeth had not been able to see past his own ambitions, but it was not the time for such a statement. She made a response that was germane but not direct. "Did you know Macbeth's lady? I served her until I went to England. When I returned yesterday they told me she is dead."

"Is she," Miriam responded. Her face showed pity but not sadness, and she spoke bluntly. "She and I were of an age, but I found her cold. It might have been my Arab blood that made her shun me, but I sensed something within the lady herself. Once Macbeth married her, we saw him less and less frequently."

Again Tessa could have said more than she did. Looking at Miriam, one would think her ancient, as she herself had at first, but she was of her parents' generation — old, certainly, to one not yet nineteen, but not ancient. Her summation of Gruoch's character was acutely drawn. Tessa's aunt had had no warmth for those around her except Macbeth himself. Despite the fact that Gruoch had indeed loved her husband, she had perhaps destroyed him with her love, demanding more of him than he could give and leaving him the creature Tessa had last seen: haunted, bestial, devoid of the human kindness that might have saved his kingship and his life.

No, Tessa corrected herself. Macbeth had chosen his own way and it would be wrong to blame his wife for his crimes. But sometimes people chose mates who brought out their worst parts. Through his own weakness and his wife's, Macbeth had become a man of blood.

Tessa's face must have shown something of her dark thoughts, for like a good hostess Miriam changed the subject to more neutral things, asking politely about young Jamie's family and Banaugh's health. When the meal was completed, however, she invited Tessa to accompany her to a "ladies' bower."

She excused herself, telling Tessa's companions, "We dine simply at Arleigh, and there is no entertainment most evenings. Still, the men of the household will share some passable wine with you if you will stay and share your experiences of the world with them." With that Ayla pushed the lady's chair from the great hall, and Tessa followed.

They ascended a small ramp that ran alongside six steps leading to a half-story section of the crannog. Ayla saw Tessa's look of interest and explained the layout of the structure. "Beneath this level is the pier where you entered and a storage area that includes some underwater shelves as well as dry ones. It keeps things cool and slows spoilage, like a root cellar. That space allows a raised section on this level for Lady Miriam, who finds the damp painful." They entered a small room in which a cheerful fire burned in a metal brazier. A window view opposite the doorway took Tessa's breath away. The moon had risen over the tarn, throwing ever-smaller images of itself in gold on the gently moving water.

"It is beautiful," Tessa murmured.

"Yes," the lady agreed. "Some have wondered why I stayed on in Scotland when my husband died. There are many reasons, but that view is not the least of them."

"It must have been hard for you," Tessa said, thinking how much worse this woman's situation was than hers had been in London. She had felt she did not belong there at times, but to be of another race, another faith! Among provincial Scots who had no understanding of her background, Miriam had probably been snubbed and criticized at every turn.

"Oh, sometimes it was," the lady admitted now with a dismissive gesture. "But I count it all worthwhile since I had the love of a wonderful man and a beautiful daughter." As she smiled at Ayla, Tessa mentally chided herself. She should have guessed. The girl looked Arabic but dressed and spoke like a Scotswoman. Her retiring demeanor had caused Tessa to take her for a servant, and she had not identified herself as the daughter of the house. Ayla smiled shyly as she took in Tessa's expression. "I misled you only to please my mother, who is sometimes overly concerned for my safety."

"Ayla is my overseer, bailiff, and a hundred other things as well as my daughter," Miriam explained. "But I am careful when strangers visit, lest she become the subject of wagging tongues. Since I have become crippled, as you see me, she has taken over most of the work as thane of Arleigh." Her eyes softened. "Her life has not been easy, I know. There is nothing here for a young woman, no friends, no parties —"

"Mother, I want none of that," Ayla hastened to reassure her. "I am content here with the beauty of the place, the people around me that I love, and my studies."

Miriam looked proud, her rather hooked nose almost meeting her lips. "Later Ayla will show you her library. Do you read, by any chance?" Her tone was doubtful.

"I do," Tessa was proud to answer. "My father believed in education, although my mother did not approve."

Miriam sniffed in dismissal of such a mother. "We had only Ayla, but I have seen to it that she lacks nothing that would advance her education."

Tessa smiled. "My father had six daughters, but I was the only one interested in books." She added in half-hearted defense of her dead mother, "Most Scotswomen see little value in that sort of learning."

Miriam's face clouded. "It is sometimes so in my homeland also, but my father provided me with an education. Because my husband agreed, Ayla reads Greek and Latin as well as English, and she has mathematics." Ayla, standing behind the chair, gave Tessa a look that conveyed the universal exasperation of young women whose mothers sing their praises to an embarrassing degree.

Tessa, obliging both her hosts, complimented them and changed the subject. "You wished to know more of Macbeth's situation." She quickly related her coming through Birnam Wood, the warning she carried to Macbeth that had sent Hawick scurrying away, and the attack, ending with the king's order that Jamie take her to his village.

"I know the place," Miriam said when she mentioned Dunangus. "It is not much. You are welcome to stay here with us if you prefer. It will be more comfortable."

"I thank you for that," Tessa replied, "but I must go on. The boy's parents will hear of the English attack and worry about their son. Besides, I would not put you in any danger. Malcolm's men might seek me here, but they will not suppose I would hide in a lowly place like Dunangus." She shrugged, "I do not know how much danger there is. I am the king's niece, but I have no power . . ."

"Oh, but you are wrong there," Miriam interrupted. "I see a way in which you would be very valuable to the English. You would link Macbeth's clan to Malcolm, solidifying his claim to the throne."

Tessa felt a surge of panic: again to become a pawn in the machinations of power! The lady was not timid in sharing her opinion of the new king. "Disloyal puppy! To ask English invaders into our country to help him do what he could not do on his own. Whatever Macbeth had become, he was no traitor to his own people."

Tessa was surprised that Miriam defended her uncle. All she had heard since returning north were complaints of his erratic behavior and rumors of deaths at his hand. Miriam continued, "I know what they say of Macbeth, and perhaps it is true. If he killed old Duncan, then it may be that he deserves to die. But who is to say that Malcolm himself did not kill his father? Was he not at Inverness too, and is that not what Macbeth claims happened?"

"Yes, but —"

"Don't be too quick to believe rumor and gossip. Malcolm and Donalbain fled after Duncan's death. Malcolm went to England to raise an army, but where did his brother go? It may be that he stayed behind to begin a secret campaign against Macbeth, whispering lies and doing deeds that undermined his kingship."

Tessa considered this, then shook her

head. "I have seen him, though, seen the changes in him. He was quite distracted and plagued with guilt."

Miriam nodded. "I witnessed his changed demeanor as well. Still, leadership is difficult, and everything a king does affects hundreds, even thousands, of lives. The strain may have been too much for Macbeth, and other forces may have contributed to his madness as well."

Tessa's mind returned to the three wild women who had teased both her and her uncle with predictions for the future couched in confusing terms. Had they been toying with them, trying to see how far each would go to make the predictions come true? Macbeth had certainly become obsessed with their words.

"We should not draw hasty conclusions," the lady finished. "Macbeth was a good man when I met him twenty years ago, as good as his brother Kenneth, although different. They had served the old king well, the man Duncan killed to take the throne for himself."

Miriam stressed the last words, reminding Tessa that Scottish kings were often as not born of violence. The lady gave her reason to believe in her uncle, to conclude that he was innocent of some, maybe most, of what was being said of him. Victors would tell the story in their way, but she did not have to believe it. Even if she could not convince herself of his innocence, there was at least justification for Macbeth's taking control of Scotland if Duncan had indeed grown weak and endangered the country. It helped to at least allow these possibilities into her mind, and she was grateful to Miriam for pointing them out.

"I am, of course, prejudiced," the old lady admitted. "When I came to Scotland, only Macbeth treated me with true friendship, having seen a bit of the world himself. I continue to worship in my own way, although I allow equal observance of Christian and Muslim traditions. Macbeth took an interest in my religion, even read the Qu'ran, and understood that the God we both worship is the same.

"When Arbeen was alive, your uncle often came here to visit, saying it was a restful spot where war and bickering did not intrude. He loved the things I'd brought from my father's home, the tapestries, rugs, and furniture." She chuckled ironically. "Of course, I had no idea I was bringing them for a reason. At home they were merely familiar objects that I loved. Here, they serve to keep out the cold winds and the

Scottish winters. But we did have good times, both here at Arleigh and back in Spain, when your father was there, too."

"I'm so glad you knew them as they were, before . . ." Tessa thought of her harassed father, trying to please a shrewish wife and provide for six daughters. How carefree his days in Spain must have seemed.

Miriam smiled. "When Duncan killed the old king and took the throne, your father was sickened by it. That is why the three set off to see the world. They accepted Duncan's right to rule, but Kenneth in particular found it difficult to do so. While they were gone, their own father was killed and his lands taken by some relative. When the news came, Kenneth vowed he would serve no man, although he would take no part in a rebellion."

Miriam coughed with a dry, useless spasm that seemed to cause her pain. "They had a terrible argument over the situation, Macbeth feeling that it was their duty to avenge their father's death, and Kenneth saying there had been enough Scottish blood shed already. In the end they returned home, and Kenneth went off to the mountains. Macbeth won back his lands and progressed to the fore among Duncan's generals. That is the most telling thing about the brothers:

341

Kenneth rejected the world's values and Macbeth embraced them."

Tessa now understood the last piece of her family's puzzle, why her father had had no contact with his only brother. Distance had separated them, true enough, but the real separation had been deeper, a difference in their understanding of the demands of manhood. Macbeth's understanding, whatever one might believe about his actions, had led him to violence, very possibly to a violent death.

Later Tessa went with Ayla to the library mentioned by her mother. It was indeed impressive, with many books that Tessa would have loved to read had she time. As they perused them, Ayla touched the covers of certain favorites lovingly, and Tessa recognized the affection that many a lonely person naturally has for books that relieve daily tedium, transporting the reader to other worlds.

"I have read this one many times," Ayla told her, indicating a volume of Ovid's poetry. Tessa was privately amused that a girl with such Arabic features produced a Highland burr similar to her own. "It has many verses concerning love between a man and a woman." Her dark eyes met Tessa's. "Have you ever been in love?"

Recognizing a need in the girl to confide in someone her own age, someone who might feel as she did about things, she answered honestly. "I have, but I'm not sure it was a wise love."

Ayla's round face dimpled in a smile. "Is love wise? One has no ability to choose. It simply exists."

"That may be, but should it not be extinguished if it is a foolish love? If the other is unworthy of affection?"

Ayla's brow furrowed in sympathy. "Is this what you experienced?"

"Yes," Tessa answered, although her heart did not accept it still. Feeling a desire to share her misgivings with a stranger, one whom she would never meet again, Tessa went on. "I met a man who treated me badly —" Seeing the girl's horror, she hastened to explain. "Oh, he did not abuse me, but he betrayed me, separated me from my family."

"From the king?"

"Yes. I went to England and lived there for a year. When I returned to Scotland, we met again, and I realized that I loved him. I thought he loved me in return, but then he again betrayed me, plotting against my uncle, even planning to assassinate him."

Ayla's eyes grew round. "That is a serious

thing, if you are sure that he did so."

"Banaugh and I heard two of the assassin's men saying that 'the Englishman' had suggested a way to kill Macbeth. Jeffrey was the only Englishman within miles."

"But if he is an enemy of your uncle, that does not make him your enemy, especially now that . . . things may have changed."

"No matter what has happened to the king, I cannot forgive Jeffrey's treachery. He pretends to care for me when we are together, but there are other women that he also cares for. He changes, like a lizard my father once described to me that can change its color to suit its surroundings." She thought of that first night she had seen Jeffrey, when he played the part of an insipid fop, and of the glimpses she had seen of the real Jeffrey, his anger when she read his journal, his frustration as he tried to remember his past, his determination to free her from Hawick's clutches. There was good in him, but how could she forgive his plotting Macbeth's death, his consorting with Mairie and Hawick, his betrayal of his own brother with Eleanor, his brother's wife?

Ayla, having no experience with such things, had no comment, and Tessa turned the discussion. "And is there a special man in your life, Ayla, to make you speak of love?"

The girl blushed, her cheeks turning a deep rose. "There is a man I find attractive, but he does not notice me," she said earnestly.

Tessa felt like she was back in London giving lessons to Mary in how to flirt. "Men can be very slow to reveal their attraction to a woman," she said, frowning at their perversity. "Sometimes it is the female who must begin, for men are shy in love for all their courage in other things. How often do you see this man?"

"Every day." At Tessa's look of surprise, Ayla smiled. "It is Hamish, the one who brought you here. He seems stern at first, but he is very sweet."

So the dour Hamish had another side, or maybe he was attractive to Ayla only because there were no other choices available. Whatever the case, the girl's face beamed when she spoke his name, so Tessa continued her impromptu lesson.

"With a man like Hamish you might begin by asking for his instruction in something. He will feel it his duty to assist you, and the two of you can get to know each other better in that way. Does Hamish have a bow? You could become interested in archery."

The girl's face crinkled in disbelief. "I could never manage Hamish's bow. It is far too strong for me."

"As it would be for a child, but they are taught with smaller, more pliant ones. Tell Hamish you wish to learn so that you can entertain your mother." Tessa rose and paced the room, warming to her topic. "It is perfect, because he will have to stand very close to you to teach the proper technique, and it is not a skill learned in a few days. He will spend time with you each day, and eventually you will overcome his reserve." With a face and form like Ayla's, no man could be immune for long.

Ayla was skeptical. "What if I am not very good?"

"All the better. It will take more time, and he will feel superior, being the better shot."

The girl had one more question. "And if I become very good and can outshoot him, what then?"

Tessa grinned. "First, you will find out what sort he truly is, for if he can accept defeat at the hands of a woman gracefully, you have a gem among men. Then, you give all the credit to him for being the best of instructors, and you have won him back again."

"You are very wise," Ayla said with a

laugh. "I will begin tomorrow on my campaign."

"Will your mother approve?" Tessa hoped she hadn't added fuel to a fire the lady would rather see fading.

Ayla's face sobered. "My prospects are not many, as you might guess. We are mostly shunned by the Scots as foreigners, some say witches. Our strong site and a few loyal retainers protect us, but most are older men who served my father. Hamish comes from a good family. His father was Arleigh's friend, and he has been invaluable since my father died, keeping strict watch on what occurs around us, because we have . . . a bit of wealth."

It was a not a confidence she would not have shared with most visitors, but Tessa had noticed the signs of prosperity, some of them Arabic, some Scottish. Evidently the marriage had united two well-to-do families.

"We keep to ourselves so that few are reminded of two women defending a castle. If Hamish and I were wed, it would strengthen our position, and our children would be more accepted as second-generation Scots. My mother would never force me to marry Hamish, but if we find we suit each other, she will be glad to have my future settled."

Ayla's manner was typical of girls of the age. Hamish was the man she should fall in love with so she had, as a good daughter and steward of her people's welfare.

The girls talked far into the night, each finding in the other something she had lacked, a confidante, a peer, and a sounding board for ideas. They spoke of books, of people, and of the world, finding they agreed on most things but comfortable with the minor variances they found in their opinions. Ayla was more idealistic, having little experience outside her books, and Tessa was more prone to be critical, especially of the place of women in the world. She told Ayla of Eleanor, of her sister Meg, and even of Auntie Madeline, women with much potential that went unappreciated. Ayla listened but in the end disagreed with Tessa. "The talents of the women you speak of are not ignored. They run their households, they raise their families, they gain the love and respect of those around them. They seem to have won your love and respect as well. Who can count that as failure?"

Tessa had to admit the truth of that, but she still wondered at a world where half the inhabitants' voices were muffled by the very fact that they were women and therefore unworthy of serious consideration.

At last Ayla left Tessa to herself, giving her a warm hug and exclaiming, "I have enjoyed my time with you, and I feel that I have known you my whole life. I am so glad that you came!"

Tessa didn't remind her new friend that it had not been her choice to stop at Arleigh and forgave the threat implied in Hamish's invitation. She too had learned much, and found two new friends as well.

CHAPTER TWENTY-THREE

At breakfast in the morning, Tessa and Lady Miriam talked of many things until Ayla came in white-faced and tense. "I am sorry to intrude," she said, her dark eyes troubled. "There are visitors, men who demand to see you immediately in the name of . . . Malcolm, King of Scotland."

To Tessa the name felt like a blow, and at the same time she heard the older woman gasp. Miriam spoke urgently. "Quickly! Hide yourself in there." She pointed at a tapestry. Tessa did not at first understand, but Ayla hurried to the wall hanging and pulled it aside to reveal a small door. Without hesitation Tessa opened it and found herself in a small room stacked with linens and blankets. Leaving the door ajar, Ayla dropped the hanging back into place as the sound of heavy steps told Tessa that someone had entered the hall.

"My lady," said a man's voice. "I greet

you in the name of Malcolm, King of the Scots, and bring you the joyous news that the tyrant Macbeth is dead."

Tessa had known it was coming, but she almost sobbed aloud. Miriam, however, seemed unaffected as she answered, "When a tyrant rules, then news of his death must indeed be joyous. May I ask your name, sir?"

"I am Thomas Perth, my lady. My thane is Ian Hawick, newly made laird of Glames." So the man was one of Hawick's louts, the haughty seneschal, by his voice, and Hawick had ingratiated himself with the new king already. Things grew worse and worse for Tessa. Had she mentioned Hawick to Miriam last night? Would she recognize that this was Tessa's worst enemy?

The man came quickly to the point of his visit. "I seek three criminals who escaped the king's justice, an old man and two young ones. One is a servant boy who saw his chance to pilfer items before fleeing the castle. He is not important, but he guides the other two. The third looks like a boy but is in truth a woman, and a most wicked one at that. This woman is responsible for crimes against my master, King Malcolm, and even the erstwhile king, Macbeth. She stole a large sum of gold from him that will belong to the person who turns her over to me. However, anyone who is caught concealing the girl will be branded traitor to the new king and suffer the consequences."

Tessa shivered in her hiding spot. The carrot and the stick had been cleverly offered. If the lady surrendered her guests, she would have gold and the gratitude of the new king. If not she could lose everything.

Miriam never even thought about it, from the readiness of her response. "I am willing to help you, Sir Thomas." She flattered him, for he was no knight. And I will watch for the three you describe. However, my captain has brought no word of anyone's passing. We are vigilant, but seldom see anyone in this backward place. If Hamish had seen them, he would have told me."

"This man of yours is reliable?"

Miriam sensed Perth's doubt. "Would you like to ask him yourself?"

"I would, in case he neglected to mention it." The man's tone hinted that in Hamish's place he would not feel compelled to keep this wreck of a woman informed of current events.

Miriam made no comment, and there was a period of silence during which Tessa assumed Ayla went to fetch Hamish. Soon the sounds of his approach could be heard, and he was introduced to the newcomer.

"Hamish," Miriam said in a calm voice, "this gentleman seeks three criminals who might have passed by on the tarn. Two boys and an old man, you said?" Perth must have nodded. "Have these people — or any others, for that matter — passed this place in the last day or so?"

"No, milady. No one has passed this place at all." Hamish's voice was clear and convincing although Tessa would not have thought the stiff young man capable of a lie. Then it came to her. Hamish sounded truthful because he was. Miriam had phrased the question carefully. They had not passed by due to Hamish himself.

Perth was reluctant to let it go. "And these people did not stop here to ask for your help?" he tried.

"They did not," Hamish replied, again completely truthfully. Tessa prayed that Perth would drop it, for if he asked if those he sought were within the walls of the place right now, how would Hamish react?

Perth, however, was no student of human nature. He chose to proceed to the method he knew best. "We will search the place."

Tessa heard Miriam's voice rise, but there was no real fear in it. "I protest. Arleigh has always cooperated with those who seek justice, and I would not hide criminals in my home. However, if you insist upon searching, do so quickly. I dislike having my routine disturbed."

Tessa heard heavy feet moving through the place, and there followed a long time of anxious waiting. It was hours later when the curtain was pulled back and Ayla peered in. "They have gone."

Miriam sat in her chair, looking weary. Hamish stood beside her, his hand on her arm as if to lend her some of his strength. Behind him, Jamie and Banaugh entered the room, and Tessa ran to them, hugging both at once. "They hid us i' th' space twixt the water an' th' floor," Banaugh told her with some delight. "We culd see Hawick's slime as they left, bu' they saw nothing o' us."

Tessa turned to Miriam. "How can we ever thank you? You have put yourselves in danger for us. If they discover that we were here —"

"My people are completely loyal," the lady responded with conviction. "No one will say a word. Only if you are caught will your pursuers know where you have been."

A servant entered and whispered a few words in the lady's ear, at which she smiled ironically. "I did not think they believed we had not seen you. Hamish had a man skirt

354

the edge of the tarn, following the direction Perth took. They have set themselves at the mouth of the river, hoping to catch you when you leave."

Tessa's mouth set in a grim line. They could not go back, and if Perth was watching the tarn . . .

"You must leave at night, when darkness hides your escape," Miriam concluded Tessa's thought, as if having read her mind.

"But the moon is full. They will see us coming."

"They will see what they see," the older woman replied cryptically. Then she told them her idea.

Just after dark, a small boat left the water entrance of the crannog, its oars dipping quietly. Three figures inside were illuminated faintly in the moonlight. The craft skimmed the calm water, heading toward the spot where the river flowed into the tarn from the west.

As the oarsman maneuvered into the river's mouth, there was commotion in the shallows. Several men appeared from either bank. One grabbed the prow, two others seized an oar each, and among them they pulled boat and its passengers to the shore. There stood Thomas Perth, looking smugly satisfied with his prediction of events. As the boat was hauled up on the sand, one of the figures broke and ran along the lake edge. It was no man, Perth guessed with satisfaction, nor boy either, despite the clothing.

"Bring her back," he told his men, and three of them took off down the beach. In minutes, he heard a scream, and shortly they returned with their quarry. Perth, having ordered a torch lit in the meantime, found himself face to face with a girl, but his grin faded at the sight of her.

"This isn't macFindlaech's kinswoman!" he snarled. "It's the cripple's daughter."

"How dare you attack me?" Ayla spat at him.

"What are you doing on the lake at this hour?" Perth demanded. "And where is the girl I seek?"

Ayla's usually sweet face contorted with disdain. "My mother told you that no such girl passed by our home or sought our help. I have every right to fish on my own lake, and you have no right to frighten me as you did. Thinking you brigands, I ran for my life!"

Perth was at a loss, but it did not matter, for Ayla seemed determined to give him a long lecture on her rights and his sins. By the time she was finished, all he could do was stammer a cold apology and order his men to ready her boat for her departure. Ayla and the two young servants who accompanied her set off for the crannog while Perth faced the grins of his companions at the abuse he had taken. What none of them knew was that the three they truly sought had skirted the edge of the tarn, portaged their boat along the opposite bank while Ayla provided a diversion, and were now above them on the river, heading upstream as fast as they could row.

Once again dressed as a boy, Tessa had hugged Ayla warmly before leaving, then taken Miriam's twisted hands in hers. "I have much to thank you for, and if all goes well tonight there will be even more," she remembered saying as she bent to kiss the older woman's cheek. "I hope someday to repay at least a part of it."

"Nonsense, girl," the lady chided. "Kindness is not to be repaid but to be passed on. Seek not to balance the acts of others but to do as many good things as ever you can." And with that she had bade them goodbye.

The boat moved slowly up the river but eventually, at dusk of the next day, they arrived at the hamlet of Dunangus. There they were accepted stoically by Jamie's parents, an old couple who had served at the king's castle until the year before. The man was sinewy and gnarled as an old tree, the woman rosy-cheeked and softly rounded. They let Tessa know that whatever his faults, Macbeth had treated them with generosity, and they were willing to repay him by hiding her. It warmed the girl's heart to find a second place where there was no hatred of her uncle. The parents clucked and shook their heads at the tale Jamie told, saddened to hear of the king's death.

"Ye shall bide wi' us," the woman told Tessa. "A band of Malcolm's men ha' already been here. I doot they will return. When i' is safe, ye can decide what ye will do."

To herself Tessa wondered what that might be. Where did she belong? She could return to her sisters and live quietly if only Hawick would forget about her. Did he still believe they were married? Did it matter? She wished she knew the answers.

The people of the hamlet seemed only mildly concerned with events at Scone. A new king was not such a novelty in Scotland, even one steeped in blood. Their lives were taken up with preparing for winter, gathering crops, repairing homes and byres, and seeing to the provision of food and clothing necessary for the months of cold.

For a week Tessa and Banaugh lived among the villagers of Dunangus. When Jamie admitted rather shamefacedly that he had indeed ransacked Gruoch's things before leaving the castle, Tessa assured him that it had been reasonable to take things no longer useful to the dead queen but valuable to his people.

He offered Tessa the parcel, which he had stuffed under the prow of the boat. She was pleased to find that there was one fairly plain dress that she could use, several combs of which she took one, and other small things that made her feel less like a pauper. Most of the dresses she gave to the old woman. Although she had no use for such finery, she could sell or trade them to make life easier. Tessa told Jamie to spread the rest among the villagers after she was gone. Maybe they would think well of the macFindlaechs that way.

After a week Tessa and Banaugh decided that Malcolm no longer had time to pursue Macbeth's niece. His way to the throne was clear. Macbeth had no male kin to avenge his death or lead people to rebellion. Stories of the final battle reached them by way of a passing soldier loyal to Macbeth who had been knocked unconscious in the fray and woke afterward to find himself surrounded by corpses. The man told his story around the firelight, still shaken from the experience.

"I lay on the battlefield when I came to myself, but it was over by then. There was blood in my eyes from this gash on my head, and those who sort things out took me for dead." Groups of soldiers checked the field after a battle, rescuing their own men and often as not putting an end to the enemy's wounded. It was not an altogether unkind thing to do.

The man went on, fingering the cut on his scalp that had been stitched together by a village woman. "I thought to myself that perhaps I was dead and in hell, it was that bad. All my comrades lay dead around me, and the king's head . . ." He stopped, unwilling to put words to the memory. Tessa, whose identity was unknown to most of those around, bit her lip to keep from sobbing.

"I crawled ever so slowly into the wood, afraid every moment that Malcolm's troops would find me and finish me off. But they paid little attention by then, for they celebrated their victory. Once I was hidden, I rested and watched for a while. Young Malcolm took two swords, his own and one he'd taken from a man he killed, and crossed them on the ground. With pipers playing, he danced in celebration of his victory over the two swords, with his men cheering him on and the English watching coldly like the curs they are. I didna stay long, but crept away in the dark and began my way up-river." He rubbed a beefy hand over several days' growth of beard. "My home is in Glencoe. They will take me in there, and I will be safe."

The soldier feared Malcolm's revenge, even on lowly troopers, but word reached them a few days later that he would take a middle road, dealing fairly with those who had served Macbeth. The image of boyish enthusiasm created by Malcolm's "sword dance" had pleased many among the Scots, causing them to whisper that this young man would be a welcome change from the dour Macbeth.

Word also came that a coronation ceremony would be held soon. Tessa hoped she could quietly travel north to her home and take up life in the Cairngorms again. Hawick would be too busy trying to curry favor with Malcolm to worry about her whereabouts.

CHAPTER
TWENTY-FOUR

As she once more donned boy's clothing, Tessa wondered if she would ever be able to dress as a woman again and wear the silks and laces that made her feel beautiful. Rolling what necessities they could carry into tartans bartered from Jamie's kin, she and Banaugh bade the old couple and the boy goodbye, starting yet another trek.

They followed the track of the river, which bent to the northeast. Their host had given Banaugh directions to a ford where they could easily cross and start on their way due north, toward home. As they walked, Tessa wondered idly whether the Cairngorms were truly home anymore. Did she belong there? Did she belong anywhere? She had been in many places over the last year; which was home?

Ahead of them a steadily growing roar indicated a fast-flowing river, and the thought of a cool drink made them hurry forward toward the noise. Tessa drew a few paces ahead as Banaugh stopped to disentangle his clothing from some brambles. Tessa had thrown back the uncomfortably hot leather hood that hid her bright mane of hair. Therefore it was she alone, and quite recognizable, who stepped out from the trees to find herself gazing across the river at a small hunting party standing over a stag.

They had evidently tracked the deer to the spot where it had fallen dead. Tessa silently cursed herself for carelessness as she took in a dozen faces surprised at seeing a young woman in breeches opposite them. English troops! She had only time to turn and signal Banaugh to stop before a man pointed and shouted something and the chase was on. She ducked back into the woods, stopping just long enough to call, "Banaugh, hide yourself. They will think I am alone. If I am caught, you must return home. If not, I will circle back here by morning." With that she was off running. Half a dozen men had already mounted their horses and were crossing the ford after her. Banaugh melted into the trees as the horsemen sped by, praying they would not harm the lass if they caught her.

Tessa ran desperately, turning and twisting among the trees to avoid capture, but her bright hair was like a beacon in the dull autumn woods, and they were too many. They saw it as sport to capture this strangely dressed girl, shouting to each other and laughing at her efforts to elude them. Twigs lashed her face and the sharp thorns of berry bushes dragged at her clothing, slowing Tessa's progress. After only a few desperate minutes, she was scooped up by a grinning soldier and hauled across his saddle. The man's comrades congratulated him heartily while Tessa heaped on him all the curses she could remember. It made no difference, though, and he splashed across the river to the main party, dumping his prize on the ground before two men. A soldier put a hunting horn to his lips and blew two short and two long notes, a signal to the rest that the quarry had been captured.

Tessa looked up dazedly and despaired even further. Gazing down on her were Ian Hawick and another man who could only be the new king of Scotland, Malcolm Canmore.

"Mistress macFindlaech, is it?" Hawick sneered. "I wondered if we two would meet again."

"This is the one you mentioned who is kin to Macbeth?" the young man asked Hawick. Tessa looked at him with some interest despite her predicament. He was young, perhaps seventeen or so, but he looked strong enough and had a determined set to his chin. She knew little of Malcolm, but she guessed he would not consider her a possible ally. "Pretty thing."

"For a snake, I suppose," replied Hawick. "This chit tried to enlist my aid to fight for her wicked kinsman, and when I told her I was King Duncan's loyal subject and therefore yours, she attacked me in my own home."

"You pig!" Tessa spat at him. "Tell him how you have cheated both Scots and Englishmen all your miserable life. Tell him how you planned to rape and even kill me! Tell all these fine English soldiers how you hold one Jeffrey Brixton, Englishman, prisoner and demanded ransom money from his family!"

"Hear how the girl lies, sire?" Hawick bellowed. "Am I to stand for this?"

"God's hooks, who is one to believe?" Malcolm frowned, looking from Hawick to Tessa in bewilderment. One of the men standing nearby stepped up and whispered something in his ear. His face cleared, and he raised an eyebrow at Tessa. "It seems that you have chosen badly in your lies, lass. This fellow served with Jeffrey Brixton and knows for certain that the man is dead, washed overboard in a storm off the coast a year ago. Tie her," he spoke to a soldier. "We will decide what will become of the tyrant's niece when we reach Scone."

Unable to think of anything that might make Malcolm listen to her, Tessa said no more. At least Banaugh had escaped. The man tied her hands and set her on a stone while they finished the ritual of field-dressing venison.

The procedure was strictly spelled out by tradition, and any man who did not know the steps necessary would have been heaped with ridicule. The stag was split open and the entrails carefully removed along with the windpipe. The carcass was then cut into large chunks. The head was removed and flung into the bushes for the birds. A piece of gristle at the end of the breast bone was also tossed aside as the "raven's fee," an ancient tradition of paying off the dark powers of the earth represented by these birds. The eyes, liver, and entrails were given to two large hounds that accompanied the group. The meat was then divided among the party according to rank. It was bloody work, but the men went at it cheerfully, having captured both meat for the castle and an interesting prisoner in one day's hunting.

While the others were absorbed in what they were doing, Hawick wandered over near Tessa and stood, apparently gazing at the river. He spoke out the side of his mouth. "Well, lass, you've been quite a trial to me, but I have won at the last."

"At least Macbeth died fighting and not by your slimy hand," Tessa responded.

"Aye, well, he's dead either way, isn't he?" Hawick sneered. "It's too bad, though, that your friend Brixton couldn't come. He decided to stay behind and keep my sister company."

"More likely he is locked up again in the barn. Isn't that how Mairie keeps her men nearby?"

Hawick laughed. "I assure you, lass, he stayed of his own accord. When news came north that Sir William is dying, Mairie was quite interested. My sister has always had her eye on a title, and Lady Brixton would suit her well. As I left to go north, they were preparing to set off for York. Together."

He wandered off, glancing slyly over his shoulder to see if his words had hit home. Tessa sat stiffly on the adamant rock, letting no sign show of her inner turmoil. Mairie had commented that she could love Jeffrey if he was someone important, and now he had hopes of a title. If Mairie could get Jeffrey Brixton, she could have him, Tessa decided furiously. However, the thought of that perfect face smiling up at Jeffrey as he escorted her into Brixton Manor would not make the ride to Scone any easier.

Hawick approached Malcolm as the troops rinsed their hands in the river and prepared to depart. Tessa, watching from the corner of her eye, could tell she was under discussion. What would be Hawick's recommendation? Her death? Certainly he would be safest if she were silenced and could not recount his crimes. Her thought was interrupted as a trooper picked her up and set her roughly onto a horse behind another man who snickered, "Hold on, girl. It's a wild ride you'll get with a man like me!"

He was right. It was all she could do to keep from falling as they rode through bracken and bush. The horse's constant twists and turns through the wood and her inability to see around the man in front of her made the ride miserable. Despite her humiliation, Tessa had to hold on to the soldier's belt, for her tied hands left no other means of balance. Thus she headed toward the ancient place of Scottish kings, where

Macbeth, her kinsman, had been crowned king of Scotland only a year before.

The party arrived in Scone after riding hard the rest of the day. The castle sat in the growing dusk like a large, gray frog, its mouth open wide and its twin tower "legs" rising against the setting sun. Before the castle the small hill where the stone of Scone sat was being decorated with dozens of flags in preparation for Malcolm's coronation. It was clear that Malcolm was anxious to complete the ceremony before some other nobleman decided he might have the qualities necessary for kingship. A pavilion frame had been constructed, and around the base of the hill merchants had already staked out places for themselves to sell their wares to the crowds who would gather to watch.

The gates of the castle closed for the night behind them. Curious faces took in the unusual return, wondering quite naturally what prisoner had been brought back along with the venison. Tessa held her head high and tried not to show any emotion. A glance into the crowd made her heart jump — Jeffrey! But it was not he, for the man was shorter, much heavier, and wore the plainspun brown robe of a priest. He regarded her with no sign of recognition or interest.

Inside the castle, Tessa was escorted into the great hall where Malcolm, after being seated comfortably behind a large table, refreshed himself with a cup of wine. She was not even offered a drink of water to relieve her thirst. She looked with longing at the stone jug but said nothing.

On Malcolm's left sat several Scottish thanes, none of whom she recognized except Hawick, who smirked at her as usual. To the right sat the English, men in a delicate position. England was Scotland's sometime enemy, and they had helped a rebel defeat a crowned king. The fact that the defeated king had been unloved did not endear invading English troops to the Scots by any means. Scottish politics was in its usual quagmire, and England's current government not much better. These men had to set about making Malcolm king of Scotland in fact as well as in name, and no one envied them their task.

Siward, the general who headed the English troops, mourned the loss of his oldest son, rumored to have died at Macbeth's own hand. The old man was dignified in his grief, but implacably set against the clan macFindlaech. When Tessa's name was mentioned, the old man's eyes settled on her with animosity. His son was lost. Would he take revenge on the dead Macbeth by demanding the execution of his kinswoman? She met the old man's eyes calmly and saw in them no such demand. He was a soldier in the truest sense and did not make war on women.

More dangerous was Macduff, whom Tessa had never met but remembered from her uncle's description. He had rejected Macbeth's claim to the throne, escaped to England to avoid pledging allegiance, and his whole family had died for it. The man's eyes revealed that he was half-mad with grief. Not just grief, she thought, but guilt, too. If he had known Macbeth's ambition, why had he left his family in its way? Wrapped in his own thoughts, the man said little in the discussion of what should be done with Tessa.

Some, including a thane called Ross, counseled Malcolm to do away with Tessa to prevent future problems. "She is loyal to her uncle's cause," he maintained. "She will breed sons and teach them to hate you."

"I had not thought to kill women on my road to rule," Malcolm replied with judgment wiser than his years would have predicted. "The question is what to do with her? She is a threat, I admit that."

"You could marry her," said a young man

who sat next to Malcolm. He had said little thus far, and Tessa noticed that his voice broke, causing him to blush furiously. The lad could not have been more than fifteen, and since he spoke in council, must be Donalbain, Duncan's younger son.

Malcolm's lips twitched. "Marry her, brother? That is your solution to the problem?"

The boy blushed even deeper but made his argument clearly. "She is Macbeth's kinswoman. You are Duncan's son. Uniting the two clans would end the arguments on either side."

Miriam's astute observation had come to shocking reality. Once again she was to be the pawn of men's political hopes. Would she never be considered as a person, allowed choices about her own future?

"My lord —" she began.

"Speak when you're spoken to," Malcolm barked. "Brother, I am listening."

"If you marry this woman, you fulfill our father's wish that you would be king, as well as continuing the line of Macbeth, who was, if nothing else, a strong king. In time you would have sons with the blood of both families to cement their claim to the throne."

"And the streak of madness," Ross put

in bitterly.

Another lord spoke rather timidly. "Macbeth was driven mad, it is said, by witches who live on the moors, but we all know he was once a good soldier and a lively comrade." His comment fell rather flat. No one else was about to speak well of the man they had just defeated. The man lapsed into embarrassed silence.

In the quiet, Macduff said surprisingly, "I once called him friend." It was said with wonder, with no understanding of the demons that pursued Macbeth macFindlaech to the depths where his life ended.

Another voice spoke from behind her. "Might I suggest, my lord, that this council continue without the lady? She is fatigued almost to fainting."

It was the monk. With his cowl thrown back, she saw him more clearly. His expression was kind and concerned for her, and Tessa realized that she had been holding herself erect with great difficulty. Fear, exhaustion, and tension sang in her blood, making her light-headed.

Malcolm waved to a trooper, who stepped forward. "Take her to a cell and see that she is fed."

Tessa was not privy to further discussions of her fate, nor could she summon up much concern. After so many betrayals, Malcolm could do nothing to bring further shock or despair. Food was brought, some cider, and even a small pitcher of water with which she could wash away the dirt of the road. After she had rested, Tessa sat quietly in the small cell as night darkened its corners. It was overgrown with lichen and damp but otherwise tolerable, and she had seen no rats yet. What would the decision of the council be, death or marriage? It was almost funny. To some girls, marriage to Malcolm would have been the height of ambition. Tessa could find little interest in either possibility.

CHAPTER
TWENTY-FIVE

She must have dozed for a while on the narrow pallet that offered little in the way of comfort or warmth. It was uncertain how much time had passed when she heard the protesting scrape of the bolt being pushed back and the accompanying squeal of the door opening. Tessa came awake quickly and sat up. Morning was breaking, but it was still very gray, and little light penetrated the cell in any case. The figure that stood silhouetted in the doorway was the one she least wanted to see, Hawick.

"I've come to tell you, lass, you'll not be wife to the king." She could not see his face in the gloom, but she could hear the smile in his voice. "It seems the English have a spare princess for the lad. Old Siward made her sound like the alpha and the omega, so unwilling was he to have Macbeth's bloodline continue on the Scottish throne."

Tessa sat immobile, unwilling to give

Hawick any sort of response. The outlaw moved into the cell, shutting the door behind him with a low word to someone outside. With a feeling of dread, Tessa saw the man's large shape loom closer, and then his face was close to hers.

"I'm thinking, then, that Malcolm will not mind if you and I have our delayed wedding night. After that he may kill you or not, as he likes." Strong hands reached out and gripped her arms.

Tessa knew that screaming would bring no help. Hawick had arranged this with the guards. She was of no use to anyone here, and therefore of no concern.

She tried to scratch at the man's eyes, but he did not retreat an inch, merely slapped her so hard that she staggered back. He caught her arms and pinned them tightly behind her with a callused, callous hand.

"I've come to show you what you missed before . . . and to pay you back for the ridicule I took after you escaped me and left me tied like a Christmas goose." His voice shook with anger, but he pulled her close, and it softened. "Come, lass, you would not die without knowing a real man?" His grip tightened as she continued to struggle, knowing it was useless but refusing to give in.

"I don't believe she is destined to die any time soon," said a voice, and they both looked toward the door. It opened and a man appeared, carrying a torch that lit the cell and revealed the monk Tessa had seen twice before. Hawick reluctantly let go of Tessa and turned to him.

"Get out, monk. You have no business here."

"But I do. My lord Malcolm sent me to speak with this woman at first light to tell her of the council's decision. It was gracious of you to undertake the task, but not necessary. His highness your king has given me specific instructions for dealing with her situation, and I am to report to him when I leave her."

Hawick almost argued. He clearly wanted to. For a second time he was denied the prize that he felt should be his. Still, the monk stood calmly and waited expectantly, so there was nothing for Hawick to do but leave the place, which he did with no good grace whatsoever.

For a moment the monk stood in the doorway uncertainly, watching Hawick go. Then he stepped farther into the cell. The door shut behind him with a clang that caused him to glance back at it, but finally he moved toward Tessa.

The man was robed, as before, in a hooded garment of coarse brown cloth, the hood thrown back. He had the traditional monk's tonsure, the hair around his ears a deep black. Tessa thought still that he seemed vaguely familiar, like a portrait of someone well known but poorly done, the features not quite in correct alignment. He spoke softly, as one who is practiced in keeping his emotions in check, yet there was an urgency about him, too.

"Are you all right? I saw Hawick going this way and feared he might have something evil in mind."

"He's your friend, not mine," Tessa responded.

"No friend of mine nor of Malcolm," the man asserted. "Hawick is an ally, which is not at all the same."

Tessa had had all she could take in silence, and her bitterness bubbled out in a rush. "I'm sick to death of men and their games of politics, marriage, and war. People are always hurt, but mankind goes on plotting the next step in the game." She was close to tears. The incident with Hawick had frightened her badly, and this man, although kind, was an enemy. She would not respond to his kindness.

"Child, I must speak with you."

"I asked for no English priest," Tessa responded brusquely. Despite the fact that he had saved her from Hawick, he came from Malcolm and the new king's council, and that could not be good for her.

"I come not as a man of God. Rather I come for your help, if you will give it." He paused, but she did not answer, so he went on. "I understand that you claim to have seen a certain Englishman."

"I have seen too many Englishmen. Would that I should never see another!"

"Please, I am not trying to upset you, but you mentioned a name to the king, and that name was repeated to me. I come from the abbey at Bury Saint Edmonds, where I study the healing arts. When the English troops have need of me, I travel with them to treat the wounded and minister to the living and the dead. Since your story was repeated to me, I have not stopped thinking about it. You claim to have seen Jeffrey Brixton."

"I do, but no one believes me."

"What did this man look like?"

Tessa grimaced and rolled her eyes. What did it matter? Still, the man leaned toward her earnestly, and her answer seemed very important to him. "He has black hair and blue eyes, and he looks —" She stopped.

"He looks like you, in fact." Her eyes widened, and the monk smiled for the first time. When she had first seen his face in the courtyard, she had thought of Jeffrey. The familiarity was real! "Are you . . . ?"

"Jeffrey is my brother. I was once Ethelbert Brixton, although I am now called Brother Philip."

"You *are* his brother. I can see it now." Tessa nodded. "Your smile is like Jeffrey's, only not so ironic."

Ethelbert chuckled. "True, Jeffrey is the cynic of our family. Still, he and I are close — at least we were as boys. Life has given me few chances to see him of late."

Ethelbert did not say that William had forced his brothers to fend for themselves, making them unwelcome in their own home, but Tessa knew of it from her time with Eleanor. Now Ethelbert chuckled. "There was not much trouble the two of us couldn't get into back then. We were the mischief-makers, while William was full of his dignity and Aidan overly serious. Jeffrey was the daring one, of course, but I was born with more patience with the ways of the world."

"Like Auntie Madeline," Tessa suggested, and he smiled again. He had a nice smile, like Jeffrey's when he was not on his guard.

"You know my family?" He sat down on the wooden cot, ready to hear the whole story.

"I stayed with them for a year, with Eleanor, until she died."

Ethelbert's face sobered. "I was in Denmark at that time or I would have been there. Eleanor was dear to us all. I have come to be a traveler like Jeffrey, only he travels as soldier and I as healer. We have never crossed paths, but when I heard he was drowned, I could not believe it. I thought I would feel it if my youngest brother were dead, and I did not. Now you tell me my doubts were correct, and he is alive." Ethelbert's suntanned face was bright with joy at the prospect.

"He was alive when last I saw him, a prisoner of the man Hawick, to whom your pet Scot Malcolm pays heed. Unless Hawick has done away with him, Jeffrey lives." Her voice hardened. "He is a hard man to kill, very slippery and quick with a story. It has served him well in assuring that he continues to draw breath."

Anger returned as Tessa recalled Jeffrey's lies and half-truths. He had dallied with his own sister-in-law, with Mairie, and with who knew how many others. At times he had seemed to care for her. Now he was

381

Mairie's again, according to Hawick. Tessa noticed the monk's keen gaze, his eyes very like Jeffrey's, only not blue but grayish, and pulled her thoughts back to her own situation.

"I can tell you where your brother was when we parted," she offered, "but you must get me out of here."

"That is the most interesting part." The monk's eyes glinted with humor as he spoke, and he folded his hands together. "I do have some official capacity in this visit. You see, the new king of Scotland does not want the death of a woman on his hands. He cannot simply let you go, however, since Hawick lays all sorts of crimes at your feet. Many of the thanes have rancor against Macbeth and would like to see vengeance taken on any convenient scapegoat. So" — here he spread his hands — "it is to Malcolm's advantage that you disappear. I am to assist as I can. He asks only that you leave Scotland and never return so long as he is king."

Tessa looked into the gray eyes. "Is this a trick?"

"It is not, on my honor as a man of God. You know that I have dedicated my life to the church, so you may trust me in this. You say Hawick is an outlaw. I will warn the king, but it is all that I can do. Malcolm must decide for himself who and what his allies are. He'll need to step carefully to put your poor country back together, and I do not envy him the task."

There was little Malcolm could do for Jeffrey. Either he was dead at Hawick's hand or he had returned to England. Quickly she told Ethelbert what Hawick had said about William's illness and Jeffrey's return to England.

The monk sighed. "I suppose there is no use in going to look for him, then," he concluded. "If he's gone to Brixton, I will hear word when I return to the abbey. Still, I thank you for the information, which I for one believe is true. I will watch Hawick and warn Malcolm, as I promised. Now we must get you on your way to safety."

Tessa considered the man's motives for a moment. This escape could be a ruse to get her away from the castle and kill her secretly so that no one could blame Malcolm for her death. She had heard of those who were men of God in name only, had even met one at Hawick's, she remembered with disgust. Men like that would cooperate in such deeds. But from what she knew of Ethelbert from his family, he was truly devout and had pledged himself to the service of mankind. It only took an instant for her to make up her mind. To die attempting escape was better than meekly going to her execution.

"Tell me what I must do."

Ethelbert had worn two robes into the cell, one over the other. He now removed the outer one and handed it to Tessa. "You are much smaller than I am, but this will hide you, I think. You will leave first. There is no guard at the door. Hawick saw to that. Make your way out in a leisurely fashion. I will leave when you have had time to get away. If God is with us, no one will realize that you are gone for some time. Can you travel on your own?"

"I have done so before," was her answer, but privately Tessa wondered where she would go. She must leave Scotland. Returning home would bring danger to her sisters, whom no one had thought of yet. They would be safe in the Cairngorms if she drew no attention to them, but her peril would end only when she was out of the country. That meant going to England, for where else could she go? She didn't even have what was left of Macbeth's gold, for Banaugh had kept it hidden in his pack.

Tessa felt a wave of determination. She would not give up now, would travel to

England on foot if she had to. Once there, she would make a life for herself somehow. Adjusting the cowl of the robe so that it hid her face completely, she told Brother Philip, "I am ready."

It was easier than she could have imagined. No one paid the slightest attention to the monk who moved out of the building at a slow, steady pace and across the courtyard. The figure stopped at the gate and looked around briefly, then stepped in alongside a donkey pulling a cart filled with turnips. Patting the animal, the monk walked through the gate with it. The guards paid little attention, being more interested in who was coming into the castle than who was leaving it.

Once away from the wall a fair distance, Tessa slowed and let the cart pass her, then disappeared into the trees that lined the road. Stopping to consider her options was distressing. She had no money, no food, no belongings, and she was far from the border. After some deliberation she decided first to get her bearings, then find something to eat. She began with the sun, dimly seen through the haze of clouds above. Its position helped her to decide, rather tentatively, that she was facing north. She pointed herself in the opposite direction and began a circle around the castle, concealing herself in the trees and moving quietly.

It took the better part of half an hour to reach the far side of the castle, where she would have been in the first place if she'd planned more carefully and exited by the south gate. There was a small village outside the walls. Neat peasant huts lined the road, and fields now empty of crops were laid out in patches edged by posts that signified which tenant farmed the piece. Farther out were the larger fields that belonged to the manor and were farmed in common. There were no more woods. She would have to cross the open distance in her monk's robe and hope no one accosted her. As she was about to step out of the trees, a hand grabbed her robe, pulling her back. Reacting quickly, she flailed out at the arm, bringing a muted grunt from the arm's owner.

"Lass, it's me," Banaugh cried, and Tessa stopped in amazement.

"Banaugh! You came for me!"

He grinned, showing several gaps where molars had once been. "Did ye think I'd just go on without ye? Followed ye here, I did. I was havin' a devil of a time figurin' how I wuld get in t' free ye, an' then I heard this crashin' through the wood, like a bear or a stag i' panic. Imagine m' surprise when it was only a tiny little monk wi' an overlarge robe, an' where's his tonsure, I ask m'self?"

Tessa pouted briefly. "I was *trying* to be quiet," she told him. "*You* try stepping over brambles in this heavy woolen thing." Of course, that is exactly what was needed. Banaugh handed over his cap, and in only a few minutes a much more realistic-looking monk emerged from the wood with a boy beside him, and the two made their way through the village and off to the south without much notice being taken whatsoever.

CHAPTER
TWENTY-SIX

The two made their way along the river, having concluded that a ship was their best choice for the voyage south. Tessa tried to convince the old man that he did not have to accompany her to England. He was safe in Scotland if he simply returned to his hills.

Banaugh would have none of it, though. "I wuld see ye away from this poor country," he told her as they walked southward, keeping to the trees as much as possible. "There's too much danger here for ye. Yer father was th' wiser man o' th' two brothers, I ken tha'. He knew tha' life is worth livin' only if a body is content. Wantin' more an' more leads only t' trouble, an' them tha' gae too much oft canna' live wi' themselves afterward. It is said tha' Macbeth's wife pu' an end t' her own life for tha' verra reason."

"She was very distressed when last I saw her, poor thing. Indeed, they were a sad pair at the end."

Banaugh shook his head. "I'd nae trade places wi' noble folk. It seems ambition is a disease wi' them. Beggin' your pardon. Not ye, o' course."

Tessa seldom thought of herself as nobility. True, she was of Scotland's upper class, but she did not feel any different from Banaugh. Hill chieftains were not far removed from their people, financially or socially. And she had no ambition to be better than anyone else. She wanted only to be herself and to be loved for that reason.

It was a short way from Perth to the town of Dundee, where Banaugh arranged passage on a boat ready to depart the next day for the south. War with the English had not stopped the constant flow of goods between the two countries, and boats left for London regularly loaded with hides, flax, salmon and dried cod.

London was the most logical destination for them, Tessa and Banaugh decided. It would be easiest to find work there, Tessa was somewhat familiar with the place, and she did not want to go anywhere near Brixton Manor. "Although I must get a message to Auntie Madeline somehow," she told Banaugh.

"Then we must go t' London, lass," Banaugh said with certainty. " 'Tis a large place, bu' ye know a bit o' it. I ken we shall make our way there somehow."

"Oh, Banaugh, I'm sorry that you must leave your homeland for me. If only I weren't Macbeth's kinswoman."

"Och, dinna fash yersel'," the old man replied. "I've ever had a secre' yen t' see a fine big city, and here's m' chance. It will only be for a few months. Ye'll see. Once Malcolm settles in, many o' Macbeth's auld supporters will start creepin' home. It is th' way o' things."

Early next morning, the two left Dundee, sailing out the Tay Estuary and along the coastline to London. They had some nervous moments as they boarded the ship, fearing capture, but no one paid them much heed at all. "The monk must have been telling the truth," Tessa remarked. "Malcolm only wants me gone."

"Aye, it is Hawick tha' ye must fear, lass. Ye've escaped him again, an' he is nae a man who likes bein' made th' fool."

Once again the trip was difficult for Tessa due to having to hide the fact that she was female. Banaugh provided distractions and excuses, usually citing his ancient constitution. One evening the boat moored at Whitley Bay, where they took on a third passenger. The man looked familiar to Tessa, but she couldn't place him until he offered to sing for the sailors. It was the bard who had sung at Hawick's the first night they were there, now traveling south for the winter. He looked quite different in travel attire, which was much plainer than the colorful costume he wore while performing.

"I travel the Lowlands all summer," he told those on the ship, "but when autumn comes, it's back to England for me. Winter is too damp by far in Scotland for a man whose voice is his living, you see."

He sang them the story of the "Twa Corbies" and several other lays, his thin face reflecting the emotions of the stories within. He had delicate hands on the lute and thin legs that looked as if they would break easily, yet he covered hundreds of miles in a year, spending a week at this castle or two at that, earning his keep and whatever else the thanes or their ladies saw fit to give him. What made a man choose such a rootless life? The faces of the crew as they sat listening to him were rapt and almost magically changed. That might have been the best reward of all.

After he had sung the evening's last song, the crew moved away to make their beds on the ship's deck. Having paid passage, the three of them, Banaugh, Tessa, and the bard, were given space beneath a leather awning that kept out most of the sun and some of the rain. The singer smiled at them now that some privacy was afforded and asked, "Did I not see the two of you at Ian Hawick's?"

"Yes," Banaugh admitted. "We visited a while back."

"Your visit caused much ado if I remember," the bard commented wryly. "Or, more precisely, your departure." The two did not know what to say to that, having no idea how much the man knew of their story. "Don't worry," he assured them. "A bard has no loyalties. I merely observe what happens around me and move on to a new place. They hardly notice me when there's no entertaining to be done."

Tessa looked beseechingly at Banaugh, who asked the question she was thinking. "When did you leave Hawick's stronghold, then?"

"Just over a week ago. As I said, it was in a state of confusion. Once this young . . . person left," he said, quirking a satiric eyebrow at Tessa, "there was cause to believe the authorities might descend upon the place. Hawick and his men rode north, believing that the escaped person would head that way and hoping to head off any chance of warning certain people." The man was certainly careful not to take sides or to appear to know too much, although Tessa sensed he knew most of it. "Mistress Mairie made plans to travel south with Master Brixton. I considered traveling with them, for safety, but had not made up my mind."

So it was true. Mairie had gone to York with Jeffrey, hoping to become Lady Brixton. Tessa's face fell, and the bard looked at her meaningfully.

"Of course, plans do not always go as one would wish," he continued. "Once Hawick rode away to the north with the main body of his troop, there were only eight of his men left at the castle. Two stayed on guard while the others went in search of the person I spoke of earlier. Two went east, two more west, and the last two south." The bard fell unconsciously into his storytelling voice, making the telling sound almost like the historic sagas of old.

"I was awakened early one morning by the lady Mairie's screams. At first I thought she was in danger, so I hurried into the courtyard. The two guards who had stood at the gate were bound and gagged, struggling like two worms on the ground inside the bailey. The lady screamed in anger, not in fear, and I have never heard such language from any who calls herself a lady, I must tell you.

"In the stable we found two more of the men, who had evidently come into the castle after completing their search only to be attacked and trussed up like two over-large pheasants hung to age. Although the castle was searched, and well, too, there was no sign of Jeffrey Brixton, and one horse was missing. Later they found two more men on the road to Jedburgh. They did not fare so well as the others. There was evidently a pitched battle. One was dead and the other senseless.

"That left the lady with no gentleman and a depleted escort for her trip to England. I tell you, she was in a fine state! I excused myself as soon as I could, saying I was expected in Jedburgh. When I left, she was preparing for a journey, although to where I cannot say, since I imagine that York was no longer a possibility." He stopped with an ironic smile. Loyalties or no, Tessa could see that the bard was not upset to see Hawick's prisoner escape and Mairie's plans thwarted.

His feelings could not compare to Tessa's. Despite herself she rejoiced that Jeffrey had escaped the wicked Hawick, killed one of his brutes, and rejected Mairie. She lay down to sleep on the hard planking with a smile that neither Banaugh nor the bard missed.

Several days after they'd left Dundee, Tessa and Banaugh found themselves on a crowded dock at London's east end. The bard had left them at Saltburn, wishing them well as he tossed his leather-wrapped lute over one shoulder. They had continued down the coast and up the Thames with fair weather but deadly dullness. Now, standing unsteadily as her legs got used to firm ground, Tessa saw nothing familiar. Any experience she had of London was far away from the docks, where smells, sights and sounds of all kinds made her head ache. Here were the industries not allowed in the City itself: brewing, bleaching, dying, and vinegar making, whose odors offended the sensibilities of the populace. They were far from the house William Brixton kept in Highgate, and she had no idea which direction to go to find lodging.

"Have we any money at all, Banaugh?" she asked the old man, who had gathered their belongings.

"A verra li'le. Enow for a night's lodgin' and a meal, if the first is nae grand an' the second nae large."

"Very well, then. We'll walk into the city

and hope I see something familiar."

It was not long until Tessa realized that her knowledge of London was not as extensive as she had thought. The city was large and constantly changing. Shops burned or were enlarged, sometimes into the street, changing the traffic patterns. They wandered among the narrow pathways, twice ending up in a close with no exit except the way they had come. Banaugh was encouragingly cheerful and unconcerned, enjoying the sights and sounds of this new place. It took two hours of walking and several helpful passersby before Tessa saw a place she recognized. "There! Banaugh, I went to a party at that house."

"Well, it's a fine house, lass, bu' will they recognize ye th' way ye're dressed?"

Tessa looked down at her trousers and loose shirt, now filthy. "No, and what's more, I don't know what Sir William told people about me, so I'm not sure what kind of reception I would receive if they did." She was near to tears with fatigue and worry.

"Lass, we'll ge' a room nearby and ha' somethin' t' eat. In th' morn, ye'll change yersel' into m' bonny Tessa and see wha' happens. It's tae much t' think on noo."

As usual, Banaugh was right. They found

a fairly clean, inexpensive inn that allowed them a room to themselves, since there was no large crowd in London at the time. The evening meal was a simple lamb stew with more vegetables than lamb, but it was warm and nourishing. After supper Tessa found that, without the constant motion that had bothered her on the ship, she fell asleep quickly and had no thought for the morrow until it came.

When she awoke, Banaugh had already gone looking for hot water so she could wash. He left her to her toilette, returning when she was done to use the same water to shave and wash himself.

Once they were refreshed and had broken fast with some bread from the night before, Tessa decided that it might be useful to observe the goings-on at the house she had recognized. Reluctant to knock on the door in case she was mistaken or rejected, she hoped that someone she knew might pass by. That person's reaction would help her gauge what her reception would be among those who had known her in London. She hoped Cedric had obtained an annulment to the marriage when she fled before the marriage could be consummated. Whatever the case, she had to know what had been said of her by Cedric, by William, and perhaps now even by Jeffrey, if he had indeed returned home.

Determined to find someone who could tell her all this, Tessa returned to the narrow wooden house that sat wedged between others much like it, only the door making it unique. This door was painted blue, with pails of water set on either side of it in case of fire, as demanded by law. While other homes' pails were plain and serviceable, the paint on these pails was blue to match the door, someone's attempt to beautify necessity.

A well with a roofed arch was located nearby, offering shelter and a place to sit. Taking up a position where she could see the blue door, Tessa began her watch while Banaugh explored the area. He returned every hour or so to report what he'd seen. Tessa was glad to see him enjoy himself, marveling at wonders he'd only heard of.

"Why, lass," he said after the first hour. "A body can buy anythin' i' the world i' this London. There are carts t' take ye anywhere ye'd like, if we'd only money left, and there's women sellin' food I ne'er saw afore." Then he was off in a different direction to sample new delights.

Tessa sat regarding the door of the house she remembered. Who had lived there? She really didn't recall, only had a vague memory of being introduced to a big-bosomed woman and a portly man. Carlyle? Himden? There had been so many in such a short time.

Twice the blue door opened. Once a serving girl in a plain muslin gown stepped out and bought something from a peddler. The second time a man came out, perhaps the man she remembered, although it was hard to tell from a distance. He looked prosperous in a wine-colored robe and a black velvet tunic and hat. The man paid her no attention and went off in the opposite direction.

Finally, just before noon, the door opened a third time. From it stepped two women, an older woman with a large bosom, almost certainly the woman Tessa had pictured so dimly. The other was . . . her heart leapt. The other was Mary Brixton. Of course! She had been engaged to marry Francis, her stammering swain, and that wedding must have taken place by now. The house was her in-laws', and either Mary lived there or she was visiting them.

Tessa was so preoccupied that she almost failed to grasp that the two women were walking away from her. When she did, she pondered for a moment what to do. Banaugh was off on one of his explorations. If he returned to find her gone, would he worry about her? She decided to leave a simple message. Tearing a bit of decorative ribbon from her shift, she tied it in a neat bow around the handle of the bucket that hung in the well and set out after Mary.

The two women ahead of her looked content and prosperous. Both wore heavy cloaks against the cold of November, but below could be glimpsed long dresses trimmed with elegant braid and soft leather boots. Their heads were covered completely by wimples over which decorative caps of fine fabric were set. Tessa herself had resorted to cutting the monk's robe into a cape for herself as the weather had cooled, but without the proper tools, the best that could be said for it was that it was service-able.

She followed the two women at a distance, watching Mary and discerning that she had become an attractive wife with a comely look and pleasant manner. It took a while to accomplish Tessa's goal, which was speaking to Mary alone. She and the older woman entered several shops, buying ribbon and thread in one, paper in another. Finally, they entered a boot maker's shop, where apparently the older lady was to have shoes made. She and the clerk went into the back of the shop while Mary looked idly at the wares in the front. Seizing her chance, Tessa went inside and approached her.

"Mary, is it you?"

At first confused by the tattered girl who accosted her, Mary frowned in curiosity. Then her eyes grew round and lit with delight. "Tessa! Oh, Tessa, we've been so worried about you!" Mary threw herself into Tessa's arms, and all doubts and fears faded. Mary was glad to see her, and she'd said "we!" *All* the Brixtons hadn't rejected her!

"Quickly, Mary. What's the situation with Eleanor's family and with you?"

Mary blushed. "Well, I have married Francis Hope, whom you know. His stammer is not nearly so bad lately . . ."

"Of course not," Tessa assured her. "Many a young man stammers. It takes only time and love to cure it."

Mary's plain face glowed. "I knew you'd understand. Oh, I have missed being able to talk to you. You are so brave, and a wonderful friend beside. My mother-in-law" — her voice dropped to a whisper — "thinks I'm a mouse."

"Then she does not know you well enough as yet, I say. You are wonderful, too, Mary.

If you knew how it cheers me just to see you!"

"Well, there was a terrible scene when you left, I can tell you. Uncle William was on about how you'd deceived poor Eleanor, and Sir Cedric was in a rage because he looked the fool, but Auntie Madeline said you must have had good reason for what you did, despite their ranting. Not that we believed William, who ever looks out only for himself. But we were very worried about you."

"I'm back now, but my circumstances are even worse than before. My uncle the king is dead, his family despised. I have nothing, Mary, and I don't know where to turn." Tessa's shame almost overcame her to admit this to her friend, but she could hide none of it.

Mary's glance took in Tessa's brown skin, thinness, and the makeshift cloak, and her face became serious. "I am sorry to hear it." There was little Mary could do for her friend. As a young wife, she was very much under the control of her husband and her in-laws. She could not simply open her home to Tessa, much as she might want to.

Her face brightened again with a thought. "Aidan will help. He was quite fond of you; I know it. He's in York now, though, at William's sickbed."

"I had heard that Sir William was ill." So Hawick had told the truth about that much, anyway.

"Oh yes, very. They say he won't last much longer. He's gone home, where Auntie Madeline nurses him. It seems Aidan will soon be the heir to Brixton, with Ethelbert renouncing his title and Jeffrey gone —"

"But Mary, Jeffrey isn't dead. I found him in Scotland, held captive by outlaws. He is well — at least he was when last I heard news of him."

They heard noises from the back of the shop, signaling that Mistress Hope had finished her business. Mary stared at Tessa as she digested the information. When she could speak, she whispered, "That's wonderful news. We must speak again. Francis and I live in Oxford, and I must return there this afternoon, but I will send word when next I come to London and we will meet. Where are you staying?"

"The Mace and Thyme," Tessa answered.

"I shall return in three days' time, then," came a voice, and Tessa shot Mary a warning look.

Mary understood, and when the lady emerged from the back, said only, "How nice it was to see you again, my dear," as if speaking to a former servant. She took Tessa's hand briefly before leaving with her mother-in-law. When Tessa looked down, there were coins in her hand, and Mary's backward glance indicated she should not worry, for she had friends in London.

Banaugh was waiting at the well when Tessa hurried back. "I saw t' ribbon an' figured ye meant me t' bide here," he said. "If ye'd been in trouble, I doot ye'd tie sae nice a bow."

Quickly telling him about Mary, she showed him the coins. "She gave me this, enough to pay for our lodging and food for several days."

"We shall soon pay 't back, lass, for I ha' taken employment." His grizzled face showed pride in anticipation of her reaction.

"Employment? Banaugh, you were only gone an hour!"

"True, bu' God looks after us both. I wandered by a dram shop, an' inside was an auld woman tryin' t' move a barrel int' place an' havin' a devil o' a time of it. Natur'ly I stepped in t' help. She tells me tha' her husband has died, leavin' her th' shop, but it's powerful hard on her t' do 't all. So I says, 'Wha' aboot a Scotsman tha's honest, hard-workin' a' knows a bit concernin' whiskey?' An' th' old woman giggles an' says, 'Well, I macht give a man like tha' a try, then.' So I come back here t' tell ye tha' I'll be takin' up m' new job as soon as I hae ye settled back a' th' inn. The pay's nae much, bu' I can live i' th' back o' th' shop an' take m' meals there, too."

He grinned again and smiled at Tessa, who struggled to comprehend so much news so quickly. Banaugh had a job, Mary was yet her friend. Could things turn out well after all? She felt the tension inside her relax a little as she hugged Banaugh's bony shoulders in congratulation.

CHAPTER
TWENTY-SEVEN

Tessa awoke the next morning with a strange feeling. After days of travel and the constant companionship of Banaugh, she was alone.

She dressed quickly, for the room was bitterly cold. Another winter was on its way. Getting dressed wasn't much of an effort these days, for she had only one simple gown that she'd carried rolled up in her blanket from Scotland. It needed repair, and her poor sewing skills were going to have to do, for she had no cheerful Cecilia to guide her.

Tessa had a moment of intense longing for the days at Brixton before Eleanor's death. They had all been so happy then, and it had seemed like home to her. Life did not stay the same, however. It changed without regard for happy times or sad ones, and that was probably good. With a sigh, she went downstairs and found the landlord's daughter.

"Might I have a needle and some thread?" she asked the girl of thirteen or so.

"What for?" the girl asked dully.

"I must mend my dress." The girl stood looking blankly at Tessa, and she indicated a large tear near the hem of the gown. "Here. I would like to mend it so that it does not get worse."

The girl looked sullen. "I s'pose. When I get time."

"I will be very grateful." The girl waited to be offered something for the favor, but Tessa had nothing to spare for such a little thing as the loan of a needle and a yard of thread. She returned to her room.

The girl's discourtesy reminded Tessa that she was nobody. With no money, no family, and no power, she could expect this sort of treatment the rest of her life. Aidan had not been wrong in insisting that he was her best hope for a comfortable life, but she had rejected his offer. She was not sorry either, for she could return only affection for his love and would rather have nothing.

As she combed her hair she let herself think of the events she'd experienced, especially those concerning Jeffrey Brixton. What was he to her? It didn't matter. He might be dead at the hand of Ian Hawick if the outlaw or his men had caught up with him.

The thought bothered her more than it should. After all, he'd never said anything to indicate he cared for her. He'd made love to at least two beautiful women. How many more had there been? He claimed he'd forgotten Eleanor and had never loved Mairie, but what girl didn't know that men were apt to lie to the woman they gazed upon at the moment? She of all people knew that Jeffrey was a natural actor. He had played a part at Macbeth's the first night she met him, and he had played the brainless fool at Hawick's for months. What was to prevent him from playing the lover if it gained him what he desired at the moment?

She wondered also where Ian Hawick was and whether he still meant her ill. If Mairie came to England, Hawick would soon follow. It was essential that Tessa avoid him, but London was a large enough city that she hoped it would be possible. She had no social circle now. She was shut out from the Brixtons, who had introduced her to society, as long as Sir William had anything to say about matters.

There was a light knock at her door, and she opened it to find the landlord's slovenly daughter. "There's a gentleman to see you," she said, her face plainly indicating what she thought of women who received male guests. "Shall I send him up?"

"Certainly not." Tessa frowned. "I will come down." Her curiosity was piqued. A gentleman? Had Hawick found her? She peered round the corner of the stair and breathed a sigh of relief and joy. The man who stood waiting was dressed in a new suit, much finer than anything she'd seen him wear before. "Aidan!"

Aidan opened his arms, taking Tessa into them with great warmth. "Tessa! Tessa, my wandering Scot! We were so worried about you."

"With some cause, I must say," she answered, able to laugh at it now. "Still, I am returned with no harm done."

"Let me look at you." Aidan stepped back and examined her. "A bit thinner, quite browned by the sun, but still beautiful." His admiration made her glad she'd taken the time to plait her hair neatly.

"How did you find me?" But she knew the answer before she'd finished the question, so they both said "Mary" at the same time, which made them laugh.

"I went to visit her as soon as I got to London yesterday, to tell her of William's death," Aidan said soberly. "She had gone

409

home to Oxford, but she left word with a servant that an invitation must be sent to Tessa at the Thyme and Mace to visit on Thursday next. It didn't take me long to conclude it must be you. I sent the news of William's death with the servant and came here myself."

Tessa wasn't hypocritical enough to express sorrow at the death of a man who'd hated the sight of her, so she tempered her sympathy. "I'm sorry you must deal with another death, Aidan. It seems Eleanor was with us just yesterday, yet I've missed her over these long months."

"I too," Aidan agreed. "William, I think, loved her more than he could admit. He became listless after her death and drank more than was good for him." He sniffed ironically. "After all his lectures to me. His health declined rapidly, and soon he moved home to York, where Auntie cared for him with all kindness."

"She is a good woman, Auntie Madeline."

"My brother died six days ago," Aidan finished. "At the end he was quite changed, less concerned with outward show. He requested a small funeral, so we buried him quietly next to Eleanor. I am here in London now to take up the business of the Brixton estate. Imagine my joy to find that you are here also. Perhaps I can convince you to consider again my earlier proposal."

Tessa was surprised at his broaching the subject so soon. "Your proposal? But surely you know that — I mean, have you forgotten Cedric?"

"I will wager that we needn't worry on that account. William and Cedric put their heads together after you disappeared. They decided it was best not to let the truth of the matter be known outside the family, mostly because it made them both look ridiculous to have been fooled by a 'Scottish seductress,' if you'll forgive me for quoting my brother." Here he did a fair imitation of William's pompous manner to soften his words. "They announced that grief for the death of Eleanor had made you ill, and you returned to your family to recover."

"A fine lie." How like William, and Cedric too.

"I'm sure Cedric will agree to a quiet annulment now that the gossip has died down. With two fortunes between us, he and I will accomplish it with discretion and speed, and you will be free."

Tessa felt relief flow through her. She'd dreaded meeting Cedric here in London, but now it seemed Aidan was taking charge of the whole matter. Then his reference to two fortunes penetrated her consciousness. Aidan had paused for a moment, but words burst from him impetuously. "It never mattered to me that you weren't Eleanor's sister, and I know you married Cedric out of desperation. I love you, Tessa, for courage, liveliness, and beauty. When we are married, you'll be my proudest possession."

Tessa stiffened at the word. Possession? She recalled what Eleanor had said of Sir William: he had wanted her only to show off to other men, to make them jealous. Was that all a woman was to her husband? Once she had convinced herself that it would be enough, but now she felt differently. Eleanor had been correct that a woman might be herself with two types of men, but Tessa could only be happy with one: a man who loved what she was, not the way she looked or the name she bore.

Aidan realized from her expression that something was wrong. His face showed concern, and for the first time she wondered what kind of man he really was. Handsome, charming and intelligent, to be sure, and he had served William loyally. She could not help but wonder, though, if he shared William's lack of feeling for others. Now that William, the man who had controlled him all his life, was gone, what real Aidan would emerge?

"I will be no man's possession," she said softly.

Aidan saw his error immediately. "Of course, my dearest. I meant nothing by it, only that now I can give you what you want. Do you realize that I am heir to the Brixton holdings? Ethelbert has renounced the title, and I am the surviving son. Now I can offer what you deserve. Take Eleanor's place as Lady Brixton, and you will never want for anything again." His eyes blazed with emotion, and he seemed more alive than she had ever seen him. "You will have everything that Eleanor planned and more."

Suddenly Tessa's mind focused and she realized that this discussion was all wrong. She had to tell him what he could not know, having missed Mary at her in-laws. "But Aidan, Jeffrey is alive!"

There was a stunned silence as Aidan's face showed several emotions: surprise, shock, and what might have been anger. Then the features composed to something like a mask, the lips white and the skin around the cheekbones tight. "How do you know this?"

"I saw him — in Scotland. Jeffrey helped me to escape from the outlaws who had held him prisoner since his accident. I have reason to believe he escaped also, but we were separated, so I don't know where he is now."

"You went to Scotland and found Jeffrey." Aidan's voice was as expressionless as his face. "You must care for him very much."

Tessa turned away, staring at nothing. "Aidan, I don't know anymore what I feel for Jeffrey."

"My brother certainly seems able to capture the affections of women."

Tessa had to agree. "The outlaws might have killed him had it not been for Mairie's interest," she murmured.

"Mairie?" Aidan looked shocked for a moment. "What an odd name. Is it Scots?"

"No," Tessa replied. "She is French. At least her mother was. She kept Jeffrey alive by persuading her brother — the outlaw lord — to spare him once William refused to pay the ransom. If Jeffrey has escaped, he will return to Brixton as soon as he can."

There was a pause. "To Brixton or to you?" Aidan asked pointedly. "Did you not tell me that my brother dallied with Eleanor, and now you would take her leavings, knowing that it is only because she is dead that he has turned to you?" His voice bitter, he threw everything he could at her to make her change her mind.

Tessa was firm, knowing she must convince Aidan to stop dreaming that they would someday wed. Facing him squarely she said, "My feelings for him have nothing to do with Eleanor, nor anything to do with you and me. I told you before, I cannot promise myself to you — someone I care about — knowing that I cannot return love for love."

Tessa moved toward him instinctively, pleading for understanding. Aidan moved suddenly, almost as if he'd been asleep and jarred awake. He smiled and his face softened, melting the tension between them. "It seems I must again accept your decision, although I hope that you will consider my offer seriously when you have time to think. Remember, if Jeffrey does return, he will be master of Brixton, and he may not see you in the same way as he did when he was simply the youngest brother of Sir William Brixton. I, however, will love you no matter who you are and who I may become. Think on that, will you, Tess?"

His words, although phrased delicately enough, were a warning. Jeffrey as Lord Brixton could have any woman he wanted. Why would he look to one such as she, who lived in a cheap inn and wore the same dress every day? It was a thought to be considered, and Aidan meant well by it, trying to make her see the hopelessness of her longing for Jeffrey. He picked up his cloak and shrugged it on.

"Well. It is wonderful to hear that Jeffrey is alive and has escaped Hawick. I must return to Brixton immediately to discover if my brother has indeed returned." He was himself again, warm and charming. He smiled down at Tessa and his eyes glowed as he said, "Make use of the house here in town. It is yours for as long as you like."

"Oh, Aidan, I couldn't —"

"Nonsense. As I've said, the world still thinks of you as Eleanor's sister, so you have every right. If you like, I will bring Cecilia with me when I return so you shall be properly chaperoned."

It was tempting, and she knew Eleanor would urge her to accept, although William would turn over in his newly made grave. "Thank you, Aidan. I will consider it, but for the moment I shall stay here." Unencumbered by favors owed, her mind finished the thought.

He was gracious, and, giving her a formal little bow, left the inn briskly, already occupied with the future.

Poor Aidan, Tessa thought, to be sure he'd finally reached the prize for which he'd evidently yearned, and then to find it might not be his after all. He was older than Jeffrey, but illegitimate. That meant the title went to Jeffrey first. Tessa hoped he wasn't too downcast at the turn events had taken. Something he had said seemed odd, but she could not settle on what it was. She returned to her room as the thought pestered her, but the answer never became clear.

Banaugh came that afternoon, as promised, and they walked together to the shop where he now worked. He introduced Tessa to Mrs. Goode, the proprietress, a woman whose thick figure and gray hair did nothing to diminish her engaging manner and pleasant expression.

"Fergus tells me you are responsible for him comin' to London, so I must thank ye, mistress. Since my husband died, I've had offers of assistance from several men, to be sure, but every one had his eye on a prosperous business and an easy life with his wife doin' the work. Now Fergus here" — odd, Tessa thought, that she'd never known his first name — "be willin' to work, and for a woman as well, and that's a blessing."

"He will be a treasure," Tessa replied. After a pleasant visit, she left alone, assuring Banaugh she could find her way back safely. She was actually a little sad. Banaugh and his new employer got on very well, and it was obvious he'd found his place in London. Of course, he would keep an eye on her, but he didn't *need* her.

The next few days were spent peacefully, resting and recuperating from the months of travel and strain that she had experienced. Tessa's hair regained its luster, her fingernails grew back, and the skin on her nose and forehead stopped peeling from too much exposure to the sun. She received with joy a basket from Mary that included creams, soaps, and other sundries that ladies find worthwhile, and she did her best to repair the ravages of her days in the wilderness.

Chapter
Twenty-Eight

Late one afternoon Tessa was resting in her room when once again the child rapped on the door. "You've a visitor," she announced, her voice conveying adolescent resentment of so many trips upstairs on Tessa's behalf.

"I thought Aidan had gone to York," Tessa muttered.

"Not that man, a different one this time," came the terse response.

Following the girl down the stairs, she entered the inn's common room to find Jeffrey pacing the small space like a caged tiger.

"Jeffr— Master Brixton," Tessa said, aware of the landlord's daughter staring at them coolly. She dismissed the girl with a nod of thanks. "How did you find me?"

Jeffrey's blue eyes flashed in his tanned face. "Mistress macFindlaech, I have been over half the island of Britain searching for you." Pacing back and forth, he recounted his movements in a low voice as Tessa stood rapt. He had been searching for her! "I went to Jedburgh as soon as I escaped Hawick's. You were not there and no one remembered seeing you, either as miss or lad. Then I went north, thinking you had returned to your family. On the way I asked about an old man and a boy everywhere I stopped. Finally a sheep herder remembered you, riding on fine horses, he said, like the one I rode. Banaugh had asked directions to Scone. I was hardly able to believe that you would go directly into such danger, but I traveled to Scone myself, arriving just after Malcolm's coronation. There I met my brother Ethelbert, of all people, who had a story to tell of a captive who had assured him that I was alive. Where had she gone? I asked him. All he knew was that you had promised to leave Scotland."

Jeffrey ran a hand through his hair again at the memory. "I could have shaken him for letting you go blithely off on your own, although I should have known Banaugh would look after you. Finally I rode to Saint Andrews and began questioning ships' crews. Banaugh was wise enough to leave a message with your ship's captain that led me to London. A maid at Mary's in-laws directed me here, having heard Mary mention your presence at the Mace and Thyme."

His face showed the frustration that he had experienced in the last weeks. "In short, I have had a devil of a time tracking you down. Now, what in the name of heaven were you doing at Scone?"

Tessa wanted to talk but sensed a half-grown witness lurking around the doorway. "Let us walk. We have things to discuss." She asked the girl to fetch her cloak. Jeffrey gave her a small coin, which had a positive effect on her speed, and they went out into the chilly autumn evening. She quickly told Jeffrey of Banaugh's new position and suggested they go to the shop, where the old man could listen and they could keep warm.

They were largely silent as they walked, Tessa's head filled with uncertainty of how she felt about Jeffrey's visit. Part of her whispered to reject any contact with this man that she was so unsure of, but another part of her sang with joy that he had sought her out. Perhaps she should have sent him away, but she knew that she could not do it.

The shop was half-filled with what looked like regular custom, men with roughened hands and serviceable clothing. They looked curiously at the two, the well-dressed man and the striking girl, but went back to their own pursuits as Banaugh escorted his friends to a table at the back. Introductions had to be made for the benefit of Mrs. Goode. Then she went off, assuring Banaugh that she could handle the trade for an hour. Banaugh told Jeffrey some of their adventures, making light of the danger and giving Tessa much credit for her bravery and her stamina. She said little, and finally Banaugh invited Jeffrey to tell his story. "So, Master Brixton, your escape went well?"

Jeffrey unfolded his long legs and regarded his feet, now drying in the fire's warmth, before answering. "Not as well at first as I'd hoped, but well enough," he said without looking at either of them. "They were so concerned with catching Tessa that they quite forgot about me."

"Did they learn that you'd helped me escape?"

"Hawick had no idea I was hiding in the room. He is sure you had a weapon hidden in the sleeve of your gown."

Tessa chuckled despite herself. "If I'd thought of it, I would have done so."

"Once you escaped, Hawick rethought his plans and decided to throw his lot in with Malcolm." It was the first jarring note to Jeffrey's homecoming, since his listeners had heard Hawick's man say that the decision had come at Jeffrey's instigation.

Banaugh's eyes slid to Tessa's face to

gauge her reaction. Seeing her jaw clench, he rose to leave them alone, but not before he let Tessa know his feelings about Jeffrey. "Ye're a good man, an' a lucky one t' ha' lived sae long among tha' pack o' dogs an' come oot wi' yer whole skin, Master Brixton. Now I'll be off t' help Mistress Goode, an' ye twa can speak t' each other alone." He went off, leaving Tessa staring at the rough plank table.

"What is it, Tessa?" Jeffrey asked. "Have you something to say?"

"No."

"Is something amiss between us?"

She straightened and looked at him directly, her chin up. "No. We are as we have always been, two people with vast differences between us."

Jeffrey's head cocked to one side as he tried to figure that one out, but he left it alone for the time being. "You have not told me what it was that took you to Scone, into the mouth of danger. Truly, I thought you would go home to the Cairngorms."

She took a deep breath, deciding that the truth was best, no matter what the consequence might be. "I had to find my uncle, Jeffrey. You see, Banaugh and I heard Dougal talking as they searched for us on the road. After that, we went north to warn

Macbeth of your advice to Hawick that he assassinate the king."

Jeffrey's eyes widened and a frown furrowed his brow. "*My* advice?" Then he scowled even more. "Tessa, do you really believe that I would plot the murder of your uncle, enemy of England or not?"

She was thrown into confusion. "I . . . I didn't know what to believe. We heard Dougal and the other man say that it was your idea."

"Well, they were wrong or you misunderstood."

"Banaugh heard it too. They said the Englishman advised that assassinating Macbeth would prove Hawick's loyalty to Malcolm."

Jeffrey slapped the table sharply and his face cleared. "There, I knew it. Are there not other Englishmen in the world beside me, Mistress macFindlaech?"

Tessa felt relief and embarrassment at once as the truth dawned. "You mean —"

"I am not the Englishman they spoke of. In truth, I have some suspicion as to who the man might be, but I cannot prove it yet." Jeffrey leaned toward Tessa, his hands spread out on the table between them. "In my time of captivity, Hawick referred to an English partner who dealt in stolen goods and other worse things. He was careful never to mention the man's name. He was simply called the Englishman when they spoke of him, but the man regularly sent information to the outlaws to help them plan their crimes: ship's routes, wealthy travelers near the borders, things like that. The box that you brought to me at Hawick's contained Eleanor's suspicions of a certain person, which confirmed my own. Having no proof, I will not say his name, but it was he, I am sure, that Dougal spoke of. He must have advised taking Malcolm's side after gleaning information at Court about the invading army's strength and leadership."

"So he advised that Macbeth's army would be defeated. Hawick hoped to gain favor by handing Malcolm the throne."

"Yes. Once you escaped, he must also have feared what you might tell your uncle about him. He would have had no chance with Macbeth after mistreating you as he did."

Tessa nodded. "I see. What a snake that man is."

"You need not tell me that. I struggled to stay alive in his snake pit for many months. At Scone, I told Ethelbert about Hawick and this associate in England. He said he had relayed what you told him to Malcolm

Canmore, and he would add my information to yours. As yet the man's position as king is so fragile that he dares not accuse Hawick, but once he is firmly in control, Malcolm has promised to root out the robber lords like Hawick, even those who purport to have done him service."

"Such action would be good for both our countries."

Jeffrey looked into Tessa's eyes earnestly. "I promise you it was not I who hatched that plot. I know not what kind of man Macbeth was, but I would never be party to assassination, and besides, he was your uncle. A mercenary I may be, but I would not betray . . . a friend." This last was almost something else, but Tessa could not decide what other word he might have wanted to use.

The mention of his occupation brought to Tessa's mind word of William's death. "I am sorry to have misjudged you," she apologized. "But Jeffrey, I have news that will affect you greatly." She told him everything: her capture and escape from Scone, her meeting with Ethelbert, and finally Aidan's visit. "Your brother William died, not over ten days ago, which means you are heir to Brixton."

When she had finished, Jeffrey stared into

the fire for a few moments. "I never thought to hold the title. I'm not even sure if I want it." She sat quietly, giving him time to think things through. Finally, he asked, "Aidan came to see you?"

"Yes, he came shortly after I met Mary on the street."

Jeffrey frowned. "Why did my brother visit you?"

Momentarily nonplussed, Tessa hesitated. How much of Aidan's conversation should she reveal? "He . . . was concerned for my welfare and he . . . expressed hope that the future will be better." It sounded weak, even to her own ears. "Why do you ask?"

Now Jeffrey answered too vaguely: "I only wondered how he took the news of my return. It may be hard for Aidan, after thinking he was heir to Brixton, to find that I am alive. Of course, I will be more generous to him than William ever was, but still, to be master is more desirable than to be second, no matter to whom."

Tessa nodded agreement. It would be hard for Aidan to accept Jeffrey's return, considering the circumstances. She'd felt his disappointment at the news when she'd revealed it. Still, Jeffrey was his brother, and Aidan seemed a man who had always adjusted to what life demanded. He would simply have to adjust once more.

Another question formed in Tessa's mind, and she had to ask. "Jeffrey, did you truly lose your memory after you fell into the sea?"

"Yes, that was no act." His face reflected the pain of it. "I did not know who I was or where I came from. Things came back to me, but only in bits. I remember almost everything now." His eyes told her he recalled how their relationship began. "After I saw you that day dressed as yourself, the pieces of my past began to form into a comprehensible whole. You, Eleanor, and Brixton, the things I care about."

Tessa chose to ignore his inclusion of her in the listing of things he cherished. "Yet you gave no sign that you knew me then."

Jeffrey's eyes crinkled as he grinned at her. "One of the more vivid images was of a furiously angry girl vowing to someday avenge her grievances against me in any way possible. How could I be sure that same girl would not take the opportunity to have Hawick throw me into his donjon for eternity?"

Tessa blushed as she remembered. "I have forgotten that vow, Jeffrey, and I wish you no harm."

"I came to that conclusion soon after, but

then I was forced to betray you to Hawick to save your life when he learned you carried gold." Jeffrey frowned in curiosity. "Why did you not use Macbeth's gold to ransom me?"

"After meeting the people in that place, Banaugh and I decided that Hawick would probably take the money and kill us all anyway. Besides, I — I thought you were content at Hawick's with . . ."

Jeffrey smiled again. "Again you suspected my relationship with Mairie? Oh, Tessa, if you knew how evil that woman is."

"I have had some words with her," Tessa responded, "and I have an inkling."

"She wants nothing more than wealth and power." Jeffrey scowled. "I amused her, but when my brother showed no interest in paying ransom, my usefulness at Hawick's was much in doubt. I was trying to work out a plan for escape when you arrived."

"Better if I had not come. Then you'd only have had yourself to consider."

"Mistress macFindlaech, I would not have missed those moments locked in the storeroom with you for anything," he teased, and she felt the warmth rise in her face.

"And the buffet in the eye, did you enjoy that too?" Tessa grinned, then grew serious. "I wish now I'd given Hawick a few like it."

Jeffrey's face sobered also. "You must watch for Hawick, for I fear he'll show in London soon."

"Hawick come here? But why?"

"Mairie hinted as much to me once. They have their sights set on wealth and power, and they will use the connection with Malcolm to advance themselves. The king will soon return to England to wed Princess Margaret, and the English will be forced to accept his entourage and treat them as guests, even men like Hawick."

"I see."

Jeffrey's dark brows bent in thought. "This Englishman that Hawick deals with has gained the trust of people in high places, for his information is reliable and valuable to the outlaws. If Ian joins with him here in England, they could make even more trouble than before. One thing is sure. His presence can bode no good for you."

"What do you mean?"

"Tessa, he is your husband, whether willingly or no."

Tessa felt her neck and cheeks turning pink. Jeffrey had to know the truth.

"No, he's not." Her voice was low, and she stared down at her hands, tracing the last of the Scottish bramble scratches, almost completely healed.

"What?"

"Hawick is not my husband, although he thinks he is. I was . . . married to someone else before I left England."

Jeffrey's face looked like it had turned to stone. "Really," was all he said.

How could she explain her feelings of desolation over Eleanor's death, William's callous treatment of her, and the news of Jeffrey's disappearance and assumed death? She saw that he was controlling his anger by sheer force of will. "Who?" came out between clenched teeth.

"Cedric . . . Lord Acton."

Jeffrey sat perfectly still for a few moments, struggling to control the flush that spread across his cheekbones. He swallowed once and his eyes closed slowly, like curtains falling over a stage. When he opened them a change had come over his face, and she saw the old look of amused scorn. "So, the little Scot caught herself an English lord. Well done, Tessa macFindlaech. I needn't have worried, it seems. You land on your feet like a cat, every time." Pushing back his chair, Jeffrey stood and bowed ironically. "Your servant, Lady Acton. Perhaps you, your husband, and I shall meet at court from time to time."

"I am not Lady Acton. At least I will not

be for long," Tessa hurried to explain. "An annulment is being sought. Aidan said it won't take long —"

It was the wrong thing to say, for Jeffrey came to the obvious conclusion. "So you hoped to exchange Lady Acton for Lady Brixton. Even better. Although Cedric is the wealthier, you'll have a much easier time controlling poor Aidan, besotted as he is with you. I did not believe him that day at William's London house when he told me that you and he —" Jeffrey stopped, again getting the better of his anger. "Good night, Lady Whoever-you-may-be when it is finished. I wish you well in your quest for a wealthy mate."

Tessa fought for something to say to make him stay, to make that look disappear from his face, but he was gone as she sat with her mouth open, still trying to form the correct words.

CHAPTER
TWENTY-NINE

Tessa remembered nothing of walking back to the inn that night. She had a dim memory of Banaugh's questioning face and Mrs. Goode's kind inquiry into her health. She could not bear to talk about it. She'd reassured them and gone quickly from the warm little shop into the cold, not noticing it at all. Banaugh followed her to the inn to protect her from scoundrels, but she was unaware of it.

Questions flooded her mind. How had she gotten into this situation? What should she do now? How much longer could she take the range of emotions that knowing Jeffrey Brixton caused her? She had gone from fear and despising to admiration and — when she would admit it — love, but now what was left? And what were his feelings for her, to cause such a reaction at her confession? Did Jeffrey truly love her after all, and had that love been killed by the news of her hasty marriage to Cedric?

In her room at the little inn, Tessa paced for hours. She finally accepted fully that she believed nothing ill of Jeffrey at all. She saw his past actions with new clarity. His abduction of her that long-ago night at Inverness gave proof of good character rather than evil. A bad man would have simply killed her and saved himself much trouble. In a situation fraught with danger for himself, Jeffrey had done what he could to protect Tessa, taking her to Eleanor where she had been treated well and protected.

At the times when she'd seen his cool, amused exterior torn away, beneath it was a man of strong emotions. She could still feel the passion he'd shown when he'd let down his guard. The stoically proud person he showed to the world hid Jeffrey's pain at the maltreatment he'd received from William, his shame at having nothing to call his own, and the pain of his true love, Eleanor, being beyond his reach, now forever. If he had begun to care for her, his pride had kept him from declaring it, believing as he had that he would remain landless for years, perhaps forever.

Recalling the look on his face tonight threatened to break her heart. One minute he'd been her friend, and the next, he had shut himself off from her completely.

Another thought sent her mood even lower. Jeffrey would soon become Lord Brixton. Even if she weren't attached to someone else, what would he want with a penniless Scotswoman whose family was disgraced? Jeffrey was now a rich man with his pick of English girls. It was a miracle he'd even come to see her at all. Things would change quickly when he took up his new title.

Looking at the night's events more clearly, Tessa convinced herself that he had come only in gratitude for her attempted rescue at Hawick's castle. Her heart hated the thought, but nothing she had experienced indicated love on Jeffrey's part. Gentlemanly concern for a lady's welfare sometimes, desire at others, but not love. Turning her face to the wall, Tessa willed herself to once again accept a future without Jeffrey Brixton in it.

Proof of Tessa's conclusions became ever more real over the next few days as there was no sign of Jeffrey. She moped around the inn, feeling more confined than she'd ever felt before. A note from Mary asking her to visit Hope House on Thursday lifted her malaise a little. Bursting for some word of Jeffrey, she accepted the invitation despite the dread of meeting old acquaintances.

Tessa didn't know what to expect from the Hope family, but she was welcomed politely by the older Hopes and with warmth by Francis. Mary, of course, was thrilled to see her. Francis blushed and fell back into his old stammering ways but eventually became more at ease in her presence. Mistress Hope, typical of overbearing mothers everywhere, dominated the conversation with pronouncements about the dire state of the world and vague faults of "the young," to which the only rejoinder needed was an occasional nod. After a polite hour or so, the older woman left to do some visiting of her own, and Francis and his father went to another room to examine some correspondence, leaving Mary and Tessa a chance to really talk.

"Tessa, how is it with you?"

"Mary, I thank you for the loan that you so kindly provided. It saved us, my old friend and me. Now he has employment, and we shall soon pay back the money."

"It is not necessary," Mary smiled. "I was so glad to see you again after wondering for months if you were dead or alive. I still consider you part of the family." She glanced slyly at Tessa. "And I think someone else would like to make that relationship official.

Am I correct?"

Her heart leapt for a moment until she realized that Mary meant Aidan, not Jeffrey. "It . . . was hinted that there were certain feelings present, but —"

"Aidan is going to have that silly marriage to Cedric annulled, since it was never consummated." Tessa thought that Cedric might be willing now that she had no connection to the Scottish throne and his dream of siring kings. "Oh, Tessa, how wonderful it would be if you were in truth a part of the family. Just think, we would be cousins and could be godparents for each other's children —" Mary broke off, blushing.

"Is there something you'd like to tell me?" Tessa teased, and Mary's even deeper blush said all that was needed. "I am so happy for you!"

"Francis is thrilled, and his father makes the most ridiculous suggestions. That I should not look directly at ugly people or animals, lest the babe take on the look of them. Even my mother-in-law is pleased with me for once."

They discussed her pregnancy for a few moments, but Mary finally returned to the former topic. "I do hope, Tessa, that you and Aidan make a match. He loves you, I think, and Jeffrey will be more generous with him than William ever was, so he'll see that you have everything you could wish for. Aidan has been wonderful through William's illness, seeing to things and helping out where he could. I used to worry about him, but I believe he will settle down once he has a wife."

It seemed Tessa had not convinced Aidan that she would not marry him, for Mary obviously had been told otherwise. "He had to go to York, but he said he would return today or tomorrow, so as to meet with Cedric," Mary went on.

Tessa paled. "Lord Acton is here in London?"

"Oh, yes." Mary smiled sympathetically. "I'm sure it will be awkward for you, but you must eventually face him. It is about the annulment that Aidan plans to speak with Lord Acton."

Dear Aidan, always efficient, always trying to be helpful. Knowing he had his own motives for wanting her to be free of Cedric, Tessa wasn't as enthusiastic as Mary. Still, his help would be welcome if he was successful. She turned the subject again to Mary.

"Please tell me more about this child you are carrying. When will he make his appearance, as near as you can tell?"

As Mary chatted on about the baby, Tessa's mind wandered in several directions. If she were free of Cedric, what would she do? Where was Hawick and what trouble was he plotting? Would Jeffrey ever forgive her for marrying Cedric? To the last question, sadly, she thought she knew the answer. The Lord of Brixton Hall did not want to see her again, and she must forget the feelings she had begun to allow to grow in her heart. The Brixton she wanted would not have her, and the one who wanted her aroused only feelings of affection, not love.

Mary was still talking, and Tessa came back in time to hear the end of her sentence. "— so I mentioned to her that I happened to know you had recently returned to London and suggested she invite you. If only to satisfy her curiosity, I'm sure you'll be asked to their celebration, possibly this afternoon."

Tessa smiled ruefully. "I'm sorry, Mary, but I . . ." She couldn't put into words her embarrassment, but she looked down at the only dress she owned. It was clean, but that was about all that could be said for it. Travel had left it forlorn, its ribbons missing or frayed, the hem dirty beyond redemption.

"I am such a simpleton! How could I be

so thoughtless? You must come with me to my room and pick out some gowns. I shan't be needing them for, oh, seven months or so!" Mary led the way to her chamber and there found Tessa three gowns that could be altered to fit her, two for daily wear and one for evening. "The green is most flattering to your coloring," Mary declared of the latter.

"But Mary, I'm not sure this is the right thing to do." Tessa for once was less confident than her friend.

"Of course it is. You must re-enter society, so that when Aidan asks for your hand, you will be ready to take your place as a Brixton. To Lord Acton and his mother you must be gracious and make no comment on where you have been for the last few months. I'm afraid Scotland is even less popular at the moment than usual. Young Siward, the old general's son, was killed in the fighting with Macbeth, and of course others among the English as well. Still, you have charm. Most people won't remember who your uncle was, and with your looks the men, at least, won't care."

"Mary, there is something I must tell you. It is true Aidan has asked me to marry him when I am free of Cedric, but I have refused his offer."

Mary's face showed surprise, "But Aidan

said —"

"Aidan thinks I can be persuaded, but I tell you, I will not marry him. I care too much for him and for all of you to make a marriage where there is no love. In fact, I don't believe now that I can marry without love. I have learned things in the past year, and I no longer believe that security at any price is what I want from life."

"I see." Mary frowned thoughtfully. "He seemed so sure. Perhaps he means to ask again when you are more settled and have had time to think things over."

Tessa knew what Mary was thinking. What other prospects had she? Even with an annulment, her reputation would be questionable after running away from her first husband, she had no dowry to make a man overlook her odd past, and her bloodline was not one that would win her many friends in England at this time. Mary dropped the subject, but Tessa was sure her friend thought her mad for not taking Aidan's offer. Marriage to him would be comfortable despite his lack of a title, and he would care for her as Eleanor had intended.

She could not explain it to Mary any more than she could to Aidan. Tessa simply knew that she would never marry at all unless it was to a man who'd won her heart. Rich or poor no longer mattered.

When she returned to the inn that afternoon, the invitation Mary had mentioned was there. The Ballards were having a masque at their home to celebrate the harvest. The estate was near Oxford, close to Mary and Francis's home. Tessa would journey to Mary's house, stay a few days there, and attend the party with the young couple.

She and Mary had great fun making their masks, which seldom concealed anyone's identity for long but were popular just the same. Tessa's was silk of a deep green that matched the dress Mary had lent her, and she added twists of rose-colored ribbon as complements. The dress itself had sleeves fitted to the elbow, which then flared into wide V's with a filmy white lining. The rounded neckline was cut low to reveal a gleaming white shift with embroidered trim. The draping skirt was pulled up in graceful scallops across the front to show an underskirt of the same white fabric as the sleeve linings. The points at which the skirt was gathered were adorned with ribbons that fell over the white below them with charming effect. Tessa's hair, which was still quite short, was pinned back with combs and false curls added to make her more presentable. Mary despaired of her tanned face, adding powder to lighten it until Tessa sneezed repeatedly.

The manor was dazzling as they entered the main hall. Candles everywhere cast light and shadow, making the moving, masked figures seem mysterious at some times and colorful at others. Ladies in elaborate gowns with trailing skirts and bright trims moved smoothly across the hall, while gentlemen in tight hose and velvet tunics watched appreciatively.

Roger Ballard, a man of large proportions in every way, bawled out greetings, kissing the ladies greedily and slapping the men on their backs hard enough to make some of them wince. Dame Ballard, her husband's physical opposite, was as small-boned and thin as Tessa remembered her, still looking as if she were always cold, both inside and out. Her main topic of conversation remained the divine Beatrice, the supposed twin to Tessa whom she had yet to meet.

Having strong feelings of discomfort about the whole evening, Tessa waited for Dame Ballard to launch into the questions that were sure to be invasive and offensive. Surprisingly, not a question was asked about where she had been for the past months. When greetings were exchanged, the lady began at once commenting on the resemblance between Tessa and her daughter. In her high, nasal voice, few things sounded like compliments, however. Something — or someone — had explained away Tessa's past misdeeds, it seemed, and she was spared explanations of her flight, her absence, and her reappearance. Aidan's work, she decided, breathing a sigh of relief.

It was not to last, however, for although she had no questions about Tessa's recent travels, Dame Ballard had news that shook Tessa to her very core. "And did you suspect when you stayed with the Brixtons, my dear, that there was a criminal in that very household?"

A lady who stood nearby tried to shut the old woman up. "Barbara, you mustn't say such things. They are only rumors, after all. No one knows the truth of it yet."

Dame Ballard was not to be silenced, as usual. "I have had it from an excellent source that he has dealt with an outlaw in Scotland for years, feeding the brute information so that he could rob and kill loyal Englishmen. He stole from his own brother, too. It is true, because as soon as his so-called drowning occurred, the embezzlement stopped as well. I for one always thought he was suspicious, a little too hand-

444

some, a little bit above those around him. Pride goeth, as they say. He may pretend all he likes. The man is a thief and as good as a murderer, and he'll never be allowed to take the title. Why, he'll be lucky to escape hanging. If he were before me at this moment, my best recommendation would be that he return to Scotland, where they're all murdering heathens." The woman's pale face registered suddenly the realization that she had gone too far, and she murmured in Tessa's direction, "Present company excepted, of course," as if that excused the deadly insult to Scots in general.

There was a shocked silence as Tessa tried to make sense of what she'd heard. The dame's insult had no effect on her. The woman was a bigot of the worst kind and stupid to boot, but the import of the rest of it . . . The Englishman who'd plotted with Hawick — Dame Ballard seemed to be saying that it was Jeffrey. Impossible!

Did people actually believe that Jeffrey would collaborate with Hawick? *You did, at least at times,* her thoughts reminded her. *But I didn't, never truly,* she decided. Aware that those around her were waiting to gauge her response to Dame Ballard's usual lack of tact, she stammered out a weak response. "I am sure you meant no disrespect."

In spite of her oblivious personality, the lady sensed that a change of subject was called for. "And here you are back among us after months and months," she whined. "Now you shall meet Beatrice, and she shall understand what I have told her, that you are her very double."

She dragged Tessa across the room to meet a lady of some forty years who, at least once upon a time, had hair the color of Tessa's and green eyes. There the resemblance ended, but the doting mother made everyone nearby judge how exactly alike the two were. They had to take off their masks and stand side by side, which certainly did no favors for poor Beatrice. Once, however, her eyes met Tessa's and a light of amusement sparked in them. Beatrice was used to humoring her mother. So, it appeared, were many others, for murmurs of faint agreement were made, placating the old lady and allowing Tessa to escape her clutches. Dame Ballard wandered off to greet the newest arrivals.

Tying her mask on again, Tessa stood among strangers, making polite conversation and discreetly searching for Mary in the crowd. Her eye lit upon a man standing aside, his black silk mask extremely plain. The clothes he wore were also black, and although finely cut, quite nondescript, as if he wanted to call no attention to himself. She had the feeling that he was staring at her, even though she couldn't see his eyes. His head tilted an inch, and she recognized the movement. Jeffrey! Looking directly at him she bowed her head slightly, acknowledging him. In answer, he made a slight movement of his head toward a hallway at his back, then turned and disappeared down it. Glancing around, Tessa saw that no one paid heed to her at the moment. She hurried after him.

Down the passage were three rooms. The first was empty. The second was locked, and she went on to the third. As soon as she stepped into the room, the door closed behind her. It was a small office. A desk with writing materials neatly arranged on it stood near the window, a cabinet set into the left wall had a key protruding from the lock, two chairs sat against the far wall on either side of a cold fireplace. That was all, except that Jeffrey Brixton stood behind her, leaning against the door he had just locked.

"Tessa." He had removed the mask, and his face was serious, even haggard.

"Jeffrey, you should not have come. I have just heard the most ridiculous —"

He threw up a hand to stop her. "I know.

I have been accused of monstrous crimes, and I must defend myself. There are rumors that I will be arrested if I show my face. I have been staying with friends, trying to work out a plan to clear my name. But I had to come. I must speak to someone who will surely be here, to find out why this is happening." His face tensed. "Although I have deduced it."

So he had not come to see her. It had been a silly thought. If he'd wanted to talk to her, he could have come to the inn. "I did not know you would be here," he said.

"Mary . . . it is Mary's doing. She is determined that I shall be accepted in society."

"And what of Cedric?"

"That was a mistake, as I tried to tell you. There is to be an annulment." Tessa could not help herself. Her pride did not matter at this moment. "Jeffrey — I thought you were dead. Eleanor died. I had no one, nowhere to go! I —" His fingers touched her lips, and she stopped as he took her in his arms, his head bent over hers.

"I am sorry," he whispered. "As soon as I left you that night, I knew in my heart that you had done what you had to do. Only it was such a blow to believe that you were lost to me. Just when I had decided that nothing mattered except — I mean, I had intended —"

Suddenly he was kissing her, and she was lost in the press of his lips on hers. The world stopped and nothing mattered, not the accusations against him or worry about the future — nothing. When he finally released her she stood mute, flooded with a thousand emotions, relief and happiness among them, but strongest was love, the love she had felt almost from the first, the love that she now knew Jeffrey felt too.

Voices in the passageway brought them both back to their present situation. Jeffrey replaced his mask hurriedly and moved toward the window, pushing it open. "I must go. If I am successful tonight, my name will be cleared and I will come to you a free man. If not, I do not know when we shall meet again."

"Jeffrey, what will you do?"

His face hardened. "I will put a stop to these lies about me. I know who is behind them and will deal with him tonight."

"Please be careful. If someone works to harm you —"

"Then someone had better understand that I do not take such things lightly." He spoke grimly, and he was gone.

Tessa left the room in confusion. Jeffrey

did love her, but he was in grave trouble. He seemed driven, almost murderous in his intent to stop whoever had slandered him. And why would anyone say those things about Jeffrey? He was no thief, and he was not Hawick's ally, she was sure. Who would want the world to believe such things?

CHAPTER
THIRTY

Tessa wandered through the crowd, the joy of the evening gone for her. The room was hot with the crush of people, and a nearby door stood ajar a few inches, letting in fresh air. Needing to escape the laughter and merriment, she stepped out the door and found herself in the garden. Cool air immediately chilled her flushed skin, but she welcomed it. To her chagrin, she came face to face with Cedric Acton, mask in hand as he attempted to rethread the ribbon that had come untied from one side.

His discomfort was as great as hers, it seemed. "Well, well, my lady wife. How goes it?"

Tessa turned to go, but Cedric grabbed her arm in a tight grip. His eyes were hard, but he smiled and tried for a light tone. "I was most distressed by your unannounced departure from our wedding. It has taken some explaining, especially to my mother, to quiet the questions that arose from your disappearance."

Tessa was for an instant sympathetic to Cedric's situation. Lady Acton must have given him fits. "Cedric, I am sorry. It was a mistake for us to wed. You don't love me, and I discovered that I could not be the wife you hoped for. I'm sure you understand that it will benefit both of us to have this marriage annulled quietly and quickly."

"That is impossible, as I told your *friend* Aidan Brixton." Cedric's large chin set with decision.

"But —"

"If we separate now, I will look a fool," Cedric interrupted. "First you leave me on our wedding day, then you return to London and never bother to inform me. I have to hear it from Brixton, who comes to tell me you will be his bride as soon as you are free from me."

"That is not true. Still, ours is no true marriage."

"It is as much a marriage as many people get. You have done what you wanted, gone off who knows where. Now it is time that I get what I want, my wife in my home and my bed, pretending at least to be content if she cannot pretend happiness."

"I don't understand. I heard you say that

marriage to me would bring you power in Scotland. There is no possibility of that now, so why?"

Cedric's eyes flashed with the understanding of what had caused her to run from him. "I see. Eavesdropping, were you? Well, it is true enough, but it is not all. If you must know, I have spoken with young Malcolm, who would be most grateful, he tells me, if you were under the care of someone who would prevent your return to Scotland, at least until he is firmly established. Stories have spread of your heroic ride across the Lowlands to warn Macbeth of danger, and the Scots love nothing more than a good tale to fire their blood. Malcolm fears you would become a rallying point for rebellion if you were nearby."

"I promised him I would not return. Is that not enough?" Tessa stormed.

"Apparently he cannot trust his own subjects — yet." Cedric set his large chin truculently. "In addition to that, you are my wife. The world knows you as such. Since you are here tonight, we will quiet their yammering gossip by appearing together publicly. You will have all you desire of my wealth, fine clothes, and lovely things, but you *will* play your part. Once we have sons, I may even leave your bed. Other women will be glad of my company."

Tessa tore her arm from his grip and massaged the bruises where his fingers had been. "Then go and find one of them now. Annul the marriage."

"I repeat, I will not be made fool of. You will make amends to my reputation by taking on your proper role. Young Brixton shall not have you. You are mine." So that was the truth of it. Aidan had seemed over-eager and made Cedric angry. "He shall see us together as man and wife tonight, and he will have to accept it. Is he here yet?"

"I have not seen Aidan," she answered dully. She was again a prisoner, this time of Cedric Acton. As her lawful husband, he had the right to claim her, body and soul. Who might help her? Aidan, but then she would be beholden to him. What a tangle she had got into. A sudden thought flashed through Tessa's mind. Cedric had betrayed great interest in Scotland on the day of their wedding. Was it possible he was the Englishman that Hawick dealt with? He certainly was more ruthless than he had seemed all those months ago when he courted her. By marrying Cedric in her haste to solve her problems, she had made them worse, and she was now under his control.

The conversation with Jeffrey returned.

He had asked her directly how she felt about Cedric. Was it because he suspected him, too? With his ties to William, Cedric might have been able to frame Jeffrey, but to what purpose?

Cedric had replaced his mask and his manner became brisk. "Now then, shall we go in to dinner? It will be the first time the world has seen the new Lord and Lady Acton, so be sure to keep yourself composed."

Tessa had no choice but to accompany him. He led her inside, his hand on her elbow. What should she do? Run? Where? She was not welcome in Scotland, and in England she was this man's property. Woodenly she stood by as Cedric chatted with several people as if it were not the oddest thing to have a captive wife by his side.

To make matters worse, as they moved across the hall, they met a beautifully dressed creature in a fantastic mask of feathers and silk. The woman was dressed in blue, long associated with faithfulness in myth and story, which was ironic, for Tessa recognized Mairie behind the mask. Tessa's mask was off, and Mairie's eyes widened, then narrowed as she considered what to do about the situation. Finally, she decided to brazen her way through. Smiling ironically, she removed her own mask.

Mairie was more impressive than ever tonight. The blue gown was sewn with hundreds of tiny pearls and draped snugly over her form. The neckline was low, showing much of her white neck and bosom. Over her dark hair a jewel-studded net of gold fell loosely, shining in the torchlight. Her eyes were enlarged by subtly applied cosmetics, and her lips were their usual, unnatural red. She looked Tessa over speculatively, taking note of the green velvet dress and matching ribbons braided into her hair. *Plainer than mine,* her look said, but Tessa reflected that her borrowed costume was better than one that was in all likelihood stolen.

Mairie spoke first, her voice low and seductive, but Tessa had a moment's amusement picturing her tantrum over Jeffrey's escape as the bard had related it. "Mistress Tessa, is it not?"

Cedric was not about to be forgotten. "The lady is my wife," he said decisively. Mairie's eyebrows lifted in surprise, but her face took on a sly look. Was she considering blackmail? Probably, but she didn't know the circumstances.

Tessa smiled at her brightly. "Mistress Hawick, this is my husband Cedric, Lord Acton. We were married last spring, before I came to Scotland and was graced by your brother's hospitality. Husband, this is Mairie Hawick, of both France and Scotland."

Mairie absorbed the information with interest but did not react beyond a slight narrowing of the eyes. "I offer my congratulations on your marriage, Lord Acton, Lady Acton." Excusing herself regally, she moved off into the crowd. Tessa wondered if Hawick was nearby and would soon learn the news. Perhaps when he knew she was not his legal wife he would forget about her and return to Scotland.

Supper was announced at nine, and Tessa by that time had located Mary and Francis. Mary looked surprised to see Cedric, but he spoke cheerfully to her and the four of them went in together. They approached long tables set up in three rows with a head table perpendicular to the others. Cedric went in search of the seneschal to exchange his place so that he would be seated beside Tessa.

"We will of course make our greetings to Mother," Cedric informed Tessa, "but we will do it after supper or her digestion may be upset." He moved off fussily.

Mary raised an eyebrow at Tessa, but she could not think of a way to explain things briefly in this public place. Francis seated them both and Tessa waited glumly, wondering what could possibly make matters worse. A masked figure touched her shoulder, and when she turned, there was Aidan.

"Forgive me for not seeking you out sooner," he apologized, removing a dark blue silk mask. "I had some things I had to do, and only now have been able to turn my thoughts to pleasure. And pleasure it will be to sit beside you, Tessa."

She had only time to give him the briefest of explanations, telling him he could not sit beside her because of Cedric's insistence that they play the married couple, but his face showed understanding . . . and anger.

"I spoke to him yesterday, and I feared he would make things difficult for us," he whispered grimly. Tessa hoped he would not make a scene, and thankfully he did not. "I must tell you something else. I have spoken to Jeffrey, who is here this evening in disguise!" Tessa tried to appear surprised as Aidan continued. "He says he is not guilty of the terrible things that are said about him and is determined to put an end to the matter tonight."

Tessa murmured, "I hope that is possible."

"As do I, my love, but I have come to doubt it. The evidence against him is strong, and although I tried not to believe it myself,

I can think of no other explanation."

"Could someone else who knew William's affairs have done these things and then blamed them on Jeffrey?"

Aidan appeared to think about it. "I don't know who."

"Cedric seems to have been close to William."

"Hmm. It's possible, but Cedric has no need of William's money." He considered again. "Could he be jealous of . . . you and Jeffrey?"

Tessa shook her head. "There is nothing to be jealous of. Besides, Cedric knows I don't love him. He still has dreams of influencing things in Scotland."

"If we convince him that you can not help with that, he will agree to the annulment. You will see." Aidan kissed her hand and retreated as the host called for silence and the speeches began.

As the host bawled what he took to be witticisms about those assembled, Tessa glanced about the room at the masked figures. A large woman in an overdone costume glared back at her from several tables over, and she recognized Lady Acton despite the mask of peacock feathers she wore. Her animosity was obvious, and her masculine body fairly bristled with indignation at Tessa's presence. Another reason she should not have come, she chided herself.

As the meal progressed, the chair beside her remained empty. Cedric did not return. Although she had quite lost her appetite, they were served course after course of exotic foods: meats carved into odd shapes, puddings studded with currants and dried cherries, and finally, tiny cakes decorated with paper castles that yielded trinkets when cut open. Tessa received a pendant of rose quartz, and Mary a tiny silver bear. As Tessa turned to put the items into her reticule she saw Jeffrey, his mask covering his face, sliding into a seat two tables over. He watched her grimly as he waved away the servant with the cakes. Although she could not see his face for the mask, his shoulders and neck were held stiffly upright, as if he were tensed for something — escape? Resistance? His eyes took in the empty chair beside her and then Mary said something to Tessa. When she looked back, Jeffrey was gone.

After dinner there was entertainment, but still Cedric did not take his seat. Scanning the crowd that watched three acrobats perform feats of balance and strength, Tessa saw no sign of Jeffrey, either. Her gaze traveled over the room idly, identifying people she knew now that the masks were removed.

She again met the gaze of Lady Acton, as imperious as ever. When their eyes met, the old lady's face stiffened and she turned away. At least there might be an ally there in the argument for annulment.

Mairie Hawick sat near Lady Ballard, two smitten men on either side of her vying for her attention. Evidently she had been watching Tessa, for when their eyes met, she raised an eyebrow and smiled, her nose lifting in disdain. Tessa held her own face immobile — at least she hoped so — and turned to speak to Mary and Francis.

The acrobats gave way to a bard, who had hardly begun his tale when Tessa felt a tug at her sleeve. She turned to find Aidan, white-faced and intense. "Tessa, come quickly," he hissed in her ear. His eyes warned her to silence, so she merely touched Mary's arm and whispered that she would return. She rose and followed Aidan from the room, threading her way around guests, servants, and hounds blocking the way.

Once they were outside, she asked, "What is it? Where are we going?"

Aidan turned to her, his eyes still wide with excitement. "Tessa, you must be calm. I have something to tell you, and you must try to understand it. There has been an . . . incident."

"An incident? Aidan, please slow down. I can't keep up." He was hurrying down the path toward the stables, and in the gloom of night she almost lost sight of him from time to time.

"Aidan!"

He stopped and waited for her to catch up at the stable door. There was a light inside, and she could see that his eyes glowed feverishly. Tessa did not know what to think until she looked past him into the stall closest to the door. A man's legs were visible in the faint light of a lantern that had been hung on a post nearby. From their position, it was obvious the man was not conscious. Aidan stopped in the doorway. Tessa stepped closer, into the stall. The man was Cedric Acton, and he lay face down in the straw, a knife protruding from his back. Tessa looked at Aidan, whose eyes were fixed on her, gauging her reaction.

"Aidan, what happened?"

"Tessa, you must forgive him. I'm sure he didn't mean to kill Cedric. He was upset when I told him that Acton intended to hold to his marriage to you. I had all I could do to keep him from attacking the man at the banquet, in front of everyone. I walked with him outside, thought I had calmed him down, but you know Jeffrey. He has a terrible temper."

Tessa gazed at Aidan in disbelief. "Are you telling me that Jeffrey did this?"

"I'm afraid so. He said something about Cedric taking you from him. I believe he has lost his wits — the blow to his head, you know. Did he not seem morose and changeable of mood to you?"

"I . . . I don't know." Tessa was at a loss to understand what was happening. Yes, Jeffrey had been changeable, sometimes helping her and other times setting her back, but he had explained all that.

Aidan looked down at Tessa, his eyes sad. "My dear, I fear that he intends to harm you also. He said as much."

"You spoke to him? He admitted to this?" Tessa gestured weakly at the body.

Aidan put his hands on her shoulders. "I know it is a shock, Tessa, but you must understand. Jeffrey is a man of great pride. He would not let Cedric rob him of a woman he considers his." Aidan ran a hand through his hair and looked out into the darkness, avoiding the scene of death beside him. "I had business with Cedric, so I went looking for him. Jeffrey met me in the garden, wild-eyed. He told me what he'd done, and why. I came to try to help Cedric, but it was too late. Then I thought more clearly and came to warn you. He intends harm to you also, believing you have betrayed him."

Tessa's mind was finally taking in what she had seen. Could Jeffrey have killed Cedric? He certainly had reacted badly to the news of her marriage to him. She forced herself to look at the body again. Poor Cedric. She had not been fond of him, but to be . . . She had a sudden revelation.

Cedric had been stabbed in the back! That did not make sense. Everything she knew of Jeffrey Brixton cried out that if he had intended Cedric's death, it would have been accomplished by face-to-face combat, not by stealth. Even Hawick's men had been merely tied up and left behind during his escape, except the one who had died in actual fighting. It couldn't be Jeffrey. Someone else had done it.

Understanding dawned. Aidan said Jeffrey had admitted it. Aidan said Jeffrey intended to harm her. Aidan had forced her to leave the ball with him, alone . . . and now she was at Aidan's mercy. With a jolt she realized that only one man had much to gain from Jeffrey's fall: Aidan, his own brother. She had not considered it possible, never thought that he would betray a blood relative, but if Jeffrey were convicted of a crime or forced to flee England, Aidan would become Lord Brixton, take control of the properties associated with the title, and be able to win the woman he seemed to desire, Tessa herself.

How could she not have seen it, having heard stories all her life of bloodshed among families to gain power? It was the same here, the same everywhere. But Aidan, who seemed so helpful to his family, so kind? She tried to find other explanations, anything.

No, it was true. Aidan had stayed in the background, doing William's bidding, for years. He now believed he deserved to be Lord Brixton, and he was willing to destroy his brother to reach that goal. Suddenly the niggling feeling from days before that something was wrong became clear. She had mentioned an outlaw as Jeffrey's captor, and Aidan had supplied his name: *Hawick,* he had said. He knew the outlaw, had known him all along. Aidan was the Englishman Hawick dealt with!

Tessa's face told the story of her thoughts, and Aidan, as always, was watchful. He said nothing, but she saw the brown eyes harden until there was no kindness in them at all, and his lips curled into a sneer.

"*You* did this," Tessa accused.

Aidan seemed unfazed. "We were hoping you would believe me. It would have been so much easier if you had."

"We?"

"My friends, actually, some old friends of yours, as well —" He raised his voice a notch. "My dear? I believe you know Mistress macFindlaech?"

"But of course," said a voice from the shadows, and Mairie stepped out from her hiding place. "I told you she would not believe Jeffrey did it."

"And you were correct, mademoiselle. I admit it." Aidan's voice betrayed his impatience with the situation. "There's nothing for it now but to do as we planned. I will return as soon as possible. Give me a few minutes and then do your part."

Mairie nodded. "Hurry then. The entertainment will end soon, and some may start for home. You will not want her screaming and kicking when there is the possibility she will be seen."

Tessa finally grasped their intention to abduct her, and she made a lunge for the door, hoping to duck past Aidan before he could stop her. Aidan simply raised his arm and cut her off, a wicked smile across his face. He encircled her waist with the other arm. Coming up behind Tessa, Mairie handed him a looped rope that he dropped over her shoulders and pulled tight. Mairie quickly tied the sky-blue sash from her dress over Tessa's mouth.

A horse stood in the shadows of the farthest stall, already saddled. Aidan mounted then leaned down, easily picked Tessa up, and set her before him. "Give me a minute to get away, then scream your heart out," he told Mairie, steering the horse out the door. Tessa caught a last glimpse as the woman stood, perfectly composed and lovely as always, smiling after them.

Taking a little-used path that circled behind the house and came out a quarter mile down the road, Aidan urged the horse to a gallop. Within minutes of leaving the masque, Tessa was on her way to an unknown destination, farther and farther away from help as the horse's hooves pounded along the road in the moonlight.

CHAPTER
THIRTY-ONE

As they traveled, Tessa considered her options. She could try to slide off the horse, but with her arms tied to her sides she would probably be hurt, and Aidan had only to turn around and come after her. If he removed the gag she could try to talk to him. Was he beyond reason? If he had killed Cedric and blamed his own brother, what else was he capable of? In the end, she rode on passively, hoping for a chance to escape at some point.

After a long and uncomfortable ride, Aidan allowed the horse to slow to a walk as he looked for a turning. When he found it, they made their way down a descending path little used and uneven, with washouts making it obvious that rainwater followed the same course to a large river. Knowing vaguely that both the Ballards and the Hopes lived along the lane, Tessa judged that they were approaching the River

Thames, which flowed through Oxford and on to London. A light showed in front of them after some moments, and Aidan called softly, "It's I."

"Come on, then," replied a voice, and Aidan made his way onto a sandy bank where the sound of flowing water could be heard. A small boat was tied to an ancient dock, and beside the boat squatted Hawick, warming himself over a small fire.

"So she didn't believe your story," he commented when he saw Tessa. His fore-knowledge of the night's events revealed that Aidan had cold-bloodedly planned the murder of Cedric. It had been no sudden crime of rage.

"It was worth a try," Aidan replied, "but your sister will see to it that my brother takes the blame."

"Right. It would have been nice if she had come willingly, but a woman is a woman anyway, say I. Once you are lord of Brixton, she'll come along right enough."

Tessa's mind screamed *"Never,"* but she told herself to concentrate on taking in her surroundings in case a chance came to free herself.

"I must return as soon as the messenger arrives, so I can add my sad tale to Mai-rie's." Aidan spoke to Tessa for the first time. "We had hoped for your help, unwitting though it might be. If you had believed in Jeffrey's guilt, it would have added to the evidence that I have been heaping up against him over time. Now I must add a bit to my part." Aidan couldn't resist explaining. "Everyone will be shocked to find that my poor deranged brother tried to kill even me. It is obvious that he is a madman." He rolled his eyes in pretended horror. "Being no match for him, a professional killer, I ran away, but I shall return and reluctantly tell the truth of the matter, matching Mairie's story in every detail, which of course I could not have heard. In fact, I've never met the woman before in my life, as far as anyone knows."

Hawick confirmed what Tessa had guessed. "I may have mentioned in your presence a certain Englishman with whom I have had some business. That gentleman stands before you, mistress."

Aidan continued the story. "As William's agent, I had access to information and networks that allowed me to supply Hawick with specifics that have been profitable for us both. Since I had intimate knowledge of the crimes, it was easy to blame them on my brother when the necessity arose. With poor William dead — and poison will do that to a man — and Jeffrey imprisoned, I will finally be what I have worked all my life to become." His voice was triumphant, and he turned with fervor to Tessa. "And tonight is your last chance to share it with me." Aidan untied the sash that acted as a gag. "Leave me alone with the lady for a moment, Hawick."

The outlaw moved off with a leer, joining one of his men who had come from the boat and squatted by the fire. Aidan gently removed the rope that tied her arms. Tessa spoke in an agitated whisper. "Aidan, Hawick is not to be trusted. He forced me into a marriage with him —"

Aidan put a finger to her lips, smiling patronizingly. "I know all about Hawick's mistakes. First, he was supposed to assure that my brother Jeffrey never returned to England, since it was obvious that you were — are — infatuated with him. He failed in that because Mairie took an interest in Jeffrey, and Hawick can deny his sister nothing.

"Secondly, he took an interest in you, not knowing of my affection. Since things worked out as they did, there is no harm done. The marriage is invalid. You were married to Cedric at the time, and now Cedric is no more, so you are, as they say, an eligible candidate. Hawick is not perfect, but he suits my needs at the moment."

Aidan took Tessa's arm and walked her to the bank of the river. "Now, when we were last together, I proposed to make you Lady Brixton. I was, of course, premature in that pronouncement, not knowing that you had found Jeffrey. Why ever did you do such a thing?"

"Eleanor asked me to give him some letters."

Aidan reacted with a spate of anger. "Yes, that is how he knew of my affairs. The bitch was spying on me. Still, he has no proof. I found the box in his room and burned it." Aidan turned to look at her, his face quite clear in the moonlight. "Oh, Tessa, I have planned this for so long. Playing the faithful lackey to William, the charming nobody to the rest of the family. And then you came along, and I knew I had found someone who would make it worth the chances I had taken, and others I must take, to make my plan work. It helped that you thought Eleanor and Jeffrey were lovers. It kept you from him just long enough for me to arrange his accident."

"But —" Tessa began, and then stopped herself. When she had mentioned Jeffrey's love for Eleanor to Aidan, he had at first seemed surprised. She'd taken it for shock that she knew of the affair, but now she realized it was surprise at the thought itself. Cleverly Aidan had played along, pretending he knew of the affair and making her doubt her feelings for Jeffrey.

He laughed aloud now at the stunned look on her face, his character quite different now from the self-controlled man she had known. "The pious Eleanor and the noble Jeffrey — that's a humorous picture! No, my dear, they were never lovers. Jeffrey felt sorry for Eleanor, and rightly so, for the way William treated her, but there was only affection between them. I know, because William kept spies in his household at all times, so jealous was he of his wife. She was a saint, as she appeared to be."

His face showed contempt. "I understood Eleanor's decision to play William's docile servant, her desire to have a place in society, and her acceptance of his wealth and security, because I had those same needs. Yet nothing I did honestly brought me what I wanted. I had little chance of becoming Lord Brixton, I did not have two coins to rub together, and I did not win your love. So I have turned to other means, which have worked out well."

Tessa made no answer and Aidan went on,

intoxicated with the sound of his own voice. "I wish you had not been so diligent about Eleanor's wishes. The letters she sent to Jeffrey alerted him to my plans, so he was able to escape arrest when he found that the box was gone. If he had been surprised and taken prisoner, he would have been unable to stop me. I have been very careful to impress the right people with my earnestness and diligence, all the while working secretly with those who can assist me to get the things I've always wanted." He turned away, looking at the darkly moving stream before them, invisible except for the occasional shimmer of light over the changing surface.

Aidan's voice became dreamy, almost wistful, revealing the boy inside the man who felt cheated by the accident of his birth. "You truly cannot know what it is like to be the bastard brother. Oh, they were all very correct and never mentioned it, but people talk. Servants, neighbors, even the tutor Father hired to teach us our letters made it clear that I was the least of the sons." His shoulders shrunk together at the memory.

"And of course, I couldn't inherit unless everyone else in the family had his chance first. William used me as a clerk who came cheaply, since he didn't have to pay a salary.

Still, over time he did begin to trust me and left things in my care, which was an advantage. I began casting about for ways to make money, and I met certain men like myself, who make money as they can."

"Men like Ian Hawick," Tessa supplied scornfully.

Aidan sent a glance over to where Hawick and his man stood warming themselves by a small fire in the sandy bank. "Yes, men like Ian. When Hawick sent a messenger to demand ransom for Jeffrey, I knew he was one such as I. You see, Jeffrey did not go overboard by accident. It's just that he has the most damnable luck. He was rescued by some fishermen and came into Ian's hands. A word with Dougal after he left Brixton Manor gave me the story. My brother did not know his own name. In the end, for certain exchanges of information, Hawick agreed to see that he did not return to England. Quite by accident in the meantime, Eleanor found out about my dealings with . . ." He paused to think of an acceptable term.

"Criminals," Tessa put in again.

"As you say." Aiden bowed ironically. "She wrote to Jeffrey, informing him of her suspicions. Because of the family tie, she did not expose me publicly, and because she knew what William would do if he found out, she did not give the information to him. Eleanor trusted Jeffrey. She wasn't to know that he would not return from that last trip." His teeth showed white in the moonlight as he smiled knowingly. "I, of course, congratulated William on not wasting his money to ransom a brother that those terrible outlaws had probably already killed."

"So you plotted to cheat one brother and kill the other?"

"The idea first came to me when Ethelbert took the holy orders. I realized that I was one step closer to the title, and one step is a beginning. For three years I have been preparing my way, investing the profits from my business dealings where it will do me good at Court. Soon I could have been happy, with Brixton . . . and with you."

"But when Jeffrey returned —"

Aidan nodded as if she were a pupil who had learned her lessons well. "He had to be dealt with. To free you from your ridiculous marriage and get rid of him at the same time, what could be better than to arrange his apparent guilt in Cedric's murder?"

They had walked in a circle as Aidan explained all this and were back where they'd started, with the horse standing patiently by. At that moment, Tessa, who hoped that Hawick had moved far enough away to be no immediate threat, brought her knee up sharply to Aidan's groin, as she'd seen a boy do in a fight once years ago, causing him to double over with a yelp of pain. She grabbed the horse's bridle and swung herself into the saddle, at the same time turning the animal's head and kicking it fiercely in the side. The horse bolted up the bank clumsily, with Tessa still trying to get a good seat in the saddle. She never saw the arm that swept her from atop the horse. There was the sensation of flying through the air, and then she landed on the sand and knew nothing.

Aidan, still crouched over in pain, looked up the riverbank to see Dougal pick up the small, limp frame and heave it over his shoulder. "Put her in the boat," he gasped through tight lips. "She shall pay for that." The man turned away to hide the smile that crossed his face. She had humiliated them all, but she was theirs now.

Tessa awoke to the sound of lapping water and a bumping of wood on wood. She was in the boat, she discovered, and the boat was still tied to the decaying pier. Every few seconds the movement of the water caused it to hit the mooring post with a soft clunk. She opened her eyes just enough to see her surroundings dimly. A few yards downriver was a large tree whose roots extended into the river, creating the small cove of still, shallow water where the old dock sat.

In the relative protection from wind and current provided by the tree sat Aidan, talking softly to Dougal and warming himself by the fire. Dougal must have been standing guard at the top of the bank earlier, unnoticed until she tried to escape. A second man stood on the bank at the prow of the boat, waiting patiently. The boat, a mid-sized vessel commonly used to move goods up and down the Thames, was loaded with several wooden boxes, a dozen small barrels, and some bundles wrapped in waxed cloth, ready for departure. What was her destination? The question was answered when Aidan, noticing she was awake, approached.

"Tessa, my love, are you well?" He said it as if it were not he who had caused her situation. "We have not much time, so here is what I have in mind. You have said you do not want me. I accept that, although *I* want *you*. I believe that you could learn to love me, especially when I am Lord Brixton and you are my lady.

"Here, then, is the choice left to you. You may accept my proposal, and we shall be married tomorrow. There may be some scandal, with your husband newly dead, but many will find it romantic that we could not wait to be together. You will be Lady Brixton and have everything my wealth can provide."

Aidan stopped here to let his words sink in, but Tessa gave him no reply, so he went on. "Or, if you prefer, you may sail to Scotland with Hawick and his men. If you choose this option, of course, I have no further business with you, and Hawick, I fear, may treat you rather badly. Perhaps his men will, too. I couldn't say. A fate worse than death, I believe it is called, though death will probably come eventually." The man beside him guffawed but thought better of it when Aidan shot him a look.

"I might add that nothing you can do will save your precious Jeffrey. If you leave with Hawick, your death at my brother's hand will be assumed by all, once I tell my story. However, if you become my wife, I will do my best to help him escape England. He will do well in Normandy or some such place where men of military experience are prized. Word from Mairie should arrive within the hour. You have that long to consider, then stay or sail away, as you choose."

Tessa fought back despair and fear. How could she choose? Aidan was mad, driven by his lust for her and his hatred for the Brixtons. How he must have despised them all! Still, he'd been clever, appearing to be meek and helpful. It was only when he drank too much that he'd showed his true, bitter self. She remembered both Mary and Eleanor commenting on it, but they'd dismissed it as the effects of wine, not realizing that it was when his inhibitions were removed that Aidan showed his depravity.

Could she live with a madman? The alternative was so frightening as to make her blood run cold, but at least Hawick would probably kill her in a few days, once they tired of her. With Aidan she would have years of torture, might even bear his children. Her mind could not accept all that had happened, and she feared she would go mad herself. Curled up on the deck of the small ship, she lay shivering and fighting back tears. Aidan returned to chatting calmly with the outlaws, ignoring her.

Suddenly Tessa felt something tug at her dress. Startled, she gasped and looked down toward her feet. Rivulets of water ran from behind a stack of crates on the deck. Someone had come swimming through the frigid water and climbed aboard. Glancing at the four men, Tessa assured herself that they had noticed nothing, paid no attention to her. "Please help me," she whispered.

"Are you hurt?" came a whispered reply.

"No."

"Can you swim?"

"Y-yes."

"When I tell you, jump overboard and let the current take you downstream. Can you do that?"

"Yes." She was more confident now. Better to drown in the river than deal with two equally appalling choices.

"When the water slows, you will be at Oxford. Someone there will help you. I will come for you when I can."

"Jeffrey?"

"Yes."

She almost sobbed aloud. "Jeffrey —"

"There's no time, for we must act quickly. Are you ready?"

"Yes." She pulled her legs beneath her, ready to spring.

"Now!"

With all of her strength, Tessa pushed herself up and with the same motion dived into the river. She heard the cries of surprise and anger from the men on shore, but she was too busy fighting the current, the cold water, and her own skirts to pay much attention. When affirming that she could swim, she'd been thinking of days in Scotland, cooling herself in the shallow burns in only her shift. It was quite another matter to stay afloat fully clothed in the mighty Thames. Kicking off her slippers, she concentrated on keeping her head above the water, trusting the river to carry her away without further effort on her part.

CHAPTER
THIRTY-TWO

As Tessa did as ordered, Jeffrey Brixton launched himself at the outlaws on the bank. The guard at the boat's prow he hit directly, full force under the chin with his lowered shoulder, hoping to knock him unconscious before the others could react. As he had hoped, the man fell limply onto the bank with a grunt. Jeffrey rolled over, the damp ground cushioning his fall, regained his footing, and assessed the situation. He had cursed his lack of weapons at least five times in the last hour. They had been taken from him earlier in the evening. Now he stood defenseless while Aidan faced him calmly, a smile on his face and a knife in his hand. At his side, Dougal hefted his sparthe menacingly, all business. Hawick was not in his line of vision, but there was danger there, too.

Tessa, in the water, heard a splash nearby and looked up to see Hawick wading into the current downstream of her. He had acted quickly for his size, and although she tried frantically to avoid him, it was difficult to maneuver with her skirts tangled around her legs. Hawick reached out, got a hand on the fabric floating around her, and began pulling her out of the current. Once in the cove, he clenched a powerful arm around her neck, towing her backward as he strode powerfully toward shore. She beat at him with both arms but could get no strength behind the blows without solid ground beneath her feet. Ignoring her struggles, Hawick dragged her into the shallows of the small cove. He had some trouble pulling her along, so heavy were her clothes, but he finally accomplished his task and stood over her, both of them fighting to catch their breath.

"Stupid wench!" he shouted, striking her once across the face. Tessa glared at him, unwilling to show any fear. "You've made trouble for me for the last time." Seeing his intention, Tessa tried to avoid his grasp, but strong arms pushed her shoulders down, sending her head under water, and he held her there, his furious face hovering over hers as she fought against him.

Jeffrey frantically parried blows from Dougal's battle-axe with a piece of driftwood snatched from the bank. It was too short to be very effective, but he had no other choice. Aidan danced on the outskirts of his reach, hoping to get a chance to step in when his brother was absorbed with fighting off the axe. Jeffrey was dimly aware that Hawick must be nearby, and he knew he had to quickly defeat at least one of the two who faced him or have all three to contend with. He said a quick prayer that Tessa had gotten away safely.

Dougal made a mistake at that moment, swinging the axe with all his weight at the spot where Brixton was, but Jeffrey antici-pated his move and ducked to one side. Dougal's momentum carried him past his target with a grunt, and Jeffrey brought the stick down smartly on the man's head as he stumbled by, dazing him and knocking him to the ground. Knowing Aidan would take that moment to make his move, Jeffrey spun quickly around, catching Aidan's extended arm with the stick as he tried to stab Jeffrey from behind. With a howl Aidan dropped the knife to the ground. Both men dove for it, both missed, connecting instead with each other, and they went down, rolling on the ground in a desperate struggle for domi-nance.

"Why didn't you die in the sea, like a good

brother?" Aidan panted, his face close to Jeffrey's.

"You were my brother once," Jeffrey said through clenched teeth, "but no more." He gave a powerful shove, and Aidan went sprawling onto his back, where he lay, winded, as Jeffrey got to his feet. To his dismay, there was Dougal, who had recovered from the blow on the head and came at him with a roar. He caught Jeffrey in the chest and they both went down. Dougal got his hands around his opponent's throat, and they struggled on the wet bank, Jeffrey fighting for breath. He tried to pummel the huge Dougal's ribs but could not get much leverage from underneath the man's bulk.

At that moment, Jeffrey heard Aidan scream, "No, no stop!" Dougal, surprised by the shout, relaxed his hold on his opponent's throat for an instant, which was what Jeffrey needed to make a final effort. Putting both hands on the man's chest and pushing with all his might, he threw the outlaw to one side and rolled to his feet, readying himself for another attack. Aidan, to his surprise, rushed past him and down the river's edge.

There Jeffrey saw what Aidan had seen. Hawick held Tessa's head under water as she clawed and scratched at him wildly. So far she had managed to gulp air as Hawick dodged her flailing arms, but she grew weaker by the moment.

Jeffrey followed Aidan frantically, not knowing his intent. Aidan, still screaming "No!" threw himself at Hawick, causing the outlaw to release Tessa as he tumbled onto the bank. Aidan was on him in an instant, and the two rolled to their feet as Jeffrey reached them. "See to her," Aidan growled at him, and Jeffrey waded into the stream to pull Tessa, to the shore. Aidan circled Hawick, the two measuring each other's remaining strength.

"You should have let me finish her, lad," Hawick said with a grin. "She's been nothing but trouble from the first."

Aidan made no answer but lunged fiercely at Hawick. As he did, his facial expression became first surprised, then pained, then blank as his knees buckled and he toppled forward. Even Hawick stood frozen for a second, then scrambled out of the way as Aidan fell face first in the mud. Dougal's battle-axe, its blade glinting dully in the firelight, protruded from his back. Looking in the direction from which the weapon must have come, they saw Dougal standing upriver, panting from exertion.

Jeffrey rose, his body tensing, as Dougal

looked around him and spotted the knife Aidan had dropped on the ground. He reached it just as Jeffrey did, and the two struggled again on the ground for control of it.

Tessa tried to rise, her mind telling her she must do something, but her knees would not hold her, and she retched water from her burning lungs. She crawled toward the two men wrestling in the firelight, determined to help. Seizing the same branch that Jeffrey had used as his weapon, she held it aloft, trying to gauge the moment when she could be sure of hitting only the outlaw and not Jeffrey. It was a mere matter of moments, however, until she heard a strangled sound from Dougal. Jeffrey rose to his feet as the last breath bubbled out of the man's body.

Jeffrey's chest heaved as he pulled in great gasps of air. One arm was bloody, but he was alive. He looked carefully both up and down the bank. Hawick was nowhere to be seen. Finally he staggered down to Tessa, who came unsteadily to meet him, arms outstretched.

"Jeffrey! Are you all right?"

"I will mend," he answered grimly. "And you?"

"I am alive, thanks to Aidan," she said

between gasps. "But Aidan killed Cedric! He is . . . he was mad." She was sobbing and talking at once, and Jeffrey held her tightly, feeling her shivering through her wet clothes. Leaving her briefly, he strode to the fireside, found a cloak and a blanket that had belonged to the outlaws, and brought them over, wrapping the blanket around Tessa and pulling the cloak around himself. Finally he replied to her statement.

"I know. Eleanor's letter planted the suspicion, and I began watching him carefully after my return, looking for proof. I had no idea he was planning to blame all his crimes on me. When the box with Eleanor's letters came up missing I was alerted, then a friend warned me of my impending arrest and I went into hiding. I did not dare to seek him at Brixton for fear of arrest, but I thought I owed it to him to face him with my accusations. Learning that Aidan was to be at the Ballard's tonight, I was determined to make him confess. Then I saw you there, and things became more complicated."

"Why?"

"Aidan has lied to us both all along. He told me before I was lost at sea that you and he . . ." Jeffrey let the words trail away.

"He hinted that you were having an affair with Eleanor," Tessa murmured, aware that it was her own conclusion but that Aidan had encouraged it.

"Eleanor and I? No, I loved Eleanor as a sister only, as she deserved. But when I returned to Brixton Manor after seeing you in London, Aidan told me that you and he were to be married. He led me to believe that you were in love with him. I did not want to take away your chance at happiness again, if that were true. I had ruined your life once and did not want to do it again."

"I never loved Aidan. I tried to tell him that months ago, but he —"

"I know. Aidan was focused on two things in life: becoming Lord of Brixton Manor and having you as his lady. Tonight, after our conversation . . . I convinced myself that you were not in love with my brother. I knew then that I had to decide how to expose him. Aidan had carefully arranged the evidence. Only crimes that could be placed at my door were revealed, and none seemed to have occurred once I went missing. He even cast himself in the role of innocent dupe. Supposedly I had convinced him to let me handle some of William's affairs, which I turned to my own profit."

"He admitted to me tonight that he poisoned William."

"I wondered," Jeffrey murmured sadly. "It

was well known I had no love for William's treatment of me, so many concluded that I had got back a bit of my own by cheating my brother. The fact that I spent a year at Hawick's also incriminated me, for who is to say that I was a prisoner if Ian and Mairie say otherwise?"

"I would!" Tessa vowed.

"If your husband would allow you to speak," Jeffrey reminded her.

"So you came to the masque tonight to face Aidan?"

"Yes, but I ran into some unexpected complications. First, I saw Aidan talking to Mairie and decided that they must be plotting something, the three of them. If Mairie was in England, Hawick would not be far away. I didn't realize they were counting on my coming there so that they could frame me for Cedric's murder as well as other crimes. Mairie recognized me despite the mask, and she lured Cedric to the stables. I didn't realize how long you'd been gone from the hall until it was too late to stop Aidan from carrying you off. When the crime was discovered, Mairie accused me. You should have heard her tears and screams."

"She was quite calm when she faced me over Cedric's corpse," Tessa commented, shaking her head wonderingly. "What fiends she and her brother are!"

"Because of her story I was taken into custody by Sir Roger and locked in a room." He smiled grimly. "His wife was ready to have me drawn and quartered at dawn. Then Lady Acton wanted the crime laid at your door. She swore you had paid me to murder her Cedric. Fortunately, Francis — Mary, of course — didn't believe a word of it."

"Mary has ever defended you, even from me," Tessa said with a smile.

"And for that I am grateful to her also." Jeffrey touched Tessa's face tenderly. "At any rate, Mary and Francis distrusted Mairie, so they decided to watch the woman once she thought she had accomplished her purpose. Francis saw her hand a note to a churl for delivery to her confederates. He stopped the man and took the note, which revealed enough to prove my innocence. However, once I was freed, Mairie was nowhere to be found. As usual, her instinct for self-preservation was strong."

"Then how did you find me?"

"The hired messenger was easily persuaded to describe his destination. Francis went for help, but I knew I had to get to you."

"That was wise on your part. They would have been gone in a short time."

"I am sorry that it was my brother who brought you to this." Jeffrey said, disbelief still in his voice.

"But he saved my life at the last," Tessa reminded him.

"He truly loved you. Aidan made a good choice for his last act on earth, even if his earlier choices were deplorable."

Tessa found herself smiling despite all she had been through. "And a very good choice you made, Lord Brixton, coming to my rescue. I believe that evens the score between us. Once upon a time you ruined my life, but you have redeemed yourself and saved me — more than once."

Jeffrey put his hands into Tessa's dripping hair and turned her face up to his. "Mistress macFindlaech, we have a conversation unfinished between us. I could not let our chance to settle things between us be confounded by circumstances, could I?" He kissed her then, with a warmth that made them both forget the cold around them.

"Hallooo!" came from above the bank, and they clung to each other as sounds of Francis and the other rescuers drew closer in the night.

CHAPTER
THIRTY-THREE

Mary insisted that Tessa stay with her for several days, sending word to Banaugh so that he would not worry. A day later he showed up at Mary's side door, asking humbly to see "his lass." Running down the stairs to meet him, Tessa hugged the grizzled old man, causing him to turn various shades of red and sputter, "Now, Tess," several times.

"I hope things are well at the grog shop," Tessa said with raised eyebrow.

"Oh, aye, things are well enough, there," Banaugh replied. "That widow is qui' a woman, ye know."

"I like her very much," Tessa said honestly.

"Do ye, lass?" He seemed ready to say more, but scratched his head and was silent.

"I also think," Tessa continued, "that she is quite taken with you."

Banaugh let a small smile cross his features, but he shook his head. "I've no business at m' age t' be takin' a woman. Besides, I've got ye t' look after."

Tessa crossed to him again and hugged him even harder than before. "Banaugh, you have done more for me than anyone else could have. But now you have a chance to be happy with this widow of yours, and I believe that I have a chance at happiness, too. We shall always be friends, but you must marry Sarah Goode if it pleases you."

"Ye are certain?" He was torn, it seemed, between duty and desire.

"I can stay here with Mary as long as I like, she says. I will go wandering no more and will need no strong protector, I promise."

Banaugh looked innocent and sly at once. "I'm thinkin' that there be one nearby, if ye have need."

Tessa said nothing. Jeffrey had gone to Brixton, and she had no idea what was next for the two of them.

"I will tell ye this," the old man said, his eyes narrowing with conviction. "Sarah Goode is truly qui' a woman, bu' she'll never tak' th' place i' this old heart tha' is yours, lass, an' that's God's truth."

Once Tessa reached London, she had sent word to Miriam and Ayla Arbeen that she was safe. At the Mace and Thyme Inn, Banaugh had found a letter for Tessa from them, which he now handed her. She read it aloud so he could hear the news.

Ayla wrote,

My dear Tessa, we were most happy to hear of your safe return to London and your luck in locating friends there. We have had no further troubling visitors since the night you left. My mother is well and sends her best regards. She says you will understand that she is, under present circumstances, considering a return to her homeland. I will accompany her on the journey in the spring and then return to Arbeen, for I am to be married at the new year to a man I believe you can identify. I will only say that, as well as being affianced, I have become quite expert with a bow over the last few weeks.

Tessa stopped reading briefly to explain the courtship of Hamish to Banaugh.

"Why is it ye can gie others all sorts o' advice i' matters o' th' heart bu' canna tell yer own man hae much ye love him?" Banaugh asked her. "It seems t' me —"

"Never mind, Banaugh," Tessa reproved teasingly. "I am waiting for the right moment, and I believe it will come soon."

She returned to reading. *We hope when you return to Scotland, as I am sure you will someday, that you stop to visit. We would be most glad of your company. Your friend, Ayla Arbeen.*

"A fine lassie, i' spite o' her bein' ferrin," Banaugh announced. "It took courage t' do wha' she did tha' night, an' we are beholding t' her and her mother." Tessa nodded agreement, promising herself that if she did return to Scotland, Arbeen would be one of the places she would be sure to visit.

A few days later a messenger arrived from Brixton Manor with a packet for Tessa. Her heart leapt, but the feminine handwriting on the outside told her it was not from Jeffrey. Still, she was pleased when she opened it to find a letter from Auntie Madeline, and within that, a note from her sister Meg. She read the note first:

My dear sister,

I have asked Father Madoc to write this for me, and I will send it by messenger to the Brixtons of York whom you spoke of in hopes that they will know where to find you. We are all well, and no harm has come to us under the rule of King Malcolm. He asked only that

Donwald, representing the clan macFindlaech, swear fealty to him on Moot Hill at Scone, bringing soil from our land-hold in his boot heel, as is customary. That done, we are free to live as we wish. The castle at Inverness has been granted to one of Malcolm's clan, I am told.

I hope that you have found what you sought when last we met, and that you will someday return to your home in the Highlands, to visit us or to live, whichever pleases you.

Your loving sister, Meg

Below her name was a mark such as Kenneth macFindlaech had used to identify his sheep, which made Tessa miss her home vividly for a moment. Scotland was a beautiful land, and again she promised herself that she would return there someday.

The letter from Auntie Madeline was longer, and the hand that wrote it a bit shaky. Still, the old lady's warmth came through as she wrote:

My dear Tessa,

Jeffrey has told me of your adventures since you left Brixton, and I marvel at what you have done. He tries to stand on dignity, but his pride in your courage and determination shows in his every word. I, too, am proud of you, although distressed at Aidan's treatment of you. He ever resented his brothers, but now it is over. May God have mercy on him. Cecilia is here with me now, the last of my girls, and she will soon marry. Alice is very happy with her young man, and I believe you know Mary's little secret. I am so thankful that all of them had their chance, and it was largely due to you, Tessa. You were the impetus that nudged dear Eleanor into action, and because of it, all the Brixton girls benefitted. I only wish she were here to see them well matched, each according to her own choice.

Ethelbert visited on his way back to the abbey. What a surprise to hear that you and he met. He will spend some time in renewal and then be on his way. Healing is a gift he has discovered in himself, and so he is content with his choice in life.

Jeffrey has been very busy setting things to rights on the manor. He insists on making amends for the girls not having a proper dowry settled on them, and he has made a large gift to Ethelbert's abbey as well. The house is being repaired, and the sound of hammers and saws dins at one's ears from morning to night. I believe he looks forward to something, but I cannot say what, it not being my affair.

Please, come to see an old woman when you can.

Yours with affection, Madeline Brixton

Tessa sat back in the window seat of the solar, the two pages clutched in her hand. She had been so lucky in her life to have around her warm, caring women: her sister Meg, the beautiful Eleanor and the kind Auntie Madeline, and Miriam and Ayla Arbeen. Women were judged in the world by their ability to capture a husband, and yet these women were very different. Meg had married for love and found happiness, Eleanor had married for security and been required to make her own happiness, and Auntie had made a life for herself without marriage and seemed happy with that. Miriam had been happy despite society's disapproval of her marriage, and Ayla would make herself content with Hamish, having known no other eligible man at all. Each one of them was loving and loved, no matter what her marital situation. Society was wrong. It was not marriage that showed a woman's worth, but the woman herself.

The weird sisters danced again through Tessa's memory. They had been correct in their predictions, she knew not how. She had come to England, she had married two men who never possessed her, and the man she loved had forgotten her name. Had they been trying to trick her, help her, or were they merely creatures who spoke the words given to them with no intent one way or the other? Tessa decided that the answer probably was the last. They had not meant to destroy her or her uncle. The information given was just that: information. How one acted upon the information made all the difference. If Macbeth had chosen to perform evil deeds while trying to make their prophecies come true, that had been his mistake. For men as well, happiness came from within. She hoped God would forgive him for not listening to his own heart.

Over the next week the story of Aidan's association with Ian Hawick became public. Unfortunately, Hawick had disappeared without a trace. By morning two dead bodies, the boat, and marks in the mud of the bank were all that was left to tell the tale. Hawick had melted into the darkness. "Best for him," Mary commented, "and for you, too, Tessa. You need never see them again."

CHAPTER
THIRTY-FOUR

Jeffrey came to visit a week later. By that time Tessa was almost sick with wondering what was to come. She had tortured herself with thinking he might have reconsidered his relationship with her now that he was established as Lord Brixton. Would he be embarrassed to take as his lady a Scottish girl with no prospects, one whose family was despised in England? When he arrived at Mary's door, Tessa had steeled herself to accept his rejection calmly if it came. After all, she wanted him to be happy, and if he chose to look elsewhere . . .

Ushered into the room by a blushing servant, Jeffrey looked wonderful, although he flinched when Francis, forgetting himself, slapped him on the shoulder playfully. He wore a brown tunic of fine brocade over tan leggings and a white undershirt, all cut to fit perfectly. Over it all hung a short cape lined with fur and dyed a deep green. Tessa had enough notice of his visit that she had dressed carefully in another of Mary's gowns, a dark blue velvet with a square bodice and a silken drape of paler hue that set it off nicely.

They sat in the great room with Mary and Francis, Jeffrey updating them with news of what had been learned. "There was a report of a French woman taking passage across the channel to Calais from a London dock, traveling alone except for two servants."

"Did one of the 'servants' have a huge torso and disproportionately small legs?" Tessa asked.

"You are very perceptive," Jeffrey said, smiling at her suspicion.

"From there they could return to Scotland or stay in France," Francis commented. "I'm afraid they've quite escaped. There's little enough pursuit of justice in England *or* France these days, and even less in Scotland with conditions as they are there."

"Malcolm is probably glad to be rid of Hawick and the problems he created as an ally to the king," Tessa surmised.

Jeffrey made no comment except to thank Francis for his help once more. He chatted about the changes he was making at the manor for a few moments, but it was obvious he had something on his mind. After refreshments, he offered Tessa his arm. "Mistress macFindlaech, shall we walk among Mary's flowers?" His eyes shone with humor, for of course there were no flowers in the garden. It was almost advent. Tessa, understanding his desire to speak with her alone, hurried to fetch a warm cloak.

They passed along pathways between empty flowerbeds and leafless bushes. A light snow had fallen, and a slight wind gusted over it, making swirls around their feet. Tessa held Jeffrey's arm and felt no chill at all.

"I have been a fool," Jeffrey said finally. "Not once, but several times."

"Oh?" Tessa answered innocently. "I had not noticed it."

Jeffrey looked at her seriously. "It's true. I knew, I think, from the first time I met you, that beside your obvious beauty, you were that most wonderful creature on earth, a person of character. I remember your spirit when you refused to dance with the English fop at your uncle's banquet, and that first morning when you struggled to escape my grasp . . . Everything was against me, but I loved you even then. However, you hated me, and I could not blame you for it. Later, when Eleanor groomed you for a brilliant marriage, I became angry. I wanted you for myself, but I had nothing to offer."

"I would have taken you for yourself."

"No man wants the woman he loves to suffer deprivation on his account," Jeffrey countered. "I thought if I could win a grant of land or an official post, I would have some future to offer you."

So his pride had stood in the way of his speaking that day in William's London home. "So you sailed off into the North Sea," she murmured.

"Yes, and lost my memory."

"You forgot my name."

Jeffrey looked confused. "What?"

"Oh, it was something some old women told me once. One said I would travel to England, and you came along and brought me here."

"Against your wishes," he admitted.

"I have forgiven you that," Tessa told him. "The second woman said I would find happiness only among the dead. When I believed you dead it broke my heart."

"But you searched for me anyway," Jeffrey said gently.

"The third woman said that the man I loved would forget my name, and you did — twice."

"Twice?" he echoed questioningly.

"The one, of course, I must forgive, for you had a blow to the head and forgot everything. But before, when first you brought me to Eleanor, you had to ask me my name. That is harder to forgive."

"I was so blinded by your beauty that I failed to hear it properly." Jeffrey grinned. "Will that do for an excuse?"

"I see you are in truth no longer a rough soldier, but speak beautiful lies as well as any lord I ever met," Tessa answered with matching humor. "I'm sure the prediction referred to the other forgetting, when you lost your past there in the borderlands."

"But you, Tessa of the Highlands, came to find me. When I saw you by the old oak at Hawick's, things that had floated through my mind made sense at last. I knew somehow that I loved you, yet you denied we were lovers. I heard, in my head, your voice promising revenge and knew I had done you a great wrong. It took days before my poor brain put all the fragments together, and by then you were gone again. I came back to London to find you, hoping we could start anew . . ." He stopped, uncertain of how to continue.

Tessa gazed up at him, understanding. "You found that I was married to Cedric. It must have been difficult to think me other than a fortune hunter."

Jeffrey smiled. "William's papers reveal his investigation into Eleanor's claim that you were her sister. With her death, you were forced to make hard choices. In her letter, Eleanor told me that she hoped I would come home and marry you myself. I think she knew that I loved you before I did."

"I was foolish to think that your affection for Eleanor was love," Tessa admitted.

"I did love Eleanor, as my sister, as a friend. But not as I love you." Tessa's heart did strange things inside her. "Then later, of course, Aidan announced that you and he were lovers. He described the inn and hinted that he had been there many times."

Tessa said sadly. "I'm sorry to say it, Jeffrey, but your brother was a very able liar. All along I thought him kind and helpful, always at my side when I needed him. Only once or twice did I see the mask slip, and I was stupid enough to brush those glimpses of the real Aidan away, thinking them only moments of frustration."

"It appears Aidan had long been a cheat." Jeffrey shook his head in disgust. "Now that I know what to look for in William's records, I have found that he was being fooled repeatedly by Aidan. Money was siphoned off, information sold to the highest bidder, and many other betrayals lined Aidan's pockets."

"How upset he must have been when you came back from the dead."

"And how much more upset when he learned it was you who was responsible," Jeffrey said with a chuckle. "At the last, though, he proved his love for you."

"Yes, we must remember that final good," was all Tessa replied. She had not told anyone of Aidan's threat to give her to the outlaws for sport. Jeffrey had enough to deal with regarding his brother's perfidy as it was. Would he really have done it, or had it been merely a threat to make her choose him? She did not know.

"Well, he's gone," Jeffrey finished. "It is time to speak of us."

Tessa mind ran ahead. Jeffrey had confessed that he loved her, but now he was a lord and she a pauper. Did it make a difference? Evidently it did not, because suddenly Jeffrey was on bended knee before her.

"Mistress Tessa macFindlaech, of the bloodline of kings and the pride of Scotland, will you be my wife, give up your homeland, and live in England for the rest of your days?"

Tears sprang to her eyes. Suddenly she

understood that what they had gone through together had united them so that changes in status meant nothing to either. She had been a king's kinswoman when Jeffrey was nothing but a man. Now he was a lord and she nothing but a woman. What they were to each other was enough.

"My lord, she answered him, "I would be honored to be your wife."

Along the moor's edge, three odd figures strode, calmly facing the winter's wrath. The one in the lead turned suddenly, facing the other two, and stopped them by holding up a crooked finger.

"It is done," she pronounced.

The second nodded. "One wed, one dead."

The third finished it: "Fair is foul, and foul is fair." Solemnly, the three continued their progress to nowhere.

AFTERWORD

The facts are sketchy, but here are some that help to separate the man from the myth.

Macbeth (1005–1057 A.D.) was king of Scots for seventeen years, from 1040 until his death. His correct name is Mac Bethad mac Findlaech (son of Findlaech). His father, a local king, was killed in 1020, possibly by his brother, Gille Coemgain. When his uncle died, Macbeth married his widow, Gruoch, and took in her son, Lulach.

The character we know as Duncan was probably Donnchad, who took the throne in 1034. The king was not old, but he is characterized in the *Prophecy of Berchan* as "the man of many sorrows." In 1040, Donnchad was killed by Macbeth in a battle near Elgin. Macbeth became king, although strife over the kingship continued, not unusual in eleventh-century Scotland. Some reports indicate that Donnchad's wife fled the country with her sons Mael Coluim and

Domnall, both future kings of Scotland.

Once Macbeth had cemented his position, he made a pilgrimage to Rome in 1050, where he was noted for his generosity to the poor. In 1052, an English conflict overflowed into Macbeth's territory with the result that Siward, earl of Northumbria, invaded Scotland. A bloody battle resulted in which 3,000 Scots and 1,500 Englishmen died, including one of Siward's sons. Macbeth survived the English invasion but was defeated and mortally wounded in a battle with Mael Coluim mac Donnchad, the son of the former king, in 1057. He was succeeded by his stepson.

No reports from the time indicate Macbeth was a tyrant. He is called "Mac Bethad the renowned" and described as "the generous king of Fortrin" by contemporaries. A poetic history of the time describes Macbeth as "The red, tall, golden-haired one. Scotland will be brimful west and east during the reign of the furious red one."

Shakespeare was a master of the docudrama, the practice of turning history into compelling fiction. In a time when a Scottish king ruled England (James V claimed to be descended from Mael Coluim III), it could be expected that a writer who depended upon the king for his livelihood would glorify that king's ancestry. Macbeth therefore became a tyrant in the play, a man so depraved that it was a boon to his people to remove him from office. It is interesting to note, however, the playwright found far more interest in the character of the tyrant, in his fall from brave warrior to depraved maniac, than in the righteous Malcolm. Although Shakespeare's *Macbeth* is a disservice to the historical king, who was no better or worse than other kings, the character created on the stage in "the Scottish play" is compelling in his all-too-human desire for power, which leads to the release of his unfortunate alter ego, "the secret'st man of blood."

Source of this information: Holinshed, Raphael. Holinshed's *Chronicles of England, Scotland, and Ireland (Volume V, Scotland)*. London: J. Johnson, *et al*, 1808.

ABOUT THE AUTHOR

Peg Herring is a writer of plays, mysteries, and romance who once taught high school English and history. In her spare time she travels with her husband of thirty-seven years, gardens, directs choral groups, and works to keep her hundred-year-old home from crumbling away.